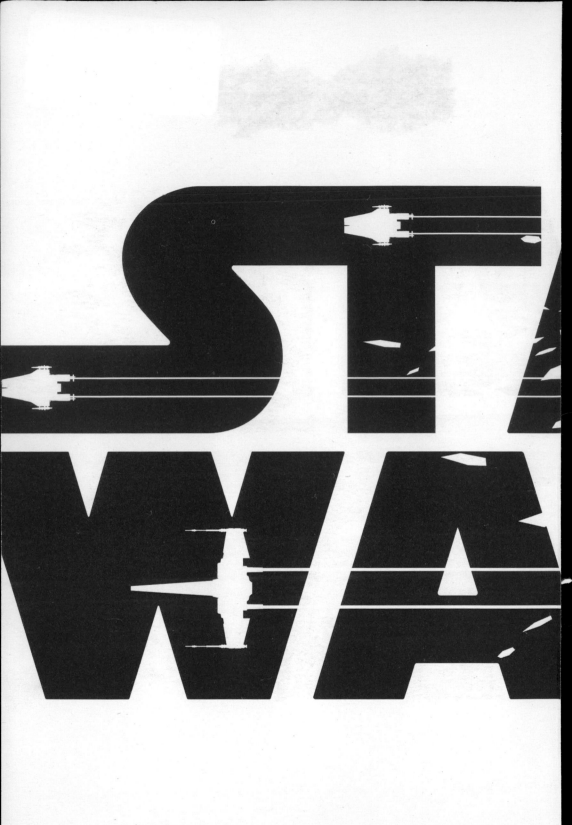

™

By Jason Fry

STAR WARS

The Essential Atlas

The Clone Wars: Episode Guide

The Essential Guide to Warfare

Star Wars in 100 Scenes

Moving Target: A Princess Leia Adventure

The Weapon of a Jedi: A Luke Skywalker Adventure

The Force Awakens: Rey's Survival Guide

The Force Awakens Incredible Cross-Sections

The Servants of the Empire Series

THE JUPITER PIRATES

Hunt for the Hydra

Curse of the Iris

The Rise of Earth

STAR WARS

THE LAST JEDI

™

JASON FRY

Based on a story by Rian Johnson

CENTURY

1 3 5 7 9 10 8 6 4 2

Century
20 Vauxhall Bridge Road
London SW1V 2SA

Century is part of the Penguin Random House group of companies whose addresses
can be found at global.penguinrandomhouse.com.

First published in Great Britain by Century in 2018

www.penguin.co.uk

A CIP catalogue record for this book is available from the British Library.

Hardback ISBN 9781780898414
Trade Paperback ISBN 9781780898421

Book design by Elizabeth A. D. Eno

Printed and bound by Clays Ltd, St Ives Plc

Penguin Random House is committed to a sustainable future for our business,
our readers and our planet. This book is made from Forest Stewardship
Council® certified paper.

STAR WARS

TIMELINE

I THE PHANTOM MENACE

II ATTACK OF THE CLONES

THE CLONE WARS (TV SERIES)

DARK DISCIPLE

III REVENGE OF THE SITH

CATALYST: A ROGUE ONE NOVEL
LORDS OF THE SITH
TARKIN
THRAWN
A NEW DAWN

REBELS (TV SERIES)

ROGUE ONE

IV A NEW HOPE

BATTLEFRONT II: INFERNO SQUAD
HEIR TO THE JEDI
BATTLEFRONT: TWILIGHT COMPANY

STAR WARS

TIMELINE

A long time ago in a galaxy far, far away. . . .

The FIRST ORDER reigns.
Having decimated the peaceful
Republic, Supreme Leader Snoke
now deploys his merciless
legions to seize military
control of the galaxy.

Only General Leia Organa's
small band of RESISTANCE fighters
stand against the rising
tyranny, certain that Jedi
Master Luke Skywalker will
return and restore a spark of
hope to the fight.

But the Resistance has been
exposed. As the First Order
speeds toward the rebel base,
the brave heroes mount a
desperate escape. . . .

PROLOGUE

Luke Skywalker stood in the cooling sands of Tatooine, his wife by his side.

The strip of sky at the horizon was still painted with the last orange of sunset, but the first stars had emerged. Luke peered at them, searching for something he knew was already gone.

"What did you think you saw?" Camie asked.

He could hear the affection in her voice—but if he listened harder, he could hear the weariness as well.

"Star Destroyer," he said. "At least I thought so."

"Then I believe you," she said, one hand on his shoulder. "You could always recognize one—even at high noon."

Luke smiled, thinking back to the long-ago day at Tosche Station when he'd burst in to tell his friends about the two ships sitting in orbit right above their heads. Camie hadn't believed him—she'd peered through his old macrobinoculars before dismissively tossing them back to him and seeking refuge from the relentless twin suns. Fixer hadn't believed him, either. Nor had Biggs.

But he'd been right.

His smile faded at the thought of Biggs Darklighter, who'd left Tatooine and died somewhere unimaginably far away. Biggs, who'd been his first friend. His only friend, he supposed.

His mind retreated from the thought, as quickly as if his bare hand had strayed to a vaporator casing at midday.

"I wonder what the Empire wanted out here," he said, searching the sky again. Resupplying the garrison at Mos Eisley hardly required a warship the size of a Star Destroyer. These days, with the galaxy at peace, it hardly required a warship at all.

"Whatever it is, it's got nothing to do with us," Camie said. "That's right, isn't it?"

"Of course it is," Luke said, his eyes reflexively scanning the lights that marked the homestead's perimeter. Such caution wasn't necessary—no Tusken Raider had been seen this side of Anchorhead in two decades—but old habits died hard.

The Tuskens are gone—nothing left of them but bones in the sand.

For some reason that made him sad.

"We've hit our Imperial quota for five years running," Camie said. "And we've paid our water tax to Jabba. We don't owe anybody anything. We haven't done anything."

"We haven't done anything," Luke agreed, though he knew that was no guarantee of safety. Plenty of things happened to people who hadn't done anything—things that were never discussed again, or at least not by anyone with any sense.

His mind went back to the long-ago days he kept telling himself not to think about. The droids, and the message—a holographic fragment in which a regal young woman pleaded for Obi-Wan Kenobi to help her.

Let the past go. That's what Camie always told him. But staring into the darkness, Luke found that once again, he couldn't take her advice.

The astromech droid had fled into the night while Luke was at dinner with his aunt and uncle. Fearing Uncle Owen's fury, Luke had taken a risk, slipping away from the farm despite the threat of Tuskens.

But no Sand People had been on the prowl that night. Luke had found the runaway astromech and brought it back to the farm, pushing the landspeeder the last twenty meters to avoid waking Owen and Beru.

Luke smiled ruefully, thinking—as he so often did—about everything that could have gone wrong. He could easily have died, becoming one more foolhardy moisture farmer claimed by the Tatooine night and what lurked in it.

But he'd been lucky—and then lucky again the next day.

The stormtroopers had arrived just after Luke returned from working on the south ridge's balky condensers—Owen and Beru's source of aggravation then, his and Camie's now. The sergeant was making demands even before he swung down from his dewback.

A band of scavengers sold two droids to you. Bring them. Now.

Luke had almost needed to drag the droids out of the garage. The astromech hooted wildly, while the protocol droid kept babbling that he was surrendering. They'd stood in the relentless heat for more than an hour while the Imperials picked through the droids' memory banks, with the stormtroopers curtly refusing Owen's request to at least let Beru sit in the shade.

That was when old Ben Kenobi had appeared, shuffling out of the desert in his dusty brown robes. He'd spoken to the stormtroopers with a smile, like they were old friends running into each other at the Anchorhead swap meet. He'd told them, with a slight wave of one hand, that Luke's identification was wrong—the boy's last name wasn't Skywalker, but Lars.

"That's right," Owen had said, his eyes jumping to Beru. "Luke Lars."

Ben had lingered, telling the stormtroopers that there was no need to take Owen in for questioning. But they'd refused that request, and forced Luke's uncle into the belly of a troop transport alongside the droids, with the astromech letting out a last, desperate screech before the hatch slammed.

They released Owen three days later, and he'd remained pale and silent during the long ride back from Mos Eisley. It was weeks before Luke got up his courage to ask if the Empire would compensate them.

Owen snarled at him to forget it, then tucked his hands under his elbows—but not before Luke saw that they were trembling.

A meteor burned up overhead, shaking Luke out of his reverie.

"What are you thinking about now?" Camie asked, and her voice was wary.

"That somehow I got old," he said, tugging at his beard. "Old and gray."

"You're not the only one," she said, hand going to her own hair. He offered her a smile, but she was looking off into the night.

No one had ever seen old Ben again. But there'd been rumors—whispers about a gunship flying low over the Jundland Wastes, and fire in the night. In Anchorhead they dismissed that as cantina talk, but Luke wondered. The troops at the farm had been real. So were the ones who'd come to the Darklighter farm and taken Biggs's family away. The Darklighters had never returned—the farm had been stripped by Jawas and Sand People, then left for the sand to bury.

Weeks had turned into months, months into years, years into decades. Luke turned out to have a knack for machinery, a feel for the maddening complexity of Tatooine growing conditions, and a talent for good outcomes, whether it was bargaining with Jawas or choosing sites for new vaporators. In Anchorhead, the boy once teased as Wormie was more often called Lucky Luke.

Camie had seen that, too—just as she'd noticed that Fixer talked a lot while doing little. She'd married Luke and they'd become partners with Owen and Beru before inheriting the farm. There'd never been children—a pain that had dulled to an ache they no longer admitted feeling—but they'd worked hard and done well, building as comfortable a life as one could on Tatooine.

But Luke had never stopped dreaming about the girl who'd called out for Obi-Wan. Just last week he'd woken with a start, certain that the astromech was waiting for him in the garage, finally willing to play the full message for him. It was important that Luke hear it—there was something he needed to do. Something he was *meant* to do.

After the stormtroopers took the droids, Luke assumed he'd never learn the mysterious young woman's identity. But he'd been wrong. It had been blasted out over the HoloNet for weeks, ending with a final report that before her execution, Princess Leia Organa had apologized for her treasonous past and called for galactic unity.

Curiously, the Empire had never shared footage of those remarks, leaving Luke to remember his brief glimpse of the princess—and to wonder what desperate mission had caused her to seek out an old hermit on Tatooine.

Whatever it was, it had failed. Alderaan was a debris field now, along with Mon Cala and Chandrila—all destroyed by the battle station that had burned out the infections of Separatism and rebellion, leaving the galaxy at peace.

Or at least free of conflict. That was the same thing, or near enough.

He realized Camie was saying his name, and not for the first time.

"I hate it when you look like that," she said.

"Look like what?"

"You know what I mean. Like you think something went wrong. Like you got cheated, and this is all a big mistake. Like you should have followed Tank and Biggs, and gone to the Academy like you wanted to. Like you were meant to be far away from here."

"Camie—"

"Far away from me," she said in a smaller voice, turning away with her arms across her chest.

"You know I don't feel that way," he said, placing his hands on his wife's shoulders and trying to ignore the way she stiffened at his touch. "We've made a good life, and this is where I was meant to be. Now come on—let's go inside. It's getting cold."

Camie said nothing, but she let Luke lead her back toward the dome that marked the entrance to the homestead. Standing on the threshold, Luke lingered for a last look up into the night. But the Star Destroyer—if that was indeed what it had been—hadn't returned.

After a moment, he turned away from the empty sky.

Luke woke with a start, instinctively scooting up to a seated position. His mechanical hand whirred in protest, echoing the thrum of the insects that lived in the hardy grasses of Ahch-To.

He tried to shake away the dream as he dressed, donning his woolens and waterproof jacket. He opened the metal door of his hut, then shut it quietly behind him. It was nearly dawn, with the pale coming day a glimmer like a pearl on the horizon, above the black void of the sea.

The oceans of Ahch-To still astonished him—an infinity of water that could transform from blank and placid to roiling chaos. All that water still seemed impossible—at least in that way, he supposed, he was still a child of the Tatooine deserts.

Farther down the slopes, he knew, the Caretakers would soon rise to begin another day, as they had for eons. They had work to do, and so did he—they because of their ancient bargain, and he because of his own choice.

He'd spent his youth resenting chores on Tatooine; now they gave structure to his days on Ahch-To. There was milk to harvest, fish to catch, and a loose stone step to be put right.

But not quite yet.

Luke walked slowly up the steps until he reached the meadow overlooking the sea. He shivered—the summer was almost gone, and the dream still had him in its grip.

That was no ordinary dream, and you know it.

Luke raised the hood of his jacket with his mechanical hand, stroking his beard with the flesh-and-blood one. He wanted to argue with himself, but he knew better. The Force was at work here—it had cloaked itself in a dream, to slip through the defenses he'd thrown up against it.

But was the dream a promise? A warning? Or both?

Things are about to change. Something's coming.

PART I

CHAPTER 1

Leia Organa, once princess of Alderaan and now general of the Resistance, stood in a jungle clearing on D'Qar, a throng of officers and crewers on either side.

Their heads were down and their hands clasped. But Leia could see them stealing looks at her, and one another. Just as she could see the way they shifted uneasily from foot to foot.

War was coming, and they knew it. And they were worried that in her grief she'd forgotten.

The idea offended her. Leia knew all too much about war and grief—she'd lived with both for longer than some of these fretful officers had been alive. Over the five decades of her life, in fact, war and grief had been her only truly faithful companions. But she had never let either stop her from doing what had to be done.

The anger felt hot and sharp, and came as a relief after the hours of rudderless sorrow that had left her feeling empty, like she'd been hollowed out.

She didn't want to be standing here in the steaming jungle—she hadn't wanted to hold this ceremony at all. She'd stared balefully at Admiral Ackbar when the veteran Mon Calamari officer had taken her aside in D'Qar's war room to deliver his message.

Han is dead, at the hands of our son—and you want me to give a speech?

But Ackbar had faced down even worse things than an angry Leia Organa. Her old friend had held his ground, apologetic but insistent, and she'd understood what he was thinking. The Resistance had so little in terms of resources, whether one was talking about soldiers, ships, or credits. It had just won an enormous victory at Starkiller Base by destroying the First Order's superweapon. But the euphoria had been short-lived. The New Republic was all but destroyed, and the First Order was now free to unleash its fury on the Resistance.

Whether Leia liked it or not, the Resistance's greatest strength— its one indispensable asset—was her. Her leadership, her legacy of sacrifice, her *legend* were what held this fragile movement together. Without them, the Resistance would disintegrate before the First Order's guns.

Her people—and they *were* her people—were facing the greatest test in their history. To stand firm, they needed to see her and hear from her. And they needed her to look and sound strong and determined. They couldn't suspect that she felt broken and alone. If they did, they would break, too.

If that struck her as cruel, well, the galaxy was often cruel. Leia didn't need anyone to explain that to her.

So she had returned to the landing field where she'd said farewell to the *Millennium Falcon*—and what was the battered, saucer-shaped freighter but another piercing reminder of what she'd lost? Slowly and somberly, she'd read the names of the pilots who'd never returned from Starkiller Base. And then, trailed by her entourage, she'd walked slowly to the edge of the jungle for the second part of the ceremony Ackbar had insisted on.

One member of that entourage—a slim protocol droid with a gleaming golden finish—was more agitated than the others, or perhaps just doing a worse job of hiding it. Leia stepped forward and nodded at C-3PO, who signaled in turn to an old cam droid.

The hovering droid accompanied Leia as she stepped forward and looked down at the object she'd placed among the roots of one of

D'Qar's sprawling trees. The droid's sensors tracked her gaze, and its lens focused on a crude wooden figurine, whittled by an inexperienced hand.

Han had carved the figurine while she lay against his shoulder in an Ewok hut, the night before the Battle of Endor. He'd meant it to be her, wearing a primitive dress and holding a spear. But he hadn't told her that, and she'd asked innocently if it was one of their Ewok hosts. Han had tossed the carving aside in embarrassment, but she'd quietly retrieved it and had it in her pocket when the second Death Star exploded in the sky overhead.

It made for a pretty sorry memorial. But then Han had always traveled as if determined to avoid making much of a footprint. She'd first slipped inside his cabin on the *Falcon* during the journey to Yavin 4, hoping a look around would give her some understanding of how someone could be at once so charming and infuriating, and found a chaotic mess: worn spacer gear, stacked flight manuals, and bits of equipment shed by the *Falcon* during innumerable malfunctions. The only personal touch she'd found aboard the whole ship was the pair of golden dice hanging in the cockpit.

Leia turned to face the Resistance members, automatically waiting for the whir of the cam droid as it repositioned itself in front of her. She stared into its lens, her gaze steady.

"Han would hate this ceremony," she said, knowing her voice was clear and firm, as it had been during countless Senate sessions. "He had no patience for speeches or memorials. Which was to be expected from a man who was allergic to politics and suspicious of causes."

She saw a smile creep onto General Ematt's face. That was something. But then Ematt had fought alongside Han during the days of the Rebellion. So had Admiral Ackbar and Nien Nunb. Others, such as Commander D'Acy and Lieutenant Connix, knew of Han only through his connection to her, which had been severed years earlier. They were there for her, and waiting stone-faced.

"I once told Han that it was tiresome watching him do the right thing only after he'd exhausted every alternative," she said. "But sooner or later, he'd get there. Because Han hated bullies, and injustice, and cruelty—and when confronted with them, he could never stand down. Not in his youth on Corellia, not above Yavin, not on Endor, and not at Starkiller Base."

In the distance she could hear the whine of speeders moving heavy equipment—she had agreed to speak if Ackbar, in turn, agreed that her speech wouldn't halt the evacuation preparations. They'd both known the First Order had somehow tracked the Resistance to D'Qar—which meant its warships would be coming.

"Han fancied himself a scoundrel," Leia said, smiling at that last word. "But he wasn't. He loved freedom—for himself, certainly, but for everybody else in the galaxy, too. And time after time, he was willing to fight for that freedom. He didn't want to know the odds in that fight—because he'd already made up his mind that he'd prevail. And time after time, somehow, he did."

C-3PO turned his golden face toward her, and for a moment she worried that the droid might chime in with some anecdote about Captain Solo being particularly reckless—despite being programmed for etiquette and protocol, C-3PO had a singularly awful sense of diplomacy. So she pressed on before the droid could activate his vocabulator.

"Han didn't want to know the odds when he and Chewbacca flew back to the Death Star in time to save my brother Luke—and the last hope for our Alliance," she said. "He didn't ask about them when he accepted a general's rank for the ground assault at Endor. He didn't want them calculated when he fought for freedom at Kashyyyk. And he refused to think about them when he saw a way to fly through the First Order's shields and infiltrate Starkiller Base."

And when he agreed to reach out to our son, she might have added. *To reach out and try to draw him back out of the darkness.*

But she didn't say that. Leia had given everything she had to Alderaan, and then to the Alliance, the New Republic, and now the Resistance. But that was hers alone.

Leia saw Ematt's eyes on her and realized she was blinking hard, her lower lip trembling. She forced herself to breathe in, then out, until she knew from years of practice that she once again looked calm and composed.

Almost there.

A transport lifted into the sky above the Resistance base, its ion exhaust riffling the tops of the trees and sending a flight of sonar swallows skyward, warbling in protest. The faces around her watched the starship shrink into the distance before turning back in her direction, and she felt the anger return. They all knew how little time they had and everything that needed to be done. And yet she knew not one of them would dare to stop her if she talked all day, undone by grief and loss, until finally a First Order barrage silenced her forever.

Leia had been horrified to hear the Resistance called a cult of personality—that had been her New Republic critics' choice of words when they sought to dismiss her as a warmonger and a relic. They'd been wrong about most everything, but the criticism had a grain of truth: Leia and her fellow leaders had struggled to find the time or resources to make the Resistance anything else.

Well, no time to fix that one right now. And anyway, all my critics are dead.

"So many of you have offered me your sympathy, and I thank you for your kindness," Leia said. "But now I ask you to focus once again on the cause we all serve."

They were nodding now. Good. It was past time to finish this, and release them. The sooner she did, the sooner she could escape their endless parade of questions and demands, if only for a little while, and be alone with her private grief.

"We face long odds," Leia said. "The New Republic is leaderless, and the First Order is on the march. I can't tell you what those odds are—and I don't want to know. Because nothing could change my mind about what we have to do now."

She said nothing for a moment, letting her words hang there for the audience to consider.

"We must return to the fight," she said. "We do so because, like Han, we believe in justice and freedom. And because we will not accept a galaxy ruled by cruelty. We'll fight for those ideals. We'll fight for each other, and the sacred bonds we've forged serving side by side. And we'll fight for all the people in the galaxy who want to fight but can't—who need a champion. They're calling to us, in terror and grief. And it is our duty to answer that call."

Leia nodded at the officers around her, then at the cam droid and all those watching.

"We all have our sorrows," she said. "And we will never forget them, or those we have lost. In time, we will honor them more fully and properly. But we must save our sorrow for after the fight. Because right now, we have work to do."

CHAPTER 2

On a chilly planet in the galaxy's Outer Rim, two sisters huddled in a space designed for one.

Refnu's wharves were thronged with Resistance crewers trundling carts of black spherical magno-charges, directing plodding power droids to charge ports, and running diagnostics on the eight Star-Fortress bombers that would soon leave their berths.

Crammed inside the ball turret of the bomber *Cobalt Hammer*, Paige and Rose Tico had an excellent view of the activity around them. But the transparent ball shut out all sound, turning the Resistance's preparations for war into a pantomime. At least for these last few precious minutes, the sisters could pretend they were alone.

"I hate to think of you flying without me," Rose said, looking up at Paige. "What if you forget how the guns work?"

Paige laughed and patted the gunsight mount.

"You just checked them," she pointed out, then yawned and stretched as much as the turret's cramped confines allowed. "I pump these triggers, and the bad guys go away."

The twin cannons attached to the ball turret were locked down and didn't so much as twitch. But a gold, teardrop-shaped medallion wrapped around the gunsight mount did. Rose heard the *tink* the medallion made against the shaft and reached into the top of her jumpsuit to touch the similar medallion she wore on a cord around her neck. They represented the emblem of the Otomok system—the sisters' home.

Paige looked over and twitched her shoulder to bump her little sister out of her reverie.

"Besides, you've got work to do," Paige said. "If your bafflers can keep our other ships safe from detection, it could be a big advantage against the First Order."

Rose looked down, embarrassed. "All the bafflers do is hide engine emissions. Anybody could have done what I did. And probably better, too."

"Not this again. You know that isn't true."

"Fine, maybe it isn't. But I want to go with you."

"You'll be with me," Paige said with a smile, reaching up and tapping her medallion.

Rose looked up, her hand on her own medallion. "It's not the same."

"Maybe not. But it won't be long. I'll see you aboard the *Raddus* once the D'Qar evacuation is finished."

"Right," Rose said, clutching her medallion hard now. She could feel tears pooling in the corners of her eyes and threatening to spill down her cheeks.

"Rose," Paige said, one hand reaching for hers. "I'll be fine."

"I know, Pae-Pae," Rose said quietly, using her pet name for her sister, the one left over from their childhoods. "You're the best gunner in the whole Resistance, after all."

Paige just smiled and Rose closed her eyes, trying to lose herself in the familiar warmth and weight of her sister's body against hers. Their breathing had fallen into the same rhythm, their shoulders gently rising and falling together.

On their first mission aboard *Cobalt Hammer*, Rose had left her flight engineer's station once the bomber had entered hyperspace, clambering down the ladder from the flight deck and squeezing herself into the ball turret beside Paige. They'd spent hours staring out at the tumbling blue-white infinity around them and talking about everything they'd do once the galaxy was at peace—the planets they'd visit; the animals they'd raise; the homestead they'd build on some world with a kind warm sun, gentle breezes, and good grass.

If the rest of *Cobalt Hammer's* crew thought that odd, they soon accepted that the Ticos had a bond that would have been extraordinary even between twins. Since Rose's birth the sisters had rarely been apart for more than a couple of days—not growing up on Hays Minor in the Otomok system, and not while serving in the Resistance after fleeing their homeworld and its First Order occupiers.

That was about to change.

Refnu had no berths large enough for the *Ninka.* The frigate waited in low orbit, a glimmering star in the deep violet of the gloomy planet's perpetual twilight. Rose was scheduled for the transport after the next. The bombers would launch not long after that, fueled and stocked and armed, and coordinate hyperspace jumps with the *Ninka.* Paige would spend the journey to D'Qar in the ball turret, suspended in a little bubble surrounded by unimaginable cosmic forces. Rose ached to make the journey with her, but it was too late—she had agreed to stay aboard the *Ninka,* showing the techs how her baffler technology worked in the hope it could be adapted for other craft.

"What made you decide to say yes?" Paige asked, sensing her sister brooding.

"I wanted a new flight suit," Rose said.

That got a little laugh from her sister, as Rose had hoped. But then that was Paige—she'd be calm even with one engine offline, an unresponsive rudder, and space around her filled with turbolaser fire, coolly sizing up the situation and figuring out what needed to be done. Whatever genetic lottery had bestowed Paige with such poise had passed Rose over, leaving her empty-handed. Battle terrified her, and the hours waiting for it made her stomach clench and heave.

That's why you're a Resistance hero and I'm a maintenance tech, Rose thought about telling Paige, but it wouldn't help and there wasn't time. So she talked instead of bravery and responsibility—at least until she heard herself and admitted the real reason she'd agreed to take on her new assignment.

"I thought you wanted me to," Rose said. "I thought you were ready to let me take responsibility for *myself*."

"I want you to be yourself," Paige replied. "But of course that means being my sister, too."

She reached up, the motion precise and efficient as always, and freed her Otomok medallion from the cannon's gunsight mount, slipping it over her head.

"Nothing can change that," Paige said. "We're connected to each other, and to home. We don't have to be in the same place for that to be true."

The sisters hugged—it was time to go, and they both knew it.

"See you after the evacuation," Rose said, begging whatever power governed the universe to turn that bland prediction into an ironclad guarantee.

"See you then, Rose," Paige replied. It was what she always said before a mission—a deliberately casual farewell that Rose had come to believe was their good-luck charm.

Then Rose was levering herself out of the ball turret, careful not to step on her sister or knock the gunsight mount out of alignment. She emerged at the bottom of the bomber's ventral stalk—what crews called the Clip. The bomb bay doors at her feet were open, while a ladder led to the flight deck above her, climbing past racks of magno-charges. There were more than a thousand in all, enough to crack the crust of a planet or batter down the shields and blast open the hull armor of a capital ship. Many of the magno-charges had been decorated with cartoons or hastily scrawled words—gallant invocations of the Resistance cause were racked next to obscene suggestions for the First Order's leaders.

Rose counted six rows up from the bottom, then five magno-charges in from the edge until she found the black sphere she and Paige had marked with a stylus. The message they'd chosen was simple: JUSTICE FOR OTOMOK.

Rose heard the whine of a shuttle lifting off. That meant hers would be inbound. She lowered herself through the bomb bay doors, dropping to the deck, and glanced up at her sister in the ball turret. Paige was going over her preflight checklist, her datapad's screen bathing her face in pale white light. As she studied it, she reached up and tucked a stray lock of black hair under her padded cowl.

That gesture—familiar and unconscious—pierced Rose in a way their conversation hadn't. She looked wildly around the wharves, hunting for the silver-skinned bulk of Fossil, the squadron's hulking commanding officer. She'd tell Fossil that this had all been a big mistake and she'd fly aboard *Cobalt Hammer* as a backup flight engineer, or do anything else that needed doing, but she wasn't leaving Paige.

And if Fossil said no? Then Rose would wait until she wasn't looking, climb back into the Clip, and conceal herself in a maintenance locker until they were in hyperspace and it was too late to get rid of her.

But then Paige turned, saw her sister, and smiled and waved. Like nothing was wrong. Like there was no danger whatsoever.

As the shuttle that would bear her away descended, Rose forced herself to wave back.

See you then, Paige.

CHAPTER 3

Even though she was standing on the landing field outside the Resistance base, Kadel Ko Connix knew the moment the First Order warships emerged from hyperspace above the planet.

Every comlink around her begin squawking and squealing—a chorus of urgent calls that struck her as oddly similar to the nighttime calls of D'Qar's brilliantly colored tree-lizards.

Beside her, PZ-4CO's eyes brightened. The bright-blue protocol droid shuffled her feet and looked down at Connix, the servomotors whirring in her elongated neck.

"Comm/scan reports three *Resurgent*-class Star Destroyers and a larger capital ship," PZ-4CO intoned, her voice cool and pleasant as always. "Unknown class, Dreadnought-sized. Preliminary estimated length seven thousand five hundred meters."

Connix winced. The Resistance had known the First Order was building warships and armies in the Unknown Regions, beyond the galactic frontier. General Organa had sent a steady stream of holographic footage and intelligence data providing evidence for that conclusion to New Republic senators, hoping to batter down the galactic government's stubborn insistence that reports of a First Order military buildup were at best a figment of the general's imagination and at worst exaggerations. But a capital ship of that size? That was worse than the darkest imaginings of the Resistance's intelligence analysts.

So was Starkiller Base. What else has Snoke been hiding out there?

"I am troubled by the apparent limitations of our threat database," PZ-4CO said.

Connix had to laugh.

"I'm troubled by a lot of things these days, Peazy. Such as the fact that where we're standing is going to be a blast crater when the First Order gets here. What's left on our to-do list?"

PZ-4CO's eyes brightened again. Connix spotted Flight Officer Jones hurrying across the landing field toward them.

"Approximately thirty percent of the deep fuel reservoir remains to be siphoned," the droid said as Jones caught his breath. "Scuttle procedure for mission-critical computers is incomplete. And maintenance stocks are still being transferred from lower-level stores."

"There are still thirty pallets of cannon shells in C bunker," Jones said.

Great. Add one more thing to the list.

"Time to completion?" Connix asked, her eyes jumping from the transports still on the landing field to the Resistance crewers and droids hurrying in and out of the portals to the subterranean base.

"Approximately ninety minutes," PZ-4CO said.

"We don't have ninety minutes. We may not have nine."

Slow down and think. Panic doesn't solve problems; it just creates new ones.

General Organa had taught her that—and so much else.

"Forget the cannon shells and the remaining maintenance stocks," Connix said. "Anything still down below is staying."

"Quartermaster Prindel will be extremely agitated by this decision," PZ-4CO said.

"Bollie will have to take it up with Snoke. Give the order, Peazy."

PZ-4CO's head swiveled and Connix knew the droid was transmitting the new instructions. She bit her lip, unable to resist another peek skyward, and considered the remaining tasks.

The Resistance ships that had answered General Organa's plea for assistance were low on fuel—every drop in that reservoir might prove critical. Yet siphoning it out was an agonizingly slow process.

No easy answer there.

Then there were the computers, and the information in them that might be recoverable after an incomplete purge. The First Order might bombard the base from orbit, finishing the Resistance's job for it. But it might also send down slicers and data retrieval droids to scour the databanks. What they found could endanger everyone from Resistance allies elsewhere in the galaxy to the families of those who'd pledged themselves to the cause.

No easy answer there, either.

So what would General Organa do? Fortunately, Connix knew.

She'd say perfect information is a luxury you can rarely afford. All you can do is make the best decision with whatever imperfect information you do have.

"Jones, tell the scuttle team to use the computers for target practice and get out of there," Connix said. "Peazy, prioritize the fuel transfer. But I want that tanker and all remaining transports airborne in ten minutes."

"Given our fuel levels, ten minutes may not be—" PZ-4CO objected.

"We have to get the fleet into hyperspace," Connix said. "Once we make the jump, the First Order won't be able to track us and will have to begin hunting all over again. That'll give us time to figure out how to replenish our fuel stocks."

"This decision—"

"Has been made," Connix said firmly. "Give the order, Peazy."

Named for a long-dead rebel admiral, the *Raddus* was the Resistance flagship, a bulbous MC85 Mon Calamari star cruiser bristling with guns and augmented shield projectors. Measuring nearly thirty-five hundred meters from its pointed beak to the cluster of engines at the stern, the *Raddus* would have been a mighty warship even during the years in which Emperor Palpatine had turned the Empire into an unparalleled military-industrial complex.

But the *Raddus* was puny compared with the massive First Order Dreadnought cruising slowly through space toward D'Qar, accompanied by three Star Destroyers. Aboard the Resistance warship's bridge, Admiral Ackbar stroked his barbels and gazed down at a hologram table showing the situation above D'Qar. Beside him stood Leia, the starfighter pilot Poe Dameron, and C-3PO.

The Resistance's three other warships—the *Anodyne, Ninka,* and *Vigil*—were moving out of low orbit, having taken on most of the transports bearing evacuees up from D'Qar's surface. But the First Order arrivals were closing quickly.

"They've found us," said a Resistance monitor.

"Well, we knew that was coming," Poe said, his gaze sliding from the holographic table to a viewscreen. "Connix, is the base fully evacuated?"

"Still loading the last batch of transports," Connix replied. "We need more time."

Poe looked at Leia, but the general had anticipated what he was going to say.

"You've got an idea," she said with a weary fondness. "But I won't like it."

Poe opened his mouth to make his case, hoping something eloquent would come out. But Leia had anticipated that, too.

"Go," she said.

General Armitage Hux stood on the bridge of the First Order Star Destroyer *Finalizer,* gazing out at the blue-green planet hanging in space.

Four ships hung in orbit above the planet, below its asteroid rings—a bulbous Mon Calamari cruiser, an angular frigate, a cargo ship with a rounded front and a jagged rear, and a smaller ship with an oversized bow like a broken crescent.

Hux automatically assessed and cataloged the Resistance warships, drawing on years of training. He knew the Mon Calamari craft: It was the *Raddus*, which served Leia Organa's rabble as flagship and mobile command center. The next-largest ship was a Nebulon-C frigate, from a line built for the New Republic after the accords that ended its conflict with the Empire. The ship with the rounded front was some kind of cargo frigate, heavily modified. The ship with the crescent bow was a model Hux didn't recognize, but it was clearly a warship, bristling with point-defense cannons and ordnance pods.

Within a few minutes it would be academic: All four would be space dust.

The *Finalizer*'s gleaming black bridge was a model of efficiency, with controllers and monitors briskly exchanging information from the Star Destroyer's targeting computers and sensor suites. Hux smiled at the thought of himself as the center of all that activity—a slim, dignified figure in black, uniform perfect, standing at parade rest.

"We've caught them in the middle of their evacuation," said Peavey, the *Finalizer*'s captain. "The entirety of the Resistance, in one fragile basket."

Hux suppressed a surge of annoyance. Edrison Peavey was old—a veteran of Imperial service who'd served with Hux's late father. He and a handful of Imperial loyalists had managed to escape the New Republic's hunters by venturing into the uncharted stars of the Unknown Regions.

Those men and women had been useful in their time. But that time was at an end—the First Order had decapitated the New Republic leadership with a single demonstration of its technological might.

True, Starkiller Base had then been destroyed, but Hux told himself that was merely an unfortunate setback—one that had been less a military defeat than the product of incompetence and treachery within the First Order. Those failures had been dealt with, or near enough. Most of those who had failed Hux and Supreme Leader Snoke had been vaporized with the base; those who'd escaped punishment would get what they deserved soon enough.

Hux smiled thinly. Truthfully, it didn't much matter. The New Republic Senate was in ashes, the heart of its fleet was incinerated, and the Resistance vermin who'd had the temerity to assault Starkiller Base had been careless enough to leave a trail back to their nest. Once these few remaining insurgents had been destroyed, no one in the galaxy would dare oppose the First Order's dominion. Hux would be free to build a dozen new Starkillers—or a hundred.

And in the meantime, the First Order had no shortage of other weapons—including ones Imperial commanders such as Peavey had only dreamed of.

That was it right there, Hux thought. Peavey and his generation saw the First Order's impending triumph as a restoration of the Empire, not realizing how that only proved their obsolescence. They couldn't or wouldn't see that the regime they'd served was not merely gone but superseded. The First Order was the fulfillment of what the Empire had struggled to become. It had distilled and perfected its strengths while eliminating its weaknesses.

Or at least *most* of its weaknesses, Hux thought, eyeing Peavey. But there would be time for another culling. In the meantime, a reminder of Peavey's station would have to suffice.

"Perfect," he said. "I have my orders from Supreme Leader Snoke himself. This is where we snuff out the Resistance once and for all. Tell Captain Canady to prime his Dreadnought. Incinerate their base, destroy those transports, and obliterate their fleet."

The order was transmitted and received by Moden Canady aboard the bridge of the *Fulminatrix*, the enormous *Mandator IV*-class Siege Dreadnought at the heart of the First Order formation. On Canady's command, the two massive cannons slung beneath his ship's belly began to slowly swivel, reorienting themselves to fire on the hot spot of transmissions and energy emissions that sensor crews had detected on the planet below.

Canady's warrant officer, Bascus, was gazing at the holographic screen and tracking the cannons' progress with something akin to ecstasy on his face. Canady scowled. His crew was half his age, with scant experience outside of battle sims. That they were untested wasn't their fault; that they were arrogant and undisciplined was.

"Reorient the topside batteries to target the Resistance fleet," Canady ordered. "And prep our fighter squadrons for launch."

"General Hux ordered no fighter deployment," objected Bascus. "He feels a demonstration—"

"Do I need to explain the difference between 'prep for launch' and 'launch'?" Canaday asked Bascus.

"Captain!" called a scope monitor from the bridge pit, his surroundings lit red for ideal visibility during battlefield conditions. "We have a single Resistance X-wing fighter approaching. It's moving to attack formation."

The X-wing's call sign was *Black One,* befitting its black fuselage and eye-catching orange flares. Those colors were more muted than Poe would have liked—his beloved fighter had returned from Starkiller Base with a bad case of carbon scoring, frayed fire-control linkages, and a host of other minor maladies. Goss Toowers, the perpetually dismayed starfighter maintenance chief, had looked over the fighter and offered Poe a choice: His overburdened techs could repair the battle damage, or they could install the piece of experimental equipment Poe had asked for, the one that hadn't quite been ready for the Starkiller raid.

Poe had opted for the experimental equipment, and stuck with that choice even after the sad-eyed Goss reminded him that it was somewhere between possible and likely that it would kill him the first time it was engaged.

After all, everybody knew the only thing that made Goss more miserable than pilots was pilots having fun.

Not that Poe was having fun, exactly—in fact, hurtling alone through space toward three First Order capital ships struck him as an aggressively bad idea.

Even as part of a squadron, flying a starfighter was both physically and mentally exhausting: Stress, g-forces, and changing gravity beat up your body, while the constant need for situational awareness, multitasking, and improvisation taxed your brain. It was simultane-

ously an ever-shifting puzzle and an endurance test, with fatal consequences if you flunked.

But at least behind the control yoke Poe had something to do.
And that was preferable to being stuck on the bridge of the *Raddus,*
fidgeting uselessly and getting in the way. Poe would never admit
this, not even to Leia, but with a starfighter around him, the galaxy
made sense in a way that it too often didn't otherwise.

Judging from the mournful beeping of BB-8 in the droid socket
behind the X-wing's cockpit, his astromech felt differently.

"Happy beeps here, buddy," Poe said. "Come on—we've pulled
crazier stunts than this."

BB-8 didn't dignify that with a response.

"Happy beeps," Poe said again, this time more to himself.

"For the record, I'm with the droid on this one," Leia said over his
comm channel.

Poe almost laughed. "Thanks for your support, General."

"A single light fighter?" asked an incredulous Hux, peering into deep
space. "What is this?"

The bridge crew said nothing. Hux looked from one side to the
other, exasperated by the impassive faces around him.

"Well . . . shoot him!"

Before the gunners could carry out this order, a ship-to-ship
transmission crackled over the *Finalizer's* audio pickups.

"Attention, this is Commander Poe Dameron of the Republic fleet,"
the voice said. "I have an urgent communiqué for General Hugs."

Hux felt all eyes turning his way, and red threatening to bloom in
his cheeks. He knew that pilot's name all too well—Dameron had
fired the shot that destroyed Starkiller Base, and he'd been an irritant
long before that. Hux had sworn he'd see the pilot back on a First
Order torture rack one day soon—and that this time he'd oversee the
interrogation personally. Where Kylo Ren and his sorcery had failed,
Hux and his technological prowess would triumph.

"Patch him through," he snapped. "This is General Hux of the

First Order. The Republic is no more. Your fleet are rebel scum and war criminals. Tell your precious princess there will be no terms. There will be no surrender."

He was proud of that last part and made a note to revisit it during the tribunals that would be carried live over the HoloNet to the entire galaxy. But Dameron, to his bafflement, didn't reply.

"Hi, I'm holding for General Hugs?" the pilot asked after a moment.

"*This* is Hux. You and your friends are doomed! We will wipe your filth from the galaxy!"

Another moment, and then the reply: "Okay, I'll hold."

"What?" Hux looked around in consternation. "Hello?"

"Hello? I'm still here."

Hux glowered at a communications officer. "Can he hear me?"

The officer nodded gravely.

Peavey, Hux noted, seemed less concerned with whatever was wrong with his ship's short-range communications than he was with the readouts displaying the distance between the lone X-wing and the First Order battle line—a number that was steadily shrinking.

"Hugs—with an *H*?" Dameron asked. "Skinny guy, kind of pasty?"

"I can hear you, can you hear me?" Hux replied.

"Look, I can't hold forever," Dameron said, sounding exasperated. "If you reach him, tell him Leia has an urgent message for him. About his mother."

Hux could faintly hear something else in the transmission—it sounded like an electronic chortle.

"I believe he's tooling with you, sir," Peavey said.

Hux glared at the *Finalizer*'s captain and found that the older man's face was a carefully expressionless mask—as was the face of every other officer on the bridge.

"Open fire!" he screamed, bringing his fist down on the nearest console. It hurt abominably, but fortunately all eyes on the bridge were fixed ahead as a web of turbolaser fire filled the emptiness of space, searching for the X-wing and its infuriating pilot.

When his energy counter hit full, Poe yelled for BB-8 to punch it. A moment later *Black One* leapt forward as if kicked, propelled by the experimental booster engine grafted to the starfighter's stern.

For a moment Poe feared he'd black out, overcome by g-forces like nothing he'd ever experienced behind the stick. But then the acceleration compensators kicked in and his vision cleared. Ahead of him loomed the First Order's massive Siege Dreadnought, laserfire arcing up at him from the turbolaser cannons that dotted its upper hull.

"Whoa—that's got a kick!" Poe yelled as his fighter skimmed over the warship's nose, at the apex of the giant wedge.

The *Fulminatrix*'s cannons had been designed to be able to target enemy starfighters, but *Black One* was moving at speeds no First Order point-defense crews had ever experienced, even in the simulator. Poe juked and weaved over the battleship's hull, getting a sense of how much more lead time he needed to hit his targets. Once he had the timing down, a single pass over the topside reduced several of the cannons to smoking scrap. As Poe wheeled around for another run, he activated his comlink and switched over to the general Resistance channel.

"Taking out the cannons now—bombers, start your approach!"

Aboard the *Fulminatrix*, Canady watched grimly as the lone X-wing eliminated cannon after cannon, stripping his ship of its dorsal defenses. A hologram of Hux flickered to life.

"Captain Canady, why aren't you blasting that puny ship?" the First Order general demanded.

Canady hadn't accumulated a lengthy Imperial service record by being ignorant of the chain of command or unaware of the damage a vengeful superior could do to a career. But being lectured by a vicious child—and one who'd favored grand gestures over basic military tactics, at that—was too much for him.

"That puny ship is too small and at too close range," he told Hux scornfully. "We need to scramble our fighters."

As Hux considered this, Canady turned away from the hologram. "Five bloody minutes ago," he muttered.

"He'll never penetrate our armor," Goneril said, peering disdainfully at the X-wing closing in on them.

Canady allowed himself a brief fantasy in which he shoved the adjutant out of a conveniently located air lock.

"He's not trying to penetrate our armor—he's clearing out our surface cannons," he told Goneril icily.

In a different situation, the offended incredulity on his adjutant's face would have been something to treasure. But not today—not when Canady had a pretty good idea what would happen next.

"Captain!" called Bascus. "Resistance bombers approaching!"

"Of course they are," Canady said.

CHAPTER 4

The bomber crews of Cobalt and Crimson squadrons had spent hours at battle stations, waiting for a launch order from the *Raddus's* bridge. It hadn't come—not when the chatter about transports and supplies became frantic, or when First Order TIEs began harrying the Resistance fleet, or when the sensor officers started yelling about warships closing on their position. Aboard the eight bombers, backs were sore, bladders were full, and tempers were short.

All of which was forgotten when their communications systems crackled to life and Fossil barked at them to go, go, go.

Suspended in the ball turret below *Cobalt Hammer's* bomb magazine, Paige felt the faint jostling as conduits and hoses were uncoupled. As always, she felt a momentary flutter at the sight of the flight deck a mere meter below the seemingly fragile glass globe enclosing her. If the repulsorlifts cut out now, she'd be pulped against the deck by the weight of the ship above her.

But Finch Darrow was a capable pilot. He'd do his job, just as she'd do hers.

Cobalt Hammer gave a little lurch, and Paige couldn't resist reaching into the collar of her flight suit to touch the medallion around her neck.

Then there was nothing below her but black and endless space.

Every muscle in Paige's body tensed during the fraction of a second before her brain was able to process that she wasn't falling. Then she was pressed back in her seat as *Cobalt Hammer* accelerated to attack speed.

"Releasing weapons lock," Finch said in Paige's ears. "Spennie, Paige, look sharp."

Paige rotated her dual laser cannons—left, right, up and down, nodding at the purr of her ball turret's gimbals.

"Guns hot, systems green," Spennie said coolly from the rear turret.

"I'm good to go," Paige said. Her eyes slid from the bombers on either side of *Cobalt Hammer* to the green globe of D'Qar to the X-wings and A-wings beyond them. Rose's bafflers couldn't hide the bombers during an attack run, so the equipment had been stripped out, leaving the bombers relying on fighter escorts. Far ahead, Paige could see three brighter stars that she knew were the First Order attackers.

"My scope's negative for bandits," Spennie said. "Where are the enemy fighters?"

"Feeling lonely, Spen?" asked Nix Jerd, *Cobalt Hammer*'s bombardier.

"Cut the chatter," Finch said. "We'll have more company than we want any minute now."

Paige's headset crackled and a new voice was in her ear—that of Tallie Lintra, the squadron commander.

"Bombers, keep that formation tight," she warned. "Fighters, protect the bombers—don't get drawn into dogfights. Let me hear you say *copy that*, Starck."

"No fun, copy that," replied Stomeroni Starck, Tallie's wingmate.

"All right then. Let's do some damage and buy our fleet some time."

Paige's turret was barely big enough for her, let alone a holographic tank like those found on warship bridges and in ready rooms, offering a computer-constructed overview of a battle and its participants. Fortunately, she didn't need one. She knew the formation the squadron had assumed for their attack run—she'd reviewed it repeatedly during the briefings on Refnu and while traveling through hyperspace to D'Qar.

The dots of the First Order warships were larger and brighter now. Paige forced herself to breathe in and out, slowly and deeply. For now, the bombers and their escort fighters were flying straight at the enemy, their formation rock-solid and undisturbed by enemy fire.

The quiet was unnerving—because Paige knew it was about to be shattered.

Aboard the *Raddus,* Ackbar studied the holotank that Paige Tico was only able to see in her head.

Once, Ackbar would have rejected a bridge holotank as a crutch for inattentive commanders. But his vision wasn't what it had once been, and in recent years he'd noticed that he was no longer able to process information with the same speed and precision he'd once taken for granted.

He didn't like to admit it, but denying it was folly: He'd grown old.

In a kinder galaxy, Ackbar supposed, that would have meant it was time for him to retire to a grotto in a warm lagoon on Mon Cala, surrounded by schools of descendants who'd take turns pretending to be interested in his war stories. But he didn't live in that galaxy. This one was full of surprises, most of them unpleasant of late, and its people still needed him, regardless of the blurriness at the edges of his vision or the details that no longer proved so simple to organize.

Self-pity is for humans. You can float in your own tide pool later. For now, stiff fins and sharp teeth.

The *Raddus* and the three other Resistance capital ships had responded to D'Qar's distress call at all speed after the Starkiller raid, delivering bombers and starfighters to defend the evacuation Ackbar knew would be a necessity. Now the *Raddus* was at the rear of the Resistance formation, where it could interpose its augmented shield envelope between the smaller ships and the First Order attackers.

The bombers and starfighters were beyond the shield envelope's protection, moving at top speed toward the Siege Dreadnought—the most dangerous enemy ship on the battlefield. As soon as the evacuation was complete, those bombers and fighters would need to be recalled so the fleet could jump to hyperspace.

With any luck that would be soon—those eight StarFortresses were the only bombers the Resistance had left. They'd been unavailable for the Starkiller raid, forcing Ackbar and the other Resistance leaders to improvise an attack by commandos and starfighters to crack the First Order's defenses. The plan had worked, but it had been a near thing—and Ackbar didn't want to be left hoping for favorable currents again in the future.

Still, galactic history was filled with commanders who'd lost today's battle by worrying about tomorrow's. The transports were carrying essential Resistance equipment and personnel, and they'd needed the bombers to buy time to get them off D'Qar. It was that simple; there was no point complicating it with anxiety about a future that might never arrive.

So how much more time did they need to buy? Ackbar reached out and tapped the tank's controls, accessing PZ-4CO's data banks. He tugged at his chin barbels, trying to derive a time estimate from the droid's data. Bollie Prindel could have made sense of it much more quickly, but the quartermaster was busy directing the stowage of supplies brought up from D'Qar.

As he pondered PZ-4CO's information, Ackbar overheard some of the younger officers—he often called them the fry, to General Organa's amusement—speculating about why the First Order hadn't launched fighter squadrons and seemed content to let its battlewagons trundle into position above D'Qar.

It was the right question to ask, but Ackbar knew the fry would come up with the wrong answer. As the young so often did, they were arguing about tactics but failing to consider personalities. Hux's principal concern wasn't winning an engagement, but demonstrating the First Order capabilities and might for a galactic audience. He envisioned his massive Dreadnought coolly incinerating the Resistance from orbit, a spectacle he imagined would cow those worlds not already stunned into submission by the destruction of Hosnian Prime.

Ackbar inflated his gular sac in disapproval, the gurgle drawing a startled glance from one of the young humans. Hux was a vicious little squig, but yet to grow into his teeth—he had the ruthlessness of age but none of its wisdom. A veteran commander worried about *winning*, not playing to an audience. Narratives were far easier to shape than battles, and they could be composed in safety and at leisure.

Hux was a fool—but a fool with vastly superior forces at his command.

The data window from D'Qar began blinking. Ackbar accessed it and looked up from the tank, allowing himself a fingerling's pride at being the first to deliver good news.

"The last transports are in the air," he said.

Leia Organa's eyes—tiny, pathetically inadequate for use in low light, and ignorant of other, richer wavelengths—jumped to his. She spoke into her comm: "Poe, the evacuation's almost complete. Just keep them busy a little longer."

As she spoke, dots winked into existence around the First Order ships.

"One cannon left," Poe said. "And here comes the parade."

The Dreadnought had finally launched its fighters.

Dozens of TIEs swarmed around the Siege Dreadnought, but only three of them veered off from their initial vector to pursue Poe across the warship's topside. His instinctive surge of relief quickly turned to alarm—the other TIEs were headed for the approaching bombers, which were far more vulnerable than his X-wing.

Stay on target, Poe reminded himself. The best way to support the bombers was to destroy that final cannon, rather than run off chasing TIEs and leave it free to wreak havoc. And the cannon would be in his sights in another moment.

Poe rolled *Black One* slightly for a better angle, but the lead TIE pilot had anticipated that, and the three fighters swooped up from below, blasting away at the X-wing's undercarriage. Red lights flared on his console.

"Damn! Beebee-Ate, my weapons systems are down. We need to take out that last cannon or our bombers are toast. Work your magic!"

Behind Poe in the starfighter's droid socket, BB-8 was already dealing with a lengthy list of mostly irrelevant alerts from the X-wing's central computer. That was nothing new: Every astromech in the Resistance droid pool could tell you that *Black One* was a prickly, vainglorious machine.

The X-wing had used its very first processor cycle after BB-8 jacked into the droid slot to flag taking off without having completed the preflight checklist as a mission-critical risk. BB-8 had deleted that alert, only to discover *Black One* had elevated twenty-eight maintenance alerts to the top of its priority queue. BB-8 patiently reslotted them below action items such as engine ignition and shield generator start, only to see the maintenance items reappear atop the list one by one. The astromech had solved that through brute force, locking *Black One* out of the maintenance subroutine entirely—which had generated an entirely new round of complaints.

With an electronic sigh, BB-8 extended various tools from his six swappable tool-bay disks, using everything from magnetometers to ion pulse tracers to seek out the source of the malfunction while fielding a new alert from *Black One*: The starfighter thought it was important to warn BB-8 about possible danger to its gyroscope from solar flares.

Solar flares? *Really?*

The Resistance astromechs classified *Black One* as a high-communications-volume interface. BB-8 searched his memory for an organic equivalent of that classification, and found a high-confidence answer almost immediately.

Black One was a pain in the ass.

Poe, of course, knew none of this—BB-8 would have been a sorry astromech indeed if he had. The pilot was corkscrewing the X-wing through increasingly dizzy spins, trying to throw off his pursuers while leaving himself in position to whip around and target that last First Order cannon.

"Tallie, heads-up!" he called.

In her A-wing, Tallie saw the TIEs rocketing toward her in skirmish formation and grimaced.

"Here they come!" she yelled. "Gunners! Look alive!"

Then the black-hulled starfighters were hurtling through the formation, like dire hounds loose among the whellays back home on Pippip 3. An X-wing in Kaiden Scorbo's flight was stitched by laserfire and sheared in two, the pilot's scream mercifully cut short. Zanyo Arak's pilots doubled back to fire at the First Order hunters, while the bombers' rear and belly turrets opened up, filling the emptiness around them with crisscrossing fire.

"They're everywhere!" yelled Jaycris Tubbs, panic cresting in his voice. "I can't—"

Tubbs's transmission vanished into static. A TIE dropped onto the tail of C'ai Threnalli's X-wing, forcing the Abednedo pilot to break formation and leave Cobalt Squadron's portside flank unprotected. Tallie cut that way, noting approvingly that Starck had matched the maneuver perfectly. Her A-wing's cannons severed a TIE fighter's solar panel and sent it careening away from the bombers, out of control and doomed.

"We're not gonna get old out here, Poe!" she warned. "Gimme good news!"

"Negative," Poe replied. "Hold tight. Beebee-Ate, we've got to kill that last cannon! I need my guns!"

He shed altitude, dropping his X-wing to just a few meters above the Dreadnought's hull, ignoring a new set of flashing red warnings and hoping the TIE pilots wouldn't have the nerve to follow him.

BB-8 squawked in frustration, deleted six new proximity alerts from *Black One,* and swung his head into a nook in the X-wing's fuselage. *There* was the problem—a smoking junction box in the narrow space below the reactant fusion and ionization chamber. Fortunately, repairing the short would take a couple of seconds at most. BB-8 extended a welding arm, but other circuits began to spark. BB-8 extended several more arms from his chassis, but the malfunctions were cascading faster than he could repair them.

The astromech squalled in frustration.

On the *Fulminatrix*'s bridge, Canady stood with his hands behind his back and his feet half a meter apart, watching the tiny figures of bombers and starfighters pirouetting in the holotank. As always, he found himself struck by the beauty of a battle reduced to a ballet of angles and vectors. At such a remove it looked bloodless, an ever-changing exercise in geometries and probabilities.

Commanders could get hypnotized by what Canady knew was an illusion. Pilots were dying out there—pilots under his command. The less time they spent out there, the more of them would come home.

"Are the auto cannons primed?" he asked.

"Primed and ready, sir," Goneril said.

"What are we waiting for? Fire on the base."

The *Fulminatrix* quivered beneath Canady's feet as the enormous turbolasers roared. Those weapons dwarfed anything he'd had available to him in the Imperial Starfleet, and had been built to scour planets of life. A single shot could obliterate planetary shields as if they were an afterthought and turn a hundred cubic meters of crust into vapor and slag.

"Bring up the orbital imagers," Canady ordered.

A controller routed the feed onto a viewscreen. A fiery cloud roiled and churned above the planet's surface, a miniature hurricane of destruction. Around the storm, the jungle was in flames, with new conflagrations erupting in chains extending for kilometers away from the blast zone. The Resistance base on D'Qar had been erased.

Goneril stood frozen, staring at the screen in adoration.

———

Aboard the *Raddus*, Ackbar ignored the worried outcry from the fry as the First Order opened fire on D'Qar. The base had served the Resistance well, but it no longer mattered—Ackbar only had eyes for the bulbous loadlifters on final approach to the *Raddus*'s main hangar. Four remained to be brought to safety, then two, and then—at long last—none.

"The last transports are aboard," he announced. "Evacuation is complete."

"Poe, you did it," Leia said into her headset. "Now get your squad back here."

"No! General, we can do this! We have a chance to take out a Dreadnought!"

Ackbar gurgled in disapproval. That was just like Dameron—for all his skill as a pilot and his promise as a leader, he remained an impulsive youth, with too many impulsive-youth mistakes left to make. Such as thinking of himself as the predator when he was actually the prey.

Ackbar's old friend Leia Organa, on the other hand, had been stripped of her youth by burdens almost too painful to bear.

"*We* need to get the fleet out of here," Leia told the rebellious pilot.

"These things are fleet-killers! We can't let it get away!" Poe shot back.

"Disengage now. That's an order."

A blinking light indicated that Dameron had disconnected the transmission. In the holotank, his tiny X-wing swerved around for yet another pass at the Siege Dreadnought's last remaining cannon.

Ackbar swiveled one eye at Leia. Every officer on the bridge seemed transfixed by the cold fury on her face.

Leia, suddenly conscious of their attention, stared down the gold-plated protocol droid standing next to her.

"Threepio, wipe that nervous look off your face," she ordered.

That order, at least, was obeyed.

Poe and Tallie saw the second wave of incoming TIEs at the same time. Another X-wing was blasted apart, and laserfire tore a bomber in two. There was real fear in Tallie's voice now—even if the bombers escaped the prowling TIEs, they were too slow and sluggish to avoid point-defense fire from the Dreadnought. Even one cannon would be enough to pick them off one by one.

Which meant that cannon had to go. Poe aimed *Black One*'s nose directly at it.

"Beebee-Ate! Now or never!"

With inventiveness born of desperation, BB-8 had lowered the elevator he used to assume his station in the droid socket halfway, which required that he delete three improper-operation alerts from *Black One*, and rolled into the cavity of the fuselage, as close to the short in the junction box as possible.

Ignoring an improper-operation alert from his own systems, the astromech retracted his welding arm, depolarized the magnetic casters that kept his head attached to his spherical body, and used the welding arm to swing the head out and down, like a man doffing his hat. It smashed into the sparking junction box, primary photoreceptor swirling with electronic feedback.

Poe saw the trigger lights come to life and mashed his finger down, his X-wing's S-foils opening up at full power. The Siege Dreadnought's cannon emplacement vanished in a pillar of flame, and Poe yanked on the X-wing's control yoke, feet jammed against the pedals, grimacing as g-forces slammed him into his seat.

The maneuver ended with three TIEs in front of *Black One*'s nose. A moment later all three were glittering motes of space dust.

"Yeaaah! All clear! Bring the bombs!"

"Happy to," Tallie said in his ear. "Here we go!"

To Canady's disgust, Bascus was still monitoring the destruction on D'Qar—admittedly impressive but now thoroughly irrelevant—even as the Resistance bombers closed on the *Fulminatrix* and her now-defenseless topside.

Canady ordered the second wave of TIEs to double back and protect the ship, then called for the auto cannons to be recharged—and to target the Resistance flagship.

If that interfered with Hux's carefully planned demonstration, well, Canady would accept the consequences.

He had a ship to save.

In the belly turret of *Cobalt Hammer,* Paige clutched her dual triggers and sent blast after blast of fire into space around her.

Every shot rattled the glass ball encapsulating her—between that and the impact of near-misses from marauding TIEs, she'd bitten her tongue more times than she could count. The temperature was rising inside the ball, sending sweat running down her forehead and into her eyes. She wanted desperately to wipe it away, but didn't dare let go of the triggers.

An MG-100 StarFortress flew like a torpid asteroid, and so each bomber relied on its neighbors for protection, flying so the rear and ball gunners could overlap their fields of fire.

But as Fossil had taught her, a plan only lasted until you got punched. Three bombers had been destroyed, forcing Cobalt and Crimson squadrons to shift their positions. And still the TIEs kept coming, dueling X-wings and A-wings that wheeled and circled around the bombers, trying to protect them from the relentless First Order fire.

A TIE smashed into the clip of one of Crimson Squadron's bombers, detonating its payload and taking out two neighboring bombers in a devastating chain reaction.

Over the shared channel, C'ai Threnalli yelped in Abnedish, warning Poe that they couldn't hold off the attackers.

"Yes we can!" urged Poe, speeding toward the dogfight in his X-wing. "Stay tight with the bombers!"

Paige pumped bolts at a TIE wheeling across her vision, the belly turret swiveling smoothly to follow the enemy fighter's path. Laser bolts pierced its ball cockpit, sending its solar panels spiraling off in either direction.

Rose would have gotten a kick out of that one—on their first bomber missions, Fossil had lectured her about needing to pay attention to her flight-engineer duties and not to her big sister's prowess as a gunner. But Paige had no time to exult—another TIE was pinwheeling toward her, emerald laserfire lancing out in search of *Cobalt Hammer*.

Ahead, the Dreadnought's nose was approaching like a shoreline.

"We're almost there!" Tallie said. "Bombardiers, begin drop sequence!"

Above her on the flight deck Nix Jerd would now be inputting commands into the bombardier's pedestal, initiating the bomb sequence and activating the remote trigger he carried. Paige knew his command would send more than a thousand magno-charges tumbling out of *Cobalt Hammer*'s bomb bay, drawn to the target below. She would be able to watch them all the way down, and would feel the familiar lurch as their bomber shed its payload and rose, freed of the proton bombs' mass.

If they reached the target.

Brilliant white light flared to starboard and *Cobalt Hammer* was slammed sideways, the bomber's fuselage groaning under the strain. Paige had instinctively thrown up her hands to protect her face and was left fumbling for the triggers, frantically trying to blink away the spots in her vision.

The First Order pilots had taken advantage of her lapse to dive at *Cobalt Hammer*, near-misses shaking the bomber. Paige fired back frantically, turning to check the position of the other bombers.

There were no other bombers.

Cobalt Hammer was the only StarFortress left.

"Auto cannons aimed," Bascus said.

"Forty seconds to full charge, Goneril added."

Canady stopped himself from ordering his sensor officers to review the Resistance flagship's schematics and calculate its most vulnerable points. It didn't matter—the *Fulminatrix*'s cannons would chew the enemy warship apart in mere moments.

Canady grimaced—he was thinking like Bascus, or Hux. He surveyed his instruments and scowled at the lone StarFortress still flying above his Dreadnought's hull, at the center of a decaying fighter escort.

"Destroy that last bomber," he said.

A black X-wing passed below Paige's turret, close enough that she could see the astromech in its droid socket.

"Cobalt bombardier, why aren't your bay doors open?" Poe demanded. "Paige, come in!"

Paige saw, to her horror, that the doors at the bottom of *Cobalt Hammer*'s bomb magazine were shut. She called for Nix, then the other members of her crew, but heard nothing.

When was the last transmission she'd received from another member of her crew? And why wasn't Spennie firing?

Below her, the Dreadnought's hull was a vast expanse.

Moving quickly, Paige released the magnetic lock on the ball-turret hatch and scrambled up into the bomb bay, manually opening the doors below her. Through wisps of smoke she saw Nix lying on the catwalk overhead, the trigger clutched in his hand.

"Nix!" she screamed. "Nix!"

"Drop the payload!" Poe shouted in her ear. "Now!"

Paige scrambled up the ladder to the flight deck. Nix, she saw immediately, was dead. She'd just pulled the remote trigger from his grip when a blast shook *Cobalt Hammer*. Her foot slipped and the remote tumbled out of her grasp as she grabbed for the edge of the catwalk—and missed.

She slammed into the deck at the bottom of the bomb bay, ten meters down. Her eyelids fluttered and she tried to move her legs but couldn't. Above her, through vision gone blurry, she could see the trigger where it had come to rest on the very edge of the catwalk.

Everything hurt. She wanted to sleep and fought desperately not to, forcing her foot to rise and slam into the ladder. High above her head, the catwalk rattled and the trigger twitched.

"Auto cannons fully charged," Bascus said, leaning forward eagerly.

"Fire!" Canady shouted.

Paige drove her foot into the ladder again, pain shooting up her leg. Had the trigger moved? She couldn't tell. Her legs were shaking. She willed them to be still and aimed one last kick at the base of the ladder.

The trigger bounced and fell off the catwalk. She reached up a trembling hand, trying to follow the trigger as it tumbled through the air, bouncing this way and that off the magno-charges in their racks.

Somehow, it fell into her hand.

Click.

The rack safeties opened with a whine. Paige's hand crept up her flight suit to her collar, hunting for the Otomok medallion around her neck. She found it as the bombs fell like black rain out of the racks, drawn magnetically down toward the distant landscape of the Dreadnought's surface. Found it and held it tight as *Cobalt Hammer* shuddered, lost power, and plummeted into the fire and ruin below.

As the dreadnought broke apart, the Resistance starfighters peeled off and raced for the safety of the *Raddus*, pursued by TIEs.

Poe whooped in triumph, opening the throttle up as he raced toward the distant Resistance fleet.

"Start the lightspeed jump, now!" he yelled.

Fire lanced out from the Star Destroyers behind him. Ignoring BB-8's squalls and the red lights all over his flight console, Poe flew into the *Raddus*'s fighter hangar at full speed.

A moment later the Resistance ships had vanished, leaving the laserfire from the First Order warships to bisect empty space.

On the bridge of the *Finalizer*, jubilation was replaced by shocked silence. Hux stood and stared at the empty space where the Resistance fleet had been a moment earlier, then turned his head to regard the burning remains of Canady's shattered Dreadnought.

"General, Supreme Leader Snoke is making contact from his ship," called a communications monitor.

Hux forced himself to look impassive, not daring to wonder if he'd succeeded.

"Excellent," he told her. "I'll take it in my chambers."

But a moment later a huge hologram of Snoke's head had appeared on the bridge. The leader of the First Order's face loomed over Hux, his startling blue eyes blazing.

"Oh good, Supreme Leader—" Hux began, but an unseen force slammed him into the polished black floor of the bridge.

"General Hux," Snoke said. "My disappointment in your performance cannot be overstated."

Hux fought to rise and reclaim his dignity.

"They can't get away, Supreme Leader!" he insisted. "We have them tied on the end of a string!"

Finn woke with a start, yelling Rey's name—and immediately banged his head.

He looked around wildly, expecting to find himself in the snowy forests of the planet that the First Order had gutted to transform into Starkiller Base. That was the last thing he remembered: the slim figure of Rey standing her ground as a bloodied Kylo Ren advanced on her, his crimson lightsaber spitting and snarling.

That same lightsaber had struck Finn from behind, making every nerve in his body spasm in agony. It had left him lying in the snow, smelling his own burnt flesh, his body trying to fold itself in half around a line of fire carved up his back. He'd tried to force his arms and legs to move, to get him back on his feet.

As a soldier must.

No, as a friend must.

Finn looked around, confused. This part of the forest was strangely different. There was still snow everywhere, but it was warmer, and the underbrush was oddly angular. Because—

Because it wasn't a forest at all.

He was surrounded by white, but it wasn't snow—it was the walls and ceiling of a room. He was lying on a gurney, with a transparent medical cocoon above his head. Around him were crates and equipment, scattered haphazardly.

And there was no sign of Rey.

Finn shoved the medical cocoon's bubble aside. His arm creaked strangely as he did so, and an odd smell—briny and oceanic—made his nostrils flare. He realized he was wearing a bacta suit of clear flexpoly, ribbed and shot through with tubing. It was an old suit—the First Order would have fed it into a trash compactor long ago in favor of a newer model.

But then he had escaped the First Order and his life as FN-2187 to follow Rey from Jakku to Takodana and then to Starkiller Base. He'd returned to the heart of the First Order's war machine to rescue her from Ren, only to find she'd rescued herself.

Had she done so again, after Finn lost consciousness in the snow? Had she saved him? It was entirely possible—Rey was impulsive, stubborn, and short-tempered, but also self-reliant and capable.

If that was what had happened, perhaps she was nearby.

Finn scrambled to his feet and promptly fell over. When he got himself righted again, healing bacta fluid was spurting out of the suit and pooling around his feet. His back ached dully and his mind was foggy.

He stumbled across the cluttered space to a window filled with blue radiance—the unmistakable signature of hyperspace. That answered one question, at least—he was aboard a starship.

Trying to focus, Finn turned away from the window. He found a door and fumbled with its controls, emerging in a hallway. Soldiers hurried past, wearing the patchwork uniforms of the Resistance. Before he could force a question from his befuddled mind they had vanished down the hallway, ignoring him completely.

Finn followed them as quickly as he could, calling Rey's name.

The moment Poe set *Black One* down on the flight deck of the *Raddus*'s fighter hangar, the X-wing began bombarding BB-8 with action items that it insisted had to be immediately put right by competent technicians.

This time, the astromech simply uploaded all 106 action items to the Resistance's starfighter maintenance-request database. Goss Toowers could deal with the temperamental X-wing for the next couple of hours. Maybe he'd even schedule a much-needed memory wipe.

The cockpit canopy rose and a weary Poe removed his helmet.

"Well done, pal," he told BB-8.

As Poe climbed down from his X-wing, BB-8 began disengaging his linkages. But *Black One* wasn't done. That booster engine was obviously a dangerous, shoddy aftermarket product that never should have been installed, but since it had been, had BB-8 recorded the starfighter's top speed during the just-completed engagement? And wasn't it the top speed ever recorded for a T-70 X-wing?

BB-8 had to admit to mild curiosity about the question. The answer came back from the *Raddus*'s tactical database instantly—it was. No sooner had BB-8 passed that along than *Black One*, being *Black One*, had another query: Was it the top speed ever recorded for *any* starfighter?

That was a more complicated query, one BB-8 immediately decided would be a waste of his processing cycles, let alone those of the Resistance flagship. So the astromech assured *Black One* that it had set that record, too.

If that was true, good for *Black One*. And if it wasn't? Well, the X-wing was overdue for a lesson in humility.

BB-8's visual sensors flagged something odd in the corridor beyond the hangar door. The astromech reviewed the data and tootled at Poe in puzzlement.

"Finn naked leaking bag what?" Poe replied. "Your chips all right?"

But a closer look revealed that was indeed a Finn Naked Leaking Bag shuffling past the hangar door, streamers of bacta jetting from innumerable ports in his suit. Poe ran toward the former First Order stormtrooper.

"Buddy!" he called. "Let's get you dressed. You must have a thousand questions."

But when he finally seemed to recognize Poe, Finn only had one.

"Where's Rey?"

PART II

CHAPTER 5

The stairway was built from ancient stones, cracked with age and grooved by the tread of countless feet. It rose from the edge of the sea and wound its way up the peak above Rey's head, a black line against the green, obscured here and there by wisps of cloud.

Rey picked up her staff and adjusted her satchel where it hung from her shoulder. She imagined she could feel the weight of the lightsaber inside it—the mysterious ancient weapon that had called to her beneath Maz Kanata's castle, and that she had carried with her to this stormy planet of gray seas dotted with green islands.

A planet identified on BB-8's map with the legend AHCH-TO.

Rey eyed the first of those broad stones—the beginning of the end of her long journey from the sands of Jakku—and looked behind her, where the battered, saucer-shaped *Millennium Falcon* stood on its landing gear. The ship's bulk all but filled a wide, flat area just above the sea.

Chewbacca stood at the foot of the freighter's ramp, the astromech R2-D2 at his side. The Wookiee called out encouragement to Rey, while R2-D2 whistled and rocked on his two stubby legs.

Well then. It wasn't like she'd come thousands of light-years to stop here. She started up the stairs, the wind whipping her dark hair across her face.

After Jakku, Ahch-To seemed like something plucked from a dream. The air was damp, with the tang of salt, and the island's steep slopes were a vivid, verdant green. A few days earlier, green had been a color Rey had only dreamed of—now she was surrounded by variations on it, from the tufts of emerald grass to the grayish moss that clung to slabs of rock.

The ocean was a study in seemingly impossible colors, too, but these were forever morphing and changing: Here the water looked black or gray, while there it was green or blue, and everywhere it was dappled with yellow whorls of reflected sun or the white crescents of wave tops. When she'd first stood outside the *Falcon*, Rey's brain had insisted on interpreting the water as a surface, and her stomach had rebelled at that surface's refusal to be still. Now, surrounded by the sea, she realized that what she was seeing was just the uppermost layer of something deep, vast, and eternally in motion. She'd thought of the island as a tiny dot on the water, but that, too, was a misperception—the island was the pinnacle of a mountain that began in darkness, rising from the bones of the planet far below.

She looked back and was surprised by how small the *Falcon* already looked—and amused to see Chewbacca offer her a wave. The Wookiee had declined to come with her, explaining that the *Falcon* had years' worth of malfunctions, breakdowns, and ill-advised modifications that needed to be put right.

R2-D2 had been more willing, but had gotten no farther than the base of the first step before retreating with an electronic sigh.

The slopes around Rey were full of life. Sticklike insects regarded her inscrutably as they picked their way through the grass, while birds rode the winds above her head. Many of the rocky outcroppings she passed were rookeries for small, chubby avians. They were curious about the intruder, peering at her with big, liquid eyes and challenging her with fusillades of squawks. Their flying struck Rey as a triumph of determination over ability—they looked like airborne rocks, hurtling themselves off the cliffs and flapping their stubby wings desperately until somehow leveling out centimeters from disaster.

Rey stopped to catch her breath—she was used to scaling the towering ruins of Star Destroyers, but the climb was still a long one. The *Falcon* was an off-white circle far below her now; above her, the stair continued its roundabout ascent.

She told herself just to climb and not to think about what awaited her at the top, but that was impossible. It would be a cruel cosmic joke indeed to find that Jedi Master Luke Skywalker—the man she'd assumed was a myth—had packed up some time ago. But something told Rey he hadn't. Somehow she was certain of his presence—it was like a fleeting something captured in peripheral vision, or the tickling sensation between the shoulder blades that hinted at a presence behind you.

She'd been *meant* to come to this planet, to land on this island, to climb this stair. She was sure of it. Her whole life—all those desperate days hunkered down in Jakku's heat and dust, all those desolate nights adrift in its cold and loneliness—had been a prelude to this.

A wall rose beside the stairs, which passed through a clearing nestled against the cliff. Several modest stone huts filled the space, conical assemblages of painstakingly corbeled stone, with narrow doorways. They were ancient but well cared for. Some doorways were open and empty, while others had simple doors of weathered gray wood. And one had a door of pitted, rusting metal, adorned with faded red stripes.

Rey glanced at the huts, but knew this wasn't her destination—not quite.

She followed the stairs up a grassy slope until they ended in a saddle between towers of rock. A figure shrouded in a simple cloak and robe stood at the edge of a cliff, facing away from her out over the endless sea.

After a moment the figure raised its head and turned slowly, peering out from under a cowl. The face above the graying beard was wrinkled and weathered, seamed and etched by hints of extreme climates. But the eyes were a bright blue.

Rey walked toward Luke Skywalker as he pushed back his hood. His left hand was flesh and blood, the right metal and wires. He stared at her, his gaze direct and intense, his expression strange. She couldn't tell if that was anger, despair, or yearning on his face.

Without breaking eye contact with the man she'd come so far to see, Rey slung her staff over her shoulder, reached into her pack, and removed the lightsaber. She held it out to him.

An offer. A plea.

Emotions chased themselves across the Jedi Master's face. After several moments he took a tentative step forward, then another. He reached up and took the lightsaber from her hand.

Rey stepped back, her breath catching in her throat, as Luke regarded the ancient weapon. Then he lifted his eyes to hers. She forced herself to hold that powerful gaze and stand her ground.

Then Luke tossed the lightsaber off the cliff.

Rey's eyes followed its arc through the air, then turned back to Luke, wide with shock.

He walked past her without a word, his strides long and deliberate.

"Uh, Master Skywalker?" she managed, but he had vanished down the stairs.

She hesitated, then hurried after him, to the clearing with the huts. She arrived just in time to see the rusted metal door slam, leaving her alone with the keening birds.

Rey edged up to the door and tapped on it tentatively.

"Master Skywalker, I'm from the Resistance," she said. "Your sister Leia sent me. We need your help. We need you to come back."

There was no reply.

"Master Skywalker?" she tried again. "Hello?"

This couldn't be happening, not after all she'd gone through to get here. She felt like she'd fallen into a bad dream, one in which she spoke but her words made no sound. After a few more moments of silence she began banging on the door.

"Hello?"

———

Rey found the lightsaber in the grass far below the cliff from which Luke had hurled it. Several of the curious, chubby birds were inspecting it, warbling at one another in puzzlement. She shooed them away and retrieved the lightsaber, rubbing the knuckles left swollen by hammering on the Jedi Master's door in vain.

Below her, she caught sight of a shape under the waters of a shallow bay—a shape too angular to be natural. She realized it was an X-wing fighter, corroded by long immersion in salt water.

She looked the lightsaber over and was relieved to find it undamaged. She replaced it gently in her pack, her thoughts returning to the Jedi Master sulking in his hut atop the mountain. Had she done something wrong? Offended him in some way? Failed to perform some secret Jedi ritual no one had bothered telling her about?

Rey had no idea—and no inkling about how to fix things. And it was a long way back up the mountain to be ignored for who knew how long.

She gazed morosely at the submerged X-wing. So that was where the door had come from—Skywalker had salvaged one of the wings. Had he stripped it of anything else? Her practiced eye picked out the location of antenna coils, maneuvering repulsors, static discharge couplings, and other gear that she once might have removed and bargained for rations.

I don't think that's salvageable. Zero portions.

She smiled slightly at the idea of Unkar Plutt gaping at a starfighter that was now more reef than vehicle. The reactor would still be outputting residual heat, but that would do no one any good except nearby fish and crustaceans. Maybe some of the wiring and conduits would still be intact, inside their protective jacketing. Everything else, though, would be junk.

Granted, that didn't necessarily mean you couldn't clean it up and try to pass it off as operational—plenty of unscrupulous dealers back in Niima Outpost had eked out a living that way. But the result would be a malfunction or a breakdown waiting to happen.

Malfunctions and breakdowns, hmm.

If Master Skywalker wouldn't talk to her, she'd arrange a conversation with someone he couldn't ignore.

She strode off in the direction of the *Falcon*.

This time, at least, the knock on the door got a response—an annoyed order to go away.

A moment later the door had been separated from its hinges, bouncing of the far wall, and an angry Wookiee was storming into the hut, snarling and roaring.

Rey followed Chewbacca inside, peeking around the *Falcon*'s first mate. Luke had changed clothes, and was now dressed in rough-hewn woolens and leggings. She had to admit the shock on his face was satisfying.

"Chewie? What are you doing here?"

Chewbacca, still angry, subjected Luke to another round of bellowing.

"He says you're coming back with us," Rey said.

Luke spared her an annoyed glance.

"I got that," he said, before turning his attention back to the Wookiee. "You shouldn't be here."

Chewbacca snarled indignantly.

"How did you find me?" asked Luke, still acting as if Rey weren't there.

"Long story," Rey said. "We'll tell you on the *Falcon*."

"The *Falcon*? Wait . . ."

Rey recognized the instant he realized what was wrong.

"Where's Han?" Luke asked Chewbacca.

The Wookiee's anger drained away, leaving him slump-shouldered with misery. He moaned pitifully. Rey hesitated, then stepped forward. The least she could do was spare Chewie this part. But that meant it was up to her to tell Luke that Han Solo was dead.

CHAPTER 6

As the turbolift doors shut, General Hux tugged at the cuffs of his uniform, even though he knew they were perfect. He tried not to think how long it had been since Supreme Leader Snoke had summoned him to his throne room aboard the enormous warship known as the *Supremacy*.

The *Supremacy* was a massive flying wedge, measuring 60 kilometers from wingtip to wingtip. Its designers had anointed it the first of the galaxy's *Mega*-class Star Destroyers, but such a classification struck Hux as essentially meaningless. True, the *Supremacy* could deliver the destructive power of a full fleet. But that was a decidedly narrow perspective from which to assess its capabilities. Within its armored hull were production lines churning out everything from stormtrooper armor to Star Destroyers, foundries and factories, R&D labs and training centers for cadets. The *Supremacy*'s industrial capacity outstripped that of entire star systems, while its stores of everything from foodstuffs to ore ensured it could operate independently for years without making planetfall.

All of which was by design. Snoke had been steadfast in his refusal to designate a world as capital of the First Order, explaining icily that he had far more in mind for his regime than ruling the handful of sectors it claimed in the Outer Rim or colonizing clusters of worlds beyond the frontier.

Such ambitions would make the First Order no different from the various nonaligned states that had sprung up in the wake of the Galactic Civil War, or the hermetic kingdoms of the Unknown Regions—many of which had been dismantled or destroyed by the First Order during its secret rise. No, Snoke had a grander destiny in mind—the First Order would restore all that had been stolen from the Empire, and then build upon that rebuilt foundation.

But until that promise was fulfilled, the First Order's capital would be mobile. It would be the *Supremacy*.

It was a strategy Hux had helped formulate. The *Supremacy* couldn't be cut off from its supply lines, as it carried them with it. Besides, Hux had seen the dangers of fixed capitals—they had their own gravity, drawing in everything from fleets to economic muscle to intellectual talent. They were cultural centers but also sinkholes—and that made them vulnerable.

Hosnian Prime had proven that vulnerability, Hux thought, a smile playing at the corner of his lips. The former capital of the New Republic was now a charnel house—the churning ember of a star, orbited by shattered planetary cores being slowly drawn into rings of dust and ash. Millennia from now, the Hosnian system would remain as a monument to the day the First Order had swept away the Republic's weakness and dishonesty, reestablishing the principle of rule through strength and discipline.

And the name of Armitage Hux would be remembered, too—of that he was certain. It would be exalted as builder of the First Order's armies, architect of its technological revolution, and executioner of the New Republic.

And, very soon, the destroyer of the Resistance.

For which he would earn another reward, Hux mused.

Commander of the *Supremacy* would be an excellent title . . . surpassed only by that of Supreme Leader Hux.

Hux almost whispered those three words to himself, but caught himself in time. Snoke had spies everywhere in the First Order—

including, quite possibly, electronic ones in the turbolift leading to his private domain at the *Supremacy*'s heart.

The doors opened and Hux stepped into that domain, one of the few beings ever accorded the privilege of seeing Snoke in the flesh. The First Order's leader sat on his throne, flanked by eight members of his crimson-armored Praetorian Guard. Banners bearing the regime's emblem hung overhead, reflected in the gleaming black floor, and red curtains veiled the chamber's viewports. In the throne room's shadows, Hux glimpsed droids attending to their duties and the mute, purple-robed aliens that had helped the First Order blaze hyperspace lanes through the Unknown Regions.

As soon as Hux dropped to one knee, Snoke's blue eyes were upon him, glittering in his ruined face.

"General, I handed you a war hammer and you pointed it to a nug-gnat," he said.

"As I assured you, Supreme Leader, the setback is merely temporary," Hux replied.

Snoke studied him appraisingly. The Supreme Leader wasn't the towering figure seen in his holographic broadcasts, but he still dwarfed a human. The face was asymmetrical and the body hunched, but Snoke radiated power. A malign energy seemed to emanate from him, one that Hux imagined he could feel sending questing tendrils into his brain.

Hux knew the Force was real—his body still ached from being slammed to the deck of the *Finalizer*. But such sorcery was a last dying echo of ancient history, unreliable and unpredictable where technological prowess delivered certainty. Snoke commanded no legions of Force warriors, as the Jedi once had. No children were plucked from the ranks of First Order stormtroopers after displaying abilities beyond those of ordinary beings. There was just Snoke, and his loathsome creature Kylo Ren.

And Skywalker, whom Snoke and Ren had hunted so avidly, at the expense of much else that needed doing.

"After your failure today, General, your assurances do not inspire confidence," Snoke said.

Hux's shoulders tensed at the icy anger in his voice. He forced himself to remain impassive. If Snoke had wanted to kill him, he would have done it aboard the *Finalizer*, where Hux's demise would have served as an object lesson to others. He wouldn't have wasted time by summoning him here to do away with him in secret.

"You say you can track the Resistance fleet even after its escape to hyperspace—something no military force in galactic history has been able to do," Snoke said, and Hux relaxed. Now the Supreme Leader was in Hux's arena.

"No military force in galactic history had access to the technology we have created, Supreme Leader."

"The Resistance fleet will be on the other side of the galaxy by now," Snoke said. "In any of a billion star systems. The prospect of checking them all makes me weary, General."

"We need not check them all, Supreme Leader. Our tracking system's computer network contains millennia worth of data: every after-action report from Imperial history, as well as many from the Republic's Judicial Forces and Planetary Security Forces. It contains astrogation reports, briefings from scouts and commercial guilds, Separatist intel—"

"A full inventory would be tedious," rumbled Snoke.

Hux dipped his chin. "Of course, Supreme Leader. "Our sensors pinpoint the target's last known trajectory, and tracking control analyzes it against our data sets. Trillions of potential destinations are sifted and reduced to hundreds, then dozens, and finally one."

"And so why are we not headed to that lone destination?" Snoke asked.

"We are cross-checking the results of our initial analysis, Supreme Leader," Hux said. "The final calculations should be complete within minutes."

Snoke leaned back in his throne, considering that. His guards stood unmoving in their imprisoning red armor. Behind him, the alien navigators carried on their inscrutable work.

"So your solution to this ancient problem is no conceptual break-through," Snoke said. "Your invention is a product not of genius, but brute force."

"Brute force is underrated, Supreme Leader," Hux said with a smile. "The New Republic's home fleet is destroyed, and its surviving senators have dissolved the remaining task forces to protect their homeworlds. Their division makes them defenseless. No power in the galaxy can stand against us, Supreme Leader."

His comlink trilled out a high-priority alert.

"With your permission, Supreme Leader?" Hux asked, and was favored with a nod. The message was the one he had hoped to hear.

"We have the Resistance fleet's coordinates, Supreme Leader. Five-nines confidence level."

"Then go, General. You've explained how your invention works—now show me that it does. Bring Organa's rabble to heel."

As Hux got to his feet, the turbolift opened behind him and Ren stepped into the throne room, face hidden behind his black-and-silver mask. Hux couldn't resist grinning at him.

"Hux's new toy appears to be working," Snoke told Ren. "The Resistance will soon be in our grasp."

"Thank you, Supreme Leader," Hux said, and stepped into the lift.

Snoke had summoned him to answer for his failure, and sent him away praising his inventiveness. Hux knew Kylo Ren had arrived with no accomplishment that might deflect the Supreme Leader's wrath—he'd needed to be rescued from Starkiller Base as it came apart and spent much of the time since then being put back together by medical droids.

Snoke had shepherded the First Order through its years in the galactic wilds, transforming a band of Imperial refugees into a weapon forged to reclaim the galaxy. As such, he would always be remembered. But Hux knew the future would need a different kind of leader—one able to direct the galaxy's industries and nurture their innovations, while commanding its citizens' respect.

Snoke wasn't that leader. And neither was Ren.

Kylo Ren studiously ignored Hux as the black-clad general all but strutted out of the throne room. But Snoke had no difficulty sensing the anger that boiled out of Kylo at the sight of Hux's smug smile.

"You wonder why I keep a rabid cur in such a place of power," Snoke said once they were alone. "Mark this—a cur's weakness, properly manipulated, can be a sharp tool."

Kylo ignored that—he was in no mood for Snoke's teachings, not after all that had happened.

"How's your wound?" Snoke asked, making no effort to hide the derision in his question.

"It's nothing," Kylo said.

That wasn't true—the lightsaber slash to his face had been closed with microsutures, but Kylo would bear its scar for the rest of his life. And his abdomen ached where a bolt from Chewbacca's bowcaster had struck—a blow that would have been instantly fatal if Kylo hadn't instinctively contained its energy with the Force.

"The mighty Kylo Ren," Snoke said, considering his student. "When I found you, I saw what all masters live to see: raw, untamed power. And beyond that, something truly special—the potential of your bloodline. A new Vader. Now I fear I was mistaken."

Behind his mask, Kylo glowered at the tall figure in golden khalat robes.

"I've given everything I have to you—to the dark side," Kylo said, his voice distorted by his mask. *"Everything."*

"Take that ridiculous thing off," said Snoke, his voice dripping with disgust.

Shock froze Kylo momentarily. He slowly reached up and removed the mask, revealing his scarred face. Snoke rose from his throne, the slow shuffling of his feet hinting at pain that dogged every step. Kylo stood stone-faced as Snoke approached him, willing himself to remain still as one finger stretched for his cheek, then higher.

The fingertip traced Kylo's eyelid, leaving a streak of moisture behind.

"Yes," Snoke said. "There it is. You have too much of your father's heart in you. Young Solo."

Kylo's eyes snapped to Snoke's, burning with rage. "I *killed* Han Solo. I killed my . . . when the moment came I put my blade through him. I didn't hesitate."

"Petulance, not strength," sneered Snoke. "And look at you. The deed split your spirit to the bone. You were unbalanced, bested by a girl who had never held a lightsaber. You *failed*."

Kylo felt rage ignite deep inside of him—ignite and become an inferno demanding release.

But Snoke had anticipated that, too. Kylo had only taken the slightest step toward his master when lightning erupted from Snoke's fingers, blasting Kylo backward and leaving him reeling in pain. The Praetorian Guards snapped into combat stances, faceless visors fixed on Kylo.

A dismissive wave of Snoke's hand and the guards straightened again, though they still regarded the black-clad figure on the floor with wary suspicion.

"Skywalker lives!" Snoke howled at Ren. "The seed of the Jedi Order lives! As long as it does, hope lives in the galaxy!"

The Supreme Leader fixed Kylo with a contemptuous look. "I thought you would be the one to snuff it out. Alas. You're no Vader, you're just a child with a mask."

Kylo turned his back on Snoke, fighting to keep the fires of his anger banked—and so missed the cruel smile that twisted the Supreme Leader's face.

In the turbolift, doors shut, he stared down at the helmet cradled in his hands. This time the rage came without warning, a live thing that felt like it would burn and blister his very flesh. Kylo smashed the mask into the wall. The Force was howling inside him, giving him the strength to hammer his mask against the metal until it had been reduced to a twisted hunk of black and silver.

The turbolift doors opened and two frightened officers took an instinctive step backward from the seething man in black.

"Get my ship ready," Kylo snapped.

CHAPTER 7

The late-afternoon suns hung low over the islands of Ahch-To, lengthening the shadows of the old stone huts. Below, the surf sighed, a rhythmic sound like static. Luke Skywalker sat on a bench outside his simple dwelling, next to a morose Chewbacca. Rey hovered nearby, reluctant to interrupt the two old friends in their mourning.

But it couldn't be put off any longer.

"Han Solo was my friend," she said. "There's no light left in Kylo Ren, and he's only getting stronger."

The mere mention of that name seemed to pierce Luke where he sat slumped beside Chewie. For a moment he struck Rey as old and broken, drained of whatever power he had once possessed, and she felt like an intruder on his grief.

But the galaxy needed this man—needed him to rise above whatever misfortune and misery had driven him into his self-imposed exile. Rey had been sent to find him, and she had. Now she had to reach him, and make him understand the knife-edge on which everything stood.

"Leia showed me estimates of the First Order's military stock," Rey said. "It's *massive*. And now that the Republic is destroyed there's nothing to stop them. They will control all the major systems within weeks. They'll destroy the Resistance, Finn, everyone I care about. *Now* will you help us? You *have* to help us. We need the Jedi Order back. We need Luke Skywalker."

Luke's eyes were cold and flinty.

"No."

"What?"

"You don't need Luke Skywalker."

"Did you hear a word I just said? We *really, really* do."

Luke scowled.

"You think . . . *what*? That I'm going to walk out with a laser sword and face down the whole First Order? The Jedi—if you had them back, a few dozen Jedi Knights in robes, what do you think they would actually do?"

Rey looked at him in disbelief. Was he really trying to engage her in some kind of strategic debate? Did he really not understand what the Jedi meant to a galaxy in peril?

"Restore the . . . balance of . . ."

There was mild pity in Luke's glance as she fumbled to answer— but there was anger, too.

"What did you think was going happen here?" he asked. "Do you think I don't know my friends are suffering? Or that I came to the most unfindable place in the galaxy for no reason at all?"

Now Rey was angry. The problem wasn't that he didn't understand— it was that he didn't care.

"Then why *did* you come here?" she demanded.

Rather than answer, Luke got to his feet, gazing sorrowfully at Chewbacca.

"I'm sorry, old friend," he said. "I'm not coming back."

Chewbacca didn't respond—his fury at Luke was spent—but Rey sprang off her bench.

"I'm not leaving without you," she warned.

"Get comfortable, then," Luke replied as he retreated into his hut, stopping to pick up the broken door and lean it up against the stone.

Rey stepped in front of the doorway, hands on her hips, and stared defiantly at him through the gap. Let him think she'd given up—he'd soon discover otherwise. Jakku had trained her to do two things better than anyone else could.

The first was to salvage broken things.

The second was to wait.

Leia sat alone in her stateroom aboard the *Raddus,* staring out into the blue-white tunnel of hyperspace.

The Resistance fleet was dangerously low on fuel—there hadn't been time to transfer more than a fraction of the reserve stored on D'Qar to the ships in orbit. Ackbar wasn't overly concerned—not with the fleet having escaped into hyperspace. His plan was to make a short jump away to a deep-space rendezvous point once used by the Alliance, then assess their situation.

Leia automatically began reviewing the list of things that had to be done. Their first task was to let the people of the galaxy know that the Resistance had survived and would oppose Snoke and his First Order. They had to reach out through coded channels to Snap Wexley, Jess Pava, and the other pilots Leia had sent to gather the New Republic's surviving commanders. They needed to recruit allies from the Outer Rim, contact senators and planetary leaders seeking protection from the First Order, corral military forces left leaderless by the strike at Hosnian Prime, and reactivate C-3PO's network of droid spies.

It was a daunting list, but Leia found herself relieved that there was nothing she could do at the moment. For at least a little while, Ackbar and his bridge crew could handle everything.

But having finally secured a bit of solitude, Leia found no comfort in it, nor in the amplified light of countless stars churning around her. The galaxy was at war again, and every star lighting her way was a potential battlefield, a bitter harvest of misery and loss waiting to be reaped.

She had seen too many losses on too many worlds—family, friends, comrades-in-arms, allies, and innocents—and the thought of how many more losses were yet to come was a monstrous weight. There was no place in the galaxy she could go where she wouldn't be surrounded by ghosts.

Hope is a light brighter than the deepest darkness—but only we can keep it lit.

Her mother had said that—Breha Organa, the queen of Alderaan.

Breha who had been murdered by the Empire—along with every one of the people she had vowed to protect.

And is that how she'd want me to remember her? To remember them? As mere victims of the Empire?

After Endor, Leia had learned to open herself to the Force, to feel the mysterious energy field that underpinned the cosmos. Luke had told her that she'd drawn on the Force all her life without being aware of it—not just when she had heard his desperate call for help above Cloud City but in Senate sessions and Alliance strategy meetings. The Force had helped her read rooms and sense the political winds. It had lent authority to her calls for action. It had buoyed her when the burdens of office threatened to become crushing. He wanted to teach her how to access the Force consciously; after that, it would be up to her.

Aboard the *Raddus,* Leia closed her eyes and remembered.

Stretch out with your feelings, Luke had told her.

He'd explained that life created the Force and made it grow. The lessons of Obi-Wan Kenobi and Yoda had helped him understand the Force as a luminous tide, one that overflowed the boundaries of the bodies that generated it, connecting and binding all life in a web of energy that spanned the galaxy.

By learning to be calm and at peace, he said, a Jedi could feel this energy around her, tracing the ever-changing currents and ripples made by life. By opening herself to the Force, she could then guide its possibilities and do extraordinary things. But all of those feats depended on this bedrock understanding of the Force as a creation of life—and of the Jedi as merely temporary vessels for its will. Living things created the Force, but they didn't contain it—its energy spilled out of them until it imbued everything, making the very idea of individual presences border on meaninglessness.

Leia reminded herself to breathe in, then out. She visualized her-self releasing her fears and anxieties, one by one.

Her breathing slowed and she let her senses drift, as if untethered from her body. She reached out beyond the confines of her state-room, her awareness expanding to encompass the entirety of the *Raddus* as it hurtled through hyperspace.

She could feel the Force around her now, and the beings creating it, along with the wild cacophony of their emotions.

There was joy at their escape, and a jagged excitement at the pros-pect of battle. But there was also fear of the precariousness of their situation, and anxiety at the possibility that they might fail. The Force was bright with rage and a need for revenge, and roiled by the agony of having to go on without friends and loved ones.

Leia let it all wash over her, allowing its tides to carry her this way and that. Then she reached out for those individuals with whom she had an emotional connection.

On this point, Luke had explained, he had rejected the teachings of the Jedi. The Order had forbidden emotional attachments, warn-ing that they left a Jedi vulnerable to the lures of the dark side. And indeed, it was a love curdled into jealousy and possessiveness that had led their father, Anakin Skywalker, into darkness and despair.

But Luke had disagreed with Yoda and Obi-Wan Kenobi that Anakin was lost to the light. He had insisted that the very emotional entanglements that had led Anakin to become Darth Vader might also draw him back—entanglements such as the stubborn love be-tween a father and son, each of whom had thought the other lost.

Luke had been right—and ignoring his teachers had saved him, the Alliance, and the galaxy.

Leia reached out and found Ackbar—weary yet stolid, his mind sifting through worries in his usual orderly fashion. She sensed Con-nix was exhausted and uncertain, doubting. And Fossil's grief for her lost bomber pilots was so raw and open that Leia instinctively re-treated from it.

She was surprised to sense the presence of Finn, the First Order deserter who'd been placed in a coma to heal. He was awake, and a tangle of anxiety and confusion. Twinned with him in Leia's awareness was Poe Dameron, his emotions oscillating between pride and doubt.

Way too much pride, not nearly enough doubt, she thought, then let that go. She'd deal with Poe soon enough.

Leia let her mind drift farther, away from the *Raddus,* until she felt the brush of other minds, beings on worlds hurtling by in hyperspace—a constant hum of emotions and hopes and dreams and fears. She reached still farther, searching for one particular signature, one she knew would burn brilliantly in the Force.

But it wasn't there.

Once, she had been able to sense Luke's mind halfway across the galaxy, if only as a faint stirring in the Force. But it had been years since she had felt that presence.

When her family had been broken by betrayal, Luke's agony and guilt had whipped the Force until it felt like a storm-wracked sea. She had been able to feel the churn of her brother's emotions even as he had retreated, abandoning her in her most desperate hour. Overcome by her own anger and sorrow, she had let him go, and for a time she had wanted him far away.

And that's what happened. Her sense of her brother had dwindled to an echo, then a whisper, and finally to nothing at all.

She didn't know why, or what it meant. Perhaps Rey had discovered that—and was on her way back to her with the answer. And maybe Luke was with her.

Leia felt for the device she kept wrapped around her wrist, then stopped herself, lowering her hands and relying on her senses instead. Perhaps if she reached out again . . .

A moment later her eyes opened and she felt dizzy. The Force was suddenly jagged with danger. Coming for her—her and the entire Resistance.

Outside Leia's stateroom viewport, the tumble of hyperspace vanished, replaced by the blackness of space. She rose and hurried for the bridge.

Poe had brought Finn to his quarters so he could wipe away the slimy remnants of the bacta, don one of Poe's spare Resistance uniforms—and get an answer to his question.

But Poe's answer had left him even more uneasy.

"So you blew up the Starkiller Base, Rey beat Kylo, the Resistance got the map," Finn said to Poe. "You won, right? Why does this not feel like winning?"

Rolling down the corridor beside them, BB-8 blooped mournfully—apparently the astromech agreed with Finn.

"We came out of hiding to attack Starkiller," Poe said, adjusting a bundle under his arm that he'd removed from a locker in his quarters. "It didn't take the First Order long to find our base."

Finn could see his friend's attention was far away. He paused, trying to figure out how to phrase what he knew he had to say.

"Look, Poe," he said. "I believe in what you guys are doing. But I didn't join this army—I followed Rey here. I just don't want you thinking I'm something I'm not."

"It's going to be all right, don't worry," Poe said. "You're with us, where you belong."

His friend's reaction only made Finn feel more guilty. Poe didn't understand that Finn hadn't joined the attack on Starkiller Base to help the Resistance but to rescue Rey. Finn had dreamed of convincing her to join him somewhere in the wilds of the Outer Rim, where the First Order could never find them. It had been a sensible plan then and remained so now. The First Order would never stop hunting the Resistance until it was destroyed, but two fugitives might have a chance to escape its notice and create a life for themselves on some quiet backwater world.

Finn scratched at his side—it was a relief to be free of the bacta, but it still itched abominably—and so missed that Poe was offering him whatever it was he'd taken from his quarters.

It was the pilot's old jacket, he saw now—the one Finn had salvaged from a wrecked TIE on Jakku, when he'd thought Poe was dead, and that Kylo Ren had sliced through in their confrontation on

Starkiller Base. The rent in the back had been mended by a decidedly inexpert hand.

"I'm not much of a sewer," Poe said apologetically. "Plus I was, you know, saving the fleet."

Finn's face fell. It was a kind gesture, which was no surprise—Poe had never been anything but kind to him. Heck, hadn't the pilot been the one to give Finn a name? But that only meant Poe would be even more disappointed when he found out how thoroughly he'd misjudged Finn.

Finn looked uneasily at his friend, trying to work up the courage to explain. But before he could speak, a golden protocol droid rushed around the corner, startling BB-8 and nearly plowing into them.

"Commander Dameron, Princess Leia requests your presence on the bridge at once," said C-3PO. "I tried to make that sound as pleasant as I could."

CHAPTER 8

Poe couldn't remember a time he hadn't known Leia Organa. She'd been a mentor to his parents, Kes Dameron and Shara Bey, both of whom had served alongside her in the Alliance. She'd kept tabs on him as he grew up, learning to push starfighters to their limits—and sometimes beyond those limits. And she'd convinced him to leave the New Republic for the Resistance.

He knew her well enough to recognize the cold fury on her face as he entered the bridge of the *Raddus,* with Finn and BB-8 trailing behind him.

An angry General Organa was a force to be reckoned with—and one for which Poe had a healthy respect. But he felt certain he could talk her down. He always had before, after all. They understood each other. She knew he could be rash and foolish, but he knew she wouldn't have him any other way. When she'd recruited him, in fact, she'd said the Resistance could use some rashness—and added that foolishness and passion were often confused.

Poe had never forgotten those words, and he knew Leia hadn't forgotten them, either.

So it was a shock when she slapped him across the face.

"You're demoted," she said, ignoring the stunned faces around them on the bridge.

"For what?" he protested, his cheek stinging. "A successful run? We took out a Dreadnought!"

"At what cost? Pull your head out of your cockpit!"

"You start an attack, you follow it through!" Poe said.

"There are things you can't solve by jumping in an X-wing and blowing something up. I need you to learn that."

"There were heroes on that mission," Poe said, unwilling to concede the point.

"Dead heroes," Leia snapped. "No leaders."

The silence that followed was uncomfortable and seemingly endless. It was Finn who broke it.

"We're really nowhere—deep space," he said. "How's Rey going to find us now?"

The fleet had emerged from hyperspace at an old Alliance rendezvous point that was nothing more than arbitrarily chosen coordinates, and Finn was staring at a holographic chart of their position, seemingly in dismay.

Something about the plaintive need in Finn's question touched Leia. The former stormtrooper was brave and capable, but there was a childlike quality about him—unguarded and almost innocent. In a galaxy riven by war, she thought, that was something to be cherished instead of punished.

Leia smiled and lifted her sleeve to reveal a faintly glowing bauble strapped to her wrist, ready to explain what it was to Finn.

She didn't need to—he recognized it.

"A cloaked binary beacon."

Leia nodded. "To light her way home."

"All right," Finn said. "So until she gets back, what's the plan?"

"We need to find a new base," Leia said.

Commander D'Acy nodded. "One with enough power to get a signal to our allies scattered in the Outer Rim."

"And most important, we need to get there undetected," Leia added.

As if in answer, a klaxon began blaring on the bridge.

"A proximity alert!" said a startled Ackbar.

"That can't be," Poe said.

But a glance at the *Raddus*'s holographic displays showed that it was. A massive warship had emerged from hyperspace, accompanied by more than two dozen Star Destroyers.

Poe was one of the few Resistance officers who recognized the huge ship. Its existence had been revealed by intelligence brought to D'Qar just before the evacuation. He'd hoped that intelligence was somehow mistaken, but what he was seeing proved rather definitively otherwise.

"That's Snoke's ship," he said. "You've got to be kidding me. Can we jump to lightspeed?"

"We have just enough fuel for one jump," Connix said gravely, her face pale.

"Do it fast—we have to get out of here!"

But Leia held up her hand.

"Wait," she said, a grim realization dawning on her. "They tracked us through hyperspace."

"That's impossible," Poe replied.

"Yes, it is. And they've done it."

Once again, it was Finn who broke the stunned silence on the bridge.

"So if we jump to lightspeed, they'll just find us again and we'll be out of fuel," he said. "We're trapped. They've got us."

That shook Poe out of his trance.

"Not yet they don't," he insisted, then turned to Leia, risking a cocked eyebrow. "Permission to jump in an X-wing and blow something up?"

"Granted."

Poe hurried off the bridge, finding himself oddly relieved to be returning to battle. Leia had been genuinely angry with him, and he promised himself he'd find time to think about what she'd said and why she'd said it.

But she'd also remembered something more important: She really did need him to be reckless sometimes.

Like now, for instance.

The wail of the klaxon jerked Tallie out of her nap in the ready room just off the *Raddus*'s main starfighter hangar.

Fighter pilots learned the necessity of being able to nap anytime, anyplace, for as long as they were allowed, but Tallie's sleep had been fitful and uneasy. She'd kept dropping back into the same dream, one in which she had to protect Resistance bombers that didn't appear on her scopes; she'd only located them by the screams of their pilots as they died.

She looked around in befuddlement and found Starck sitting up on a cot nearby, looking equally confused.

The ready room's holotank lit up and both pilots peered at it, then at each other.

"That's practically an entire starfleet," Tallie said.

"And two of those ships are the same ones that were chasing us at D'Qar," Starck said. "Can't be right. It's gotta be a glitch."

Red dots began flashing in the emptiness ahead of the enemy flagship.

"Your glitch just launched a squadron of TIEs," Tallie said.

She pulled on her boots and her flight vest, practiced hands automatically adjusting the straps to fit snugly, then scooped up her helmet. Starck was hopping on one foot, trying to get his other boot on.

"Practice your dance moves later—we gotta fly," she called over her shoulder, activating her comlink and selecting the squadron channel.

"Boss, you seeing this?" Tallie yelled into it as she sprinted across the hangar deck, dodging squalling BB units and harried technicians who'd been working on routine maintenance a moment before.

"I know—on my way," Poe said breathlessly.

The *Raddus* shook beneath Tallie as she reached her A-wing, waving off a Sullustan tech fumbling with a ladder and scrambling onto the fighter's fuselage, then dropping into the cockpit. Starck was yelling for his astromech to load in and for the ground crew to get his fuel hoses disengaged. She made a note to remind him not to do that.

The techs knew their jobs and were working as quickly as possible—yelling at them didn't help anything.

The *Raddus* trembled again. Tallie cold-started the engines and the little fighter growled a brief protest, then began to thrum around her, as if eager to get into space and confront the fleet's tormentors. *Black One* was still empty, but the ground crew was detaching hoses from the X-wing and closing access panels with frantic speed.

As the pilots began their roll call, Tallie spotted Poe's orange-accented astromech rolling into the hangar from the main corridor. The squadron leader sprinted right behind the droid, eyes fixed on his X-wing.

Then the sensors in Tallie's A-wing flashed red, keening an urgent warning.

Missile lock? We're still in the hangar. That one really is a glitch.

Tallie's fingers reached for the interrupt. Before she could silence the alert, everything around her became heat and light.

A cannonade from the First Order task force ripped into the *Vigil*, breaking the cargo frigate's back. A moment later the warship exploded into a cloud of glittering fragments as a flight of First Order TIEs swept past. The starfighters skimmed the *Raddus*'s hull, laser fire arcing from their weapons, and the cruiser groaned and shuddered.

"Torpedo!" cried out a sensor officer. "Direct hit on the starfighter hangar!"

Leia had no time to think of the losses they'd sustained on an already unbearable day, or to wonder if Poe had reached the hangar before impact.

"Full engines ahead," she ordered, her voice cutting through the hubbub on the bridge. "Get out of range of the Star Destroyers and the fighters will fall back."

"All craft, full engines," Ackbar said. "Concentrate rear shields."

Leia nodded. The *Raddus* was at the tail of the Resistance column, its shields between their First Order pursuers and the other three ships.

And then she went rigid. Staring, she fumbled for a chair and half fell into it, the Resistance officers' worried faces turning in her direction.

Her mind had brushed a familiar presence in the Force—one she knew intimately. A presence that had once been bright but had turned black as space, becoming a soundless scream of rage and need.

She knew instantly that it was Ben Solo, her son.

Leia tried to stop herself from being drawn into her memories, even as she knew she wouldn't be able to resist.

Ben in her womb, turning and tumbling in search of comfort, an ever-expanding radiance in the Force, but one shot through with veins of shadow. Luke had reassured her that was normal—the brighter the light, the darker the shadow. She'd desperately hoped that was true.

Ben as a baby, red-faced and round. His hair had been black from birth, impossibly fine and delicate—the softest thing Leia had ever imagined.

Ben as a toddler, forever following Han. Carrying the dice from the *Millennium Falcon*—the ones his father had used to win the beloved, battered freighter—and promising anyone who'd listen that one day he would be a pilot, too, like his daddy.

Ben in adolescence, his face grown lean above a strong jaw. A boy who always seemed alone, a churning storm in the Force. And whose anger had begun to manifest in malfunctions and breakdowns and objects that fell off shelves and shattered with no one near.

Ben, her son. Who'd been stolen from her and Han, stolen by Snoke's wiles and Luke's mistakes and his own furies. Who'd become Kylo Ren, the champion of the First Order—and his father's murderer.

Ben was leading that TIE squadron. He had fired the torpedo that had killed her pilots, and now he was coming to kill her and everyone else.

———

Kylo banked his fighter—a prototype TIE Silencer with a night-black hull—away from the ruin of the starfighter hangar, his wingmates matching the maneuver.

The Resistance fleet was barely worthy of the name—his fighters' initial attack run had reduced it to a Mon Calamari heavy cruiser and two smaller craft. The smaller ships were of little consequence. The heavy cruiser had rebalanced its shield envelope to protect it against the turbolasers of the First Order vessels harrying its stern. That was a sound strategy, but it left the cruiser vulnerable to the prowling TIEs—and Kylo had just ensured it wouldn't be launching starfighters anytime soon.

"Target the main bridge," he said.

His mother would be there, he knew. It wasn't Leia Organa's style to lead from the rear, or to put her own concerns above whatever cause she held dear at a given moment.

For a moment Kylo let himself recall his parents' worried conversations behind closed doors, the ones they'd deluded themselves into thinking he wouldn't know about. Conversations about the anger and resentment that had boiled over once again in their son. Conversations in which they talked about him like he wasn't their son, but some kind of monster.

They were frightened of him, he realized. And so they got rid of him, sending him away to his uncle Luke—whose betrayal would prove far worse.

But Ben Solo was no more—Kylo had shed his childhood identity and the pathetic weakness it represented. Han Solo's days of cheating and disappointing people were over. The New Republic was destroyed. And now the Resistance—the last of his mother's causes—would follow it into extinction.

The heavy cruiser's bridge was bracketed in Kylo's sights. He glanced at his instruments, verifying that his torpedoes were loaded and armed.

His mother was indeed there. He could feel her familiar presence in the Force, and he could sense her determination and focus—along with a deep weariness. And sorrow. And worry.

It's too late to be sorry, Mother. Though you're right to worry.

His thumb hovered over the trigger, even as his senses drank in impressions from the Force. The panic on the bridge ebbed and flowed around the calm focus that was his mother. Her anxiety pulsed in the Force, in this last moment before her death . . . but she wasn't afraid.

She was worried *for* him, he realized. And she wasn't angry. She ached for him to come back to her.

Kylo depressed the trigger slightly, not quite enough to fire.

And then he lifted his thumb.

He couldn't do it.

A moment later, Kylo's wingmate fired.

The torpedo sheared through the bridge of the *Raddus* and exploded. In a nanosecond it became the center of an expanding envelope of overpressurization that hurled crew members and equipment in all directions, shattered the viewports, and buckled the bulkheads separating the bridge from the rest of the ship. Then the torpedo's payload of superheated plasma vaporized everything that the blast wave hadn't flung into space, leaving behind a ruin of twisted, blackened metal, already cooling in the vacuum.

The explosion buffeted Kylo in his cockpit. If he had known, he could have stopped the torpedo—freezing it in space with a thought. But he had been surprised. Now he couldn't sense his mother—the shock had shattered his focus, leaving him breathing hard behind his fighter's control yoke.

"The Resistance ships have pulled out of range," Hux said over his comlink. "We can't cover you at this distance. Return to the fleet."

"No!"

Kylo turned back toward the *Raddus,* determined to erase the cruiser and the rest of the Resistance fleet from existence. The Mon Calamari ship's point-defense cannons spat energy at the TIEs, and the fighter to port vanished in a ball of fire.

"Snoke's command," Hux told him. "They won't last long, burning fuel like this. It's just a matter of time."

Hux sounded patient, as if he were addressing a child. Kylo would show the arrogant general that was a fatal mistake.

The *Raddus*'s guns incinerated another TIE.

Teeth gritted, Kylo broke off the attack, streaking for the distant line of First Order warships.

Leia Organa flew through the void, arms raised as if in supplication.

She could feel the moisture in her eyes and mouth evaporating and her lungs struggling for air that wasn't there. All around her she saw debris—and members of the bridge crew. Those who weren't dead would be soon.

She could see the First Order TIE fighters, shrinking in the distance. Her son—lost to her, flying back to his master. Who was aboard one of the bright dots of light arranged in a line beyond those fighters. Those lights were Star Destroyers, relentlessly hunting her battered and beleaguered little fleet.

She could surrender, and it would all be over in a moment. She would be at peace.

Then she noticed another light nearby, drifting through space amid the wreckage. It was Rey's beacon, she realized—the one she would need to find her way back. It had come loose from Leia's wrist.

Her hand closed around its soft glow. She couldn't give up, not yet. She had to go on—for Rey and everyone else on the *Raddus*. And all those the First Order would consign to misery and despair.

Leia's eyes closed and she lowered her head, her outstretched hands tensing as she concentrated.

Feel the Force around you. Life creates it, makes it grow.

Leia reached out with her senses. She was surrounded by the remains of battle—but thin traceries of life remained around her, generated by the tiny microorganisms that lived, undetected, on and in bodies and even in the air. Their Force energy was ebbing, dying out or growing dormant, but she could sense that it formed a tenuous ladder back to the warship behind her.

Leia asked the Force to help her ascend that ladder and return to the broken bridge. Where, faintly, she could see Resistance crewers gathered at an air lock.

Even as her senses dimmed, her body rose toward the gaping maw of the shattered bridge. It slid through the wreckage and into the lock. Leia's fingers brushed the viewport, and the outer hatch closed.

Then the inner door opened, flooding the narrow space with light and air and life. Faintly, as if from a great distance, she heard contradictory commands and agonized questions surrounding her. The Force was bright and spiky with fear.

Leia wanted to tell her rescuers that it would be all right, that they should see to the fleet. But even imagining the effort necessary to do so was impossible. And so, belatedly, she did surrender, letting go and allowing herself to slide into darkness.

PART III

CHAPTER 9

The Jedi Master emerged from his hut at dawn. Autumn had come to the island and the morning was gray, hinting at worse weather to come.

He found Rey standing outside the repaired door, leaning on her quarterstaff.

"Morning," she said.

Luke didn't acknowledge her, shouldering his pack and walking up the stairs.

Rey hadn't expected him to yield that easily, and so she followed him. And she kept following him, as he ascended the island to its jagged crest to watch Ahch-To's second sun clear the horizon.

"So this is where they built the original Jedi temple?" she asked. "How long ago?"

"Go away," Luke replied.

He'd spoken! She decided to count that as progress, and smiled as she followed him back down the well-worn path, trailing him until they reached the tumbled rocks and narrow beaches that fringed the shoreline. Seabirds called overhead and the salt air was sharp in Rey's nose. On the beach, sea sows lounged torpidly in tide pools, waiting for the suns to warm them.

Luke unfastened a bottle from his pack and bent over a sow's belly, squeezing green milk from her swollen udder. He looked up from his work, a green streak on his upper lip. Rey kept watching, though that last moment had left her a little ill. The sow regarded her lazily.

"Is this like a thing where you're pretending to ignore me but secretly teaching me lessons?" Rey asked.

"It is not," Luke replied.

She was there the next morning when his door opened.

"I've never seen so much water in my life," she said.

"Don't care," Luke muttered, and began his rounds.

She suppressed a slight smile. Today he'd spoken to her immediately. At this rate they might have an actual conversation within a few months.

On the south side of the island, a narrow inlet pierced the land, its cliffs plunging down into a foamy slot of a bay. A pole leaned against the edge of the cliff, its end planted in the shallows far below. Luke grabbed the pole and used it as a lever to swing himself over the gap.

"Whoa—careful!" Rey called.

Luke landed lightly on the other side, standing on an impossibly narrow ledge, and aimed a withering look her way. He braced himself above the long drop and lifted the pole, staring down at the water. Rey edged over to the gap and peered down to where the pole's pointed, barbed end hung over the churning water.

Luke waited, utterly still, until some signal told him to plunge the pole into the water. When he pulled it up, a meter-long fish was flapping on the end, stuck through.

"How'd you do that?" Rey asked. "The Force?"

"No."

It was raining hard when they returned to the saddle at the top of the island, the great fish strapped to Luke's back. Rey trudged along a few steps behind him, peering at his back through the rising wind and the slashing rain and making sure she stayed close enough to hear him if he spoke to her.

He didn't.

A cold rain continued for most of the night. When Luke's door opened in the morning, Rey was there—chilled and weary, but there.

He hesitated for a moment, but then walked past her, heading up the worn stairs, wreathed in mist.

Rey followed, fingers white around her staff. She began to talk, at first just to keep herself warm, then so that there was some sound besides the murmur of the sea and the cries of the birds. So she let the story of her life unspool: all those years scavenging on Jakku, BB-8's arrival, flying the *Falcon*, seeing the miraculous green of Takodana, finding herself on Starkiller Base, departing D'Qar with a Wookiee for a copilot and an ancient map for a guide.

She addressed the story to Luke's back. Perhaps telling it properly would make him realize the importance of her quest, and he'd stop treating her like an intruder. And if not, well, by now annoying him was its own reward.

Then, in midsentence, she stopped.

Something was calling her—a sweet sound, whispering to her through the mist. She turned away from Luke and walked silently off in the opposite direction, eyes fixed ahead.

Luke stopped and turned. He watched her go, head cocked, curious.

The uneti tree had been massive once, but all that remained of it now was an ancient, mossy husk. In one end an opening gaped, carved by weather and time.

It was warm and dry inside. Light from a crack in the ancient trunk fell on a nook in the wood—one that held a row of ten or so very old books. Rey approached slowly, gazing at them. As she neared the books, they began to glow faintly, and she felt like the air was thrumming with energy.

She felt almost hypnotized. The books seemed to call her. But unlike the lightsaber on Takodana, that call didn't feel like a threat. Rather, it felt like a promise, one made long ago and now ready to be fulfilled.

She reached out her hand toward the books, to touch them.

"Who are you?" Luke asked. He had followed her, and now stood looking at her as if for the first time.

Rey was so entranced by the books that she barely noticed that Luke had finally acknowledged her.

"I know this place," she said. "This is a library."

Luke stepped in front of her and took one of the books off its shelf. She couldn't read the ancient runes inside, but she could feel their power.

"Built a thousand generations ago to keep these—the original Jedi texts," Luke said. "The Aionomica, the Rammahgon, a dozen other mystic-sounding made-up names—the foundation of the ancient faith. They were the first and now, just like me, they are the last of the Jedi religion."

He looked up from the book, his eyes searching Rey's face. After the days she'd spent trying to get his attention, his sudden regard was a little unsettling.

"You know this place," Luke said. "You've seen these books. You've seen this island."

"Only in dreams," Rey said.

He looked at her again, and repeated his earlier question: "Who are you?"

"Weren't you listening? I told you the whole story."

"I went in and out."

It seemed wrong to roll one's eyes in the presence of the founding Jedi texts. She managed not to.

"The Resistance sent me," Rey said.

"They sent you? What's special about you? Jedi lineage? Royalty?"

Rey was none of those things, and after a moment's consideration Luke seemed to sense that.

"An orphan," he said wearily. "This is my nightmare. A thousand wannabe younglings showing up on my doorstep, hoping they're the Chosen Whoevers, wanting to know how to lift rocks."

She silently pleaded for Luke to say something. But he just stared at her for a moment before turning and striding out of the library, reclaiming the solitude he had guarded so jealously.

"Where are you from?" Luke asked.

"Nowhere," Rey said, recalling endless days of heat and sand.

"No one's from nowhere."

"Jakku."

Luke raised an eyebrow. "All right, that is pretty much nowhere. Why are you here, Rey from Nowhere?"

"The Resistance sent me. We need your help. The First Order—"

But Luke's eyes had turned flinty again.

"You've got your youth, you've got a battle to fight, a whole universe out there to explore," he said. "Why come dig me up? Dry bones, tired old legends. Let them lie, Rey from Nowhere. Find your own path."

"That's not it . . . this *is* my path."

"Is it? Why are you here?"

There was nowhere to hide from his eyes. She took a breath, and then looked up pleadingly.

"Something inside me has always been there, but now it's . . . awake. And I'm afraid. I don't know what it is or what to do with it. And I need help."

"You want a teacher. I can't teach you."

"Why not? I've seen your daily routine—you're not busy."

"I'll never teach another generation of Jedi," Luke said. "You asked why I came here? I came to this island to die—and to burn the library so the Jedi Order dies with me. I know only one truth: It's time for all of this to end."

The words seemed to reverberate inside her head, terrible and final.

"Why?" Rey asked.

"You can't understand," Luke said, dismissively but also a little sadly.

"So make me," Rey said. "Leia sent me here with hope. If she was wrong, she deserves to know why. We all do."

It was all too much, suddenly. He had seen the connection between her and the books and stopped ignoring her, only to reject her again. To reject her, his sister, and all those who were depending on him so desperately.

She silently pleaded for Luke to say something. But he just stared at her for a moment before turning and striding out of the library, reclaiming the solitude he had guarded so jealously.

CHAPTER 10

In a corridor in the depths of the *Raddus,* Finn sat by himself on an equipment crate, looking down at the glowing beacon in his hand.

General Organa had been clutching it when the hatch to the bridge air lock opened. As crewers and medics frantically worked on the badly injured Resistance leader, the beacon had rolled across the deck, unnoticed, and come to a halt at Finn's feet. He'd picked it up and then stood back, allowing the medical droids to attend to the general and bear her away on a stretcher.

He rolled the device back and forth in his hands. Rey was out there somewhere—and when she returned, it would be to the beacon's location.

Finn got to his feet. He knew what he had to do, even though Poe and his other friends in the Resistance would never understand.

He just hoped he wouldn't regret it for the rest of his life.

Rose Tico was also sitting by herself in one of the *Raddus*'s corridors, tears rolling down her cheeks and falling into her lap. Occasionally her hand crept up to the collar of her jumpsuit, feeling for the teardrop-shaped Otomok medallion around her neck.

She had spent the journey to D'Qar showing the *Ninka*'s techs the jury-rigged system she'd developed to cloak the energy signatures of bombers' ion engines. Once that work was complete, she'd transferred to the *Raddus*. After that, she and Paige had little time together—Rose had watched from a ready room aboard the *Ninka* as *Cobalt Hammer* released its payload above the First Order's Siege Dreadnought and then vanished into the mighty ship's funeral pyre.

Paige had told Rose that they were connected to each other, and to home—and that they didn't have to be in the same place for that to be true. But now Rose's connection with her sister had been brutally severed. After rarely spending more than a couple of days away from Paige, Rose was looking at the endless, yawning expanse of a lifetime without her.

She had no idea how she was going to survive that—or if she even wanted to.

The technicians aboard the *Raddus* hadn't known what to do with her, and they were too busy keeping the cruiser running to figure it out. They'd handed her a spare jumpsuit from the Ground Logistics Division and sent her out doing droidwork—checking bulkhead doors and data conduits down on the lower levels.

Rose supposed she should have been insulted—she'd been a flight engineer aboard a bomber, after all. Paige, she knew, would have pitched a fit on her behalf—when they'd joined the Resistance, she'd refused to fly without Rose as part of her bomber crew.

But the Resistance had no more bombers, and Paige was dead.

The droidwork had turned out to be a blessing in disguise, allowing her to be mostly alone down here in the guts of the *Raddus*. She had been briefly reunited with Fossil, who was also left adrift as surplus personnel, the commander of a squadron that no longer existed. Fossil had given her a ring engraved with the logo of the old Rebel Alliance—in memory, she said, of Paige's sacrifice for the Resistance.

The hulking Martigrade's sorrow had only deepened Rose's misery; it was better to sleepwalk through her duty shifts with no company except the thrum of the *Raddus*'s air exchangers.

Then the heavy cruiser had been attacked—Rose had felt the torpedo impact on the bridge as a shudder and shimmy, followed by a deep, eerie moan that seemed to ripple through the hull. Rumors had begun flying, reaching her when she stopped in the mess or returned to the barracks. That General Organa was dead. That the Resistance and the First Order were negotiating a surrender. That the First Order had another superweapon, and more leading New Republic worlds had been targeted.

And then, for her morning shift, Rose had been handed an electro-stun prod and grim orders: Stun anyone accessing the *Raddus*'s escape pods.

She'd agreed without hesitation. Her sister had died to save this ship—to save the entire Resistance fleet—and deserters were dishonoring that sacrifice.

Rose heard something moving down the corridor and looked up from her gloomy appraisal of the ring Fossil had given her. A man was creeping down the corridor, with a canvas bag on his shoulder. He was so intent on his objective that he didn't see her.

Curious, she wiped her nose on her sleeve and followed him. He was tall and dark-skinned—handsome, she thought idly. He was wearing a Resistance jacket with a rip in the back. The damage had been repaired by a malfunctioning droid or someone whose understanding of a needle and thread would be best described as theoretical.

"What are you doing here?" she asked him.

She was only a couple of meters away, and the sound of her voice startled the man, who bumped his head on the hatch of an escape pod.

"Hi!" he said, then began stammering. Rose couldn't figure out what he was trying to tell her.

Then she realized it was *him*.

"You're Finn! *The* Finn!" she said.

He looked perplexed. "*The* Finn?"

This wasn't going well. She forced herself to stop.

"Sorry, I work behind pipes all day," she said, trying to get her bearings. But somehow that just made her feel more discombobulated.

"Doing talking with Resistance heroes is not my forte," she said, then cringed at how that had come out. "Doing talking. I'm Rose."

"Breathe," Finn told her, and she did. It helped, a little.

"I'm not a Resistance hero," Finn said. "But it was nice talking to you, Rose. May for Force be with you."

"Wow," Rose managed. "You, too."

She understood—he had things to do. Everyone aboard the *Raddus* had things to do except her, it seemed. What were they not telling her now that was so important? Was there a radiation leak? Saboteurs aboard?

Rose had gone several paces down the corridor when she decided she couldn't leave it like that. She didn't know Finn, but whatever was wrong, maybe she could help. And Finn seemed like he could use a little help.

"Okay, but you *are* a hero," she said, finding him back at the open hatch of the escape pod where she had left him. "You left the First Order, and what you did on the Starkiller Base—"

"Listen—" Finn tried to say, but Rose kept on talking, hoping to make him understand.

"When we heard about it, Paige—my sister—said, 'Rose, that's a real hero. Knows right from wrong and don't run away when it gets hard,' she said."

"Sure."

"You know, just this morning I've had to stun three people trying to jump ship in these escape pods," Rose said. "Running away."

Thinking about it made her angry all over again.

"That's disgraceful," Finn said.

"I know. Anyway."

"Well, I should get back to what I was doing," Finn said, smiling broadly.

"What *were* you doing?" asked Rose.

"Checking. Just checking the . . . uh, doing a check."

Rose's eyes jumped from his face to the bag on the deck to the open escape pod.

I am the biggest idiot in the history of big idiots.

"Checking the escape pods," she said quietly.

"Routine check," Finn said.

"By boarding one. With a packed bag."

"Okay, listen—" Finn began, but she had heard enough. She reached down, the motion practiced by now, unclipped the prod from her belt, raised it, and stunned him.

The summons came as Poe was arguing with Vober Dand about how to best reshuffle the fleet's remaining starfighters to protect the *Raddus*. Poe knew the disagreement would have been minor if both their nerves weren't so badly frayed, but he and Vober still wound up profoundly irritated with each other. They rode the turbolift in fuming silence, ignoring BB-8's querulous beeps, and found positions at different places in the crowd of officers that had gathered in the briefing room on the *Raddus*'s emergency bridge.

Taking the seat next to C'ai Threnalli, Poe spotted D'Acy and Connix—two of the few officers who hadn't been on the main bridge during the First Order attack.

D'Acy stepped forward, and the hubbub of conversation ebbed.

"General Organa—Leia—is unconscious but recovering," she said. "That's the only good news I have. Admiral Ackbar, all our leadership—they're gone. Leia was the sole survivor on the bridge."

Poe knew that, but it still felt like a punch in the gut.

"Oh dear, oh dear," said C-3PO.

D'Acy continued: "If she were here she'd say, *Save your sorrow for after the fight.* To that end, she left clear instructions as to who should take her place. Someone she's always trusted, and who has her full confidence."

Poe considered the likely line of succession. Undoubtedly Ackbar would have been next in line, but the old Alliance veteran was dead.

So who . . .

No, it couldn't be.

But he thought it could. A promotion from the starfighter corps was unconventional, but hadn't Leia always valued personalities over military hierarchies?

For a moment Poe was certain that D'Acy was looking at him. But it was Vice Admiral Amilyn Holdo who stepped forward to stand next to D'Acy, leaving Poe unsure if what he was feeling was relief or disappointment.

If Holdo was aware of the scrutiny, she didn't show it.

"Thank you, Commander," she said, a mercurial half smile on her face. Her hair was washed in purple, and she wore a dress of the same color. "Look around you. Four hundred of us on three ships. We are the last of the Resistance, but we're not alone. In every corner of the galaxy, the downtrodden and oppressed know our symbol and they put their hope in it."

As she spoke, Poe studied the other officers. They looked skeptical, he thought. Or perhaps they were all just in shock.

"We are the spark that will light the fire that will restore the Republic," Holdo said. "That spark—this Resistance—must survive. That is our mission. Now to your stations, and may the Force be with us."

"That's Admiral Holdo?" Poe asked C'ai. "Battle of Chyron Belt Admiral Holdo?"

The Abednedo pilot shrugged and muttered something in his own language.

"Not what I expected," Poe said.

As the crowd broke up, Poe approached Holdo. Her speech had been long on rhetoric but short on specifics. And she had a reputation for being unconventional—eccentric, some would say. But he also knew she was one of Leia's oldest confidantes—and one of the closest things the general had to a friend. That alone was enough for Poe to offer whatever her help he could.

"Vice Admiral?" he asked, trying to remember if they'd been formally introduced. "Commander Dameron."

Holdo studied him. Her eyes struck him as shrewd.

"Admiral, with our current fuel consumption there's a very limited amount of time we can stay out of range of those Star Destroyers," Poe said.

"Very kind of you to make me aware," Holdo said.

"And we need to shake them before we find another base. What's our plan?"

"Our plan . . . *Captain*? Not *Commander*, yes? Wasn't it Leia's last official act to demote you? For your Dreadnought plan? Where we lost our entire bomber fleet?"

Poe, astonished, found himself at a loss for how to defend himself. "Captain, Commander, fine. I just want to know what we're doing."

But Holdo wasn't finished. Her eyes bored into his.

"Of course you do. I understand—I've dealt with plenty of trigger-happy flyboys like you. You're impulsive. Dangerous. And the last thing we need right now. So stick to your post, and follow my orders."

And with that the new commander of the Resistance stalked off, leaving a stunned starfighter ace in her wake.

CHAPTER 11

Chewbacca sat by the fire, the dark shadow of the *Millennium Falcon* behind him.

Building a fire had taken longer than he'd expected—the island had few trees, just stubborn shrubs kept stunted by the ceaseless wind. At least the pudgy native birds—Luke had said they were called porgs—were easy to catch. Eager for a change from shipboard rations, Chewbacca had scooped one up to roast on a spit.

The Wookiee gave the spit another turn and took a sniff.

Done. Nicely charred, with a hint of spiciness from the firewood.

That was good. Even better, there was no shortage of porgs for future meals—the island was overrun with them, and they seemed to have no fear of bipeds.

Chewie was about to take the first bite when something caught his eye. It was a porg, standing at the edge of the firelight as if mesmerized.

A particularly plump and juicy-looking porg, the Wookiee thought, wondering if it was worth delaying his meal a few more minutes to snatch this one up, too.

The porg stared up at him with big, glassy eyes. Chewie reluctantly decided it would be wrong to eat that one. His belly rumbled and he turned away from the porg, annoyed by its seemingly sorrowful gaze.

On the other side of the fire a whole family of porgs was huddled together, staring up at him.

The Wookiee roared and the porgs fled into the darkness. Checking to make sure he hadn't missed any stragglers, he turned back to his dinner—only to find he'd lost his appetite. Something about the way the porgs had looked at him made him feel like he'd done a bad thing. But he'd only been hungry.

He was too busy feeling sorry for himself to notice the dark figure that slipped through the moonlight and up the ramp of the freighter behind him.

Luke walked slowly through the corridors of the *Falcon,* feeling like a ghost. The ring of his heels on the decking was achingly familiar. So was the smell—a distinctive blend of fuel and coolant, with a faint undertone of burning circuitry from whatever was malfunctioning at the moment.

Since the moment Rey had chattered excitedly about flying it, Luke's thoughts had been straying to Han Solo's ship, sitting on the ancient stone at the foot of the island, until finally he'd been unable to resist a visit. The *Falcon* had taken him away from Tatooine decades ago—a shell-shocked farm boy hurled into the middle of a galactic civil war he'd wrongly assumed would never touch him, his step-parents, or his friends.

He wondered what that Luke Skywalker would think of what he'd become.

Luke stepped into the cockpit, standing behind the pilot's chair that had been the closest thing to home for Han. The moonlight gleamed on the pair of dice hanging overhead and he gently removed them, turning them this way and that with his mechanical fingers.

The main hold was dim and quiet. Luke gazed at the holochess table, his eyes lingering on a familiar helmet and blast shield. He'd worn that for his very first lesson with a lightsaber, tormented by the hiss of a training remote that he couldn't see and trying to figure out what Ben Kenobi meant by stretching out with his feelings.

He sat at the game table, overwhelmed. This was where he'd wound up after Ben vanished, seemingly bisected by Darth Vader's light-saber blade. Where Leia had sought to console him as he sat in shock. He'd simultaneously seen Ben as his last link to his past on Tatooine and as the teacher who'd help him navigate the future. Without him, he'd been unmoored and adrift.

A string of familiar interrogative beeps came from the shadows.

"Artoo?" he asked, brightening, and a moment later the blue-and-white astromech rolled into view, chirping and whistling at length.

"Yes," Luke said. Decades of missions with R2-D2 had left him reasonably fluent in droidspeak, but the astromech's list of accusations was both lengthy and highly specific. "No, I—yeah, it's true."

R2-D2 squawked derisively.

"Hey, sacred island," Luke said. "Watch the language."

The droid replied with a plaintive whine.

"Old friend, I wish I could make you understand. I'm not coming back. Nothing can change my mind."

Luke rested his hand on R2-D2's dome, but the droid responded by activating his holographic projector.

Luke's breath caught at the sight of his sister as he'd first seen her—robed in white, pleading for Obi-Wan Kenobi's help.

"That's a cheap move," he chided the droid, who beeped smugly.

The recording vanished, leaving Luke and R2-D2 alone. The little astromech remained still as his former master stared into nothingness. And he stayed silent as Luke rose and made his way into the corridor and down the ramp, his footsteps slow and deliberate.

Rey woke with a start. Luke stood over the stone bench where she'd chosen to sleep, the better to intercept him before his morning rounds. Above her, his face was drawn and pale in the moonlight.

"Tomorrow, at dawn," he said. "Three lesssons. I will teach you the ways of the Jedi—and why they need to end."

PART IV

CHAPTER 12

Apparently Finn's new thing was waking up completely confused.

This time he found himself lying on his back—but for some reason the world was sliding by around him.

He lifted his head, which caused pain to flare at his temples, and saw the back of Rose's jumpsuit. She had found a cart and was dragging it and him down a corridor on the *Raddus*.

"You've got to be kidding me," Finn said, his mouth and tongue struggling to form the words properly. "I can't move! What happened?"

Then realization flooded in.

"You stunned me!" he yelped accusingly. "With a . . . *stun thing*! Oh my God, you're totally insane. Help!"

Rose gave him a look that suggested the stun thing might be part of his future, too.

"I'm taking you to the brig and turning you in for desertion," she said.

"Why?"

"Because you were deserting."

"No!" Finn protested.

She stopped guiding the cart and got in his face. They were nose-to-nose.

"My sister just died protecting the fleet," she said. "I heard what you did on the Starkiller Base. Everyone was talking about you. You were a hero for the Resistance! And you were running away?"

"Sorry," Finn said. "But I did what I did to help my friend, not to join another army."

He knew that was a mistake even as he said it. Rose's disappointment in him was palpable, and so was her anger. Finn realized he had to talk fast—or his next foggy awakening would come in the *Raddus*'s brig, and then it would be too late.

"I don't know what you know, but this fleet is doomed," he explained. "If my friend comes back to it, she's doomed, too. I'm going to get this beacon far away from here. Then she'll find me and be safe."

"You're a selfish traitor," Rose snapped.

"Look," Finn said pleadingly. "If I could save Rey by saving the Resistance fleet I would, but I can't. Nobody can."

"Yuh-huh," Rose said dismissively.

"We can't outrun the First Order fleet," Finn said.

"We can jump to lightspeed."

"They can track us through lightspeed."

That stopped Rose. "They can track us through lightspeed?"

She hadn't known. But then *of course* she hadn't known. Finn knew what it was like to spend shift after shift belowdecks on a warship, doing droidwork and being told nothing.

Hey, at least Rose hadn't been sweating herself half to death in a body glove and armor.

"They'll just show up thirty seconds later and we'd have blown a ton of fuel—which, by the way, we're dangerously short on," Finn said.

Rose was still grappling with this latest bit of information.

"They can track us through lightspeed," she said again, her mind far away.

"See? Yes! I can't feel my teeth. What did you shoot me with?"

"Active tracking," Rose said.

Finn looked up from checking that all his teeth were where he'd left them. "What now?"

"Hyperspace tracking is new tech, but the principle must be the same as any active tracker," Rose mused. "I've done maintenance on active trackers—they're single-source to avoid interference. So—"

Finn realized the implication and finished her sentence along with her.

"—they're only tracking us from the lead ship."

Rose nodded, but Finn could see her mind was far away again, pondering the problem.

"But hyperspace tracking takes a *lot* of computing power," she said. "The whole fleet would have to be computer banks, which is crazy. Unless . . ."

"Unless what?" Finn asked warily.

"A static hyperspace field generator," Rose said. "*That's* how they're doing it."

"A what now?"

Rose bit her lip. It looked like she'd forgotten he was there.

"Instead of adding lots of computers, you add lots of processing cycles," she said. "You do that by surrounding the computers with a hyperspace field generator. You could speed them up a billionfold . . . assuming nothing melts or gets accelerated right through the ship's hull. It's theoretical stuff—super-advanced tech. But if anyone could make it work, it's the First Order."

"So they've made it work. How do we make it *not* work?"

Rose looked at him appraisingly. She started to say something, then stopped. Finn cocked his head at her.

"You're going to say 'but.' I can tell. You've got that going-to-say-but look."

"But," Rose said, her brow wrinkling. "We can't get to the tracker. It's an A-class process, they'll control it from the main bridge."

"No," Finn said, and she gave him another one of her looks. "I mean yes, but every A-class process—"

This time she was the one who followed the thought to its logical conclusion and voiced it along with him: "—has a dedicated power breaker."

They looked at each other. Now Finn's teeth *hurt*. Did that mean things were getting better, or worse?

"But who knows where the breaker room would be on a Star Destroyer?" Rose asked.

Finn tapped his chest. "The guy who used to mop it. Deep in the subengine complex. If I can get us there—"

Rose tapped her own chest. "I could shut their tracker down."

"Yes! Rose! We've got to bring this plan to someone we can trust!"

"Whoa hey whoa," she objected. "When I said 'we' I didn't mean 'us.'"

"You've got to be kidding me—we could save the fleet!"

Rose shook her head. "You're a weirdo traitor. I'm maintenance. I'll file your plan."

"Poe!" Finn said desperately, worried she was about to stun him again.

"I'm Rose, remember?" she replied, annoyed.

"No. Rose. *Poe.* Take me to Poe Dameron and we'll tell him the plan. Poe. Rose, *please.*"

"Poe Dameron? He'll be busy."

"He'll see me," Finn said. "Hero of the Resistance, right?"

That was another mistake. Rose scowled, one hand creeping toward the device holstered on her belt, with its wicked-looking charge prongs.

"Just let him hear it," Finn said hastily. "If he says no you can stun me. With the stun thing."

"I totally will, you know."

Finn didn't doubt it for a second. He watched Rose making up her mind.

"I don't know why I'm trusting you," she said, disgusted.

"It's the baby face," Finn replied. "Blessing and a curse."

———

"Give that to me one more time," Poe said. "But simpler."

Rose and Finn had found him in General Organa's chambers, which had been converted into a makeshift medcenter. The Resistance leader lay motionless on a gurney, surrounded by instruments and tended to by white-plated MD-15 medical droids. C-3PO hovered nervously nearby, while BB-8 was circling the room, beeping mournfully.

Rose watched Finn prepare to walk Poe through their hastily conceived plan again, the one she was reluctantly beginning to think might not be such a terrible idea after all.

She wished Paige could have seen this—her kid sister, the maintenance tech, talking with the best star pilot in the Resistance and the galactic hero that Paige had hoped to meet one day. Paige would have gotten such a kick out of it—well, except for the part where Rose had found her hero sneaking into an escape pod.

Finn was handsome—Rose had to admit that. It was too bad about the weird traitor thing. And the bizarre crush on the friend of his. Whoever this Rey was, she had to be quite something to make you desert people you'd fought alongside and a cause you'd come to believe in.

But then, she remembered, Finn had grown up in First Order training halls, one of those luckless orphans who got numbers instead of names. Maybe that was why he'd fallen so hard for his friend. The number of people who'd ever been nice to him must be depressingly small.

"The First Order is only tracking us from one Destroyer—the lead one," Finn said.

"So you blow that one up?" Poe asked eagerly, and Rose fought the urge to roll her eyes. Fighter pilots, even aces, were all alike.

"I like where your head's at but no, they would just start tracking us from another Destroyer," Finn said.

Rose found the holoprojector built into the Leia's desk and activated it, displaying a schematic of the Mega-Destroyer that Poe had been studying.

"But," Rose said.

"But if we can sneak on board that lead Destroyer and disable the tracker without getting caught—" Finn said.

"—they won't realize it's off for one systems cycle," Rose cut in. "About six minutes."

"That buys the Resistance fleet a quick window to jump to hyperspace untracked," Finn said.

"And escape!" piped up C-3PO. "Brilliant!"

Finn ticked off the elements of the plan on his fingers. "Sneak on board. Turn off the tracker. Our fleet escapes before they realize."

Poe considered that cautiously. Rose could see him trying to calculate the odds. But BB-8 was beeping excitedly.

"You don't get a vote," Poe told him, then turned to Rose. "What do you think?"

"Somehow the fact that this was all my idea got lost in the telling," she said. "But if he gets us to the tracker, I can shut it down. I think it would work."

Poe considered that, then looked up at them.

"How did you two meet?" he asked, curious.

The look of panic on Finn's face was actually pretty entertaining.

"Just luck," Rose said.

"Good luck?"

"Not sure yet."

Poe chewed it over, his gaze returning to Leia where she lay unconscious.

"Poe, this will save the fleet and save Rey," Finn said. "We have to do it."

Rey Rey Rey. Rose really wanted to stun him again.

"If I must be the sole voice of reason, Admiral Holdo will never approve this plan," said C-3PO. "In fact, it's exactly the sort of brash heroics that would particularly infuriate her."

Poe smiled broadly. "You're right, Threepio. The plan is need-to-know. And she doesn't."

"That wasn't exactly what I—" the protocol droid objected as BB-8 whistled approvingly.

"All right, you guys shut down that tracker, and I'll be here to jump us to lightspeed," Poe said. "How do we sneak the two of you onto Snoke's Destroyer?"

"We steal a First Order shuttle," Rose said.

Finn's face fell. "No good, we need clearance codes."

Rose scowled, thinking this was the kind of problem someone familiar with First Order security procedures might have brought up earlier.

"So we steal clearance codes," she said, but Finn was shaking his head.

"They're biohexacrypted and rescramble every hour," he said. "It's impossible. Their security shields are airtight. We can't get through them undetected. *Nobody* can."

Poe and Rose looked at him dolefully. Then Finn thought of someone who just might be able to prove him wrong.

In her more than a millennium of life, Maz Kanata had been wounded sixty-seven times, with twenty-two of those wounds serious enough to nearly kill her. She'd been submerged in liters of bacta, swaddled in meters of medpatches, attached to more than a dozen droids, and spent weeks with no assistance whatsoever, relying on her own stubborn constitution and the will of the Force to avoid becoming one with it.

Absent some remarkably bad luck she didn't see coming—which, granted, was the kind that tended to do you in—this present spot of bother wasn't going to add to her tally. She'd rate the current dustup as something between a misunderstanding and a tantrum, a situation that had gone sufficiently off the rails that one party had to salve its hurt pride by shooting at the other.

That happened. She knew all the principals and was reasonably sure that within a few weeks the survivors would be in a cantina, having a grand time clanking glasses, comparing pockmarks left by blaster burns, and drinking to the memory of the unlucky departed.

But that time hadn't arrived yet. Until it did, not getting shot struck her as an excellent policy.

Maz ducked a blast that was a little too close, firing her pistol back in that direction to show her lack of appreciation, and turned one goggle-covered eye to her hologram transmitter. Four figures shimmered in the blue transmission field.

One of them was Finn, the young First Order deserter who'd caught her interest on Takodana, before his former colleagues arrived and did so much damage to her operations. She'd been curious about what she'd seen in his eyes then and wondered what they'd show her now. Was it possible he'd learned the patience he'd so thoroughly lacked then?

Maz doubted it. Finn was only human, after all. Human life spans, regrettably, were a couple of centuries too short for patience to stop being a virtue and become a habit.

Maz recognized two of the others. Poe Dameron looked like he'd stepped out of one of Leia Organa's recruiting posters, but war heroes were a decicred a dozen. He needed to fail a few times to become intriguing. As for Leia's protocol droid, he'd never been allowed to accumulate the logic snarls and quirks that might have given him something interesting to say in one of those seven million languages he was always boasting about. Still, unlike the others, he had no expiration date. A few billion more processor cycles without a memory wipe might make him into an amusing companion.

The fourth person in the hologram was a young woman wearing a painfully dull-looking jumpsuit. She was new to Maz, and broadcasting loss and confusion through the Force. But this Rose had toughness and resilience, too. Maz made a note to remember her, and take the opportunity to look into her eyes someday. She was curious to see what was in them, and to figure out in whose life she'd encountered them before.

But there wasn't time for that now—not with the galaxy in such a hurry again. And these four wanted something from her. What was it again?

Oh, right. A simple request, really—one she would have granted offhandedly in different circumstances, if only to see what currents it set flowing through Finn's and Rose's possibilities. But with things the way they were now, the two of them would have to show some initiative, instead of relying on her.

"Could I do it?" Maz asked. "Of course I could do it. But I *can't* do it. I'm a little tied down right now."

Finn struck her as more alarmed by all the blasterfire around her than a former stormtrooper should have been. But maybe that was why he no longer was one.

"Maz, what is happening?" he asked.

"Union dispute—you don't want to hear about it," she said. "But lucky for you, there's exactly one guy I trust who can get you past that kind of security. A master codebreaker, a soldier, freedom fighter, and ace pilot. A poet with a blaster—and the second-best smuggler I've ever met."

"Oh!" said C-3PO. "It sounds like this fellow can do everything!"

"Oh yes he can," Maz said, and let herself remember some of the better capers and exploits she'd helped him engineer. He really was one of her favorite beings, though she knew one of his bouts of inattention would likely be the death of him before he got truly interesting. Well, either that or his inflated ego.

But then both maladies were among the many hazards of dealing with humans. Maz had learned long ago that she had to enjoy their adventures while she could.

The crackle and tang of ionized air broke her reverie.

"*And* he's sympathetic to the Resistance," Maz said. "You'll find him at Canto Bight, on Cantonica."

"Cantonica?" asked Poe. "But that's . . . Maz, is there any way we can do this ourselves?"

So impatient, that one. If he isn't flying a starfighter, he's at a loss. It's too bad—I like that set to his jaw.

Maz surveyed the battlefield and realized her position was about to be overrun. That would be an annoyance.

"Sorry, kiddo," Maz said. "This is rarefied cracking. You want on that Destroyer, you've got one option—find the Master Codebreaker. You'll recognize him by the red plom bloom on his lapel."

She activated the jetpack she was wearing, cutting the transmission as she ascended. Soaring into the sky, Maz wondered if her friends would find the Master Codebreaker. She didn't speculate, knowing it was useless. Like everything else in the galaxy, whether they succeeded or failed—or discovered that their destiny involved neither of the two—would depend on the will of the Force.

Still, she could wish them luck.

CHAPTER 13

Dawn on Ahch-To found the island shrouded in mist, tinted a fiery crimson by the rising suns.

Trusting in Luke's promise that they would train at dawn, Rey had abandoned her vigil outside his door to sleep in a hut of her own—though the stone bench inside the structure she'd chosen offered no more comfort than the one in the clearing.

She rose, blinking at the sunlight streaming through her narrow window—and then stopped.

For a moment she'd thought she'd seen someone in the hut with her—a tall, pale figure, sitting quietly, with a dark bulbous shape hovering over it and touching its face.

And it was almost as if she felt something pulling at her own cheek, tracing a line up from her jaw.

She looked up and her eyes widened. Kylo Ren sat there, his cheek bisected by an angry red line—the wound she had branded him with in the snows of Starkiller Base. Its upper reaches were still stitched shut with sutures.

Terrified, Rey fumbled for the blaster she carried in her holster, raised it, and fired. She thought she saw Kylo flinch as the blaster spat energy in his direction, the noise startlingly loud in the confines of the stone hut.

But he wasn't there.

Rey lowered the gun, her hand shaking slightly, and stared at the smoking hole she'd blown in the wall.

There was no sign of her mortal enemy—the dark, menacing figure that had frozen her on Takodana and spirited her off to Starkiller Base, where he'd killed Han Solo and nearly killed Finn. But she knew she hadn't dreamed it—he'd been there.

She bolted out of the hut, looking in all directions. Nothing. Just the morning chill and the cries of porgs, diving in groups from the cliffs to bombard schools of fish below.

And then, instantly, Kylo was there. This time, she knew he saw her, too. He lifted his hand, staring at her, and she could hear his voice.

"You will bring Luke Skywalker to me," he said.

But unlike on Starkiller Base, no invisible fingers burrowed into Rey's brain to root through her thoughts and secrets. Unlike on Takodana, her body responded to her commands, not his. They were just words, and held no power over her.

She smirked, and Kylo lowered his hand in surprise.

"You're not doing this. The effort would kill you."

He peered at her, curious now.

"Can you see my surroundings?"

He sounded like a student contemplating an interesting problem—and expecting her to work as his partner to solve it. That infuriated her.

"You're going to pay for what you did," she said, but he ignored her.

"I can't see yours—just you," Kylo said. "So no, this is something else."

That was when Luke emerged from his hut, blinking at the morning light. Rey turned to face the Jedi Master, panic accelerating her heartbeat. Would Kylo see Luke? Would he somehow know where the last of the Jedi was? Had she done something wrong, unlocked some gate that had desperately needed to stay shut?

When she turned back, Kylo's expression told her instantly that while he might not have seen Luke, he *had* seen her reaction—and understood what it meant.

"Luke?" he asked, his eyes eager and hungry, like a predator catching its prey's scent.

"What's this about?" asked Luke.

Rey's eyes returned to the Jedi Master's face, expecting to see anger and betrayal there, but Luke just looked puzzled—until, to her horror, he pointed past her, directly at where this strange visitation stood.

She forced herself to follow his gaze, but Kylo was gone.

Luke was pointing at the hole in the side of her hut.

Kylo was gone, but she and Luke weren't alone. Half a dozen aliens had emerged from the mist and were milling about the huts, one of them inspecting the damaged wall in consternation.

Rey knew immediately that these new arrivals were real—and that they were no threat to her. They had broad faces and three-toed feet, and their stout bodies were hidden beneath simple robes of beige and white. They reminded Rey of the anchorites of Jakku, who'd found its wastes ideal for a simple life of religious observation and adherence.

She realized Luke was still waiting for an answer to his question. And so were the aliens.

Rey's first instinct was to tell him the truth, in hopes that he might be able to help her close off the unwanted connection before it became more dangerous. But something told her that would be a mistake. Luke had stopped pretending she didn't exist, but their relationship was fragile and perilous. The slightest misstep, Rey sensed, would cause him to reject her even before the first lesson he'd promised.

No, she had to tell him something else.

"I . . . was cleaning my blaster," she managed. "It went off."

Luke didn't look any less puzzled by that explanation, but the aliens seemed to accept it, albeit grumpily. Within moments they were removing fish from baskets, sharpening knives, and angrily yanking loose stones from the damaged wall.

Luke inclined his chin at the stairs climbing higher up the mountain. As Rey turned to follow him, one of the aliens glowered at her, then turned to Luke.

"*Choo-chigga chupa?*" she asked, or something like that.

"*Croopy,*" Luke replied.

The alien looked decidedly dubious.

Certain she'd made a poor first impression, Rey followed Luke up the winding steps until she thought they were out of earshot of the activity around the huts.

"What were those things?" she asked.

"Caretakers," he replied. "Island natives. They've kept up the Jedi structures since they were built."

"What did you tell them about me?" she asked.

Luke gave her a thin smile. "My niece."

"Oh. I don't think they like me."

"Can't imagine what gave you that idea."

Rey followed Luke across the grassy saddle above the huts and then up another set of winding stone steps. This staircase followed a rocky prominence that loomed above the island and the sea beyond.

She was still shaken by the manifestation of Kylo Ren, in a place she had come to think of at least as Luke's sanctuary, even if it wasn't hers.

After he'd immobilized her on Takodana, Kylo had taken her to Starkiller Base, to pry her memory of the map to Luke out of her head. He had probed her thoughts, sifting and sorting, and seen much that she would have kept from him—him and anybody else.

Her desperate certainty that her abandonment on Jakku had been a mistake, or a grim necessity that would be put right by her lost family, if only she waited long enough and patiently enough. Her terror and despair that she was deluding herself, and would spend her days in solitude, ending up as anonymous bones in the sand. Her dreams of an island amid a trackless ocean—the very island on which she now found herself.

Kylo had rummaged through these hopes and fears, things he had no right to. But as he searched, something had changed. Even as he callously rifled through her mind, he had somehow revealed his own. Rey found herself in his mind even as he invaded hers. She felt his rage, like a ruinous storm that filled his head, and his hatred, and his lust to dominate and humiliate those who had wronged him. But she also felt his hurt, and his loneliness. And his fear—that he would never prove as strong as Darth Vader, the ghost who haunted his dreams.

Kylo had retreated at finding Rey in his head—had practically fled from her. But that had not been the end of that strange, sudden connection. She had seen more—far more. Somehow, almost instinctually, she knew how he accessed some of the powers at his command—even though she didn't understand them. It was as if his training had become hers, unlocking and flinging open door after door in her mind.

But now Rey couldn't shut those doors—and she feared what had been set loose.

Kylo had urged her to let him be her teacher—had pleaded with her, almost. She had rejected him—only to be rejected, in turn, by Luke.

Until this morning.

Rey had traveled halfway across the galaxy so that Luke would help those who needed him so desperately—Leia, Finn, the Resistance, the people of the galaxy. But she also hoped he would help her.

Rose was simultaneously annoyed and amused when Poe insisted on going over the plan one more time, pulling her and Finn into a ready room off the hangar to do so.

"You could just come with us, you know," she said, exasperated.

Poe's face fell, and Rose felt sorry for him. He wanted to do just that—wanted to so badly that it was killing him.

"Someone has to stay here and keep an eye on things," he said. "On General Organa."

"Threepio can do that," Finn said.

"Well, someone has to keep an eye on Holdo, too."

Considering that, Finn reached up to scratch his chin. When he did so, Rose spotted the glow of the beacon around the former stormtrooper's wrist, the twin of the device Rey had taken with her into the Unknown Regions.

Poe saw it, too.

"Better leave that with me, buddy," he said, reaching for Finn's wrist.

Finn drew back instinctively, and Rose saw the indecision on his face. His original goal had been to take the beacon far from the fleet and the danger to it, and now he was being asked to abandon that goal.

"The general sent your friend to bring back Skywalker so he can help us," Poe said. "It's not going to do the Resistance any good if he shows up at Canto Bight."

Rose knew immediately what Finn was thinking—the former stormtrooper would have been a terrible sabacc player.

"Give that thing to Poe already," she told him. "You want to save Rey? Then save the fleet. That's why we're doing this, remember?"

Rose saw the look of surprise that crossed Poe's face, followed by dawning comprehension as the pieces fell into place.

"I just want her to be safe," Finn said unhappily.

"So do I," Poe told Finn, his voice surprisingly gentle. "But this is a lot bigger than Rey. Or any of us. It's about everybody in the galaxy. So come on—let me have that. I promise I won't let it out of my sight."

For a moment Rose was afraid Finn would refuse. But then he reluctantly worked the beacon free of his wrist, placing it in Poe's hand.

"You see?" Rose said. "That was easy."

But Finn's face told her that hadn't been true at all.

As she followed Luke up the steps, Rey saw that the stairway ended in a cave in the side of the peak.

She followed Luke inside, where an ancient mosaic was still visible in the middle of the stone floor. But this wasn't their destination—

Luke led her out onto a pair of ledges, one high and one low. It was a dizzying vantage point from which the island seemed to fall away into the endless sea surrounding them.

Luke watched her for a moment, idly twisting a reed in his hand, and Rey wondered if he somehow thought she was afraid of heights. She wasn't and never had been—she'd still been a child when she'd scaled the conning tower of her first wrecked Star Destroyer.

"So?" she asked him.

"So."

Rey tried not to scowl. So far the morning when he'd teach her the ways of the Jedi wasn't terribly different from the mornings on which he'd refused to speak to her.

"Well, I'll start," she said. "We need you to bring the Jedi back, because Kylo Ren is strong with the dark side of the Force. Without the Jedi we won't stand a chance against him."

Rey half imagined Luke would walk back into the cave and down the stairs, leaving her to wonder what test she'd failed this time. But he simply peered at her.

"What do you know about the Force?" he asked.

"It's a power that Jedi have. That lets them control people, and . . . make things float."

For a moment the only sounds were the cries of seabirds and the whine of the wind.

"Impressive," Luke said. "Every word in that sentence was wrong. Lesson One. Sit here, legs crossed."

Rey settled herself on the higher of the two ledges, arranging her legs awkwardly in a crisscross position.

"The Force is not a power you have," Luke said. "It's not about lifting rocks. It's the energy between all things—a tension, a balance that binds the universe together."

"Okay. But what is it?"

"Close your eyes," Luke told her. "Breathe. Now reach out."

Rey did as she was told and tentatively stretched out her arm, fingers grasping for purchase.

Nothing happened. Was something supposed to? Did it take a

while? Was he testing her patience? Back on Jakku, the Teedos had venerated a sun-addled local who sat unmoving atop a stone pillar all day. She'd hoped learning the ways of the Jedi wouldn't require anything like that. But apparently she'd been wrong.

Then Rey felt something strange, like a tickle on her hand.

"Ah!" she told Luke. "I feel something!"

"You feel it?"

"Yes! I feel it!"

"That's the Force."

"Really?" Rey asked. She couldn't help feeling pleased with herself—after all, she'd only been reaching out for a few seconds at most.

"Wow, it must be really strong with you."

Rey was wondering why her early breakthrough amused Luke when pain flared in her outstretched hand. She yelped, eyes snapping open, and realized Luke had whipped her hand with the reed—just as he'd been tickling her with it earlier.

Hoping her face wasn't red, she put one hand over her heart.

"You meant reach out like . . . Okay. Got it. I'll try again."

She closed her eyes and felt Luke take her hands with his rough, calloused ones, directing them to the rock on either side of her.

"Breathe," he said. "Just breathe. Now reach out with your feelings. What do you see?"

The image came to her almost immediately, and was reassuringly familiar: the island, seen as if she were one of the seabirds overhead, just as it had looked in her dreams back on Jakku.

But almost immediately, there was more. The images were vivid, almost hallucinatory, but later she couldn't be sure if she'd seen them in her mind's eye or somehow actually experienced them as her awareness expanded out from her body to encompass the island and the sea around it.

Her first impression was life—life all around her. She could sense herself, and the Caretakers pottering about near the huts, but there was so much more than that. She felt the presence of flowers and grasses and shrubs. Birds and insects and fish, and creatures too tiny for the eye to see. Her awareness of all of it seemed to crowd her senses, plunging her into something so deep and intense that for a moment she thought she might drown in it, only to realize that was impossible, because she was a part of that life.

But there was death, too—and decay. Dead flesh and vegetable matter, sinking into soil that hid bones and dry sticks from bygone seasons of the island. She shrank from this new awareness, but sensed almost immediately that there was nothing to fear. From the death and decay sprang new life, nourished by what had come before.

She could feel the warmth of the suns—not just on her face but on the rocks and the surface of the ceaseless tumble of the water. And cold, too, which surrounded the dark places where the roots of the island and the seafloor were revealed as one and the same. There was peace—mother porgs with their eggs, sheltered and safe in warm hollows—but also violence that left behind broken nests and shattered shells.

And all that her senses showed her had been but a moment. That moment was but one of trillions, part of a never-ending cycle that had begun eons before she was born and would go on for eons after she was dead. And it was itself part of something vastly larger, so enormous that her mind couldn't grasp it, an immensity even the stars were but the tiniest portion of.

Rey, her eyes still closed, tried to tell Luke what she had experienced, frustrated that her words were so small and inadequate.

"And between it all?" she heard him ask.

"A balance—an energy," she said, wanting to laugh. "A *Force*."

"And inside you?"

"Inside me, that same Force."

She opened her eyes and was faintly surprised to find Luke unchanged—a weather-beaten, gray-bearded man in workaday clothes designed for sun and salt and wind.

"And this is the lesson—that Force does not belong to the Jedi," Luke said. "It's so much bigger. To say that if the Jedi die the light dies is vanity. Can you feel that? Can you understand that?"

She could. But a new presence was calling to her awakened senses.

"There's something here," she said. "*Right* here. A powerful light—blinding."

"This is the first Jedi temple," Luke said. "A concentration of light."

Rey wondered how they'd found it so long ago, those first Jedi explorers, and thought she knew. They'd followed a whisper in the Force, plunging into the trackless churn of the galaxy's stars and trusting the Force to find pathways through them. She tried to imagine the bravery and faith they'd needed to do that.

"But there's something else," she said, realizing. "Beneath the island. A place—a *dark* place."

She could see it now, in her mind's eye. Rocky flats by the sea, ominous and cold. With a dark hole in the rock . . .

"Balance," Luke said, and there was a twinge of concern in his voice. "Powerful light, powerful darkness."

"It's cold. It's calling me."

The ledge trembled beneath her, and dust and rocks fell from the cliffs around them.

"Resist it," Luke urged her. "Rey, *fight* it!"

Dimly, Rey heard his voice calling her name. But it faded away to nothing, until all Rey could hear was the roaring of water. She was standing on the cold, rocky shore from her vision, moving as if hypnotized toward a black hole before her—the source of that roar. The sound built, reaching a crescendo as water shot out of the rock.

With a start, Rey found herself on the ledge. Luke was drawing back his hand. He had slapped her. She gasped for breath, feeling like she'd been dragged out of deep water.

Her face was wet. At first she thought it was her imagination, but her hair was dripping, and she could taste salt on her tongue.

The Jedi Master's eyes were wary—and fixed on her.

"That place can show me something," Rey managed to explain. "It was trying to."

"You went straight to the dark," Luke said. "It offered you something you needed and you didn't even try to stop yourself."

He turned his back on her, but she reached out a shaky hand to stop him. Because she had realized something else—something she knew immediately that Luke would have wanted to keep from her.

"I saw *everything*," she said. "The island, and past it I felt the stars singing. I thought my heart would explode. *But I didn't see you.* Nothing from you. No light, no dark. You've closed yourself off from the Force."

Luke stared at her, his face pale and drawn.

"I've seen this raw strength only once before, in Ben Solo," he said. "It didn't scare me enough then. It does now."

Rey shrank back from what she saw in his gaze, and was relieved when Luke walked away from her, into the darkness of the ancient temple.

CHAPTER 14

From his vantage point on the periphery of the *Raddus*'s secondary bridge, Poe kept a wary eye on Holdo and suppressed the urge to find a reason to march back down to the hangar where he'd left Rose and Finn.

All was ready, or should be. He had friends all over the ship, many of whom shared his unease about their new commander. It had been trivial to authorize a flight in a light shuttle, delete that flight from the hourly schedule, and override the resulting error message. Every logistics tech with a rudimentary sense of self-preservation had a backdoor passcode or two in case the system got finicky and locked down normal operations.

Poe shifted from foot to foot. He'd have felt better if he were behind the stick, of course, but Rose and Finn knew how to fly. Well, okay, Finn didn't. But Rose was rated for a light shuttle. Heck, even C-3PO could probably handle a light shuttle.

Besides, if something had gone truly wrong, BB-8 would tell him. Though come to think of it, Poe wasn't sure where BB-8 had gotten to.

Come on, you guys. Get that bird off the deck before the Rancor Lady calls an inspection or something.

Still, when the alert finally sounded on an operations monitor's console, Poe nearly jumped through the viewport.

"What was that?" Holdo demanded, looking up.

"Nothing, Admiral," Connix said. "Passing debris."

Holdo, satisfied, returned to her work. Connix looked up and shared a conspiratorial nod with Poe. The shuttle had launched.

"The smaller ships will run out of fuel first," Holdo said. "We need to begin evacuating their crews to the flagship. Staring with the medical frigate."

Poe surveyed the bridge. Connix wasn't the only one who had her doubts. He saw rigid backs, and eyes fixed on monitors. It was a commander's job to sense that, to read her bridge and her people. Holdo either couldn't or wouldn't.

And it made Poe angry. Leia had built the Resistance, despite the New Republic's apathy and First Order sabotage and a chronic lack of credits, equipment, and personnel. And now Holdo—someone Leia had *trusted*—seemed determined to undo all her work.

"So we abandon the *Anodyne*," Poe said. "What changes after that, Admiral? What happens when there are no ships left to abandon?"

Holdo fixed Poe with her gaze.

"You want a daring plan," she said. "Dashing hero, derring-do, single-handed day-saving. That's what you want?"

"I just want to know the plan," Poe said helplessly. "I think we all do."

"And at the appropriate time, you will," Holdo said. "But just so we're clear: There will be no idiot heroics, daring plans, or showy bombing runs on *my* watch."

Poe's frustrations boiled over. "You're going to destroy everything Leia has built."

"Captain Dameron. If you're here to serve a princess, I'll assign you to bedpan duty," Holdo replied. "If you're here to serve the Resistance, follow my orders. Somebody has to save this fleet from its heroes."

And with that she turned back to her monitor, dismissing him.

Poe, stunned, looked around the auxiliary bridge and found no other officer would meet his gaze.

Rose and Finn's shuttle emerged from hyperspace above the desert planet of Cantonica, an almost featureless globe broken by a single blue sea that reminded Rose unsettlingly of an eye, staring into the void.

"So this place is fancy?" Finn asked. "Doesn't look fancy. Looks beige."

"The beige part doesn't matter—nobody lives there," said Rose, wishing she could concentrate on her flying and not his fretting. "The town's by the blue part."

"You know this town, Canto Bight?"

"From stories," she said. "It's a terrible place filled with the vilest people in the galaxy."

Paige probably would have said that was unfair—that Rose shouldn't begrudge people a little fun. But the idea of wearing fancy clothes and gambling while the galaxy burned struck her as obscene.

"Why doesn't anyone ever hide out someplace nice?" Finn asked. "The fleet doesn't have much fuel left—we'd better hurry."

Rose unstrapped herself from the pilot's seat.

"I'm going to douse the landing runners," she said. "Don't touch anything."

Finn looked mildly offended. "I'm not gonna touch anything."

But no sooner had Rose left the cockpit than he leaned his arm on a panel—a panel that, to be fair, looked like it had nothing to do with sticks or yokes or whatever that thing Rose used to fly was—and the shuttle violently banked to port.

He lifted his arm and the shuttle swung back to the proper course—but there was a crash from the cabin behind him.

"I touched something," Finn confessed. "That was me."

Rose thrust her head into the cockpit, looking exasperated. "Without a little practice you're going to get us both killed. Let's teach you how to land a shuttle."

"I'm not a pilot," Finn objected.

"Well, time to learn. By the way, the ball droid's in the toilet."

Finn, surprised, pushed past her and peered into the tiny space. BB-8 had indeed jammed himself inside, and greeted Finn with a cheerful string of beeps. Was it his imagination, or did the astromech look a bit smug?

"Quit stalling and get back here," Rose called from the cockpit.

Finn returned, BB-8 rolling along behind him, and watched as Rose pointed at various things.

"Control yoke, throttle, brake."

"Why does everything have to be so complicated?" Finn muttered.

"It's no more complicated than your average escape pod," Rose said with a smirk. "And you were ready to fly that."

"That hurt," Finn said, feeling his face flush.

Rose raised an eyebrow, and he sighed, throwing up his hands.

"Okay. Control thing, throttle, brake. Got it. Now show me the rest."

Sirens and shouts filled the corridors of the *Anodyne*.

Poe helped two young medics push a portable bacta tank containing a wounded Resistance fighter down the corridor, the man trying to brace himself inside the tank as the bacta sloshed back and forth.

They had almost reached the medical frigate's hangar—but the evacuation was taking too long.

The *Anodyne* was already down to its last fuel reserves, if it hadn't exhausted them already. It had fallen behind the other ships in the Resistance fleet, leaving it unprotected by the *Raddus*'s powerful shield envelope. When the medical frigate's fuel was gone, it would lose headway—and almost immediately come within range of the guns of their First Order pursuers.

Poe turned back, waving for the next party of medics to hurry.

The *Anodyne* trembled and an explosion filled the corridor behind Poe with fire.

There was nothing to be done. He tried to go faster without top-pling the tank over.

Ahead, in the hangar, the starfighter pilot C'ai Threnalli stood at the bottom of a transport's ramp. Like many of the fleet's pilots—including Poe himself—the Abednedo had been pressed into service flying transports and shuttles and figuring out how to move crewers out of harm's way.

The *Anodyne* shuddered again as First Order turbolasers continued chewing through its shields.

C'ai waved for Poe to hurry.

On the bridge of the *Supremacy,* Hux gazed into the holotank, a rapt expression on his face. The First Order's task force filled the left side of the display; on the right, the *Raddus* trailed the two smaller Resistance ships.

"The main cruiser is still out of range, but their medical frigate is out of fuel and falling behind," Captain Peavey reported.

"The beginning of their end," Hux said. "Destroy it."

The order went out and the *Supremacy*'s prow turbolasers opened up. Peavy watched as the *Anodyne*'s already weakened shields flared, then died. A barrage of laserfire broke the frigate's back, snapping it in two; a moment after that the Resistance craft had been reduced to gas and superheated globules of metal.

"Target destroyed," said Captain Yago, a bit stiffly.

"Acknowledged," said Peavey, aiming a slightly apologetic nod in Yago's direction. The *Supremacy* had been Yago's command until Hux had unexpectedly been granted permission to transfer his flag from the *Finalizer* to his flagship—and brusquely informed Peavey that he was transferring as well.

Peavey had to give Hux credit for this much: The callow general knew he would be exposed without an experienced captain to lean on, and that—having been robbed of his command—Yago would give his help grudgingly at best.

Like Peavey, Yago was a veteran of the Imperial Starfleet. He'd greeted the interloper on his bridge with stiff formality, his bearing frosty but impossible to find fault with, and his dealings with Peavey had been businesslike and correct. That was the product of years of training and decades of service, the kind of thing Hux's father—mad though he had been—would have understood even as the son disdained it.

Yago would endure Hux just as Peavey had—because both men knew the general wouldn't last. He would undoubtedly succeed at destroying the remnants of the Resistance, and bask in the glory of that accomplishment for a time. But then the real challenges would begin. The First Order would have a restive galaxy to tame, one that had been plunged into chaos. And sooner or later, Hux would be undone, revealed as an incompetent officer and an intemperate leader.

Peavey smiled privately. Hux was a revolutionary, full of fire and fervor, but revolutionaries' seasons were fleeting.

Peavey looked out through the viewports, hands behind his back. The surviving Resistance ships remained just out of range of the First Order guns. If there had been any chance that those fleeing ships would be reinforced, Peavey would have recommended trying to cripple them with waves of starfighter attacks, but all the First Order's intel indicated no support was coming.

That meant there was no reason to send pilots into danger—not with the Resistance fleet unable to flee and beyond help. Hux was right about one thing—this was the beginning of their end.

Which meant Hux's own end was growing closer, too.

Far below the *Supremacy*'s bridge, Captain Phasma stood in the middle of a vast hangar. While impossibly cavernous, larger than some capital ships, it was just one of many staging areas on the enormous First Order flagship.

Phasma eyed the lines of TIEs and attack ships, the walkers being tethered to their landing craft, the stormtrooper legions, the black-clad pilots waiting in formation. They were ready—ready to be unleashed on whatever remained of the Resistance once its leaders accepted their plight and went to ground, hoping to find safety.

They wouldn't. Her troops would see to that.

Most of the galaxy's beings were soft—they grew up sheltered and spent the rest of their lives trying to make sure they stayed ignorant and indolent. Phasma was anything but soft—and by the time she could walk, she had understood there was no such thing as safety. There was only survival, which was the product of ceaseless struggle.

She inclined her chrome helmet to address her second in command.

"High alert, Commander," she said. "Their ships are dropping like flies. Our time approaches."

Poe's transport had escaped the *Anodyne* shortly before fingers of fire lanced out from the First Order flagship, eradicating the helpless frigate in seconds.

The explosion rattled the transport and lit the faces of the fighters he'd helped evacuate. Some had been helped out of the medical facilities, moved only because they would have died otherwise. They sat in silence, men and women left hazy by droid-administered sedatives or stoically ignoring what had to be terrible pain.

But the healthy crewers and soldiers barely looked up, either. They were staring at their boots, glum and miserable.

They don't see a reason to hope. Because Holdo won't give them one.

The Resistance ships flew on, but Poe wondered if the movement's spirit had already left it.

CHAPTER 15

Rey picked her way down the cracked and chipped stairs in the rain, careful of her footing—after everything she'd been through, it would be beyond ridiculous to kill herself falling down a wet staircase.

She found Chewbacca in the *Falcon*'s cockpit, fussing with the freighter's hypertransceiver.

"Still can't reach the Resistance?" she asked.

The Wookiee barked in frustration.

"Keep at it," Rey said encouragingly. "If you get through, ask their status, and . . . ask about Finn."

Chewbacca promised he would and Rey worked her way back to the ramp, wiping the rain off her forehead.

She wondered if she should have asked about the dozen porgs perched on the dashboard, watching the Wookiee work—or the porg that had been sitting companionably on his hairy shoulder.

She supposed the porgs would be dinner soon enough, and the Wookiee was using the *Falcon* as a larder. Treating tomorrow's meal as today's pet struck Rey as a bit odd, but then it was a big galaxy, and every species was entitled to its quirks.

It was raining harder now, and Rey lingered under the *Falcon*, looking out in wonder and occasionally extending a hand so she could feel the rain splashing in her palm. Water had been precious on Jakku, bartered and hoarded and fought over, and its gleeful abundance here still felt like a miracle. She knew the Caretakers would be gathering it in barrels, while the shallow roots of the island's grass and shrubs eagerly drank in as much of it as they could.

Something tickled at her awareness and she turned to stare out at the gray sea, her happiness giving way to dread at what she already knew she would see.

Kylo was staring at her.

"Murderous snake," Rey said as his eyes locked onto hers.

He came closer and she flinched, but refused to give ground.

"You aren't really here—you can't touch me," she said. "I'm safe."

"For someone who's safe, you're awfully afraid," Kylo replied. He peered at her, eyes dark in his pale face, and she realized he could see the spray bouncing up from the stone and hitting her.

"You're too late," she said, determined to break through his air of detached curiosity. "You lost. I found Skywalker."

"How's that going?" Kylo asked, amused. Then his eyes flashed. "Has he told you what happened, the night I destroyed his temple? Has he told you why?"

"I know everything I need to know about you," she countered, taken aback.

"You do?" he asked, and peered at her, eyes intent. "You do. You have that look in your eyes from the forest, when you called me a monster."

He came within a meter or two of Rey, and she wondered what would happen if she refused to move and they intersected. Would she find herself in his mind again, and have to endure his presence in hers? Could they actually touch, across a galaxy?

"You *are* a monster," Rey said, remembering the terror of her paralysis on Takodana.

She stared back at him—and found his eyes full of hurt. Hurt—and conflict.

"Yes, I am," Kylo said, and there was no menace in his voice—only misery.

And then he was gone, leaving her watching the waves breaking on the stone. She stared into the heaving sea, not sure what she was searching for, then felt another tingle of awareness. She turned, looking up at the island, up into the rain, and saw Luke waiting for her.

In the metal heart of the *Supremacy*, Kylo stood and stared at the place Rey had been. He felt something strange and looked down at his gloved hand.

There was water on his palm.

He stared at it, then balled his hand into a fist to hide it from his sight.

CHAPTER 16

Finn fell in love with Canto Bight the moment he flew over it.

He gazed down in disbelief at the sea, dotted with sleek yachts, and the graceful curve of the crescent bay, lined with stately, gorgeous hotels. Beyond them, the town was a sparkling jewel. Its broad boulevards surrounded a modern complex of tile and black glass, bathed in shimmering light of every spectrum. Beyond the complex was a warren of low stone buildings, crisscrossed by narrow, warmly lit streets.

Rose hadn't wanted to land at the spaceport for fear that the shuttle would be recognized as a Resistance craft, so they came in low over the edge of the sea. Below them, couples strolled along the boardwalk, admiring the sunset, while children ran to the edge of the gentle waves, daring the water to attack their feet before running back up the beach to their parents.

Finn was so busy looking around that he forgot to look below. The shuttle plowed nose-first into the beach, flinging BB-8 across the cockpit and wrenching Rose and Finn sideways in their harnesses before it shuddered to a stop. Finn looked up guiltily as Rose extracted herself from the copilot's chair, wincing. She'd bitten her lip and was pretty sure the restraints would leave bruises where they'd dug into her shoulders.

"What?" Finn asked. "We're down in one piece, aren't we?"

BB-8 squawked derisively. Rose just shook her head.

"I still think it's a bad idea to leave the ship here," Finn said.

"We can't afford a berth at the spaceport, remember? Or to have our identities broadcast. Besides, if you'd made that landing at the spaceport we'd be in a medbay right now—or a crater."

"But—"

"But nothing. Come on. The fleet needs us."

They hurried up the beach to the boardwalk, then headed for the lights of the casino.

Crossing the tree-lined piazza in front of the Canto Casino and Racetrack, Finn nearly got hit by two luxury speeders—muscular, powerful street machines with growling engines. One after the other, organic chauffeurs leaned out of their windows to make unlikely anatomical suggestions.

Rose responded to the second chauffeur with a counter-suggestion that would have demanded a lot more privacy, and made BB-8 hoot in admiration.

"Don't they have droid-speeders in this town?" Finn asked, pretty sure he was blushing.

Rose looked at him in surprise. "Any tourist can afford to ride with a droid," she explained patiently. "If you've really got credits, you hire flesh-and-blood help."

"I hadn't thought of that," said an embarrassed Finn as they walked up the entryway to the casino, dodging the warning flickers from parked speeders' anti-theft fields.

Finn sidestepped a hustling valet and looked from the elaborate, scented gardens to the holo-marquees greeting visitors.

"They've got a luxury hotel and a shopping concourse," he marveled. "And twenty-two restaurants. How are we going to find the Master Codebreaker in all this?"

"Maybe he'll find us," Rose said, hurrying as liveried attendants grandly swept the double doors open. "All he has to do is look for the two rubes dressed like greasy speeder jockeys."

Finn saw immediately what she meant. They were surrounded by humans and aliens of every conceivable species, from diminutive Chadra-Fan to towering, long-armed Dor Namethians. But all of them were dressed immaculately: Finn's eyes leapt from sleek chadors and billowing gowns to elegant tuxedos and lavish waistcoats with trains held high by attendants. Heads bore coronets; eyes peered through lorgnettes held in position by repulsorlifts; ears, noses, and appendages Finn didn't recognize dripped with jewels of every hue; arms and digits were encircled by bracelets and rings that glittered in the light; and feet and ventral tentacles were held aloft by footwear that struck Finn as dangerously wide, high, or both.

The riot of color and wealth was so overwhelming that the most extraordinary outfit barely registered—but every eye seemed drawn to Finn's dirty jacket and Rose's maintenance jumpsuit. Finn wanted to find a hole to crawl into, but Rose simply looked around dismissively, deflecting an attendant's offer of assistance. Then she squared her shoulders and marched across the lobby, with Finn rushing after her.

To his surprise, though, the casino's staff treated them with the same extravagant groveling as the guests wearing outfits that cost as much as a small moon. Arms beckoned in welcome and greetings were offered in rapid-fire Outer Rim tongues as he and Rose strolled onto the main casino floor, BB-8 rolling along behind them.

"This place is great!" Finn exclaimed.

"No, it is not," Rose muttered.

"Are you kidding? *Yes. It. Is.* Look at—look! And look!"

Rose glared at the rows of gaming tables, where laughing groups were wagering stacks of Cantocoins on everything from Savareen whist and Kuari zinbiddle to spins of the jubilee wheel and rounds of hazard toss. Elsewhere, gamblers carrying gleaming buckets surrounded carousels of floating slot machines, gold and glossy black with spinning reels on their faces. Bartenders juggled cocktail shakers, dealers in green tarbooshes and matching vests offered congratulations or sympathy, and server droids stepped carefully through the crowds, politely dipping heads as they nimbly rotated drink trays out of the path of the overserved and inattentive.

"Let's find the Master Codebreaker and get out of here," Rose said.

As they scanned the crowd, a small, dark-eyed alien in evening wear staggered up to BB-8 and jammed a coin in a diagnostic slot set in one of the droid's tool bays. Confused and a little offended, BB-8 drew back and squawked at the drunken gambler—who squinted at the droid and then put another coin in.

"I wish Rey could see this," Finn said as Rose pushed through the throngs of guests, hunting at each table for the crimson splash of a red plom bloom. Frustrated, she finally jumped on a table so she could scan the entire floor.

"What are you doing?" Finn asked, nervously eyeing a couple of aliens in dull-black clothing who he was pretty sure were security, as their eyes were always in motion and they never smiled.

"Our mission, remember? Stop drooling all over the scenery, stop pining for Rey, and get with it."

"I was not pining for Rey," Finn objected.

Rose looked scornful.

"Heavy pining. *Heavy.* You were ready to abandon the Resistance to help her. How can one person mean more to you than a whole cause?"

Finn looked away from a trio of jovial Suertons—no red plom blooms there—to glare at Rose.

"I was raised in an army to fight for a cause," he said. "Then I met Rey. And for the first time I had someone I cared about to fight for. That's who I wanted to be."

He braced himself for another caustic remark, but Rose's face softened.

"When she comes back, will she be a Jedi like in the stories?" she asked. "Brown robes, little rat tail?"

That made Finn laugh. "No. Rey a Jedi? Nah."

He tried to figure out where an egg-laden Xi'Dec might affix a red plom bloom, then gave up

"But she'll be different," Rose said.

"No," he insisted. Rey would always be Rey. He was sure of it, and a little annoyed by Rose's failure to see that.

Rose looked skeptically at him before returning to her glowering appraisal of the wealthy gamblers around them.

"She's on her own path," she told him. "You need to find yours."

"Thank you, wise master Rose."

"Any time, youngling."

"When I see her again she'll just be Rey."

He smiled at Rose, who shook her head and continued looking for new rich people to dislike.

BB-8 stood stock-still on the casino floor, beeping encouragingly. The inebriated alien stuck another coin into his tool bay and BB-8 warbled happily, flashing the diagnostic lights on his head, then of-fered a sad, droopy coo. Frustrated, the gambler dug in its bucket for yet another coin.

Rose had retreated to a bar on the side of the casino floor that was open to the evening breeze. A whiskered bartender in green-and-white livery readied a cocktail while gamblers sat in the shadows, studying decks of cards.

Rose glared at a pair of guests who sneered too obviously at her jumpsuit.

"I think we've covered the whole casino," Finn said. "Where is this guy?"

Suddenly a blur of motion and a thunderous clatter filled the space behind the bar, rattling the glasses and bottles.

"Were those what I think they were?" Rose asked wonderingly.

She rushed through a door, Finn hurrying after her.

"Hey, what happened to not getting distracted?" he asked.

They found themselves on a balcony overlooking an oval race-track, adjoining the casino. Spectators were cheering, their attention directed below, where twelve jockeys in iridescent livery were perched atop animals with tawny hides, long ears, and streaming tails.

"What are those things?" Finn asked, admiring the way their ears, legs, and tails parted the air. They looked like flesh-and-blood ver-sions of exotic-model starfighters.

"Fathiers," Rose said, entranced. "They were my sister's favorite animal when we were kids. She never got to see a real one. So beautiful . . ."

"Look, this whole place is beautiful," Finn said. "I mean, come on. Why do you hate it so much?"

"Look closer," Rose suggested.

Finn spotted a pair of electrobinoculars mounted on the balcony railing and peered through them. The fathiers were in the home stretch. He could see sparks as the jockeys' electro-whips rose and fell, ruthless strokes aimed at extracting more speed from their exhausted mounts.

Without taking her eyes off the racing fathiers, Rose reached into the top of her jumpsuit and extracted a medallion she wore on a cord around her neck.

"My sister and I grew up in a poor mining system," she said. "The First Order stripped our ore to finance their military, then shelled us to test their weapons. They took everything we had."

Finn looked up and found Rose clutching her medallion, pale with anger. She waved one arm accusingly at the cheering gamblers in the grandstand below.

"And who do you think these people are?" she asked him. "There's only one business in the galaxy that will get you this rich."

"War," Finn said.

"Selling weapons to the First Order," Rose said. "I wish I could put my fist through this whole lousy beautiful town."

Finn didn't know what to say. As he groped for an answer, BB-8 rolled up to them, his spherical body rattling strangely. The astromech beeped frantically.

"Red plom bloom?" Rose exclaimed. "Where?"

CHAPTER 17

Rey stood opposite an outcropping of rock, practicing sparring with her staff.

On Jakku she'd rarely neglected such practice—she needed to defend herself against threats ranging from marauding Teedos to fellow scavengers willing to kill for a valuable bit of salvage. She'd let things slide since arriving on the island, though, and now she wished she hadn't.

She was rusty, for one thing. But the exertion also helped blow away the fog and frustration that had enveloped her. Here there were no gnomic Jedi utterances or malevolent visitations to contend with—just the need to keep her staff spinning and jabbing.

Rey didn't allow herself a breather until she was sweating freely and her arms and shoulders ached. Leaning on the staff, ignoring the curious porgs circling overhead, she spotted Luke's lightsaber peeking out of her bag.

Should she?

Of course she should.

The lightsaber felt different in her hands—it was heavier and there was none of the additional momentum supplied by the counter-weight of her staff. But the principles weren't too different. And the lightsaber seemed *alive* in her hands somehow—as if something inside it were simultaneously focusing her strength and guiding her thrusts and parries. Her sense of the energy around her felt sharpened, and the song of the blade seemed to resonate with the currents of the Force surrounding her, amplifying them.

She no longer noticed the sweat running down her face, or the fatigue weighting her arms and legs. There was only the motion of her body and the lightsaber, moving as one. Thrusting and parrying, wheeling and weaving, until the distinction blurred between weapon and wielder.

"Impressive," Luke said.

The sound of his voice jerked her out of her trance. Turning to look at him, she stumbled slightly, her slash continuing so it intersected rock instead of just empty air.

The lightsaber bisected the outcropping she'd been mock-fighting and the top half slid away, vanishing over the edge of the cliff. Dirt and rock flew into the air, along with tufts of grass and indignant porgs.

As Luke watched in amusement, Rey deactivated the weapon and peeked over the cliff. The massive stone had obliterated a Caretaker's cart and left a broad scar all the way down to the sea. Below, two Caretakers chattered in dismay, then stared up at her disapprovingly.

The suns were dipping toward the horizon as Rey and Luke entered the Jedi temple, facing each other across the font in the center of the ancient space.

"So," Rey said.

"So."

She shook her head. "Nope, you start this time."

"I've shown you that you don't need the Jedi to use the Force," Luke said. "So why do you need the Jedi Order?"

Rey peered at him. Surely this was another one of his tests. She had heard the tales of what he'd been able to do with the Force. She'd seen with her own eyes what Kylo had used that energy to accomplish. And she sensed—with a mix of fear and anticipation—what her own growing powers might one day allow.

But one person couldn't stand against an army like that of the First Order. No matter how powerful they might be.

"To fight the rising darkness," Rey said. "They kept the peace and protected the light in the galaxy for a thousand generations . . . and I can tell from your look that every word I just said was wrong."

Luke smiled and studied the mosaic in the floor. She wondered how long ago it had been created, and by whose hands.

"You got 'thousand generations' right," he said. "Lesson Two. Now that they're extinct, the Jedi are romanticized—deified. But if you strip away the myth and look at their deeds, from the birth of the Sith to the fall of the Republic the legacy of the Jedi is failure. Hypocrisy. Hubris."

"That's not true!" she protested, staring at him in shock. If he was the last of the Order, the galaxy needed him to be its custodian, its preservationist. The galaxy had no shortage of those who wanted to see the Jedi discredited and buried and forgotten.

But this was no test.

"At the height of their powers they allowed Darth Sidious to rise, create the Empire, and wipe them out," Luke said. "It was a Jedi Master who was responsible for the training and creation of Darth Vader."

"And a Jedi who saved him!" Rey objected. "Yes, the most hated man in the galaxy—but *you* saw there was conflict in him. You believed that he wasn't gone, he could be turned."

She didn't understand. It was troubling enough that Luke had rejected the legacy of the Jedi. But whatever had happened to him had led him to reject his own legacy as well. Not for the first time, she wondered if he had slipped into madness during his years of exile.

But the bearded man in the rough-hewn woolens didn't look insane. Just profoundly sad.

"And I became a legend," Luke said. "For many years there was balance. I took no Padawans, and no darkness rose. But then I saw Ben, my nephew—with that mighty Skywalker blood. In my hubris I thought I could train him, I could pass on my strengths. I might not be the last Jedi."

His eyes were far away now, interrogating the past. Rey wondered if he relived those dark times every day, brooding on the top of the island as when she'd first met him, or if he never did—if it was her arrival that had forced him to confront the events that had caused him to shut himself away from family and friends and vanish.

"Han . . . was Han about it," Luke said. "But Leia trusted me with her son. I took him and a dozen students and began a training temple. And by the time I realized I was no match for the darkness rising in him it was too late."

"What happened?" Rey asked gently.

Ben Solo—no longer a boy but not yet a man—looks up in surprise and alarm. His uncle Luke has come into his chambers, at night, and now stands over him. There is no sign of trouble—Luke is unarmed—but his Master's face is creased with concern. And the Force is aboil with danger.

Ben's hand reaches up, not toward Luke but beyond him, to the stones of the ceiling. Bidding those stones to obey his command and come crashing down on Luke's head. To crush and bury him.

"He must have thought I was dead," Luke said. "When I came to, the temple was burning. He had vanished with a handful of my students and slaughtered the rest. Leia blamed Snoke, but it was I who broke that family. I failed. Because I was Luke Skywalker, Jedi Master. A legend."

He said that last word as if it were something terrible—a burden and a curse. But Rey held his gaze.

"The galaxy may need a legend. I need someone to show me my place in all this. And you didn't fail Kylo—*he* failed *you*. I won't."

Luke regarded her gravely, and when he spoke his voice was quiet.

"I don't know who's more dangerous: the pupil who wants to destroy me, or the one who wants to become me."

For a long moment there was no sound but the wind. Then Rey felt it: Something was coming. She stepped out onto the meditation ledge, high above the sea, and peered out at the horizon. Six ships—crude constructions of wood—were arrowing through the water toward the island.

Rey tensed. They'd been found.

"It's a tribe from a neighboring island," Luke said from behind her. Her shoulders slumped with relief.

"They come once a month to raid and plunder the Caretakers' village," he added.

Rey hurried to the end of the ledge, seeking to trace their course. Her heart began to pound. The ships were indeed bearing slightly north of them, perfectly positioned to skirt the headlands and land in the bay where the Caretakers' huts huddled by the sea.

"Well, come on!" she urged Luke. "We've got to stop them!"

But he just stood on the ledge, contemplating the ships and the sea. She stared at him in disbelief.

"Come on!" she said.

"Do you know what a true Jedi would do right now?" Luke asked, as if they had all the time in the world. "Nothing."

"*What?* This is not a lesson—they're going to get hurt! We've got to help!"

"If you meet the raiding party with force, they'll be back next month—with greater numbers and greater violence. Will *you* be here next month?"

Frustrated, Rey watched the ships cutting through the water, every moment bringing them nearer to the helpless village. Her senses were aflame, bombarding her with images: shattered eggs, crashing waves, splintered bones, and fire in the night.

"That burn inside you, that anger thinking what the raiders are going to do?" Luke asked. "The books in the Jedi library say ignore that. Only act when you can maintain balance. Even if people get hurt."

Oh really? Well, then the hell with what a bunch of old books say.

Rey shoved past Luke, squeezed through the entrance to the temple, and took off at a run down the ancient stairs.

Jedi Master Luke Skywalker has hidden away on the remote planet of Ahch-To for years. When young scavenger Rey comes to ask for his help, Luke refuses her, believing the galaxy is better off without him.

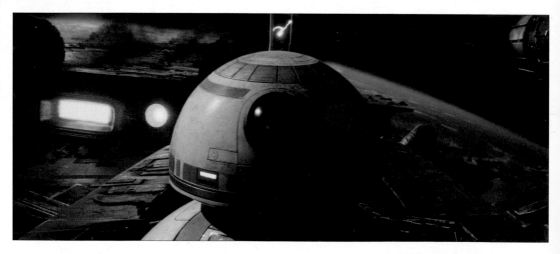

The First Order is invading the galaxy, and only the Resistance stands in their way. When the evil army attacks, Poe Dameron and BB-8 race to their X-wing to protect the Resistance fleet.

General Leia Organa has always led the
Resistance against the First Order. But after
a devastating attack, Vice Admiral Holdo is
forced to take command. Although Leia and
Holdo have been friends since childhood,
they have very different styles of leadership.

Worried about their new leader, Poe sends technician Rose Tico and former stormtrooper Finn on a secret mission. Their quest takes them to the beautiful and deadly city of Canto Bight. There they meet a skilled codebreaker called DJ who can help them with their mission.

On Ahch-To, Luke finally agrees to train Rey in the ways of the Force. But a surprising connection to Kylo Ren causes Rey to doubt Luke and his vision for the Jedi.

Rey leaves Ahch-To and travels to the First Order fleet to confront Kylo and save the Resistance. Meanwhile, Finn and Rose board the same *Mega*-class Star Destroyer and fight against their First Order foes.

The battle of Resistance vs. First Order culminates on the planet of Crait, where First Order AT-M6s and Resistance ski speeders face off above the ancient salt flats.

Rey uses her formidable Force abilities to rescue the Resistance and lead them to freedom. Although the First Order continues to grow in strength, the Resistance now has a powerful Jedi on their side and hope for a better future.

"Wait!" she heard the Jedi Master call. "Rey!"

But Rey had waited long enough.

The Master Codebreaker looked exactly like Finn had imagined: a young human, with a striking white streak in his hair and a thin, perfectly groomed mustache. He wore an immaculate gaberwool tuxedo with a leather cummerbund, a platinum ring—and, yes, a pin on his lapel that looked like a red flower.

He stood at one end of a gaming table, surrounded by riveted onlookers, cupping a pair of dice in one hand. Next to him was a tall red-haired woman whose geometric hair seemed to levitate above a cheongsam decorated with an intricate, hypnotizing lattice of lace.

The Master Codebreaker winked at the woman in lace, then let the dice fly. They tumbled across the table and the onlookers roared in delight.

Time seemed to slow down as Finn made his way through the crowd, trailed by Rose and the rattling BB-8. Somehow, he knew, everything would work out. They'd cut it a bit close, to be sure—the fleet would be running on fumes by the time they got back to it—but it would be okay.

A sour-faced Abednedo stepped in front of him, right into his personal space. More puzzled than annoyed, Finn turned to brush past him.

"Yeah, these are the guys," the Abednedo said.

Before Finn could protest or even make sense of what was happening, two police officers stepped forward, saying something about parking. Or maybe it was littering. Finn wasn't sure—he lost the thread of the conversation when he saw the cops unclip their stun prods and raise them.

This is happening way too often, he thought a moment before the jolt of electricity shot through him, the world around him shrank to a dim tunnel, and everything went black.

The stairs were taking too long, so Rey skidded down the slope leading down from the temple, then raced across the top of the island, scattering nesting porgs and digging in her bag for Luke's lightsaber.

She ran past the tree housing the Jedi tomes and reached the winding track that led down to the Caretakers' village. It was growing dark and she was breathing hard. She could see the lights below her—and, through the gloom, the shapes of the raiders' ships approaching the rocky shore.

Fear lent Rey an additional burst of speed—fear and anger. Luke had said the raiders came every month. That meant this had happened many times during his exile. How many nights had he stood brooding at the crest of the island, doing nothing, while those who served him were left to suffer?

She didn't understand how anyone could do that—and so this would be the last time it happened. She'd watched the Hosnian system burn; with the First Order on the march, other worlds were in danger of meeting the same fate. But this one village would be spared. At least in this one tiny corner of the galaxy, there would be some justice.

She hurtled a tide pool and her finger found the lightsaber's activator, its light tinting the water around her blue. Its weight felt like a promise of retribution, and the ancient Jedi weapon's hum sounded eager to her ears.

As she neared the village, kicking up loose rock, she heard screams and cries ahead. She slashed through a gate made of driftwood, lightsaber raised over her head—

—and came to a shocked stop.

Tables groaned with platters of fish, roe, and spiced seaweed. Caretaker matrons were dispensing grog into stone mugs and passing them into a crowd of males and females, dancing energetically on their spindly legs to the sound of horns and drums. The raiders, Rey saw, were the same species as the Caretakers, but wearing woolen caps and warm, colorful coats designed for seafaring.

She'd interrupted a party.

The partygoers turned to behold Rey poised like a war goddess, teeth bared and weapon raised. They greeted her with joyous cries, swinging lengths of kelp studded with phosphorescent bladders above their heads. Rey halfheartedly waved the lightsaber in the air and they cheered even more loudly.

Her sides hurt and her adrenaline had leaked away, leaving her feeling shaky and faintly sick.

On the fringe of the crowd, she spotted Chewbacca with a mug of something, one hairy fist resting on R2-D2's dome. The Wookiee called out a cheerful greeting, and the astromech beeped.

"Seriously?" Rey asked.

She was staring out over the moonlit ocean, still furious, when Luke finally made his way down the slope into the village. He stood next to her, but she refused to look at him.

"Raid and plunder?" she asked when she couldn't stand it any longer.

"In a way."

"Was this a joke?"

At least he had the good grace to sound sheepish. "I'm sorry, I didn't think you'd—you just ran so fast."

The musicians had begun a lilting song that struck her as beautiful but sad. It made her think of lonely voyages across vast and uncertain seas.

Luke held his hand out to her. He was inviting her to dance, she realized. She looked away, flustered and embarrassed.

"I've never danced before," she admitted.

Luke smiled. "You've never single-handedly fought a Bonthian raiding party, either."

"Yeah, but this is *scary*."

She took his hand, roughened by work and weather, and looked down to see how to position her feet correctly, trying to copy his stance. He gave her an encouraging smile and they began to dance, their steps forming overlapping squares across the stone and gravel, in time with the drums.

Luke, she supposed, was a good dancer. She followed his lead, their hands clasped, as the moon shone down and the party turned around them.

"I thought they were in danger," Rey said. "I was just trying to do something."

"And that's what the Resistance needs—not an old failed husk of a religion. Do you understand now?"

She let go of his hand.

"I understand that across the galaxy our real friends are really dying. That legend of Luke Skywalker that you hate so much? I believed in it. I was wrong."

And she left him alone on the edge of the party, backlit by the moonlit sea.

CHAPTER 18

Everyone in the Resistance understood that waiting patiently wasn't one of Poe Dameron's strengths.

Behind the control yoke of an X-wing, there were hostiles, friendlies, and noncombatants, and a flyby or two would sort out which was which. He knew how much damage he could deal out, how much he could take, and made decisions accordingly.

And if things went wrong, well, BB-8 could usually fix it.

Suddenly none of that was true. Most of the Resistance's starfighters, including *Black One*, were space dust—and flying one of the few remaining fighters into the teeth of thirty Star Destroyers would be suicide, even for a pilot as skilled as Poe.

Even BB-8 was gone—after a couple of hours of baffled searching, Poe realized the astromech had joined Rose and Finn on their hastily conceived mission.

Poe didn't blame the droid. It's what he'd wanted to do himself.

As for Holdo, Poe had avoided the heavy cruiser's temporary bridge since his confrontation with her—he wouldn't do anyone any good by losing his temper and getting himself confined to quarters. So he circled among the mess, the medical suites, and the ready room, checking in on his surviving pilots and trying to keep their spirits up.

But it wasn't working, and he knew it as well as they did. The heavy cruiser's lower levels were guarded now, amid reports of more demoralized personnel trying to reach the escape pods.

Poe understood their desperation. The two surviving Resistance ships remained just out of range of the First Order's weapons, but there was nowhere for them to run. The only thing changing was the level of their fuel reserves, creeping ever closer to zero. How long would it be until they ran dry? Six hours? Seven if they were lucky? And under the circumstances, would an extra hour really matter?

He checked his comlink on the vanishingly small chance that he might somehow have missed a message from Finn and Rose in the four or five minutes since he'd last checked.

Nothing.

Poe tried to imagine that was because they had just reached the tracking-control room of the flagship pursuing them, and were about to free the Resistance from its own slow-motion destruction—and not, say, dead or shackled in a First Order interrogation room somewhere.

As he wandered the *Raddus,* Poe's mind kept gnawing at the problem of Holdo. If the *Raddus*'s new commander was a friendly, she was the kind you didn't particularly want as a wingmate.

But what if she was something worse? What if she was actually another hostile?

Poe found that hard to believe—but then Holdo's intentions were beside the point. Her actions—or her lack of action—had left the Resistance rudderless and in despair, at a time when it had never needed hope more desperately.

Poe realized his wanderings had returned him to the officers' level, and Leia's stateroom. He gathered himself and thumbed the door controls, then stepped into the makeshift medcenter. Two med droids glanced briefly up from their stations by the bed next to C-3PO, then returned to their work.

Poe nodded at C-3PO and leaned over the Resistance leader. She was pale and motionless, eyes closed.

Poe was struck, and not for the first time, by just how small Leia was—a petite, delicate-looking woman, seemingly at risk of being swallowed up by the bedding and the gurney around her. It was an impression that many people had on meeting her—and that vanished the moment she engaged with them. Her determination, her ferocity, her sheer force of will belied her size and made visitors remember her as far bigger than she was.

"How is she, Threepio?" Poe asked, wanting to smooth a stray lock of hair from her forehead but not daring anything so familiar.

"Her signs are steady, Captain Dameron," the protocol droid reported. "Most of the trauma she experienced was due to the pressure wave from the blast. Though I am not programmed as a medical droid, Captain, I am of course more than able to interpret their findings for personnel who lack such expertise. Therefore . . ."

Poe's mind drifted as C-3PO rattled on about ebullism, hypoxia, and exposure to solar radiation. He stared down at Leia, trying to will her to return to consciousness, to come back to the people who so desperately needed her.

"It seems you didn't hear me, Captain Dameron," C-3PO was saying, a bit peevishly.

"Sorry, Threepio, what was that last part?"

"To reiterate, Captain—it's not my place to say, but might you put a little more faith in Vice Admiral Holdo? The princess certainly did."

"I'll take it under advisement, Threepio," Poe said.

It was true that Leia Organa's trust wasn't given easily, and her friendship was a far rarer gift than that. But everyone made mistakes—even the general.

And every starfighter pilot knew that a single mistake, if made at the wrong moment, would kill you.

CHAPTER 19

Rose wouldn't quit.

The moment she spotted the guard's gray-and-blue Canto Bight Police Department livery through the gloom of the cell block, she was at the bars yelling that she and Finn needed be released this instant, or at the very least granted access to an attorney.

"This is a big mistake!" she insisted, as the guard strolled past, aiming his glow rod at the sprawled prisoners trying to sleep in neighboring cells. "We didn't do anything!"

"You crashed your shuttle on a public beach," the guard said, not even looking at her.

"Oh, I'm sorry—what, did we break the sand? You can't break sand!"

The guard, unimpressed, continued his rounds.

"Hey, don't—augggh," Rose muttered as the guard turned the corner and disappeared.

She sagged against the bars. With the guard gone, Finn wedged himself in the corner of the cell and began pushing and pulling at the lock mechanism, trying to remember long-ago infiltration techniques from his First Order training.

Rose paced in tight circles, sizing up their surroundings yet again. As far as she could tell, the prisoners with whom they shared their cell were asleep, incapacitated, or possibly dead. There was no help there—and from what she could see, Finn's lock picking was an exercise in stubbornness, not expertise.

"So after that totally works, what's our plan?" she asked.

Finn strained at the lock. Something beeped. Rose looked over in surprise and wild hope, only to see an additional panel slide into place, covering the lock mechanism.

Finn leaned against the wall and blew his breath out in frustration.

"This thing that failed was our plan," he said. "Without a thief to break us into that Destroyer, it's shot. Our fleet's out of time. We're done. Which means Rey's done."

Rey Rey Rey, as always. Rose took a step toward Finn, determined to actually throttle him this time. What would they do if she did? Send her to jail?

"Why did I trust you?" she demanded.

"Baby face," Finn reminded her.

"You're a selfish traitor."

Finn looked up. "'Cause I want to save my friend? Yeah, you'd do the same."

"I would not," Rose insisted.

"No? If you'd had the chance, you wouldn't have saved your sister?"

That was too much. Rose turned, took two steps, and shoved him. Her fury shocked him into silence. He looked so startled—and hurt—that Rose found her anger ebbing, replaced by a sick sense of weariness. It was over. They were going to sit in this cell while the Resistance died, and whatever happened to them after that wouldn't particularly matter.

"Um, I can do it," someone said.

"What?" asked Rose, more annoyed than curious.

One of their fellow prisoners had sat up on the bench and was peering blearily at them. He was scruffy and tattered, from his rumpled stack of hair and unshaven face to his battered jacket and dirty black pants.

The man conducted a lazy inventory of his possessions—a pair of worn boots with the laces tied together and a scrofulous-looking cap—and began scratching himself, his fingers digging into places better attended to in private.

"Sorry," the man drawled. "Couldn't help but overhear all the boring stuff you were saying really loudly while I was trying to sleep. Codebreaker? Thief? I can do it."

He gave them a lazy double thumbs-up. "Yo."

"Yeah, we're not talking about picking pockets," Finn said.

A feral grin split the man's face. "Awww, yeah. Don't let the wrapper fool you, friend. Me and the First Order codeage go way back. If the price is right, I can break you into Old Man Snoke's boudoir."

"Yeah, no thanks," Finn said, at the same time that Rose assured the pile of vaguely animate rags that they were good.

The thief—if that was indeed what he was—just shrugged.

"Besides, if you're such a good thief, what are you doing in here?" Finn asked.

The thief reached down and retrieved his hat, pawing it onto his head and making a vague attempt at straightening it. A cheap metal plate on the front was emblazoned with letters that spelled out DON'T JOIN.

"Brother, this is the one place in town I can get some sleep without worrying about the cops," he said, working his feet into his boots.

Finished, DJ—that's how Rose had decided to think of him—waddled over to the cell door with the stiff gait of someone hungover or still actively addled. He looked blearily at the lock while Finn watched, amused and curious.

"Hatukga," DJ cursed. He reached over, adjusted something, adjusted something else, and slapped the lock. The door slid open noiselessly and he strolled out into the cell block, leaving Rose and Finn staring gape-mouthed at the open bars.

An alarm began to blare. Rose and Finn exchanged a stunned look, squeezed through the door, and began to run.

———

Sometimes the worst thing about being a droid was also the best thing: Nobody noticed you.

After being unceremoniously heaved out of the casino, BB-8 had watched, unmolested but powerless to intercede, as a police speeder carted off Rose and Finn. A map of Canto Bight suggested a logical destination: the local jail. So BB-8 headed that way, dodging ground-coaches and customized speeders, troubled only mildly by the coins rattling around in his innards.

By the time the droid arrived in the vicinity of the jail, Rose and Finn had been processed and an authorization issued to hold them pending identification and sentencing. Activating a slicing subroutine that had proven useful getting Poe out of more than a few scrapes, BB-8 delved into Canto Bight court records. After a moment's search, he whistled mournfully: By the time Rose and Finn were eligible for bail under normal procedures, the chances of saving the Resistance fleet would have dropped from scant to non-existent.

Well, so much for doing things by the manual.

While rolling across the speeder lot in front of the jail, BB-8 accessed his primary photoreceptor's image memory, reviewing the denomination of the Cantocoins he had accumulated while masquerading as a slot machine. Disappointingly, the amount—while able to buy several months' worth of high-quality oil baths—was likely insufficient to persuade a legal official to make the charges disappear from the docket.

That was disappointing, but not unexpected. Apparently a more direct approach would be needed—one that BB-8 concluded merited a pause for electronic consideration.

BB-8's computational suite contained tens of thousands of subroutines, from ones accessed nearly every day (facial recognition and threat assessment of organics) to others that had never been initiated (it wasn't impossible that mimicking the mating calls of Zohakka XVII's sea life might prove useful at some point).

None of BB-8's subroutines was an optimal match for the most likely scenarios that would unfold once he entered the jail—an anti-personnel tactical suite with accompanying weapons attachments would have been ideal, but the astromech didn't have one of those.

Still, BB-8 had learned a few things from Poe over the years.

Humans and other organics were dangerously error-prone in so many ways: They somehow failed to see or hear important stimuli, insisted on ignoring data they didn't like, and forgot things they desperately needed to remember. Any self-respecting droid would have addressed such failings with a quick diagnostics session and memory defragmentation.

Yet organics made up for this—at least a little bit—with a talent for tackling a problem with simultaneous bits and pieces of multiple subroutines at once, what they called improvisation.

BB-8 liked to think he had developed a knack for that.

At least entering the jail proved trivial—BB-8 consulted a map, headed for the employee entrance, and simply rolled past several officers sharing questionable strategies for betting on fathier races while exchanging rumors about the Nojonz Gang.

As always, nobody noticed a droid.

The time for improvisation came once inside the cell block—which did require BB-8 to wait for a guard beginning his shift to badge in and enter, completely ignoring the astromech rolling inside beside him. Once the new arrival finished chatting and joined a sabacc game with the other two guards on duty, BB-8 swung into action. His decontamination/foreign-body-purge subroutine allowed him to fire coins like slugthrower shells, forcing humans into a defensive crouch; his electroprod could be dialed up to an intensity level that would incapacitate them; and his liquid-cable launchers were adequate for binding them so they were incapable of pursuit.

BB-8 had just finished this work and was feeling a bit pleased with himself when the jail's alarms began to blare. A moment later an ill-dressed human who needed a bath rounded the corner and almost tripped over the astromech.

BB-8's threat-assessment matrix proved unable to categorize the new arrival—insufficient data. But judging from his appearance, he wasn't a guard.

"You do that?" the human asked, taking in the unconscious guards with what BB-8's auditory sensors identified as a mix of admiration and amusement.

Before the droid could answer, another guard rushed into the cell block, blaster drawn. BB-8 fired a fusillade of coins at the man, forcing him to raise one arm to shield his face. While he was distracted, the human brought his fists down on the guard's head, leaving him motionless on the floor.

As the grungy man began scooping up coins, he looked over at BB-8 and grinned. "So what's your story, roundy?"

CHAPTER 20

Rose ran through the cell block after Finn, grateful that at least the wailing alarms were covering the sound of their footsteps. On either side of them, grimy humans and aliens pressed up against the bars of their cells, hollering to be let out, shouting encouragement, or simply reveling in a break in the monotony of captivity.

Over the din, Rose heard shouts behind her. Finn skidded to a stop and she almost plowed into his broad back. Before she could protest, she spotted glow rods bobbing in the gloom ahead of them.

They were trapped.

Rose looked around frantically—and spotted a grating in the floor. A foul smell wafted up from it.

"Finn! Help me!"

Finn heaved, teeth gritted. The metal groaned and the grate came free. Rose scrambled down a rickety-looking ladder into the darkness, Finn squeezing himself into the shaft above her.

"Put the grate back!" she called up to him.

"I can't—not all the way," Finn said, his voice strained by the effort. "It's too heavy."

"Then forget it," Rose said, and the ladder shook as he hurried down after her.

They found themselves in a stone sewer, too low for Finn to stand without stooping slightly. Fortunately, there was only a trickle of fetid water flowing through the middle of the space.

"Which way?" Rose asked, looking left and right and trying not to gag. "Ugh, it smells even worse this way. Let's go that way."

Before she got more than a step, Finn grabbed her arm.

"It slopes down that way," he pointed out.

"So?"

"So what if it comes out in the sea?"

"Then it comes out in the sea."

"What if it comes out in the *middle* of the sea? How long can you hold your breath?"

"We'll need to hold our breath going that way, too," Rose objected. "Or we'll suffocate."

"That way at least there's air."

"*Bad* air."

They glared at each other. Then a boot heel hit the grate above them.

"We go *this* way," Finn said, pointing to the right.

"We go *this* way," Rose said at the same time, pointing to the left.

"What do you want to do, a round of wonga winga?" Finn asked.

It was the stupidest idea Rose had ever heard. And she couldn't think of anything better. She threw up her hands, scowling, as Finn held up a finger, pointing left.

"Wonga winga cingee wooze, which of these do I choose?" they recited together, Finn's finger oscillating back and forth, like a pendulum. "Stars above and stars below, show me now which way to go."

It pointed right, toward the bad air. Finn grinned. Rose scowled and hurried after him, into the foul air.

"Who knew they taught wonga winga in the Stormtrooper Corps?" Rose muttered.

Finn looked back over his shoulder, an annoyingly smug smile on his face. "Me. They also taught us you always win if you start with the choice you *don't* want."

"Cheater," Rose grumbled. But she couldn't help smiling back, just a little.

The tunnel ran on for about a kilometer, dimly lit by a strip of maintenance lighting. The smell grew steadily worse, until Rose's eyes stung and she thought she would gag. Just as Rose was beginning to worry that the tunnel would never end, they encountered another ladder—one that emerged from a dark mound whose origins Rose could figure out all too readily.

"After you," she said, turning away in disgust. It occurred to her that even Paige—who'd loved all animals from tookas to slime molds—would have opted to skip this particular experience.

Finn shrugged and scrambled up the ladder, paying considerably less attention to where he put his feet than Rose would have. She followed him up the ladder more carefully, grimacing, and emerged next to him in a dark, dimly lit space.

"That smelled great," Finn said, scraping his boot against the top rung of the ladder. He looked around, puzzled. "What is this?"

They were in a long, pillared hall of brick and stone, with wooden gates on either side of them and a floor littered with straw. Rose wrinkled her nose—there was a strong smell up here, too.

A massive, milky-white head appeared over the wooden gate next to them, regarding them curiously. It had wide, winglike ears, deep, worried-looking eyes, and a short snout.

Startled, Finn slipped and fell, winding up on the stable floor. He moaned, but Rose ignored him. The animal was a fathier.

More heads appeared above the gates. Some of the fathiers' hides were crisscrossed with pale scars.

Moving slowly so as not to startle it, she peeked over the first fathier's gate, the animal snuffling at her and murmuring something. The beast itself didn't smell bad—its odor reminded Rose of grass and sweat, but faintly spicy somehow. Its stall was barely larger than it was—it didn't have enough room to lie down or turn around.

In the middle of all this wealth, too.

Startled, a small boy sat up behind the fathier, scooting back to where his rough cot met the wall. He stared at her, frightened, and fumbled for a red button on the wall.

"No no no!" Finn yelped.

"We're with the Resistance!" Rose said at the same time.

The stableboy looked at her doubtfully from beneath a frayed cap. Rose fumbled with her ring—the one Fossil had given her in memory of her sister. She activated the hidden catch on its side, revealing the insignia of the old Rebel Alliance.

The fathier nickered plaintively. Rose held her breath as the boy studied the ring. Then a smile crept across his face.

When the police burst into the stable, blasters drawn, two things happened almost at once. First a massive door slid aside, opposite the row of fathier stalls. Then every gate on the stalls snapped open and the hapless officers were left spinning in the dust and straw as twenty fathiers leapt free of the confines of their pens, jostling to be first through the door leading to the empty racetrack beyond.

As the officers picked themselves up and stared after the departing fathiers, the stableboy grinned and crept away from the control panel he'd activated, looking down happily at the ring with the Alliance crest where it bobbled on his finger.

Rose clung to the lead fathier—the herd's matriarch, the boy had explained in halting Basic—as her first steps exploded into a full gallop. In her ear, Finn let out an astonished yelp as the world began pitching violently up and down around them.

Rose knew a grin was plastered across her face. She'd been nervous when the stableboy had hastily buckled a saddle onto the matriarch's back and indicated—with a wide grin—that they should climb aboard. But Finn had been little short of terrified.

Despite their nerves, the matriarch had accepted both Rose's presence and the unaccustomed additional weight of Finn. Her sides quivered between Rose's knees and her ears twitched, and somehow Rose knew: She wanted to *run*.

Around them, the racetrack was empty but lit up as if it were broad daylight instead of the middle of the night. Rose wanted to rear up in the saddle so her legs could better keep her in place atop the hurtling fathier, but she couldn't with Finn plastered to her back, hands locked around her waist. There was nothing to do except hold on to the animal's neck as best she could.

Rose could feel the matriarch's enormous lungs working beneath her hide, and the muscles of her neck and legs working in synchronization. It was like being atop a living machine—one built with exquisite precision to maximize speed.

She was terrified and exhilarated—and aching for Paige to have been able to see this.

This isn't a daydream or a story we're making up in the ball turret so we can forget about the war for a moment. Pae-Pae, this is real—*I'm riding a fathier!*

The fathier's head slammed up and down as she ran, her ears pushed back behind her by the wind. Rose could feel the blood pumping beneath her arms where they were pressed against the beast's graceful neck.

"Stop enjoying this!" Finn yelled in her ear.

Police speeders rose into view above the track and Rose could see their weapons rotate, trying to get a fix on the matriarch and the herd sprinting behind her. But then the fathier matriarch snorted and lowered her head, as if she had a plan.

"Ohhh—hang on!" Rose yelled as she realized what that plan was.

She ducked, pressing her head against the fathier's neck as the matriarch crossed the infield, churning up grass, and smashed through the window behind one of the casino's bars. Glasses and chairs flew, and Rose could hear people screaming. Finn's face was between her shoulder blades.

Rose looked up and saw the blur of the casino floor around them. Gamblers were diving over tables and piling up in panicked heaps, yelling in terror. Server droids stood stock-still, pivoting their trays rapidly this way and that to avoid the herd. Bouncers were screaming and trying to stay upright amid the tide of fleeing guests. Elderly women in glittering gowns managed to leap atop pazaak tables while smartly uniformed croupiers sought shelter below them. Chance cubes and cards and coins and purses and monocles and drinks and utensils and coasters and canapés wheeled in midair.

Oh, it was glorious. Every vacationing arms dealer doing an involuntary cartwheel made Rose want to cheer.

The fathiers stormed into the lobby. A valet stood, staring and paralyzed, in front of the matriarch. She shouldered him into a pond filled with ornamental fish—*carnivorous* ornamental fish, to judge from the sudden frenzy in the water. The automatic doors ahead of them obediently opened and the matriarch leapt into the air, mashing the outline of her hooves into the hood of a fancy speeder, then barreling up the boulevard.

Rose felt as if she were flying. She was pouring sweat, breathing hard with the effort of keeping herself upright in the saddle. Her legs ached and she didn't care.

Behind them, the herd pursued the matriarch, drawn out like a string in her wake. She somehow picked up the pace, her speed creating a tunnel of air and noise around Rose. Tables and chairs flew as the herd obliterated an outdoor café, separating bleary-eyed nightshift workers from their cups of caf. Behind her, Rose could hear the jangle of police sirens, the wails of terrified onlookers, the crash of windows shattering, and the hollow clomp of fathier hooves denting speeders.

Rose was laughing out loud now. How many times had she and Paige imagined themselves the heroes of adventures in which they rescued fathiers from sleazy owners, guiding them to victory and watching their abusers laid low? But the Tico sisters had never dreamed of this much delightful destruction.

Rose patted the matriarch, who quirked an ear as one of Old City's plazas rocketed by around them.

She loves wrecking this awful place as much as I do!

The matriarch lunged sideways, ducking into an alley, then leapt up onto a low rooftop. Rose yelped as the fathier hurtled the gaps between the buildings, scanning for a route across the city. Ahead of them, a rooftop skylight glowed in the night.

"No no no—" Rose yowled as the matriarch turned toward the

light. Then she was pressing her head into the warm hide as the sky-light exploded around the fathier, plunging downward with her legs braced for impact.

They landed, hard enough to knock the air out of Rose's lungs. Finn was screaming in her ear and she wanted to tell him to cut it out but couldn't. It was sweltering and the air was full of steam—they were in a sauna, she realized.

"Oh, sands," exclaimed a long-armed masseur.

A diminutive pink alien clutched at his towel, single eye staring, as the matriarch sprang back into motion. A charcoal-colored, slablike alien yelped from atop a masseuse's table as the herd turned the room to kindling before crashing back into the street in an explosion of flying glass.

"Yeahhhh!" Rose screamed, her joyous defiance turning into a moan of fear as police speeders swooped down in their path, spotlights turned on them. The matriarch rocketed into a narrow alley. Strings of decorative lights stretched and snapped, and Rose cringed at the stone walls blurring by on either side of her, convinced that her knees would be smashed at any second.

Ahead of them, the alley terminated in a dead end.

Rose could hear herself screaming—but she could also feel the matriarch's muscles coiling beneath her. Rose's stomach fluttered as she sprang into the air, the wall of Old City passing just below her belly, and landed in loose gravel and sand. The rest of the herd came down behind her, grunting and snorting, chasing the matriarch across the beach.

Moonlight glimmered on the surface of the sea.

She could see the pale shape of the shuttle, still sitting where Finn had plowed it into the beach. It wasn't far away—they might even make it.

Then it exploded, ripped apart by a fusillade of full-intensity laserfire from the police speeders.

"Aw, come on!" Finn yelled.

Blasterfire whined around them and blue rings struck the edges of the herd and one fathier tumbled end over end, stunned and helpless. The matriarch snorted and froth flew from her muzzle.

Ahead of her, the beach rose, climbing a bluff. The matriarch took it at a sprint, her hooves scrambling for purchase in the loose sand, and raced along a rocky ledge above the water.

Police vehicles were alongside them now, firing into the herd. Fathiers tumbled off the ledge, falling toward the beach.

"This is a shooting gallery!" Finn screamed. "Get us out!"

Rose yanked on the matriarch's neck, trying to alert her to the danger, but she knew there was only one way forward and sped up a crumbling path that struck Rose as terrifyingly narrow, her hooves slinging gouts of sand in her wake.

They emerged in a broad meadow, a green oasis in the middle of the Cantonican desert. The tall grass crackled and shooshed as the matriarch pounded through it, up to her flanks in greenery.

Rose leaned hard to the right, urging the matriarch that way. She raised her head and called to the rest of the herd before obeying, cutting across the field as Rose had asked. The rest of the herd remained on its earlier course.

"Is it working?" Finn yelled.

Rose watched the spotlights swing from the other fathiers to the matriarch.

"They're letting the herd go!" she yelled. "Now if we can just—"

"*Cliff!*" Finn shouted.

The matriarch skidded to a halt, digging up skeins of grass and dirt. Rose and Finn were flung over her head, tumbling through the sweet-smelling grass. Rose wound up on her belly, just short of the cliff's edge. She peeked over it, legs shaking, and saw it dropped at least a hundred meters to the water below.

"Can you swim?" Finn asked.

"Not when I'm dead," she replied. "We're trapped."

The matriarch stood in the grass, sides heaving. Behind her, the police speeders were hurtling toward them, spotlights searching the meadow.

"Well, it was worth it to tear up that town," Finn said, waiting for the speeders with his shoulders slumped. "Make 'em hurt."

Rose shot a surprised look his way. Was this the same Finn who'd seemed happy to hang around the hazard-toss tables and cabarets?

The matriarch was still breathing hard. Rose's fingers worked at the straps of her saddle, loosening it and then letting it slide off into the grass.

"Thank you," she told the animal quietly, then reached into her jumpsuit to touch her medallion.

They're even more beautiful than you said they were, Pae-Pae.

The matriarch looked at her, either reluctant to leave them or too tired to go. Rose slapped her flank and she trotted away, breaking into a canter that took her across the meadow, back toward the other members of her herd. Above, the police spotlights followed the fathier briefly, then snapped back to Rose and Finn.

Rose watched the matriarch go and smiled.

"*Now* it's worth it," she said, and waited for the police speeders to descend and take them back to jail.

A different sound reached her ears—the whining hum of well-tuned ion engines.

Rose turned and her mouth opened in shock as a luxury star yacht rose from the cleft in the bluffs, hovering in front of them.

A hatch opened on the side of the yacht and an orange-and-white astromech whistled at them.

"Beebee-Ate, are you flying that thing?" Finn yelled.

The answering beeps were accusatory.

"No, we were coming back for you!" Finn said. "Come on, pick us up!"

Then, behind BB-8, DJ stepped into view.

"Oh, you need a lift?" he asked. "Say the magic words."

Finn considered. "Pretty please?"

But Rose knew all too well what DJ was waiting to hear.

"You're hired," she said grimly.

PART V

CHAPTER 21

Rey walked alone across the meadow atop the island, beneath a full moon like a lantern. Her eyes wandered to the outcropping of the Jedi temple, a pale spike against the night, atop the winding thread of the stone stairs.

She supposed it was the last time she'd ever see it. The last time she'd walk through this grassy saddle. The last time she'd admire the craftsmanship of the cluster of ancient huts.

It made her a little sad, but she realized what made her sad was the memory of what she'd hoped to find on the island, but hadn't.

Such as a teacher—or a reason to hope.

Both had eluded her, and now she would have to explain that to General Organa.

Leia had lost so much, and Rey would add to her burdens. By telling her . . . what, exactly? That her brother had lost himself in bitterness and self-reproach? That after helping the Force find the balance it had sought, he had closed his senses to it, stubbornly rejecting its call? That he was willing to die alone on a speck of land in a nameless ocean on a forgotten planet while the galaxy burned around him?

Well, *she* wasn't willing to do that. She would do the only thing she could do: tell Leia the truth.

And then she would fight. Even if she could offer the galaxy only another day of hope—or a minute or a second—she would fight.

Rey could see the pale saucer of the *Falcon* far below her now. She dug in her bag for her comlink.

"Chewie, get her ready for launch," she said. "We're leaving."

Even as she broke the connection, she felt a familiar presence, like a change in the weather behind her. Gooseflesh broke out on her arms.

"I'd rather not do this now," she said, without turning.

"Yeah, me too," said Kylo.

Steeling herself, she turned, determined not to let her adversary into her head. This time, she would make him answer for what he'd done.

"Why did you hate your father?" she demanded, then stopped. "Oh!"

Kylo was stripped to the waist in his chambers. The angry scar she'd given him in their duel snaked down his face and neck and across his collarbone.

Her eyebrows rose, but Kylo was unruffled by the sight of her— and seemingly undisturbed by her question.

"Because he was a weak-minded fool," he said.

Rey forced herself to look into his eyes—those angry, haunted, needy eyes.

"I don't believe you," she said. "You're going to—do you have a cowl or something you can put on?"

Kylo ignored that, and Rey made herself focus.

"Why did you hate your father? Give me an honest answer."

"I will when you ask an honest question," Kylo said, and she wanted to scream at him. He wasn't her teacher—and anyway that position was no longer open.

"Why did you hate Han Solo?" she asked.

"No," Kylo said dismissively, almost bored.

But Rey wouldn't let him escape so easily.

"You had a father who loved you. He gave a damn about you."

"I didn't hate him."

"Then why?" Rey demanded.

"Why what? Why *what*? *Say it!*"

"Why did you kill him? I don't understand!"

"No?" Kylo's curiosity was genuine—and infuriating. "Your parents threw you away like garbage."

"They didn't," Rey said, and she hated the fact that even to her own ears she sounded like she was pleading. The strange contact between their minds had given her insight into his powers, and had helped unleash her own. It had also let him pillage her memories and feelings.

But there was no way the Force could have told him that, shown him that.

That was right, wasn't it?

"They did," Kylo said. "But still you can't stop needing them. It's your greatest weakness. You look for them everywhere—in Han Solo, now in Skywalker."

His gaze was hungry—and knowing.

"Did he tell you what happened that night?" Kylo asked.

"Yes," Rey said, knowing Kylo could see that wasn't true.

"No," he said.

Ben Solo—no longer a boy but not yet a man—looks up in surprise and alarm. His uncle Luke has come into his chambers, at night, and now stands over him. The Jedi Master's face is twisted in a snarl—and lit by the green blade of his lightsaber. The Force is aboil with danger. For a moment regret shadows Luke's face, but Ben can see his uncle has gone too far to turn back. He will not falter or hesitate; rather, he will bring his lightsaber down and cleave his nephew in two while he sleeps.

Desperate, Ben's hand reaches out, not toward Luke but beyond him, to the lightsaber he has constructed. Willing it into his hand, its blue blade blocks the killing blow. The locked blades buzz and spark. But Ben knows this is only a brief reprieve—he can't resist his master's far greater powers for long. Trapped, he reaches up toward the ceiling with his free hand, begging the stones to heed his plea and come crashing down on Luke's head. To save him.

"He had sensed my power, as he senses yours," Kylo said. "And he feared it."

"Liar," Rey said, but there was no conviction behind it. She could feel that what Kylo had told her was true—or at least he wasn't trying to mislead her. And hadn't she sensed Luke's guilt and self-reproach? What if he had gone into exile not because of what the apprentice had done to the teacher, but because of what the teacher had done to the apprentice?

"Let the past die," Kylo said. "Kill it if you have to. That's the only way to become what you are meant to be."

And then he was gone, leaving her alone in the night. Alone, but knowing that she had one final thing to do. Only then would she leave Master Skywalker's refuge forever.

Jaw set, Rey strode off across the rocky highlands, in the opposite direction from the *Falcon*.

Luke stood outside the temple, bathed in moonlight. Below him, the waves chewed ceaselessly at the margins of the island, continuing the slow, patient work of dissolving it into the sea from which it had sprung. Above him, the stars were cold lights, following their fixed and eternal courses.

Luke sat, his legs protesting as he forced them into position. He put his hands on the rocky ledge, where so many Jedi had meditated over the eons, and closed his eyes.

Breathe. Just breathe.

The wind filled his ears—the island's constant companion. It was a whisper now, the low conversation of autumn breezes instead of the whine of winter or the howl of a summer storm. He could hear the night birds calling as they rode high above him, and the metronome calls of insects from the grasses.

Behind him, in the ancient temple, the still surface of the water in the ancient font began to ripple and dance.

Luke could hear more now—far more. He heard the static of pebbles and sand being washed back and forth beneath the waves. He listened to the bump of the worms pushing blindly through the dirt, building their tunnels and revitalizing the soil. He heard the muttering of the season's last porglets as they turned inside their eggs, beneath the heartbeats of their mothers.

He heard the world flooding back into his senses.

Aboard the *Raddus,* an MD-15 medical droid raised its blank white head. Its patient's heartbeat had suddenly surged, accompanied by spikes of brain activity. The droid focused its photoreceptors on the subject, motionless on the gurney. Her eyes moved beneath their lids.

"Luke," whispered Leia.

The sounds grew to a crescendo, a thunderclap that was followed by a bewildering, blinding rush of images.

Seek your center. Find balance.

Luke's body felt like it was on fire. He knew it wasn't. He accepted the feeling, denying it power over him, and then let it ebb. In its place came a familiar sense of warmth, of belonging, of finding himself part of an endless lattice of connections that held him and everything else, each fixed in its proper place.

A Force.

That aspect of the Force—the Jedi had called it the living Force—was ceaseless and ever-renewing. But the Jedi had spoken of another aspect—the Cosmic Force. It had an awareness, and a purpose, and a will. A will that had been silent, dormant after the demise of the Sith, only to wake once again during Luke's exile. A will that Luke finally allowed himself to acknowledge once again.

More confident now, Luke stretched out with his feelings, his awareness slipping lightly through the island's tumult of life. He found Rey instantly—she was like a beacon in the Force, burning so brightly that everything around her seemed attuned to her.

And Luke sensed another familiar presence. This one was far away—achingly far. But nothing so meaningless as distance could ever dim that presence in his awareness.

Luke opened his eyes.

"Leia," he said.

Rey stood on a long, flat outcropping of stone that emerged from the grassy slopes of the island to end in a low cliff above the sea. In the center of the stone was a gaping hole in the rock, surrounded by reddish moss bleached gray by the moonlight.

She carefully approached the place she'd seen in her vision on the meditation ledge, the one that had been trying to show her something. Luke had warned her that accepting its offer would be yielding to the dark side, but perhaps that was because he feared the truths it might reveal.

She stared into the inky darkness of the hole. Bright as the moon was, it revealed nothing about what was below. The hole burbled and hissed, as if it were speaking to her.

Rey stopped at the edge, stooping to examine the moss, and slipped. Slipped, or was dragged inside. She didn't know if she cried out, or if it made a sound.

She fell into water, the cold like a knife in her lungs. She struggled, surfaced, and gasped, eyes stinging from the salt, then hauled herself out onto the slick, flat stone.

She was in a cave, she saw now—a long, narrow space that the sea had carved away beneath the lip of the cliff, creating a hidden place beneath the island, its existence revealed only by a blowhole where a vertical shaft had intersected the surface. The hole spat gouts of water at high tide but seemed to breathe when the tide was low, as it was now.

Before her, the sea had ground and polished the walls of the cave until the stone was like a dark mirror, cracked but glossy. Rey could see her reflection in it—a reflection repeated a thousand times in the stone's labyrinthine facets, so they created a line of Reys retreating from her gaze.

Rey gazed into the mirror—and realized it was gazing back. The Force was quavering in response to the approach of something.

She could hear herself breathing—slowly and raggedly. Then her breathing quickened as she realized she was inside the stone, within the mirror world, with several Reys between her and the soaked, shivering girl standing on the ledge in the cave.

Then that Rey was gone and a hundred Reys stood between her and the slim figure on the ledge. She turned her head and all those Reys obediently did the same, each one's turn coming a moment after the one before it, until all were staring along with her deeper into the dark stone.

Rey knew she had to go deeper—that the world inside the stone only seemed to go on forever. It was leading somewhere, and if she only had the courage to follow, that secret place would show her what she had come to see—and what she was most afraid to know.

There were Reys deeper in the stone, part of the line yet ahead of her. She told herself to follow them, to become them, to ignore the voice in her head that kept babbling that she would be trapped forever, down here in the darkness at the secret heart of the island.

She followed the line of Reys, willing the surreal succession to end, until finally it did. Until at last there was one final Rey, breathing hard and staring at a large, round, clouded mirror of polished stone like the one that had called to the girl in the cave.

This last Rey stood in front of the stone, gazing into its depths.

"Let me see my parents," she begged. "Please."

She stretched out her hand and the clouded surface of the mirror seemed to ripple, its darkness melting away. She saw two dark figures beneath its surface. As her heartbeat hammered in her ears, the two became one. Her fingers touched the stone and met the fingertips of another.

It was the girl from the sea cave, staring back at her. It was herself. Rey lowered her hand and her reflection did the same.

Then she began to weep.

She'd spent so many nights in the deserts of Jakku, an orphan in the half-buried wreckage of a forgotten war. Marking each night with a new scratch in the metal, until she was surrounded by thousands of gouges. There had been too many to sensibly mark time, but that had long ago ceased to be the point. The rows upon rows of slashes had become something else, but she didn't know what. A testament to her insistence that this vigil had a purpose, maybe. Or perhaps a ritual to hold back the solitude that was always at work on her, eroding her hope and whispering that she would wind up like everything else abandoned on Jakku—a shell, empty and purposeless.

She had felt so alone, all those nights. But never as alone as she did staring at her own reflection, beneath the island in the cold and the dark.

When her tears finally ebbed, Rey lifted her head. She knew who she had to talk to about the cave, about what she had sought and what it had shown her—someone who would understand how solitude and loss could eat away at you until there was nothing left.

Luke was afraid Rey had gone—that his awakened sense of the Force had blinded him to the more mundane world around him, and he would discover the *Falcon* had departed, taking her away with it.

"Rey, you were right," he called as he crossed the meadow in the driving rain, lightning flashing overhead. "I'm coming with you. Rey?"

Luke had shut himself off for so long, and now the Force was roaring around him. Rey was right. She needed him. As did Leia, and the Resistance, and all those desperate for hope. His grief and guilt had left him unable to see that, unable to see anything but darkness and despair. In trying to shield the galaxy from his failure, he had walled himself off from everything—including the prospect of hope.

The Force had sent Rey, of that Luke was now certain. She had arrived bearing the message he had refused to hear. But she was not just the Force's vessel. To think of her that way was to diminish her.

She was also a young woman, powerful with the Force, who needed his help—and who had believed in him even when he gave her no reason to.

He reached the huts, and saw to his relief that Han Solo's freighter was still sitting at the bottom of the long, winding stair. And light was leaking out of the door and the narrow window of the hut Rey had claimed for her own.

Relieved, Luke quickened his steps, eager to make up for lost time.

The moment Rey reached her hut she had felt him near her, in the Force. The connection between them was so raw and powerful that it reminded her of touching a live wire in the wreckage of a starship. She had closed her eyes, opened them, and found Kylo Ren there— right next to her where she sat on the stone bench. As if she could actually reach out and touch his hand, his face, his hair.

At the sight of him she'd felt relief surge through her.

Kylo listened intently, his long face impassive, as she told him about being drawn into the cave and into the stone, and how the journey had led to nothing, no revelation except how alone she was.

"You're not alone," he insisted, and she believed him.

"Neither are you. It isn't too late."

Rey tentatively raised her hand toward his, expecting to see their hands go through each other and wondering if she would feel it in the Force somehow.

But their fingers actually touched. She grasped his hand, jolted by the contact, and saw that the same shock had gone through him.

Luke Skywalker walked into the hut—to find Rey and Kylo with their hands clasped, staring into each other's eyes.

"Stop!" he yelled, and flung out his hand. A burst of power hurled every stone of the hut outward from its center, scattering them around the bench where Rey and Kylo sat in astonishment.

Rey's hand closed on nothing and she stared at Luke as rain pelted them.

She got to her feet and stared at the Jedi Master.

"Is it true?" she demanded. "Did you try to murder him?"

"Leave this island," Luke said through gritted teeth. "Now."

Then he turned and walked away—just as he'd done the day she arrived, bearing the lightsaber that had called to her.

That day she had just watched, bewildered and hurt. But that had somehow become a long time ago.

"No," Rey said. "You answer me. You tell me the truth. Stop!"

Luke kept walking—and so Rey snatched up her staff, took three long strides, and swung it flat and hard, cracking him across the back of the head and knocking him to the ground.

He stared up into the rain, surprised, at the young woman standing over him with her teeth bared.

"Did you do it?" Rey asked. "Did you create Kylo Ren?"

Luke got to his feet and Rey saw immediately that nothing had changed—he was still going to walk away from her, retreating to brood in silence. Furious, she swung her staff at him again—but Luke reached out, the motion a blur, and a length of lightning rod flew off the roof of one of the huts. Before Rey could blink he had intercepted the strike of her staff, the impact sending a jolt up her forearms, and knocked her backward.

Rey sprang back at him, her staff and his improvised weapon spinning and colliding as the rain poured down. She pressed the attack. The staff had never felt more comfortable in her hands, so much like a part of her. Her confidence grew and she smiled wolfishly as she saw the surprise on his face.

But it was a fleeting thing. Quicker than she could follow, he parried her thrust and continued the motion, flipping the staff out of her hands to clatter on the stones, leaving her defenseless.

Rey reached out, feeling the Force alive and hungry around her, and found the weight of the lightsaber in her hands. She ignited it and Luke gave ground, looking up at her as she held the blade high, rain hissing and sparking off its length.

They looked at each other for a long moment, and then Rey turned the lightsaber off, leaving them in the rain.

"Tell me the truth," she said.

Luke Skywalker looks down at his nephew Ben Solo—no longer a boy but not yet a man. He has come into his chambers, at night, and now stands over him. The Jedi Master's eyes are closed. The Force is aboil with danger. Worry shadows Luke's face as he extends his hand, reaching out with the Force—reaching into the sleeping Ben's mind.

The boy remains still, his face untroubled. And Luke's eyes remain shut. But he can see: fire, and ruin, and the sightless eyes of the dead. And he can hear: screams, and the howl of lightsabers, and the roar of explosions.

Darkness—expanding from this slim, dark-haired boy to shroud everything—and the cacophony of terror that will accompany it. Luke draws his hand back, as if burned. The Force around Ben has always been shot through with veins of darkness, but what he's seen is beyond anything he'd feared to find.

Luke removes his lightsaber from his belt and ignites the blade, his eyes grave. But then he looks at Ben and the brief, almost unwilling thought is gone. He cannot bring his lightsaber down on his sister's son while he sleeps.

And immediately Luke knows it is too late—he has already failed his student. Because Ben's eyes are open—frightened but aware. The boy's powers with the Force are already immense, and still growing. And he is a Skywalker.

He knows what Luke thought.

He knows what Luke saw.

He knows what will be.

Desperate, Ben's hand reaches out, not toward Luke but beyond him, to the lightsaber he has constructed. Willing it into his hand, its blue blade a killing blow aimed at his Master. Luke's own blade meets Ben's and the locked lightsabers buzz and spark. Then Ben reaches up toward the ceiling with his free hand, compelling the stones to come crashing down on Luke's head.

Rey touched Luke's arm.

"You failed him by thinking his choice was made," she said, her voice equal parts gentle and insistent. "It wasn't. There's still conflict in him. If he were turned from the dark side, that could shift the tide. This could be how we win."

Luke turned his eyes to her. His gaze was bleak, and for the first time in Rey's memory he struck her as old—a broken man dragged back into a storm he'd thought he'd escaped. But his voice was strong, insistent.

"This is not going to go the way you think," he warned her.

"It is. Just now, when we touched hands, I saw his future. I saw it—as solid as I'm seeing you. If I go to him, Ben Solo will turn."

"Rey, don't do this," Luke said.

Rey's answer was to hold the unlit lightsaber out to him once again—a last invitation.

She knew immediately that he would not accept it.

"Then he's our last hope," she said.

She turned and simply walked away from him.

CHAPTER 22

When the time came to evacuate the last personnel off the fuel-starved *Ninka*, some glitch had kept Poe off the duty roster. The deck officer had shrugged helplessly, then let Poe look at the datapad for himself. His name was there, and next to it the word INELIGIBLE.

Fuming, Poe had been forced to remain aboard the *Raddus* as C'ai Threnalli fired up the transport and eased it out of the hangar—a lone ship would be sufficient to evacuate the *Ninka*'s skeleton crew. He watched on the control room's monitors as the transport left the little bunkerbuster, leaving her empty in space, then looked on in agony as the *Ninka* lost headway, her bow riding up, and was cut to pieces by turbolaser fire from the First Order fleet.

The Resistance fleet had never been large enough to justify that grand-sounding term, but now it no longer existed. Only the *Raddus* remained. A single First Order Star Destroyer would have been a tough fight for the Mon Calamari cruiser, and there were thirty of them back there.

Not to mention Snoke's monstrous flagship.

And whatever else the First Order had spent all those years building in secret, while the New Republic's senators argued about nonsense.

Poe left the control room as C'ai's transport returned, figuring the least he could do was welcome the Ninkas to the *Raddus.* But his words sounded unconvincing in his own ears as he greeted the techs and soldiers, and few of them even looked up. They simply trudged across the hangar with their shoulders slumped and faces drawn.

They looked beaten.

Poe stalked angrily through the corridors of the *Raddus,* passing nervous-looking soldiers and crewers. The heavy cruiser was dim, lit in many places only by emergency lighting. That was to conserve fuel—a measure he might have agreed with, if only he knew what that fuel was being conserved for.

He reached the temporary bridge and found Commander D'Acy waiting for him, outside the doors.

"The admiral's banned you from the bridge," she said. "Let's not have a scene."

So it hadn't been a glitch.

"Let's," Poe said, shouldering D'Acy aside and storming onto the bridge. D'Acy hurried to catch up with him, but he'd target-locked Holdo and arrowed straight for her. None of the officers in his path dared to stop him.

Holdo just regarded him evenly.

"Flyboy," she said.

"Cut it," Poe spat, nose-to-nose with her. "We're running on fumes and your crew knows it and you've told them *nothing.* You've got something up your sleeve, now's when you put it on the table. *Right now.* Tell me we're not just running away until we die—that we have a plan. That we have hope. *Please.*"

Poe wondered if she'd slap him, or order the soldiers to drag him off to the brig, or simply ignore him. But she surprised him with words that he knew by heart.

"When I served under Leia she'd say hope is like the sun," Holdo said. "If you only believe in it when you can see it—"

"—you'll never make it through the night," Poe finished.

They looked at each other in silence—united, if only for that moment, by their shared regard for the woman they'd lost.

"Captain, you're mistaking rashness for bravery," Holdo said. "Follow my orders."

Poe started to say something, then stopped—one of the officers' monitors had a readout of a transport on it, like the one C'ai had just piloted back from the *Ninka*. Poe looked over the man's shoulder, trying to process what he was seeing and not wanting to believe it. Then he whirled to face Holdo, incredulous.

"You're fueling up the transports—all of them," he said, his anger building. "We're abandoning ship! *That's* what you've got? The transports are unshielded—unarmed. If we abandon our cruiser we don't stand a chance!"

"Captain," Holdo said, but he plowed on ahead.

"This will destroy the Resistance! You're not just a coward—you're a *traitor!*"

Holdo turned away in disgust. "Get this man off my bridge," she ordered, and the soldiers stepped forward to obey her order.

Rose had to give DJ this much: He'd stolen a good ship.

The yacht's nameplate identified it as the *Libertine*, a name that had made Rose wrinkle her nose and wish there was time to make some alterations with a blaster. It was nearly sixty meters from the repulsorlift vanes jutting from its prow to the rakish fin at the stern, sheathed in hull plating that had been milled, polished, and buffed to a glossy white sheen. There was an elegant lounge with the latest model of pedestal holoprojector in the center of the flight deck; trim, tastefully appointed cabins belowdecks; and an honest-to-goodness staircase leading up to the cockpit.

Someone's gonna rattle every cage on Cantonica when they find out this ride is gone.

Before leaving Canto Bight's jail, BB-8 had retrieved Rose and Finn's personal effects from the impound lot. The droid had then accompanied DJ to the city's spaceport to obtain transportation.

BB-8 had given Rose the details of the theft in a flurry of droidspeak as the *Libertine* slipped away from the desert world, the transition from atmospheric flight to space travel barely noticeable thanks to the yacht's top-line acceleration dampeners and antishock fields. There'd been a note of admiration in BB-8's beeps and whistles as he gleefully recounted how DJ had slipped past the spaceport guards and needed less than two minutes with a computer spike and a key-bypass hub to get aboard the yacht and fire up its engines.

Rose made a mental note—make that *another* mental note—to take Poe aside, should they manage to actually rescue the Resistance fleet without dying in any of a dozen ways she decided it would be too depressing to catalog. Having already proven amenable to disobeying orders, assuming false identities, and committing simple assault, the pilot's astromech was now developing a taste for larceny.

Speaking of larceny, where was DJ anyway?

She extracted herself from the pilot's seat, grimacing at the ache in her legs and back, and peeked out of the cockpit to discover that their grungy rescuer was rifling the lounge's cabinets, humming while he appraised a necklace's delicate web of diamonds.

Rose scoffed. He'd already stolen the ship—why toss its interior like an Otomok wharf rat who had to stay one step ahead of the security droids?

DJ heard her snort and looked up, eyes bright and merry. He showed her the necklace and cocked his head to one side, offering her a floppy grin.

She just shook her head and returned to the cockpit, where Finn was staring out at the tumbling tunnel of hyperspace.

"Four parsecs to go," Finn said. "This thing cooks! He must do all right as a thief if he owns a ship like this."

Rose looked at him pityingly. "Say that one more time, slowly."

"I'm saying he must be a good thief if . . . oh right, he stole it."

A moment later, still embarrassed, Finn came up with an excuse to flee the cockpit. Rose had steeled herself not to laugh at him so he could escape with at least some shreds of his dignity; once he was gone she finally let herself smile at the ridiculousness of it all.

When they were kids on Hays Minor, Paige had become briefly obsessed with the curious fact that avians on a number of worlds would imprint on the first creature they saw once they emerged from their eggs—so you'd sometimes find, say, an eager convor chick following around a very confused tooka-cat.

Rose wondered if that was how Finn's mysterious Rey felt to have this bumbling goof follow her around, mystified by everything in the galaxy that wasn't her. If nothing else, Rose hoped she appreciated Finn's wide-eyed, seemingly unconditional devotion.

In the meantime, Rose didn't know what to think about the fact that a man trained to be a First Order stormtrooper could be innocent enough to assume a feral, unapologetic thief actually owned a fancy yacht. She supposed it made her feel simultaneously better and worse about the galaxy.

On the one hand, maybe there were painfully naïve young men behind many more of those expressionless, skull-like helmets—lost boys who'd never been allowed to have so much as their own name.

On the other hand, battalions made up of those lost boys had destroyed Rose's homeworld and so many others. How much more ruin and misery would they inflict on the galaxy? How many more people would they rob of loved ones?

Rose had never heard of another First Order stormtrooper shaking off his brainwashing and refusing to carry out the murderous orders he'd been given. Maybe Finn was the only one.

Well, if that's the case, Paige would have said I should give him a break.

She heard Finn clomping around in the lounge—if he'd ever been trained in stealth, the lessons hadn't taken—and ran a finger down the almost imperceptible seams in the yacht's perfectly milled dashboard.

You would have loved him, Pae-Pae. You would have said he has a good heart.

Rose smiled at the thought.

And you would have been right.

Finn felt a bit dizzy watching DJ systematically rifle the storage compartments in the yacht's lounge.

The thief looked so mangy and sleepy that it seemed like a minor
miracle he stayed upright. But his hands moved with an easy, fluid
grace over the cabinets, alighting on locking mechanisms and security
measures that were invisible to Finn's eye. After the briefest pause, one
of DJ's hands would dart into his jacket, emerging with a computer
spike or some mysterious implement Finn didn't recognize. A moment later, the compartment would be open, leaving DJ free to pillage.

BB-8, apparently, was less impressed—or maybe jealous. Like Finn,
the astromech watched DJ at work, but just squawked unpleasantly.

"Your droid's a good judge of character," DJ said offhandedly, set-
tling himself at a data console and getting to work on its anti-intrusion
measures.

"Why do you say that?" Finn asked.

DJ offered him a crooked grin by way of reply.

"Doesn't like me," he said, extracting a small, gleaming tin from
his jacket. "Icindric caviar?"

Finn, unsure what that was, shook his head.

"So you just steal whatever you need?" he asked.

"Whatever I *want*. Don't sell me short. Now, let's see who I liber-
ated this gorgeous hunka from."

The air shimmered and a holographic diagram hovered over the
console. DJ glanced at it and his hands danced over the keys, causing
diagrams to wink in and out of existence in rapid succession.

"Well, I guess at least you're stealing from the bad guys and helping the good," Finn said.

DJ gave him much the same look Rose had aimed at him a minute
ago in the cockpit.

"Help the . . . you can't . . . look," DJ began, then stopped to put his
thoughts in order.

"The Resistance? The First Order? They're both the same
machine—and that machine's a meat grinder. Do you help a meat

grinder by jumping into it? Well, in a way you do but that's semantics, I guess. *Look.* Good guys, bad guys, them's made-up words to keep everyone fighting. Keep the money spinning around. *That's* what I steal from . . . A-ha!"

DJ grinned at something he saw on the console, then thumbed a key. A schematic of a TIE fighter appeared, followed by diagrams of a scout walker, TIE bomber, and a TIE interceptor.

"This guy's an arms dealer," DJ said. "Bought this beauty selling ships to the bad guys."

But the next diagram that appeared was a New Republic T-70 X-wing.

"And the good," DJ said, eyes twinkling.

Finn's face fell—and DJ saw the confusion on his face replaced by dismay.

"Finn, let me learn you something big," he said. "It's all a machine, partner. Live free. Don't join."

And DJ tapped the plate on his hat bearing his motto.

"Finn, get up here!"

That was Rose, and it sounded urgent. Finn bounded up the short flight of steps to the cockpit, so intent on whatever news she had that he failed to notice DJ's attention remained fixed on him as he departed.

"I got through to the fleet," Rose said. "Poe's on the line."

Finn leaned over the comm.

"Finn! Holdo's loading the crew into shuttles—she's going to abandon ship. Where are you?"

"That's what they wanted my bafflers for," Rose said, her hand reaching for her medallion. "To hide the transports from detection."

Finn tried to find the readout showing the *Libertine*'s progress, but couldn't pick it out amid the welter of screens and controls.

"We're so close," he told Finn.

"Did you find the Master Codebreaker?"

Rose and Finn exchanged a look.

"We found . . . *a* codebreaker," Finn said. "But I promise you I can shut the tracker down. Just buy us a little more time."

"All right," Poe said. "Hurry."

Poe broke the transmission. Finn could tell Rose was thinking the same thing he was thinking—and that neither of them wanted to be the first to ask.

Rose gave in first.

"How much do we trust this guy?"

"How much choice have we got?" Finn replied.

Poe shut down his comlink, breaking the connection with Rose and Finn, and looked up at Connix, C'ai Threnalli and the five other pilots in the utility room off the hangar.

"*Now* we have a chance," Poe said.

Some of the other pilots still looked uncertain. Poe could hardly blame them, given what he'd asked them to do. But C'ai was nodding, his eyes steely.

Poe knew them all—he wouldn't have summoned them to this meeting if he hadn't—though he'd only flown with a couple of them. He wished he had pilots he knew better, the ones with whom he'd flown wingtip-to-wingtip and could trust to keep him alive: Snap Wexley, say, or Jess Pava. But Snap and Jess had their own mission, and most of the other pilots he knew best were dead.

But then every pilot wanted to go into battle in a cloaked, invulnerable starfighter boasting enough armaments to crack open a planetary core. Since that never happened, you took what the ground crew could give you, relied on your wingmates, tried to get the angle, and took your shot. And you hoped it was enough.

"We tell the admiral about Rose and Finn's mission, and that we need to buy them time," Poe said. "And we hope she agrees."

"And if she doesn't?" asked one of the pilots.

"Then the conversation's over," Connix said.

"We'll do what needs to be done," Poe said. "But nobody dies. If we have to shoot, it's to stun. There are enough people trying to destroy the Resistance as it is—we're trying to *save* it."

Luke Skywalker walked across the meadow beneath the stars. The grass had been soaked by the recent downpour, and his Jedi ceremonial robes were getting wet—soon they'd be filthy with mud.

The Caretakers wouldn't like that, he knew. They were there to help him, as they had generations of Jedi dating back to when history became legend, but they weren't above sidelong looks and clicks of the tongue when they thought he'd been careless or performed some task haphazardly.

It couldn't be helped—it took more than a soggy field to stop a Jedi rite whose time had finally arrived.

And anyway, the Caretakers would have things to be a lot angrier about.

Luke activated the torch in his hand, igniting a hissing flame that guttered in the night. Ahead of him loomed the ancient uneti tree that held the primordial Jedi texts.

He'd donned the robes and taken up the torch before, only to falter and lose his resolve. Luke wasn't sure why, exactly. He supposed it was because he had spent so many years crossing the galaxy with R2-D2 as his companion, searching obsessively for ancient lore and a current purpose, at the cost of everything else. When he consigned the library to the flames, he would be consigning everything he had done since Endor with it. Vanity, again—but time after time, it had prevented him from taking that final step. In fact, Rey had arrived on the island after a failed attempt had left him brooding in the meadow, trying to summon the will to try again.

But Rey was gone. And this time, Luke vowed, he would not falter.

As he lifted his eyes to the tree, Luke sensed something behind him. He turned and beheld a shimmering presence from another time—the era he was about to declare extinct.

"Master Yoda," Luke said, feeling an instinctive surge of joy at the sight of him.

It had been many years since he had seen a manifestation of the great Jedi teacher, and Yoda appeared almost corporeal, much the same as Luke remembered from his fractious training on Dagobah, which he had cut short to confront Darth Vader. The little Jedi Master was wizened and stooped, his green scalp wreathed by a frizzy halo of delicate white hair, but now as then his eyes were penetrating, seeming to look through Luke and into his innermost thoughts.

"Young Skywalker," Yoda said.

But Luke realized his old teacher could only have appeared for one reason, and his happiness slipped away.

"I'm ending all of this," Luke warned the vision. "I'm going to burn it down. Don't try to stop me."

Yoda just looked amused.

Luke advanced on the remnant of the ancient tree, the torch blazing in his hand. He stopped less than an arm's length away from the pale, twisted bark. As soon as he stretched out his arm, the wood would begin to burn—and minutes after that the founding texts of the Jedi Order would be drifting ash.

Time is a circle. The beginning is the end.

But as had happened so many times before, Luke found he couldn't bring himself to lift his hand.

Yoda looked to the sky and raised a gnarled finger. A bolt of lightning lanced out of the night, momentarily painting the island in black and white and leaving Luke blinking frantically. When he chased away the spots on his vision the tree was ablaze.

Luke hurriedly doused the torch, nearly burning himself in the process, and looked for a way to beat out the rapidly spreading flames.

Behind him, he could hear Yoda guffawing. " 'Ending all this I am.' Oh, Skywalker. Missed you have I."

Luke steeled himself to rush into the tree and grab the books from their nook, but it was impossible—the tree had become an inferno. He slumped, turned, and stared at Yoda's shimmering form, standing placidly here, at the top of a tiny island on a forgotten planet in a nameless sector of the galaxy.

"So it *is* time for the Jedi Order to end," Luke said.

"Decide we do not, where our place in this story begins or ends. But time it is for you to look past a shelf of old books."

Despite what he had come to do, despite all he had brooded upon, Luke found himself offended.

"The sacred Jedi texts," he said.

"Read them have you? Page-turners they were not. Wisdom they held, but that library contained nothing the girl Rey does not already possess."

Yoda shook his head, and Luke felt very much like the Padawan he had been, so many years ago in the bogs of Dagobah. His master was disappointed, and he was embarrassed.

"Skywalker," Yoda said. "Still looking to the horizon. Never here, now. The need in front of your nose."

The little Jedi Master reached out with his cane, to rap Luke's nose with it.

"I was weak, unwise," Luke said.

"Lost Ben Solo, you did," Yoda said, gently but firmly. "Lose Rey, we must not."

"I can't be what she needs me to be."

"Heeded my words not did you," Yoda said. "'Pass on what you have learned.' Wisdom, yes. But folly also. Strength in mastery, hmm. But weakness and failure, yes. Failure most of all. The greatest teacher failure is."

And then he sounded faintly regretful: "We are what they grow beyond. That is the true burden of all Masters."

Luke stared into the fire, its filaments reaching for the distant stars. He stood beside his old teacher as the blaze raged on, consuming the ancient past.

CHAPTER 23

Aboard the *Millennium Falcon*, Rey finished closing a storage compartment beneath the relief pilot's bunk in the main hold and took a deep breath. None of her lengthy debates with herself during the journey from Ahch-To had led her to any other conclusion.

The Force had shown her what to do; now it was up to her to actually do it.

Chewbacca was waiting for her in the freighter's cramped escape pod bay, crouched by one of the single-person pods. R2-D2 stood nearby, lights blinking on his dome.

Rey saw that the pod was emblazoned with stenciled letters:

ESCAPE POD CLASS A9-40
MILLENNIUM FALCON

And below that was added, in poorly handwritten Clynese:

PROPERTY OF HAN SOLO PLEASE RETURN

She allowed herself a smile. She wished she could ask Han if that had ever worked.

Maybe it had—and if so, maybe that was good luck.

In which case, better not to think about the pod's unsettling re-semblance to a coffin.

Chewbacca helped her into the pod, his hands surprisingly gentle despite—or perhaps because of—his great strength. His eyes—startlingly blue in his fierce face—regarded hers uncertainly.

"As soon as I launch, you jump back out of range and stay there until you get my signal," she said.

The Wookiee rumbled, but she wasn't interested in being talked out of it.

"If you see Finn before I do, tell him . . ." she began.

Chewbacca yowled.

"Yeah. Perfect. Tell him that."

She climbed into the pod, arranged the lightsaber at her side, and gave the droid and the Wookiee a thumbs-up, crossing her arms across her chest as Chewbacca sealed her in.

Rose had known the First Order fleet would be waiting for them, but she still felt her chest tighten when the *Libertine* emerged from hy-perspace and she spotted the task force on the outer edge of the yacht's sensor cone.

"Whose brilliant idea was this again?" Finn asked.

"Don't look at me, man," said DJ, who'd joined them in the cock-pit. "I just work here. Which Destroyer do you want on?"

Rose studied the image of the flagship as the yacht's sensors con-structed a diagram of the massive ship from their scan. She still found the warship's size almost incomprehensible—the credits necessary to finance it would have made beggars out of entire sectors, and she'd never heard of a shipyard large enough to build it.

She wondered if any ore stripped from the ruins of Hays Minor had gone into that hull, or if her homeworld's minerals were part of some conduit connecting its turbolasers to its reactor. Or if the ship had been built from the wreckage of other worlds ravaged by the First Order.

And if the First Order had built this, what else had it secretly created?

"Which one do you think?" she snapped at DJ. "Do it. You can actually do this, right?"

DJ studied his grimy fingernails.

"Yeah, about that. Guys, I can do it. But there exists a pre-*Do It* conversation about price."

"Once we're done, the Resistance will give you whatever you want."

DJ eyed her appraisingly. "What you got deposit-wise?"

"Are you kidding me?" Finn asked. "Look at us."

DJ did—and Rose noticed that her medallion had drawn his attention.

"Is that Haysian smelt?" DJ asked. "That's something."

Rose put her hand over her medal, instinctively hiding it from his covetous gaze.

"No," Finn said angrily. "We gave you our word. You're going to get paid. That should be enough."

"Guys, I want to keep helping," DJ said. "But no something, no doing."

Finn started to argue, but Rose knew whatever he said wouldn't be enough—and they had nothing else of value. Eyes cold, she tugged her medallion free and tossed it to DJ.

"Do it," she said.

"Now I can help," DJ said.

The feral gleam in DJ's eye as his hand closed around the medallion made her want to hurl herself at him. She stormed out of the cockpit instead, ignoring Finn's worried look.

After a silent moment in the cockpit, DJ extracted one of his mysterious machines from his pockets and wired it into an exposed panel on the yacht's console.

"Cloaking our approach," he said. "We should be off their scopes. Now we slice a slit in their shield and slip through. 'Slice a slit in . . .'—hm. Say *that* five times fast."

Finn was in no mood. "Just do it."

"Done," DJ said.

As the yacht approached, the First Order ships grew from points of light to recognizable shapes, their details perfectly sharp in the vacuum of space. DJ accelerated and Finn looked at him in surprise, but the thief just shrugged.

"We've got the cloak," he said. "It works? Nobody sees us, we live, the doing gets done. If not? I figure just skip to the big boom."

And with that DJ grinned and wiggled his fingers, miming an explosion.

Finn glared at him, still angry about Rose's medallion. He was sure there was a reason DJ's strategy was a bad idea, but he couldn't articulate what it was—and arguing with an amoral thief seemed like a lousy way to spend his last minute or two of existence.

The *Supremacy* was a wall ahead of them that expanded until its blunt prow filled the viewports. Finn wondered what he would experience if one of the Dreadnought's turbolaser clusters fired on them. Would he see the beam, and feel the *Libertine* come apart around him? Or would he and Rose simply cease to exist—there one moment and gone the next?

He realized he was holding his breath and forced himself to breathe, studying the endless underside of the ship as it passed over them, covering them in shadow. His duty rotation had included assignments aboard Snoke's flagship, but he'd never seen its exterior—he'd come and gone from it aboard a transport, sealed inside a stormtrooper's helmet.

Finn tried to match up what he knew of the warship's interior with the hull overhead. Above them, he knew, there were assembly lines and foundries and assembly halls and training centers for cadets, like he had been. As well as more than a million crewers—the *Supremacy* was more a mobile capital than a ship.

Finn realized he felt guilty. He'd known what the Resistance hadn't: that the *Supremacy* was out there somewhere, lurking in the Unknown Regions of the galaxy. Just as he'd known about so many other things he'd seen in his years of First Order service.

He knew it was ridiculous to blame himself—when he'd arrived on D'Qar there'd been no time for a thorough debriefing. There'd barely been time for him to tell General Organa and her officers about Starkiller Base before he'd left with Han and Chewbacca aboard the *Falcon*. And afterward . . . well, there hadn't been an afterward. He'd woken up in a bacta suit, stashed in a storeroom aboard a ship that was being hunted.

Still, somehow it seemed wrong that he'd been the only one aboard the *Raddus* who hadn't been surprised to see the massive warship come out of hyperspace.

And if things had been different, would it have occurred to him to warn the Resistance of everything arrayed against them? Finn liked to think he would have done so, but he wasn't sure that was true. It was as likely, he had to admit, that he would have insisted on accompanying Rey on her Jedi hunt, or tried to convince her to join him somewhere in the Outer Rim.

An alert flashed and Finn spotted the dots of fighters on the *Libertine*'s scope—but immediately realized their heading would take them nowhere near the yacht. He tried to locate the fighters through the viewports, wondering what their mission could be. There were only three of them—if the First Order were attacking the Resistance fleet, it would have emptied its hangars.

"They're going after something," Finn said.

"Something that ain't us," DJ said. "Almost there, buddy. And check it—that's our spot."

DJ pointed, then guided the yacht to a tiny dot on the underside of the *Supremacy*. Finn couldn't see what it was—some kind of port or vent, he supposed—but it grew until the yacht slipped inside it, into darkness.

The three TIE fighters flew in close formation, their pilots' gloved fingers hovering near the FIRE button on their control yokes.

Every First Order pilot assigned to the fleet wanted to avenge the disaster at Starkiller, pitilessly dissected in after-action reports as a failure of the starfighters corps to contain a numerically inferior enemy. But the all-out blitz against the Resistance that the pilots hoped for kept failing to materialize—instead, there was this strange, sublight pursuit, with most of the pilots stuck watching.

Things had begun promisingly, with a frantic dogfight with the bombers that had destroyed the *Fulminatrix* (another round of after-action reports no one was looking forward to); and the attack run against the enemy flagship.

But the fleet had been pursuing the Resistance stragglers—now supposedly reduced to a lone ship—for more than twelve hours since then, each minute of which had been spent on high alert.

The pilots were edging beyond tired into exhaustion. Shift rotations had been canceled to guard against the possibility that the Resistance—whose spies and infiltrators were rumored to be within every droid pool and under every trash bin—might know about the switchover and use it to mount a lightning-fast raid. Pilots who should have been in their bunks were still in their ready rooms, over-stimulated by bad caf and the weird mix of hope and dread that this next minute would become zero hour, with fighters launched and battle joined. The first wave of pilots' replacements had arrived after being unable to sleep, hoping that the slow-motion chase would drag on long enough to deliver the chance at glory to them.

The alert that finally did sound had come as a relief, one that had curdled into puzzled disappointment before the TIE flight cleared its hangar: Their orders were to investigate an anomalous sensor contact.

That was it. A lone ship had come out of hyperspace between the two fleets and jumped almost immediately, ejecting something that began flying toward the First Order task force. The sensor profile indicated it was too small to even be a starfighter, so what was it?

The logical conclusion was that it was a bomb—but even a hundred devices of that size would have been incapable of doing more than cosmetic damage to the Supreme Leader's flagship. That made this the worst kind of hop—one you could only screw up.

So what was the object flying out there?

To the pilots' bafflement, it turned out to be an escape pod—one with a single life-form. As they escorted it toward the hangar, all three pilots pondered a variation of the same thought: What lunatic would head *into* a battle before abandoning ship?

Kylo Ren knew who was in the escape pod even before it opened with a hiss of vapor—her presence had been a steady pulse from the Force the moment his father's junk-heap freighter once again somehow heaved itself out of hyperspace without disintegrating. The storm-troopers behind him stood ready, but he just smiled at the sight of Rey crammed into the pod's tight confines.

His smile faded at the sight of his uncle's lightsaber.

"I'll take that," he said. "It belongs to me."

Rey was tempted to tell him to come and get it, as Finn had—and to remind him that she'd driven him to his knees at Starkiller Base and disarmed him. That he would bear the mark of that duel forever, and lived only because she had chosen not to strike him down.

But that wasn't why she had come, and they both knew it. Still, she held the lightsaber appraisingly for a moment, to remind Kylo that she was the one who had set this chain of events in motion.

"Strange, then, that it called to me at the castle," Rey said, studying the ancient weapon almost idly before snapping her gaze back to Kylo. "And not to you."

The corner of Kylo's mouth twitched in the beginning of a smile, and he inclined his head at the soldiers filling the hangar. "You're in no position to dictate."

Rey held the hilt out to him, as if daring him to take it. The storm-troopers shifted uneasily. Kylo frowned, then reached out, his scarred face momentarily uncertain. The slightest tremor disturbed his black-gloved fingers as he reached out for the weapon sitting mo-tionless in Rey's steady hand.

He snatched it away and gestured curtly for a First Order officer to approach with binders.

"That isn't necessary," Rey said.

"It is," Kylo said, hustling her into the depths of the massive flag-ship. "We have an appointment."

Rey quickened her pace to match his long strides, not wanting to be seen scurrying to keep up. Behind them, the accompanying stormtroopers' armor rattled. Rey could feel their anxiety about a situation they couldn't fit into the lockstep of their training regimens. That anxiety was shot through with fear—not of her but of the mercurial, unpredictable Kylo.

She didn't blame them—Kylo's turmoil all but filled the Force around them, roiling and churning it. The troopers couldn't sense it the way she and Kylo could, but that wasn't the same as saying they couldn't sense it at all—they were part of life and the Force, and couldn't help but be affected on some level.

Kylo stopped at a lone turbolift ringed by stormtroopers and dismissed the guards. The doors shut and left Rey alone with him. He was still contemplating the lightsaber in his hands.

She nodded upward. "Snoke? You don't have to do this."

"I do."

"I feel the conflict in you growing since you killed Han," Rey said. "It's tearing you apart."

"Is that why you came? To tell me about my conflict?"

There they were again, his usual tactics—deflection and derision. As if he were the master and she was his student, to be kept at bay and off balance by questions. But things had changed. She wasn't the young woman he'd kidnapped on Takodana or confronted on Starkiller Base. Not anymore.

"No," Rey said. "Look at me. *Ben.*"

He turned at the sound of the name he'd been born with, the one he'd abandoned. He looked lost.

"When we touched I saw your future," she told him. "Just the shape of it, but solid and clear. You will not bow before Snoke. You will turn—I'll help you. *I saw it.* It's your destiny."

She watched the emotions chase themselves across his face, echoed by jitters and spikes in the Force. Anger. Confusion. Pain. Loneliness. Longing. Sorrow.

Then he lifted his eyes to hers.

"You're wrong," Kylo said. "When we touched I saw something, too. Not your future—your *past*. And because of what I saw, I know that when the moment comes, *you'll* be the one to turn. You'll stand with *me*. Rey, I saw who your parents are."

Rey stared at him, but there was no lie in Kylo's eyes. And a terrifying realization bloomed in her mind: Kylo's churning emotions weren't just about himself. They were also about her.

The turbolift doors opened with a hiss and Kylo led Rey into the throne room, where the Supreme Leader of the First Order awaited them on his throne. His faceless, crimson-armored guards stood on either side of the throne, bladed weapons ready. Snoke himself was almost slouching—indolent in his golden robes, secure in the safety of his sanctum.

But his eyes were piercing and hungry. Rey tried to avoid them, but his gaze was like a lodestone, dragging her attention involuntarily to him. Their pull was akin to what she'd felt near the pit on Ahch-To—whispering of secrets that had been reserved for her, that belonged to her. Ancient, hidden knowledge that would destroy the weak but elevate the strong. *The worthy.*

Snoke grinned hungrily at her and she found she couldn't look away until the Supreme Leader fixed those dreadful, bottomless eyes on Kylo instead.

"Well done, my good and faithful apprentice," he said, the voice deep and slow. "My faith in you is restored."

Then his gaze pinned her once again. "Young Rey. Welcome."

CHAPTER 24

The *Raddus*'s hangar was filled with transports—Poe counted thirty of them, enough to evacuate every member of the Resistance who'd survived the evacuation of D'Qar. Crewers scurried around them, preparing them for flight—and sneaking looks at the gathering to the side of the hangar, where a small group of pilots led by Poe Dameron had approached Vice Admiral Holdo and her officers with an urgent message.

"So a stormtrooper and a who-now are doing *what*?" Holdo exclaimed.

"Trying to save us. This is our best hope of escape. You have to give Finn and Rose all the time you can!"

While Holdo tried to process what she'd been told—a missing light shuttle, a rendezvous on a distant gambling world, a codebreaker of uncertain repute, the nature of hyperspace tracking, the location of First Order circuit breakers—Poe looked over her shoulder at her officers, studying their faces in mute appeal. Some he knew—D'Acy, for one—while others were unfamiliar to him, Ninkas who'd arrived on the *Raddus* with their commander.

But known or unknown, their expressions told him the same thing: They'd stand with Holdo. It was her decision.

"You have bet the survival of the Resistance on bad odds and put us all at risk," Holdo fumed. "There's no time now."

She turned to her officers. "We need to get clear of this cruiser—load the transports."

As the transports' doors hissed open, Poe and C'ai exchanged a look.

"I was afraid you'd say that," Poe said, and drew his blaster. He was relieved to hear the other pilots unholstering their own weapons.

"Admiral Holdo, I'm relieving you of your duty for the survival of this ship, its crew, and the Resistance," he said, hoping his voice sounded cool and steady.

The officers behind Holdo looked shocked and angry, but the admiral simply gave Poe one of her appraising glances.

Poe tensed, knowing this could go either way.

Then Holdo raised her hands. After a moment, her officers did the same.

"I hope you understand what you're doing, Dameron," she said.

In different circumstances he might have explained that he *did* understand—trying, one last time, to make her see how she had lost sight of Leia's vision and how she might restore it. But he had to seize the little time that remained to them—seize it and use it to improve the odds for Rose and Finn as best he could.

"I'm going to the bridge," Poe told C'ai. "If they move, stun 'em."

The aperture DJ located led to a laundry room, of all things.

Finn had endured his share of drudgery as a stormtrooper cadet—his trainers had routinely stuck those who failed an exercise with demeaning duty shifts spent doing droidwork—but he'd never seen a First Order laundry from the inside.

The laundry, in fact, had no organic workers at all—just several auto-valet droids hard at work at their ironing stations. The multi-armed droids swiveled and turned ceaselessly: one arm grabbed a freshly washed uniform out of a bin, another ran a sensor over it to verify the fabric type, and a third manipulated a built-in steam-iron attachment.

To Finn's relief, none of the droids seemed to care—or even

notice—when three humans and an astromech emerged from the moist, lint-filled vent that wended its way to a heat sink on the exterior of the *Supremacy* in which the *Libertine* had been stashed.

Nor did they object when those same humans grabbed three washed and pressed uniforms slated to be returned to their owners; or picked out shined and polished boots, belts, and caps to go with them.

There were no mirrors, but Finn had seen enough First Order uniforms to know his looked right—tunic straight, pants flaring above the high boots, visor of his cap neither too high nor too low. The only uniform small enough to fit Rose had been a major's blue-green outfit, but it looked passable.

As for DJ . . . well, DJ's uniform was fine, but the man himself looked like he'd just crawled back into his quarters after three days' shore leave on Nar Shaddaa.

Finn scowled, but it couldn't be helped. Fortunately, hierarchy outweighed everything else in the First Order—unquestioning obedience was rewarded and independent thought punished.

"Will this really work?" Rose asked, and it was obvious she didn't think it would.

"Of course it will," Finn said with a jauntiness he knew wouldn't fool her. "Just look out for the guys in white."

"Stormtroopers?" she asked, trying to arrange her hair so her hat would sit properly atop it.

"No—white tunics," Finn said. "Those guys are First Order Security Bureau. Loyalty officers. It's their job to be suspicious. Everyone else will be looking at your rank insignia, not your face."

DJ looked dubious. So did Rose. BB-8 whistled anxiously.

"Chin up, shoulders back," Finn said. "Stand up tall, don't be slack."

Rose and DJ exchanged a puzzled glance.

"It's how they taught us to walk," Finn said, then sighed. "Brass it out, people. It'll be okay. Only problem is we don't have working code cylinders."

Rose eyed the silver capsules adorning Finn's tunic.

"Those don't work?" she asked.

"Afraid not. They've been reset to unregistered status. Probably some officers forgot to take them off and they wound up in the hamper."

Rose looked at DJ, who was cleaning his fingernails to no discernible improvement.

"Can't you reprogram them? You're the codebeaker, after all."

"In a laundry room?" DJ drawled. "Nuh-uh. That's heavy code, friends. Need a white shirt to fire it up. Mess it around elsewhere, alarms start ringing. Clang clang clang clang. Lots and lots of alarms."

Rose glared at him, frustrated, and the grubby thief raised his hands.

"The Do It? It was the Getting You Here. And the Do It has been done."

"And the getting the tracker shut off," Finn reminded him.

"And that. This, though? The stuff in the middle? Not this guy's department, friends."

"So can we even reach the tracker?" Rose asked.

"Sure," Finn said. "We just have to avoid the major security checkpoints between here and there, that's all."

"And how many of those are there?"

Finn tried to remember. "Three? No, four. Except maybe . . . look, there are a few. It'll be okay."

"You keep saying that," Rose said.

The laundry room was deep in the *Supremacy*'s lower levels, near the huge warship's stern. During the first few minutes of their journey toward the distant tracking-control room, they encountered no one—just a lone mouse droid that regarded BB-8 curiously before letting out a puzzled but cheerful chirp.

Finn eyed BB-8's scorched and dingy finish. "We should have gotten you a uniform, too. Hmm."

He paused at a technician's station by the turbolift bank and scooped up a rectangular black trash can.

BB-8 hooted derisively.

"You're kidding, right?" Rose asked.

The turbolift chimed.

"It'll be okay," Finn said. She rolled her eyes.

The lift rose silently, then opened into a massive commons area filled with control stations and swarming with officers. Rose stopped fussing with her cap and shrank back, eyes wide.

"I didn't sign up for this, man," DJ said.

"Eyes forward," Finn said. "Hey. *Breathe.*"

He reached out and realigned Rose's cap—she'd somehow gotten it on backward—then covered BB-8 with the trash bin.

"Okay, let's do this," Finn said.

He squared his shoulders and stepped out of the turbolift. Rose exchanged a dismayed look with DJ and followed him, with BB-8 gliding along beside them.

Rose was certain they'd get no more than a few meters across the vast commons before the alarm went up and stormtroopers swarmed them. But as Finn predicted, the officers barely looked at them—and the few that did seemed loath to make eye contact.

Rose was convinced that her impersonation of an actual officer was the worst acting job in the history of infiltration. Was she walking too slowly? Too quickly? With too much of a slouch? And she didn't dare look at DJ, let alone the rolling trash can next to him.

But Finn . . . Finn looked like a model officer, striding through the commons like he owned it. He practically radiated aloof confidence.

But then Finn had grown up in such surroundings, she supposed. This was the world to which he was accustomed, and by comparison the Resistance must have felt chaotic and haphazard. Maybe it hadn't just been his infatuation with Rey that had driven him to flee, she thought—maybe he'd also been trying to escape unfamiliar surroundings in which he was alone and didn't fit in.

Rose was a bit frightened of this new Finn, striding briskly in his polished boots. It was as if she were seeing the capable First Order officer he might have become—a well-engineered cog in its war machine, designed to further its murderous work.

She pushed the thought away. He had rejected that future—and with it, thrown away his entire past. He wasn't FN-2187, not anymore. He was Finn—her friend.

"Major?" someone asked, loud and insistent and far too close. "Could you okay this nav assignment?"

Major. Major. That's you, dummy!

A junior officer was standing beside her with a datapad.

Rose looked it over coldly and gave him a muttered okay and what she hoped was an officious nod—the minimum amount of time she could spare for an underling who was bothering her.

They walked on, leaving the junior officer behind. But were eyes lingering on them? And what about those mouse droids? Was it her imagination, or were they fixated on the motile trash can sliding through their midst?

"This isn't working," DJ warned under his breath.

No, it wasn't her imagination.

"Almost there," Finn said.

There. A long-nosed, scowling man with suspicious, darting eyes and a permanent scowl. A man in a white tunic. And rolling next to him, a First Order BB-series astromech.

Those BB units could see a full range of spectra, Rose knew. The man was First Order Security Bureau. And he was looking right at them.

Six stormtroopers stood at the turbolift bank, their postures indicating they were waiting and not on guard duty. Finn reached around one of them and jabbed at the lift controls.

The security officer was still looking at them.

And now he was walking toward them, not hurriedly but with determined steps. Behind him trundled the BB unit.

Rose wanted to scream. Where was the lift? They were surrounded by the pinnacle of warship evolution and the stupid lift still wouldn't come.

It finally arrived and Rose hurried inside, DJ on her heels. She turned and found the senior officer just steps away. Now he was hurrying, his eyes boring holes in them.

She stabbed at the controls, willing the doors to close.

They closed in the security officer's face.

Rose reminded herself to remain stock-still—a major didn't ex-hale in nervous relief, high-five her fellow officers, or pat the top of overturned trash cans. Even a stormtrooper might find that odd.

Still, she couldn't resist a glance at Finn—and discovered that one of the stormtroopers was looking at him, too, head cocked.

DJ's hand crept toward his blaster.

What had they done wrong? And why, out of the four of them, was Finn the one who had attracted attention?

"Is there a problem, soldier?" Finn asked coldly, but Rose could hear the fear creeping into his voice.

"FN Twenty-one eighty-seven?" the trooper asked, voice modu-lated by his helmet.

Finn's eyes widened. Rose looked at DJ, found the thief pale with fright.

"You don't remember me," the trooper said. "Nine twenty-six, from induct camp. Batch Eight. But I remember *you*."

DJ's hand was on his blaster now, trying to work it free without anyone noticing. The other stormtroopers' attention was riveted on the conversation in their midst.

"Nine twenty-six . . . please don't," Finn said.

"I'm sorry, Twenty-one eighty-seven," the soldier replied.

Rose knew it was hopeless. Even if DJ did get the drop on one of the troopers, there were five others. And anyway, the turbolift would be rated for blasterfire—a few stray bolts caroming around in this enclosed space would kill them as effectively as any public execution.

She put her hand on DJ's, stopping his draw.

"I know I'm not supposed to initiate contact with officers, but look at you!" the stormtrooper told Finn. "Never took you for captain ma-terial. Batch Eight, heigh-ho!"

And then he reached out and gave Finn a friendly swat on the butt.

Finn nodded stiffly as the doors opened.

"Batch Eight," he said.

The troopers headed in one direction and the four of them headed in the other, stopping once they were around the corner. Finn gasped in relief, and a wan-sounding beep came from beneath BB-8's trash can. As for Rose, she thought she was going to throw up.

"Let's get to that tracker—fast," she said.

"Right around the corner," Finn promised. "It'll be okay."

There were just a few officers on the *Raddus*'s temporary bridge, beneath the Mon Calamari craft's pointed nose. And none of them were prepared to see Poe, Connix, and several Resistance pilots storm in with their blasters drawn.

The Resistance officers looked aghast, but C-3PO looked up from a monitor as if nothing were amiss.

"Ah, Captain Dameron," he said. "Admiral Holdo is looking for you."

"We spoke," Poe said, nodding at his fellow mutineers. "Get them down to the hangar."

The officers were escorted out. C-3PO watched them go, obviously confused, as Poe studied the bridge consoles, longing for the simplicity of a control yoke and a trigger.

After several anxious moments of searching, he found what he was looking for. He powered down the transports in the hangar, watching the scene on the monitor in satisfaction as the lights flickered and left Holdo and her entourage peering through the gloom.

But none of it would mean anything unless Finn and Rose had found a way to shut down the First Order tracker that kept the *Raddus* pinned in place.

As Finn rounded the corner, he was grimly certain that he had made a mistake somewhere, leading them in some random direction through the *Supremacy*'s guts instead of to the tracking-control station.

But no, ahead of them the corridor ended at a formidable-looking door. Beyond it, through combat-rated viewports, he saw rows of computer banks and imposing circuit breakers rated for the power needs of an A-class process.

"This is it," Finn said, debating whether or not to tease Rose about all the worrying she'd done. He decided not to—why jinx things?

DJ studied the door control.

"Gimme a mo," he said.

"Good time to figure out how we get back to the fleet?" Rose asked.

Finn considered that. "I know where the nearest escape pods are."

"Of course you do," Rose said.

Finn rolled his eyes.

DJ pulled Rose's medallion out of his coat and pushed it into the innards of the control panel.

"Haysian smelt," he said. "Best conductor."

A moment later he tossed the medallion to Rose.

She tried to hide her astonishment. She was afraid she'd burst into tears, and there wasn't time for that—or for anything else.

"You're welcome," DJ said.

Beneath the trash barrel, they heard a muffled voice—which Finn realized was Poe's. A moment later, BB-8 extended a mechanical arm from beneath the bin, flipping the comlink in Finn's direction.

"Poe, we're almost there," Finn said. "Have the cruiser prepped for lightspeed."

"Yeah, I'm on it," Poe said over the comlink. "Just hurry."

"Is this going to work?" Rose asked. "It seems like it's actually going to work."

"Almost there," DJ said.

Poe hurriedly input coordinates into the *Raddus*'s navicomputer. The terminus of their jump didn't particularly matter—all they needed was to be close enough to a world where the Resistance could communicate with its allies and acquire more fuel. By the time the First Order's hunters found them, they'd be gone again.

C-3PO was staring at him now. "Sir, I'm almost afraid to ask, but—"

"Good instinct, Threepio. Go with that."

Then motion from the hangar caught his eye on the monitor. Smoky vapor was spilling out of a fuel hose, pierced by flashing rings of stun beams. Holdo had made her move—Poe could see her in the middle of the fight, directing her loyalists.

"Seal that door!" he shouted to a pilot by the entrance to the bridge.

The pilot did so, overriding the controls to lock out anyone trying to enter from the other side.

Now all Poe could do was wait.

C-3PO began shuffling toward the door. Poe watched the protocol droid in disbelief.

"Threepio, stay away from that door," Poe warned him.

C-3PO turned indignantly.

"It would be quite against my programming to be party to a mutiny," he huffed. "It is not correct protocol!"

Sparks flew from the juncture of the bridge doors as someone began cutting through from the other side. C-3PO executed a hasty about-face and headed in the other direction as quickly as his servomotors allowed.

Poe exchanged a glance with the other pilots, then looked worriedly at the sparking door.

"Finn?" he yelled into his comlink.

"Now or never!" Finn called to DJ.

"Now," DJ said with a look of sleepy satisfaction, then stepped back.

The door opened and Finn and Rose rushed in, with DJ and BB-8 trailing behind. Rose eyed the circuit breakers, tracing the pathways of power conduits.

Three levers, five seconds. Easy job.

Something hissed on either side of them. Two doors opened and the BB unit from the commons rolled inside, its electronic eye fixed balefully on them. A dozen stormtroopers rushed in, blasters drawn. Behind them came the security officer from the commons area.

Finn looked glumly at the stormtroopers as they clattered into the control room. There were far too many of them even to think of starting a firefight.

Then a new sound reached his ears—a dreadfully familiar one. The slow, measured tread of armored feet.

Captain Phasma walked into the control room, rifle cradled in her mirror-bright gauntlets.

"FN Twenty-one eighty-seven," she purred. "So good to have you back."

Poe was still trying to process that he'd just heard his friends being captured when sparks began to fly from the doors to the *Raddus*'s temporary bridge. He fumbled for his sidearm as the doors groaned open, then waited for the smoke to clear, keeping his blaster leveled at the bridge entrance.

Leia Organa walked through the smoke in her hospital gown, her steps a bit shaky, her face grave.

Relief flooded through Poe. He lowered his blaster.

Before he could say anything—how happy he was to see her, how horribly wrong everything had gone without her—Leia raised her blaster and stunned him.

CHAPTER 25

Interpreting visions of the future was a dangerous game. Whether Jedi, Sith, or some other sect less celebrated by history, all those who used the Force to explore possible time lines kept that uppermost in their minds. Those who didn't died regretting that they hadn't.

Snoke had learned that lesson many years ago, when he was young and the galaxy was very different. These days, what struck him was how much visions of the future left out.

For example, who would have guessed that the girl Rey would be so slim and fragile-looking? She looked lost in the throne room, dwarfed by both her surroundings and the galaxy-shaking events for which she was the unlikely and unwitting fulcrum.

But Snoke knew appearances were often deceiving—sometimes fatally so. Underestimating Rey had nearly cost Kylo Ren his life, after all. Snoke knew better. For he had his own legions of uncounted dead, their ranks filled by those who had underestimated him.

Snoke knew he himself was an unlikely fulcrum, just about the furthest thing from what the tattered remnants of Palpatine's Empire had imagined as a leader. The admirals and generals who'd survived the fury of the Empire's implosion and the New Republic's wrath had envisioned being led by someone else, anyone else: pitiless, devious

Gallius Rax; dutiful, cautious Rae Sloane; the slippery political fa-
natic Ormes Apolin; or even an unhinged but ambitious military architect such as Brendol Hux.

All of those would-be leaders had been co-opted, sidelined, or destroyed, leaving only Armitage Hux, the mad son of a mad father.
And that one was but a mouthpiece, a miscast tinkerer whose rant-
ings could only persuade the sort of rabble who blindly worshipped
rage and lunatic certainty.

Though galactic history would record it differently—Snoke would
see to that—the evolution of the First Order had been more improvisation than master plan. That was another element visions tended to
miss.

Palpatine had engineered the Contingency to simultaneously destroy his Empire and ensure its rebirth, ruthlessly winnowing its ranks
and rebuilding them with who and what survived. The rebuilding was
to take place in the Unknown Regions, secretly explored by Imperial
scouts and seeded with shipyards, laboratories, and storehouses—an
enormously expensive effort that had taken decades, and been kept
hidden from all but the elect.

But the Imperial refugees' military preparations had been insufficient bulwarks against the terrors of the Unknown Regions. Grasping
in the dark among strange stars, they had come perilously close to
destruction, and it had not been military might that saved them.

It had been knowledge—Snoke's knowledge.

Which, ironically, led back to Palpatine and his secrets.

Palpatine's true identity as Darth Sidious, heir to the Sith, had
been an even greater secret than the Contingency. And the Empire's
explorations into the Unknown Regions had served both aspects of
its ruler. For Sidious knew that the galaxy's knowledge of the Force
had come from those long-abandoned, half-legendary star systems,
and that great truths awaited rediscovery among them.

Truths that Snoke had learned and made to serve his own ends.

One obstacle had stood in his way—Skywalker. Who had been
wise enough not to rebuild the Jedi Order, dismissing it as the scle-

rotic, self-perpetuating debating society it had become in its death throes. Instead, the last Jedi had sought to understand the origins of the faith, and the larger truths behind it.

Like his father, Skywalker had been a favored instrument of the will of the Cosmic Force. That made it essential to watch him. And once Skywalker endangered Snoke's design, it had become essential to act.

And so Snoke had drawn upon his vast store of knowledge, parceling it out to confuse Skywalker's path, ensnare his family, and harness Ben Solo's powers to ensure both Skywalker's destruction and Snoke's triumph.

Now the endgame he had foreseen was at hand.

Snoke waved and Rey's binders parted and clattered to the floor—a trivial demonstration of the Force. He noted approvingly that it no longer awed her.

"Come closer, child," he said.

She refused him and Snoke reached out with the Force, whose power had waxed even as his body had withered. To his delight he found Rey strong—even more powerful than he'd imagined. Strong with the Force, and with the kind of towering will that made her able to command it.

She would have made a fitting instrument for Snoke—if he'd still had need of such crude tools.

"So much strength," Snoke said, savoring the currents of power in the room and the chaos of their collisions. "Darkness rises, and light to meet it. I warned my young apprentice that as he grew stronger, his equal in the light would rise."

Another seemingly offhand gesture and Anakin Skywalker's lightsaber ripped itself free of Kylo's grasp, tumbling past Rey to smack into Snoke's hand. He turned the weapon gently, admiring both the skill of its construction and the power coiled within it. To Snoke's eyes, the weapon's very form revealed the Jedi lineage behind its creation, a string of once mighty names that no longer had any meaning.

"Skywalker, I assumed," he said. "Wrongly."

He set the lightsaber down on the throne's armrest and pinned Rey with his gaze.

"*Closer*, I said."

She resisted him again, but this time Snoke didn't limit himself to testing her defenses. He used the Force to compel her body, yanking her centimeter by slow, unwilling centimeter toward him across the polished floor.

The rumors began flying even as Holdo's loyalists and Poe's mutineers found shelter behind equipment cases still waiting to be loaded into the *Raddus*'s transports: General Organa was ready to retake command.

But for which side? That was less clear, and led to the odd spectacle of fighters on either side of the hangar alternating firing stun blasts at each other with trying to hear what was being said over their comlinks.

The firing stopped when the hangar doors opened to reveal the slight figure of the general, followed by C-3PO and several soldiers and pilots—one of whom had Poe's limp body slung over his shoulders.

For a long moment, no one said anything.

"I just got back on my feet—if it's all right with everybody, I'd prefer to stay that way," Leia said quietly.

She walked into the middle of the hangar, between the two sides, and put her hands on her hips. "Now, where is Admiral Holdo?"

Holdo emerged from behind a stack of crates and the two women regarded each other for a moment.

"Amilyn."

"Leia."

They embraced. Slowly, in ones and twos, soldiers and pilots on both sides holstered their weapons and stood.

"We're about to make planetfall," Leia said, once they'd parted. "If the First Order follows us down, I recommend we all shoot in the same direction."

She stepped away from Holdo and began conferring with D'Acy. Holdo indicated which crates needed to be loaded first. After a few sheepish looks back and forth, the loyalists and mutineers realized that was it. They began carrying boxes, their divisions erased.

Holdo checked that Poe was breathing, then signaled for two soldiers to carry him aboard one of the transports. She turned to Leia.

"That one's a troublemaker," she said. "I like him."

"Me too," Leia said with a smile. "Now board your transport."

Holdo raised an eyebrow at her old friend.

"For the transports to escape, someone has to stay behind and pilot the cruiser."

Leia fixed her with a look Holdo knew all too well. She'd seen it on Alderaan, during the pathfinding expeditions of their youth, in the Apprentice Legislature on Coruscant, and in various impressive-looking legislative chambers as the New Republic Senate moved from world to world. Her friend was marshaling her arguments and preparing to give a speech.

Holdo had no doubt that it would be an effective one. But the time for speeches was over.

"I'm afraid I outrank you, Princess," she said, gently but pointedly. "And an admiral goes down with her ship."

Leia stopped and her chin dipped.

"Too many losses," she said quietly. "I can't do it anymore."

"Sure you can," Holdo replied, and Leia looked up in surprise. "You taught me how."

Leia looked up at her and almost smiled. Were the situation different, she might even have laughed—the full, robust laugh that had rarely, if ever, been heard in her never-ending rounds of diplomatic summits and Senate debates and military strategy sessions. But then Amilyn had always had that effect on her—a gift for saying what reached your ears as the wrong thing but turned out to be perfect.

She'd miss that. She'd miss her.

"May the Force—" Leia began, only to hear her friend was saying the same words.

They stopped, deferring to each other.

"You take it," Leia said. "I've said it enough."

"May the Force be with you always," Holdo said with a smile.

Leia put her hand on her friend's arm as the first transports rose ponderously from the hangar's deck and headed for space.

Rey tried to resist, commanding her feet to remain planted on the floor of Snoke's throne room, but it was hopeless—she was pulled closer and closer to the Supreme Leader. As on Takodana, with Kylo Ren, she found that both her mind and body had been invaded and overwhelmed. The feeling sickened her—her stomach wanted to revolt, as if Snoke were a physical malady it could purge.

"You underestimate Skywalker," she warned the gaunt, robed figure, her voice strained by trying to keep her distance. "And Ben Solo. And me. It will be your downfall."

Snoke's eyes glittered with feral amusement. Few things were more entertaining than an opponent who mistook a little bit of knowledge for the entire picture. Their downfalls were so much more satisfying—provided that before the end, they were confronted by the sheer scope of their folly and failure.

He studied Rey, still futilely struggling against his will, and decided he had time to teach her this final lesson.

"Oh?" Snoke asked, radiating mock concern. "Have you seen something? A weakness in my apprentice? Is *that* why you came?"

He laughed at the dawning horror on her face, and her attempt to hide it. There was nothing she could hide from him—not with her defenses so inadequate. Not even her thoughts—her deepest fears and secrets—were safe from him.

"Young fool," Snoke said. "It was *I* who bridged your minds. I stoked Ren's conflicted soul. I knew he was not strong enough to hide it from you—and you were not smart enough to resist the bait."

Kylo Ren had remained kneeling in the throne room as Snoke

tormented Rey, his face an impassive mask. Now he looked up in surprise, his eyes locked on his master.

Snoke ignored the pleading look on Kylo's face—just as he ignored the sickly waves of pain and confusion that rolled out from him into the Force.

But he did not ignore the fear in Rey's face. Her shock at learning Snoke's role in forging her connection with Kylo had disrupted what meager defenses she had. With her concentration broken, Snoke dragged her to his throne, her face paralyzed just centimeters from his own.

Holding Rey pinned there, Snoke considered Kylo.

He had seen his apprentice's enormous potential when he was still a child—the latent power of the Skywalker bloodline was impossible to miss. And he had also seen how to exploit the boy's feelings of inadequacy and abandonment, and his mother's guilt and desperation to contain the darkness within her child.

And indeed, Ben Solo had performed the role Snoke had envisioned for him perfectly. The combination of his potential and the danger he posed had lured Skywalker into seeking to rebuild the Jedi. His power had then destroyed all Skywalker had built and sent the failed Jedi Master into exile, removing him from the board just as the game entered a critical phase.

But what role the boy would play in the future was less clear. He called himself Kylo Ren, but as with so much else about him, that was more wish fulfillment than reality. He had never escaped being Ben Solo, or learned to resist the pull of the weak and pathetic light, or had the strength to excise the sentimental streak that had destroyed his legendary grandfather. And then there was his most glaring failure of all: his inability or unwillingness to use his power to redirect the course of his own destiny.

Snoke had once seen Kylo as the perfect student—a creation of both dark and light, with the strength of both aspects of the Force. But perhaps he had been wrong about that. Perhaps Kylo was an unstable combination of those aspects' weaknesses—a flawed vessel that could never be filled.

Snoke pushed the thought away. There would be time to consider Kylo's fate later, after the Resistance and the last Jedi had been destroyed.

And both of those goals were now at hand.

Snoke turned his attention back to Rey, still gamely struggling to fight something she had no hope of contending with, let alone defeating. It was a pity about the girl, whose unexpectedly strong powers intrigued him. But her role in the story was just about over. She had one final service to perform, after which she could be discarded.

"And now you will give me Skywalker," he told her. "Then I will kill you with the cruelest stroke."

He saw horror in her eyes—followed by stubborn defiance.

"No!" she managed.

"Yes!" Snoke replied, exultant. He raised his hand and hurled her across the room with the Force, then held her in the air as he smashed aside her resistance and began rifling through her thoughts, her memories, making them his to do with as he would. The skin at Rey's temples pulsed in waves, a physical manifestation of the violent intrusion into her mind.

"Give me *everything*," Snoke commanded.

The very air between them bent and wavered as Snoke harnessed the Force and made it his weapon. Rey thrashed in pain, screaming and seeking an escape that didn't exist.

Kylo could feel Rey's pain and panic, a bright roar in the Force that overwhelmed all else—even the dark presence of Snoke. But he did not intervene. Instead, he lowered his head and awaited his master's command.

Poe woke up slowly and then all at once. First his eyelids fluttered as consciousness returned; then he sat bolt upright, panicked, as pieces of his memory returned, jangled and misaligned.

We're in danger. Jump to lightspeed. Save the Raddus. *Hold the bridge.*

The first thing he saw was the backs of Resistance uniforms—

soldiers, techs, and pilots, as well as droids. Then, behind them, he saw the viewports of a U-55 loadlifter.

And through those windows, deep space—and the bulbous shape of the *Raddus,* rapidly shrinking.

"No!" Poe gasped, struggling to his feet. Heads turned to regard him, and his fellow Resistance members looked variously concerned, pitying, or angry.

Someone was calling his name. He knew that voice—it was General Organa.

It all came back to him—his profound relief at seeing Leia enter the bridge ahead of Resistance fighters loyal to Holdo, followed by the sight of her raised blaster and the blue concentric circles of energy that had sent him into oblivion.

"Poe!" Leia said again. "Look!"

He found her, standing in front of the windows on the other side of the transport, near C-3PO and a gaggle of officers. She was beckoning him over.

Poe forced his legs to work—his muscles were still tingling and twitching, numbed by the aftereffects of the stun blast. The officers made room for him and Leia took his hand—he wasn't sure if that was supposed to be a comfort, an apology, or concern for his shaky legs.

Filling the viewports on this side of the transport was a pale white planet adorned with dark streaks.

"What is that?" Poe asked. "There are no systems anywhere near us."

"No charted ones, no," Leia said. "But there are still a few shadow planets in deep space. In the days of the Rebellion we used them as hideouts."

"The mineral planet Crait," D'Acy said, studying the bright globe below them.

"There's a rebel base there?" Poe asked.

"Abandoned but heavily armored," D'Acy explained. "With enough power to get a distress signal to our allies scattered in the Outer Rim."

"The First Order's tracking our big ship," Leia said. "They aren't monitoring for small transports."

Now Poe understood. The transports were small—not much more than twenty meters long—and simple craft that output relatively little energy. The Resistance techs had worked feverishly to install bafflers that reduced that energy even further. With the First Order content to pursue the *Raddus* at a distance, its sensors could easily miss the stream of small craft departing the heavy cruiser.

"We'll slip down to the surface and hide unnoticed until they pass," he said. "It'll work."

But he immediately realized something else: It would only work if the eyes of the First Order sensor officers remained fixed on the *Raddus*. The transports would escape, but the heavy cruiser would not. And neither would anybody who'd stayed aboard.

Poe had a pretty good idea who that was.

"Why didn't she tell me?" he asked Leia plaintively.

Leia's eyes were gentle. He felt her fingers working at the cuff of his jacket and looked down to see she'd taken the beacon from around his wrist, restoring it to its place around her own.

"The fewer who knew, the better," she said. "Protecting the light was more important to her than looking like a hero."

Contemplating that, Poe turned to look back out the window, at the rapidly shrinking shape of the doomed *Raddus*.

Aboard the heavy cruiser's temporary bridge, Holdo stood alone at the controls, going over a checklist she'd long since committed to memory.

The *Raddus*'s system controls had all been redirected to the bridge. She could fire every turbolaser battery on the ship from here. The shield envelope was functioning properly, and a few simple commands would redirect additional power to the rear deflectors once the heavy cruiser's fuel ran out.

Holdo had no illusion that she could target enemies with anything approaching the accuracy of an on-site gunnery crew, or that the *Raddus*'s shields could stand up to a lengthy barrage once the First Order warships came within close range.

But none of those things was the goal.

The goal was to keep the ship intact as long as possible—intact and posing a threat to its pursuers. That would keep attention on the *Raddus* and not the small, hopefully undetectable craft slipping away from its belly and down to Crait.

With her people safe, Leia would know what to do—she always did. She would summon their allies, find a new base of operations, and quietly work to turn the New Republic's planetary defense forces and home fleets into a force capable of opposing Snoke and his generals.

Into a new rebellion.

The work would not be quick or easy. It would demand patience, the strength to endure the suffering of planets in the First Order's grip, and the wisdom to choose when, where, and how to fight.

But Holdo knew there was no one better to lead such an effort than her old friend—who, after all, knew a thing or two about what ragtag, fractious bands of insurgents could accomplish.

Holdo would not live to see it, and that grieved her—both because she loved life and because she knew Leia would need her in the months and years ahead.

But the faith of her homeworld of Gatalenta taught that no one who reached salvation arrived there alone—they brought along all those whose love and compassion had helped deliver them.

She had always found that thought a comforting one—the more now in the solitude of the bridge.

"Godspeed, rebels," Amilyn Holdo said quietly.

Captain Phasma marched through the corridors of the *Supremacy* at the head of a cordon of stormtroopers who surrounded Finn and Rose. DJ skulked alongside the column, obviously ill at ease.

The journey ended in a huge hangar prepared for war. Dozens of

TIE fighters were fueled and ready, tethered to their support lines. Troop transports waited to receive soldiers. Scout walkers stood in front of heavier, four-legged war machines, which were attached to the drop ships that would bring them planetside. And a full storm-trooper regiment stood in parade formation.

At the head of the troops was a man Finn recognized all too well— Armitage Hux.

Phasma led the prisoners right up to the pale, red-haired general, who was visibly seething.

Rose shot a look at Finn, who forced himself to remain expressionless. Phasma was brutal and pitiless—barracks rumors had it that she had been worshipped as the divine queen of a pre-industrial barbarian world before the First Order found her—but she was also disciplined and pragmatic.

Hux, on the other hand, was insane—irrational and perpetually enraged.

Hux eyed Finn, a muscle jumping in his sallow cheek, and then backhanded the former First Order stormtrooper.

Finn braced himself for a further assault, but Hux appeared content with the gesture—or, perhaps, the slap had hurt his hand worse than he'd expected.

"Well done, Phasma," he spat. "I can't say I approve of the methods, but I can't argue with the results."

The general's eyes were locked on DJ, who looked very much like he wanted to be elsewhere.

The *Libertine* slipped through the hangar's magnetic field, its engines whisper-quiet. Its landing gear extended and the sleek yacht settled to the deck with a stuttering of repulsorlifts, then sat silently. At Hux's command, First Order officers guided a repulsor pallet up to the ship. Atop it stood stacks of black crates.

"Your ship and payment, just as we agreed," Phasma told DJ.

Rose moved so quickly that Finn flinched. But there were too many stormtroopers between her and the Canto Bight thief. They intercepted her and held her fast, but she kept thrashing wildly.

"You lying snake!" Rose screamed at DJ.

"We got caught," DJ said. "I cut a deal."

Finn looked at him in horror. "Wait. Cut a deal with what?"

Rose bombarded him with oaths that would have made an Oto-mok stevedore blush.

DJ listened for a moment, then shrugged. "Yeah, okay. I apologize that I'm exactly who I said I was."

CHAPTER 26

No one noticed a droid.

Every day of existence brought BB-8 more evidence that this belief wasn't a hypothesis but qualified as a theory, and perhaps should even be enshrined as a cosmic law.

When the stormtroopers burst into the tracking-control room, BB-8 had frozen, waiting for someone to wonder why Finn, Rose, and DJ had bothered lugging an overturned trash can along with them. At the very least, once the threat of sabotage had been dealt with, surely some luckless stormtrooper would be ordered to take the bin to maintenance, so it could be returned to the position specified by some tediously comprehensive First Order document. With no better alternative at hand, BB-8 had decided to shock as many of the troops as possible, at full intensity, before a blaster or ion weapon ended this futile resistance.

But nothing had happened. The stormtroopers had shackled Finn and Rose and led them away. DJ had followed them. And the room had been left empty.

BB-8's first thought had been to continue his friends' mission, shutting down the tracker himself and then telling Poe to have the fleet jump to hyperspace. So the astromech had shed his trash-barrel disguise and jacked into the First Order network. He had even succeeded in freezing security protocols that would have switched the active tracking to another station if the control room's circuit breakers failed.

But that moment of triumph had been short-lived. The circuit breakers had to be thrown manually—tripping them through a power surge, even the erroneous report of one, would shut down the entire control room, with the tracking switching stations once again.

BB-8 had moaned in dismay. There was nothing he could do without his friends.

It had taken considerable gymnastics to maneuver the trash barrel back over himself—something that would have been the work of a few seconds for a friendly organic. But he'd managed it, and sped off after Phasma and her troops.

Now the astromech idled in the hallway, photoreceptors peering through the ventilation slots in the trash barrel and analyzing potential courses of action. All of them were assessed as vanishingly unlikely to succeed.

BB-8—still unnoticed but apparently helpless—whined miserably.

Inside the hangar, a First Order commander marched up to Hux.

"Sir, we checked on the information from the thief," he said. "We ran a decloaking scan and sure enough, thirty Resistance transports have just launched from the cruiser."

Hux regard DJ. He looked impressed—and surprised.

"You told us the truth. Will wonders never cease?"

The First Order general returned his attention to the commander. "Our weapons are ready?" he asked.

"Ready and aimed, sir."

Holdo's plan might well have worked, Rose thought—the bafflers would reduce the transports' engine emissions to levels that would likely go undetected, particularly at such long range and with the First Order's sensor crews tired and complacent after so many hours of pursuing the same target along the same course.

But now those crews would know where to look and what to look for. And the transports were slow, sluggish to maneuver, unarmed, and protected by only rudimentary shields.

It would be a slaughter.

Finn had reached the same conclusion. "No!" he exclaimed, horror on his face.

"Sorry, guys," DJ mumbled.

Hux was flushed with triumph.

"Fire at will," he told the commander.

"No!" Rose yelled, lunging at Hux this time. But the stormtroopers were wary of her now, and there were too many of them.

The Resistance was going to be destroyed, and there was nothing she or Finn could do about it.

The transport carrying Poe and Leia shook violently, and turbolaser fire flashed past the viewports. One of the transports vanished in a ball of fire, instantly vaporized.

Leia looked out, horrified—then turned her head to look at the surface of Crait below them. It took only seconds for her to perform the calculations.

They were moving too slowly.

There were too many transports.

The First Order knew about their ploy.

Around her, the Resistance crewers had seen the explosion—and from the dawning horror on their faces, they'd come to the same conclusion.

Poe looked over at Leia, frantic to do something—anything. He found her standing calmly, her expression stoic.

Panic wouldn't save them—or anybody else. Whatever emotions were churning beneath Leia's surface, they would remain hers alone.

Poe forced himself to try to follow her lead.

Aboard the *Raddus*, a stunned Holdo could only watch as another transport exploded.

A hologram shimmered to life at her console.

"Admiral, we're taking fire!" reported a Resistance pilot, and she could hear panic in his voice. "What do we—do we turn around?"

"No! You're too far out. Full speed to planetfall! *Full speed!*"

An instant later the hologram flared out of existence. Holdo thought she saw the pilot throw up his arms before it vanished.

Holdo choked back a dismayed cry. She had to do something. But what? There was no way the *Raddus* could defend the transports—they had moved beyond the protection of its shields.

She looked helplessly at her console, searching for some answer that eluded her. There was nothing.

A light blinked on the interface with the navicomputer.

Holdo called up the interface to dismiss whatever the alert was—it would only distract her while she tried to think—then paused.

Someone had entered hyperspace coordinates into the system, calculating a jump that had never been made. The navicomputer was asking if the coordinates should be purged.

It was Dameron, she realized—he'd rushed to the bridge as part of the plan he'd concocted, the one she'd correctly dismissed as too reckless and desperate to succeed.

Holdo called the coordinates up on her console. The Mon Calamari cruiser had kept traveling along its heading for Crait since the coordinates had been entered into the navicomputer. As a result, the entry point for the hyperspace jump Poe had calculated was now behind the *Raddus,* on the other side of the First Order fleet.

Holdo stared at her screen, trying to figure out what she had missed and concluded that her wild hope might not be completely unfounded.

Rey could feel Snoke in her head, his consciousness a live, hungry thing, carelessly sifting and sorting through what wasn't his, what he had no right to.

The Supreme Leader must have taught Kylo this ability, she realized. But he was far more skilled than his apprentice. Rey was unable to push back against him—his mere presence threatened to over-whelm her. And unlike with Kylo, she had no sense of that mind being left open to her. Snoke's presence felt like a pit, empty and cold and dark—as if the dark-side cave beneath Ahch-To had gone on forever.

Random bits of memory came back to her as the Supreme Leader scrutinized them and cast them aside. Here she was, alone at sunset on Jakku. Waking from a dream of a cool island in a gray sea. Stunned and reeling beneath Maz's castle. Holding a lightsaber hilt out in mute appeal.

She felt his interest quicken at that last moment burned into her mind. That was what he wanted: Skywalker's island, and the planet of which it was a part, and what it was called and how she had reached it.

Rey tried to blank her mind, to shut him out, to fight him off.

None of it worked. Snoke found what he wanted, took it, and dis-carded her.

She found herself on the floor of his throne room, writhing in pain, consumed by hatred for him.

He just laughed at her.

"Well, well," he said, voice oozing satisfaction. "I did not expect Skywalker to be so wise. We will give him and the Jedi Order the death he longs for. After the rebels are gone we will go to his planet and obliterate the entire island."

Rey raised her hand toward Luke's lightsaber, sitting next to Snoke on the arm of his throne. She willed it into her hand—and it flew it into the air, in a perfect arc that would end in her grasp.

Watching Rey struggle against him, Snoke smiled. Calling a light-saber into one's hand was such a trivial use of the Force—a trick for the greenest apprentice, its workings almost beneath the dignity of a master of the Force. Nevertheless, he admired the girl's resolve. She was beaten but persisted.

Such hubris would have to be punished.

Snoke twisted his fingers, altering the weapon's path so that it smacked Rey in the back of the head—then spun and continued back to its place beside him.

"Such spunk," he said, feeling the hatred swelling in her and savoring it.

It was too bad, really. The girl's power could have been catalyzed by hatred and fear, forging her into a potent weapon. In another era she would have made someone a superb apprentice.

"Look here now," he said, summoning the Force to drag Rey across the room. The red curtains of the throne room parted, revealing a curved bank of viewports. Before one of them was a lens-like oculus. Forced to stare into it, Rey saw the Resistance fleet has been reduced to one warship and a collection of small transports. The smaller ships were exploding, erased one after another by the First Order's guns.

"The entire Resistance is on those transports," Snoke said. "Soon they will all be gone. For you, all is lost."

Rey turned from the window, teeth bared. Her eyes burned like fire.

Oh yes. Such *power. A pity, really.*

"And still that fiery spit of hope," Snoke said mockingly.

Rey's hand reached out again, fingers splayed, and Snoke could feel the Force in motion around him. This time, her target wasn't Skywalker's weapon—but Kylo Ren's.

This unexpected, desperate act caught Snoke's apprentice by surprise. His lightsaber flew off his belt and across the room, the Praetorians tensing at its flight, to land in Rey's hand.

She ignited it, the crimson blade a snarl of energy, the crossguard energy channels sputtering to life a moment later, and ran at Snoke.

The guards sprang forward, blades raised, but Snoke stopped them with a raised hand, chuckling at the sight of Rey, face bathed in the red light of the unstable blade.

"You have the spirit of a true Jedi," he told her—then used the Force to fling her across the floor. She landed hard, groaning, and the lightsaber clattered and spun across the floor to land at Kylo's feet, spinning like a top.

"And because of that you must die," Snoke said, turning his cobalt-blue eyes to Kylo.

His apprentice had barely moved since delivering Rey, but his emotions had been simmering when he arrived, and begun to boil when Snoke revealed that he was the creator of Kylo's mysterious connection with Rey.

Or at least they had boiled until a moment ago. Then the tumult had ceased, replaced by an eerie calm and focus. Snoke had been surprised, but pleased. Master and apprentice had work ahead of them, and Kylo—that endlessly conflicted mixture of light and dark—had finally found himself.

"My worthy apprentice, son of darkness, heir apparent to Lord Vader," Snoke said, knowing how Kylo had yearned for such praise. "Where there was conflict, I now sense resolve. Where there was weakness, strength. Complete your training and fulfill your destiny."

Kylo rose, his unlit lightsaber in one hand and the other held carelessly behind his back. Step by step, he advanced on the helpless Rey. Snoke used the Force to hoist her to her knees, arms pinned back. He eyed Kylo, wary of some new retreat into sentiment, into the weakness that had held him back for so long. But Kylo's face was cold, and his eyes were determined.

"Ben!" Rey called out desperately.

Kylo stopped once Rey was within reach of his blade.

"I know what I have to do," he said, his voice emotionless.

Snoke laughed. Bridging their minds had been a gamble, one he had weighed for some time. But it had worked even better than Snoke had hoped. It had fooled the girl into revealing Skywalker, but it had also forced Kylo to confront his weaknesses. By eliminating Rey, he would also be excising the flawed, hesitant, weak half of himself.

Rey's eyes no longer burned. They were pleading. But Kylo wouldn't even look at her. Snoke could feel that his attention was focused on what he had resolved to do.

"You think he will turn, you pathetic child?" Snoke asked Rey. "I cannot be betrayed. I cannot be beaten. I see his mind. I see his every intent."

The Supreme Leader closed his eyes. This was a drama best appreciated through the Force, not the crude approximation offered by mundane senses.

"Yes!" he said. "I see him turning the lightsaber to strike true. And now, foolish child, he ignites it and kills his true enemy."

It was the last thing the Supreme Leader ever said.

Kylo had indeed rotated the hilt of his lightsaber so it was pointed directly at Rey's chest. But even as he did so, Luke's lightsaber was rotating silently on the armrest of Snoke's throne—unnoticed by either the Supreme Leader or the Praetorian guards.

When Kylo's fingers twitched behind his back, the blue energy blade of Luke's lightsaber sprang into existence, spearing Snoke. Then, with a flick of Kylo's hand, the blade carved through his master, cutting him in two, and flew through the air into Rey's hand as Kylo's ignited his own lightsaber.

Kylo and Rey had a moment to lock eyes. Then the crimson-armored Praetorians were blurs of motion—four sets of pairs, each pair brandishing the same variant of deadly edged weapons. It was too late to save their master, but they could at least avenge his murder.

Back-to-back, Kylo and Rey received their charge.

CHAPTER 27

Another transport was incinerated and vanished, and this time Leia flinched, closing her eyes. All those lives lost—people she had recruited or attracted to her cause, fought alongside, sent into danger and been unable to save. They were gone forever, snuffed out in an instant, and there was nothing she could do.

While her eyes were closed she felt the transport rattle and heard the stifled gasps of those around her, and knew another ship had been destroyed.

Less than half of the transports evacuating the *Raddus* remained— and they were still short of planetfall.

Leia tried to imagine a miracle—Luke arriving with a flotilla of Jedi battleships he'd discovered somewhere, or Inferno Squad returning with a task force of Starhawks. But space remained empty.

Poe, unable to stand it, hurried to the cockpit. By the time he got there the First Order's gunners had destroyed three more transports.

"Give it full thrusters! Full speed!" he urged the pilot.

"I am, sir," she replied.

He recognized her beneath her helmet: Pamich Nerro Goode. She'd been a starfighter dispatcher back on D'Qar, and rated as a pilot. Transports and shuttles, but he'd noted her ability to stay cool under fire, and seen her as fighter pilot material.

And beside her—yes, that was Cova Nell, who already was a starfighter pilot.

They had the right people, which was critical for any mission. But it didn't matter when you asked those people to do the impossible.

*

It was the sight of DJ counting his money that set Finn off.

The thief had his credits and his ride, yet he lingered, sifting through the crates the First Order had left for the *Libertine* to bear away. His reward was hard currency, of course—stacks of peggats, aurei, and zemids plundered from worlds the First Order had occupied. DJ had seen enough of the galaxy to know an electronic balance was just an arbitrary arrangement of pixels, and even an account could disappear with a few keystrokes.

Suddenly it was all too much for Finn. The yacht alone was enough to finance a fairly decent retirement, after all.

"You murdering bastard!" he howled, struggling to break the stormtroopers' grip.

DJ looked up from his work, surprised.

"Oh, take it easy, Big F," he said. "They blow you up today, you blow them up tomorrow. It's just business."

"You're wrong," Finn said.

"Maybe," DJ replied.

And it hit Finn—DJ would learn too late just how wrong he was.

Yes, there were double-dealers around the conflict—arms dealers and financiers and grifters like DJ, drawn to money and misery like mynocks to a whisper of energy in deep space.

But that didn't mean the conflict itself was their invention. It wasn't some cynical exercise beyond anyone's control. It was a show-down between those who believed in freedom, with all its messiness and uncertainties, and those who worshipped order, and saw murder on an unimaginable scale as a fair price for that order.

And everyone was caught up in that conflict, whether they admit-ted it or not. There were no bystanders and no neutrals—and no difference between what you did when faced with an evil regime and who you were.

You could pretend that regime didn't exist, or rationalize its excesses away, or seek to insulate yourself through wealth or connections, or flee it and hide, or hope that for whatever capricious reason it would crush people other than you.

And all of those things were easy to do. The harder thing by far was to fight—to attract that murderous regime's attention, and become an object of its malice.

But that was the *only* thing to do. Those who chose something else were hoping that the monster they had ignored would eat them last.

Finn had fought. It had taken him awhile to understand that running wasn't an answer, but he had figured it out. He had fought to save Rey, at first, but Poe had been right—this was far larger than one person, or two, or two billion.

And so Finn had fought for Poe, too. And for General Organa. And for Rose—who'd lost her sister and her parents and her planet and responded by fighting even harder.

He hadn't *won*—that was an annoying detail, to say the very least. But he'd fought. And here, at the end, he found he wouldn't trade having fought and lost for being DJ.

Not even if the First Order had filled a stolen yacht to bursting with coins.

Hux watched coldly as Finn struggled in his troops' grasp. FN-2187's defection had been more than an embarrassing reversal to the training program that had begun with Hux's own father—this one traitor had prolonged the search for Skywalker and given the Resistance crucial intelligence that had led to the destruction of Starkiller Base.

Hux would have liked nothing more than to consign him to an interrogation room for the better part of forever. But soon, very soon, FN-2187's treachery would no longer matter.

He eyed the young woman next to the deserter, also wasting her time battling his troops. He had no idea who she was—but the medallion peeking out of the neck of her stolen uniform struck him as familiar.

Hux stepped closer and saw he'd been correct.

"The Otomok system?" he asked, grabbing the struggling woman's face to force her to look at him. "That brings back memories. You vermin may draw a little blood with a bite now and then, but we'll always win."

He savored the fury in her eyes—at least until she bit him, hard, drawing blood from the meat of his palm and hanging on like a maddened nek.

He yelped as the stormtroopers dragged her away from him, spitting and snarling. Hux stared at the half-moon of punctures on his hand. Undoubtedly infected, given the filthy habits and utter lack of breeding the First Order had seen in that benighted star system.

Hux briefly allowed himself to return to the idea of sending both of them to the detention level for extensive interrogation. But no, his first instinct had been correct. Traitors and insurgents were vermin, and beneath his notice. He'd lingered too long as it was—a leader of his stature had far more important duties to attend to.

Still, his hand *hurt*.

"Execute them both!" he ordered, then strode out of the hangar.

Snoke's Praetorian guards advanced on Kylo and Rey in silence, their faces concealed by the faceplates of their helmets.

Rey could hear a hum from their bladed weapons and realized the edges were enhanced by ultrasonic generators. And there was something else—not a sound, but a sensation she could feel as a throb in her teeth and sinuses.

That was familiar from Jakku, somehow, and after a moment she realized what it was: an intense magnetic field, probably generated by the guards' armor. If proximity to it affected Rey this way, it had to be a source of constant pain for the beings encased in that armor.

A moment later and the guards were on them, blades whirling and whining. Rey shifted her feet, raising her lightsaber to meet one guard's polearm as he tried to split open her skull. She expected the lightsaber to cleave the weapon apart, but it merely blocked the blow, and the impact sent painful vibrations shooting up her arms and into her shoulders.

Rey fell back and dodged the segmented whip of another guard. She could hear Kylo's lightsaber spitting and crackling behind her, and his grunts of effort.

The first guard aimed a slash at her knees, which she sent wide, then turned her block into an arcing slash at his face. It nicked the brim of his helmet and he stumbled away, regarding her with new-found respect. She offered him a savage grin—only to duck as she sensed another guard aiming a windmill kick at her face.

Rey fell backward, bumping into Kylo's back. Her lightsaber rose and fell, wheeling in sweeps as the guards came at her from a bewildering variety of angles.

There were too many attacks to keep track of, suddenly, and she felt her heart begin to hammer.

A guard rushed at her with a double-bladed staff and she brought her lightsaber crashing down on its middle—then nearly fell when he yanked the weapon apart, slashing at her with a blade in each hand. Rey shifted her feet to redistribute her weight, then brought her light-saber up in a blur, knocking aside a vicious thrust from a humming voulge.

She hadn't seen the thrust coming—but the Force had warned her. *Stretch out with your feelings.*

A flurry of chops from the humming lightsaber pushed back the guard with the voulge. Rey exhaled, opening her mind to the Force, and the room seemed to snap into focus.

She sensed Kylo's excitement, and his *hunger*—as if he were a beast finally freed to confront its tormenters.

She felt the guards' coldness, mixed with determination. Their master had been undone through treachery, and they would be the instruments of retribution.

And around all of them, she perceived the ever-shifting web of the Force.

She heard a clatter of armor as one of the guards went down behind her, felled by Kylo. Two rushed Rey at once, a whip and a vicious ax flashing. The whip locked around the blade of her lightsaber, its segments sparking and flashing, but she wrested it free and batted the ax away.

Rey reached out with her hand and shoved one guard backward with the Force, then found herself spinning in the other direction. An ax struck sparks from the floor, leaving its wielder's arms outstretched in front of her.

She brought the lightsaber down hard on the armored arms and the blade hacked through them, the vibrations in her arms vanishing as the blow interrupted the armor's mag-coils and shut off the field.

The guards backed away as the ax wielder crashed to the floor. Rey risked a look at Kylo and saw him yank a Praetorian with a whip toward him with the Force, spitting him on his lightsaber blade. The man slumped and Kylo shoved his body free with his booted foot.

Rey's arm buzzed and stung as one of the guards slashed at her with his voulge, missing her with the deadly blade but striking her with his weapon's crimson housing. Rey backed off with a yelp of pain, trying to will feeling back into her tingling fingers.

She tried to anticipate her attackers' motions, using the Force to warn her where they would be. But they were everywhere now, hot and bright in her perceptions. She just barely dodged a slash at her face, so close she could smell ozone.

It was too much—even with the Force. She was tiring, and her impressions felt like they would drown her: Sensations of life, death, light, and dark poured in on her from all directions. It was too much, a challenge bigger than what her limited training had prepared her for.

So much bigger.

Rey realized she was correct—but that she'd asked the wrong question. She couldn't direct the Force well enough to last long against three elite warriors in lightsaber-resistant armor. But she could let it direct her, allow it to make her its instrument.

One of the guards rushed at her, electro-whip crackling with energy that would shock her into unconsciousness. Rey's eyes didn't track the coiling tip of the whip, but her lightsaber was there to deflect it and sent its wielder staggering away—and then the blade interjected itself between her and the slashes of another guard's twin blades.

The Praetorian with the voulge saw his opening and charged at Rey, weapon lowered to open her belly.

The lightsaber knocked it aside and found his throat.

Two left. In her hands the lightsaber was a wheel of blue fire that sent her attackers spinning away. One guard's sudden uncertainty bloomed in the Force and Rey advanced on him, his whip connecting with air, then falling from his hand as the lightsaber found a gap between his armor's segments.

Rey was breathing hard now. The guard with two blades rushed her. She dodged, but he was faster than she thought and got behind her, his weapons seeking her throat. The lightsaber spun in her hands as she switched to a reverse grip, sending the blade through her opponent's midsection. His body sagged against her back and she shrugged him off, his armor clattering against the floor.

A strange sound reached her ears—and she felt a sudden spike of fear in the Force.

Kylo had downed another guard, but the last one had him in a headlock and was forcing the edge of his weapon closer to his throat. Rey saw Kylo's black lightsaber lying on the floor where it had been dropped. He had one hand on his enemy's weapon; the other, empty, was flailing for purchase.

"Ben!" Rey called, hurling Luke's lightsaber across the room.

Kylo raised his hand and the lightsaber smacked into it as if drawn there. Kylo looked at the ancient weapon he had sought so avidly, his eyes blazing. He ignited it, then turned it off almost as quickly. The guard behind him slumped to the floor, a smoking hole in his red helmet.

Rey and Kylo stood amid the smoke and carnage, gasping for breath, then looked at each other. Rey's eyes were filled with joy.

The deck of Snoke's throne room thrummed, and the air was lit by the glow of turbolaser fire. Rey rushed to the oculus, staring at the pinpricks of light that represented the Resistance fleet.

So few.

"The fleet!" she yelled. "Order them to stop firing! There's still time to save the fleet!"

She found Kylo standing over Snoke, Luke's lightsaber in his hand. He stared down at the body of his master. Above them, the First Order banners burned.

"Ben?" she asked.

"That's my old name," he said.

"What?"

There was neither fear nor anger in Kylo's eyes now—just a deep resolve.

"It's time to let the old things die," he said. "Rey, I want you to join me. Snoke, Skywalker, the Sith, the Jedi, the rebels? Let it all die. We can rule together and bring a new order to the galaxy."

She stared at him in disbelief and horror.

"Don't do this, Ben," Rey said quietly. "Please don't go his way."

Kylo stepped over Snoke's corpse.

"You're holding on," he said. *"Let go."*

He advanced on Rey, the ignited lightsaber held loosely in one hand. But there was no threat in his approach.

Somehow, suddenly, that scared her even more.

"Do you want to know the truth about your parents?" he asked. "Or have you always known and have you just hidden it away— hidden it from yourself? *Let it go.* You know the truth. Say it!"

Rey tried to find the strength to deny him, to shove him away. But he was right. She did know the truth—and it was the same as her greatest fear, the one that had haunted her for so long.

A truth she could find no refuge from.

"They were nobody," she said.

"They were filthy junk traders who sold you off for drinking money," Kylo said. "They're dead in a pauper's grave in the Jakku desert."

Tears filled Rey's eyes. She fought to keep her emotions contained, fearing that if she released them even for a moment they would overwhelm her and sweep her away.

Kylo was a pace away now, his eyes locked on hers.

"You have no place in this story," he said. "You come from *nothing*. You *are* nothing."

And then his eyes softened.

"But not to me. Join me. Please."

He turned his uncle's lightsaber off and stretched out his hand to her.

CHAPTER 28

As Hux departed from the hangar, surreptitiously shaking the hand Rose had bitten, the stormtroopers drove Finn and Rose to their knees.

Phasma stared down at them, and Rose realized she could see herself, small and distorted, in the First Order captain's chrome gargoyle mask.

"Blasters are too good for them," she said. "Let's make it hurt."

Rose looked over at Finn, who was trying to break the stormtroopers' grip on him, and had a strange thought: At least she was dying beside him.

It was true that she'd wanted to strangle him for the first few hours after meeting him, which wasn't the best start to a relationship. But they'd fought together on Canto Bight and in the very heart of the First Order. They'd fought for the Resistance, despite Finn's initial reluctance. And they'd fought for each other.

Somewhere in that whirlwind of events Rose had started to trust him. And more than that, she'd begun to care for him.

"On my command," Phasma said, and the stormtroopers holding them in place shifted uneasily.

Did Finn know what Phasma had in mind for them?

Rose glanced over at him, and the look on his face made her wish she hadn't.

Aboard the *Raddus,* Holdo hastily rechecked that the heavy cruiser's navicomputer hadn't kicked back the overrides that she'd had to program into it. Proximity alerts flashed on the console, but she ignored them.

The First Order flagship began to slide across space ahead of the *Raddus,* outside the temporary bridge's viewports. Turbolaser fire continued to lance out from its bow, destroying the Resistance transports seeking safety on Crait.

Holdo reminded herself that there was only one way to help the evacuees—if she attracted the First Order's attention too early, her desperate gambit would come to nothing. The only thing she could do was wait.

Captain Peavey stood at attention on the *Supremacy's* bridge, watching as yet another Resistance transport vanished into flame.

"Your gunnery crews have done excellent work, Captain," he said to Yago, pitching his voice to be heard in the crew pits. "I commend them."

Yago received this praise with a stiff nod, but beneath his reserve Peavey thought the man was pleased.

The Mon Calamari warship's captain had clearly hoped that the transports fleeing its hangar would go undetected at such long range—a gambit that might have succeeded if not for a tip from Hux, of all people, to zero in on trace emissions in the cruiser's vicinity.

Once the *Supremacy's* crews had analyzed the emissions, it had been relatively straightforward for comm/scan to home in on their signatures, discover the ruse, and begin picking off the transports one by one. But at this range, the crews' accuracy was still impressive.

Yago's officers had trained them well, and Peavey intended to make sure they got the credit. Given all the work they had ahead of them, it wouldn't do to have resentments fester among the navy's top ranks.

"What is that heavy cruiser doing, though?" Yago asked, eyeing the holotank suspiciously.

Peavey glanced at the holotank, curious what the other captain had seen.

At this range, the First Order's turbolaser blasts could destroy the transports, but simply bounced off the heavy cruiser's shields—and the Mon Calamari warship's own guns were no threat to the First Order flagship. So the *Supremacy* had simply ignored the Resistance ship, dismissing it as a distraction.

"She's coming about," Yago said. "Scan the engine signature for gamma radiation."

Peavey nodded. He had expected the Resistance captain either to jump to hyperspace in the hope of drawing off the First Order pursuit, or to make a suicidal attack in order to buy time for the transports. It appeared the captain had opted for the former, though he had to know it was far too late for that tactic to succeed.

Before Peavey could consult with Yago, Hux swept onto the bridge, looking agitated. His boot heels rang on the polished deck.

"Sir, the Resistance cruiser is preparing to jump to lightspeed," a monitor called up from one of the crew pits.

Peavey turned an inquiring glance at Hux, hoping the hotheaded young general wouldn't do something rash.

For once, he didn't.

"It's empty," Hux sneered. "They're just trying to pull our attention away. Pathetic. Keep your fire on those transports."

Peavey offered Yago a look of mild surprise—carefully calibrated to be too mild for Hux to notice—and saw that Yago had reacted the same way, matching Peavey's ever-so-slightly raised eyebrow with a minute cock of the head.

Then, subtle message having been exchanged, they resumed their rigid, unimpeachable posture.

Poe watched in despair as another transport was destroyed. Just six remained—six unarmed, defenseless ships between the First Order and galactic domination. He tried to imagine anything that might change their fate, but there was nothing.

Connix looked from a sensor screen to the *Raddus*.

"Our cruiser's priming her hyperspace engines," she said. "She's running away!"

"No she isn't," Poe said.

There was nowhere to run, and Holdo knew it. Besides, Poe had been on the bridge. There'd been no courses loaded into the navicomputer—until he'd programmed one himself.

He knew what Holdo planned to do.

Ahead of the *Supremacy*, the Mon Calamari warship was turning, its bulbous nose swinging around, back toward the First Order task force that had harried it for so long.

Peavey waited for the ship to vanish, followed by the telltale twisting of space and burst of Cronau radiation that marked a hyperspace wake. He idly tried to imagine where the heavy cruiser might be heading. It didn't much matter—Peavey doubted the cruiser had enough fuel for another jump once it arrived. Once these last few transports had been eliminated, the First Order could retrieve the warship at its leisure.

But the cruiser hadn't jumped. Peavey leaned forward, curious, and realized Yago and the other officers were doing the same— horrified realization etched on their faces.

They knew what the Resistance captain planned to do.

"My God," Peavey said.

"Fire on that cruiser!" screamed Hux.

In the ruined throne room, Rey regarded Kylo's gloved hand, held out to her in supplication.

She reached out with her own—and before Kylo realized her aim, she had snatched Luke's lightsaber out of his grasp with the Force. The weapon tumbled toward her hand—and then froze in midair.

Kylo, his entreaty rejected, had flung up his own hand, harnessing the Force to arrest the lightsaber's flight.

The weapon hung in the air between them, quivering faintly. Rey stared at it, willing it into her grasp. But Kylo was pulling it toward him with equal determination.

Between them, the lightsaber shivered and danced.

They stared at each other, eyes locked.

Rey could feel the Force heaving like the sea on Ahch-To, whipped into a fury by their attempts to manipulate it. And she could feel the kyber crystal at the heart of the weapon seeking a resonance, trying to find harmony where there was only dissonance. Caught in their tug-of-war, the crystal seemed to keen in the Force, a wail that Rey could feel in her bones.

She and Kylo were sweating now, neither willing to give so much as a millimeter in their standoff.

Until, finally, the crystal sheared apart, its unleashed energy tearing the lightsaber's housing in half and filling the throne room with a flash of brilliant, blinding white.

The second he heard the tramp of boots, Finn knew what Phasma had ordered for him and Rose.

Every stormtrooper battalion had a small number of soldiers assigned to execution duty. But there was no special executioner unit—rather, the assignment was random, and any trooper could draw it. They did so anonymously—executioners' armor never transmitted the number of the trooper beneath it. Unquestioning obedience was the duty of every First Order stormtrooper, and so was enforcing that obedience.

The troopers' ranks parted and the executioners advanced, wearing the armor reserved for them: a helmet with a black stripe, black carbon shoulder bells, and a specialized chest plate with black markings.

Rather than blasters, they carried laser axes. A touch of the activation switch and each ax haft sprouted four pairs of emitter claws. Suspended between each was a monomolecular filament of brilliant cyan energy that could cut through anything.

A stuttering buzz rose from the energy filaments—a noise Finn had always found weird and unsettling. Each time he'd drawn execution duty, he'd devoutly hoped the day would end without his having to carry out such an order. He wondered if the troopers chosen today had hoped the same thing.

"Execute," Phasma ordered.

The whine of the axes change in pitch as the troopers raised them for the killing stroke.

Before it fell, the world exploded around them.

Under ordinary operations, the presence of a sizable object along the route between the *Raddus*'s realspace position and its entry point into hyperspace would have caused the heavy cruiser's fail-safes to cut in and shut down the hyperdrive.

But with the fail-safes offline and the overrides activated, the proximity alerts were ignored. When the heavy cruiser plowed into the *Supremacy*'s broad flying wing, the force of the impact was at least three orders of magnitude greater than anything the *Raddus*'s inertial dampeners were rated to handle. The protective field they generated failed immediately, but the heavy cruiser's augmented experimental shields remained intact for a moment longer before the unimaginable force of the impact converted the *Raddus* into a column of plasma that consumed itself.

However, the *Raddus* had also accelerated to nearly the speed of light at the point of that catastrophic impact—and the column of plasma it became was hotter than a sun and intensely magnetized.

This plasma was then hurled into hyperspace along a tunnel opened by the null quantum-field generator—a tunnel that collapsed as quickly as it had been opened.

Both the column of plasma and the hyperspace tunnel were gone in far less than an eyeblink, but that was long enough to rip through the *Supremacy*'s hull from bow to stern, tear a ragged hole in a string of Star Destroyers flying in formation with it, and finally wink out of existence in empty space thousands of kilometers beyond the First Order task force.

From his post at the port viewports of one of the six remaining Resistance transports, Poe saw the *Raddus* elongate into a streak of light that shot through the First Order flagship, shearing it in two and leaving a fiery trail to mark its ruinous passage through the fleet.

Soldiers and crewers cheered and hugged, but Poe and Leia remained silent and solemn, weighed down by Holdo's sacrifice.

Though ripped in two, the Mega-Destroyer continued to hurtle through space along its last heading—the *Raddus* had passed through it with such astonishing speed that what was left intact barely slowed.

The transports, now unhindered, flew on.

When Finn's eyes snapped open he discovered that Rose was struggling to drag him across the starship's deck.

Finn shook away the cobwebs and scrambled to his feet next to her, blaster raised. Around them, all was chaos—thick smoke filled the hangar, the bodies of stormtroopers littered the floor, and sirens blared. BB-8 inclined his head at Finn, obviously whistling and beeping in concern, but he couldn't hear the astromech.

He tried to figure out what had happened. He'd been tensing for whatever followed having one's head removed from one's body, and hoping the old barracks tales of severed heads studying their surroundings and trying to speak weren't true. Then the hangar had shook, hard enough that all the stormtroopers crashed to the deck around them. An enormous sound had filled his ears, the hangar, everything.

And then darkness.

"Finn! Come on!"

Rose yanked on his hand, pulling him toward a First Order light shuttle that looked intact. That was a good idea, he decided—he'd never heard of a journey aboard half a ship ending well.

An explosion rocked the hangar, sending BB-8 flying and forcing them to duck. Finn spotted a flash of reflected fire and his heart sank. A moment later Phasma emerged from the smoke, two dozen stormtroopers arrayed behind her. The troops fanned out, blocking their route to the shuttle, and raised their rifles.

Well, that hardly seemed fair.

Then Finn was stumbling backward from an eruption of heat and light that sent stormtroopers hurtling in all directions. Amid a thunderclap of sound, Finn looked over to see a two-legged scout walker struggling to free itself from its moorings. As it fired another barrage of shots, the cables holding it in place ripped away the walker's cabin, revealing BB-8 at the controls.

The headless scout walker stomped across the hangar, looking like it was going to topple over with every step—and opening up on the stormtroopers with its chin guns. Every blast sent white-armored troops flying.

"That crazy droid's given us a chance—let's go!" Rose yelled.

Finn looked at the walker in shock—BB-8 was driving that? Then he ducked a laser blast, seeking cover with Rose behind the hunks of debris littering the hangar.

As her stormtroopers hurried to set up a repeating blaster that could take out the scout walker, Phasma strode across the hangar with her rifle raised. Rose sent a hasty volley of shots her way, but they went wide as Phasma rushed their position.

One of the executioners' axes lay on the deck where its wielder had abandoned it. Finn scooped it up, slashing down at Phasma's head as she raised her rifle. She saw the blow coming and raised her blaster to intercept it.

The ax cut her rifle in two. Finn grinned as his former commander tossed the useless halves of her weapon away. But before he could press his advantage, Phasma yanked a short steel baton off her utility belt. A quick whiplike motion extended it into a double-ended spear as long as she was tall.

"You were never anything more than a bug in the system," she told him, voice dripping with contempt.

"Let's go, Chrome Dome!" Finn yelled back, taking a wild swing with the ax. She blocked it and nearly ran him through, forcing him to give ground. Behind her, the scout walker was taking apart the hangar piece by piece, the stormtroopers forced to flee from its murderous fire.

Growling, Phasma whipped her spear at Finn, alternating vicious jabs with slashes aimed at his head, chest, and legs. He parried with the haft of the ax, sparks leaping with each impact, and looked for an opening in her defenses.

But there wasn't one—she was both faster and stronger than he was. It was all he could do to keep the ax between the two of them as she rained blows on him from every direction, driving him steadily backward and forcing him to dodge to avoid tripping over the bodies of stormtroopers killed by the blast that had knocked him unconscious.

She was maneuvering him toward a shaft in the hangar floor, he realized—probably a lift for bringing heavy equipment up from a lower level. Flames were licking out of the opening.

Finn tried to dodge sideways, but Phasma intercepted him and it was all he could do to raise the ax at the last possible second before she split his skull open. But his weapon shivered and then broke.

"You were always disobedient," Phasma said, the staff in her mailed fists. "Disrespectful. Your emotions make you *weak*."

He tried to grab the spear as she brought it back down on him, but she knocked him backward, into the heat and wind boiling up from the *Supremacy*'s depths.

The chrome-armored stormtrooper had advanced on Finn with murderous single-mindedness, heedless of the scout walker or the other hazards around them. Rose had squeezed off a few shots in her direction but could do little more—she wasn't a trained sharpshooter, and the slightest mistake could mean a blaster bolt found Finn instead of his enemy.

Besides, Rose knew all was lost if the stormtroopers took out BB-8's walker. It was a miracle that the warship around them had held together as long as it had, and they couldn't push their luck any further. They had to get out, and the shuttle was the only ticket available.

Rose kept up a steady stream of fire at the stormtroopers, taking advantage of their preoccupation with BB-8 and leaving several motionless on the deck. She tried to line up a shot at the leader's caped back, but she dodged a blow from Finn and the opportunity was lost.

Finn, she saw, was being driven back toward a flaming pit in the deck. Rose yelled for him to be careful, but there was nothing she could do. As she watched in horror, the chrome-armored trooper knocked him into the inferno.

But a moment later he emerged from the flames, riding atop the turbolift platform he'd landed on and aiming a vicious uppercut with his broken ax at his attacker. The blow knocked Phasma down and split her mask open. Through the shattered chrome Rose could see a pale blue eye in a pale face.

"You were always scum," she spat.

"Rebel scum," Finn replied coolly, and a moment later the floor collapsed around his former commander. Phasma fell, vanishing into the fire.

The hangar shook, an ominous vibration rolling through it.

BB-8 had maneuvered the scout walker near Rose. She scrambled atop it.

"Hey, need a lift?" she yelled at Finn, praying he'd hear her.

Fortunately, he did.

He leapt atop the walker, which stomped across the hangar. Flames rose from vents and conduits around them.

"We need to go and we need to go now!" Finn yelled as they abandoned the walker and hurried for the ramp of the bat-winged shuttle.

"Working on it!" Rose yelled back.

"Can you fly this thing?"

"It'll be okay."

Finn looked alarmed.

"Would you rather stay here?" Rose asked.

The hangar shuddered and a gantry came loose from its moorings above, slamming to the deck behind them. BB-8 whistled urgently.

"It'll be okay," Finn said hastily.

"That's the spirit."

She hurried into the cockpit and was relieved to discover the controls were straightforward—and even more relieved when the shuttle powered up immediately. Back on D'Qar it would have been no surprise to discover that important components had been cannibalized or the fuel siphoned off.

Rose yanked back on the controls and the shuttle jerked off the deck. It shuddered as one wing scraped the wall of the hangar. Finn put his hands over his eyes.

"You're not helping! I've got it now!"

"Then punch it!" Finn said.

Rose hit the accelerator and the shuttle leapt forward, flames rising around it. It quivered as it passed through the magnetic field that kept the hangar's atmosphere contained, then steadied. Rose dipped its nose, leaving the doomed First Order warship in their wake.

After the chaos of the hangar, the silence in the cockpit was somehow unnerving—all three of them simply sat for several moments, the only sound Rose's and Finn's ragged breathing.

"So where are we going?" Rose asked.

Finn's eyes turned to the white expanse of Crait.

"Where we belong," he said.

CHAPTER 29

The decks of the *Supremacy* that had been in the path of the *Raddus*'s jump to hyperspace no longer existed—they had been excised as if with a surgeon's knife. Elsewhere, whether crewers lived or died depended on quirks of the mighty warship's construction as systems failed in cascades up and down the severed halves of the flying wings. Clouds of escape pods surrounded the remnants of the mighty ship, and all channels were jammed with frantic calls for assistance.

The *Raddus* had hit left of center, sparing the section of the Mega-Destroyer that housed the overbridge and the throne room. Which was fortunate for Hux—as the bridge descended into chaos, he had hurried to the turbolift connecting it with the Supreme Leader's sanctum. It wasn't until after he'd stepped into the lift and used his code cylinder to access the throne room that he realized it might not work.

He looked around frantically, gripped by the fear that he'd consigned himself to an ignominious end—the architect of the First Order's military domination spending his last moments trapped in a turbolift. But the lift descended so smoothly, Hux had no idea anything was wrong.

Then the doors opened and that illusion was snuffed out. The throne room was a scene of unfathomable carnage. Snoke's alien navigators had fled, his fearsome guards were dead, and the Supreme Leader himself lay crumpled in a heap in front of his throne. Kylo Ren, motionless, was sprawled nearby.

A single glance was enough to tell Hux that Snoke was dead. But Ren was merely unconscious, his chest rising and falling.

Hux stood over the Supreme Leader's body in shock for a moment, trying to process everything that had happened and calculate everything that could happen next.

The First Order's flagship—which was also its mobile capital, its greatest shipyard, its best research-and-development facility, and so much more besides—was doomed. Yet the Resistance had been reduced to a pathetic handful of ships trapped on a backwater world. And the New Republic was no closer to resurrection. The imminent end of the *Supremacy* would change surprisingly little about the balance of power in the galaxy.

But one thing was certain: The First Order would need a new Supreme Leader.

Snoke was dead. Ren was not.

Moving quietly and carefully, Hux stepped away from the Supreme Leader's corpse and looked down at Ren. His hand crept to the pistol in his holster.

Kylo stirred, his eyes fluttering.

Hux turned the move for his blaster into scratching at a phantom itch on his leg and took a step back. When Kylo's eyes opened he would find the general looking down at him with apparent concern.

"What happened?" Hux asked.

It took Kylo a moment to gather himself.

"The girl murdered Snoke," he said.

The throne room lurched sickeningly around them. Hux knew what that meant—the complex system of inertial dampeners and acceleration compensators that protected the core decks of the *Supremacy* was failing. They had to hurry. But Kylo was confused. He braced himself, staring out in disbelief at the mangled half of the flagship and the wrecked Star Destroyers beyond it.

Hux marched over to a sealed door, studying the readout next to it.

"What happened?" Kylo asked, seeing his expression.

"Snoke's escape shuttle is gone," the general replied.

Kylo considered that. Rey had recovered first. She must have realized he was at her mercy, yet she'd left him alive.

Almost as if she cared for him.

Well, it was another foolish, sentimental decision. And this one would be her destruction.

"We know where she's going," he snapped at Hux. "Get our forces down to that Resistance base. Let's finish this."

The general fixed him with a look of disdain.

"Finish this? You presume to command my army? We have no ruler. The Supreme Leader is dead."

Kylo said nothing. Screeching speeches and superheated rhetoric were Hux's departments. Sometimes action was a far more effective message.

He raised his hand, commanding the Force and directing it to coil around Hux's throat.

"The Supreme Leader is dead," Kylo said.

Hux's airway closed and the world began to go gray. He sank to his knees before Kylo, eyes wide with fear.

"Long live the Supreme Leader," Hux told Kylo.

Kylo released him, the gesture offhand and almost contemptuous, leaving Hux to gasp for air.

The First Order shuttle hung in space, bathed in the dazzling light reflected from the surface of Crait.

The command shuttle's cockpit was simple and functional. Rey had slipped away from the two halves of the *Supremacy* to a vantage point far from the First Order task force and the planet below. As long as she did nothing foolish, she knew, the craft's low profile and sensor countermeasures would keep her safe from detection until the *Millennium Falcon* arrived.

And then, she hoped, she and Chewbacca might be able to help their friends.

Rey's fingers traced the beacon on her wrist—the one Leia had promised would light her way home.

But home to what? She hadn't seen exactly how many transports had escaped, but she knew it was only a handful. The First Order commanders would be bent on destroying the survivors.

And Kylo would be one of those commanders.

It might have been otherwise.

Rey had stood over Kylo, lying unconscious on the floor of the throne room after the detonation of Luke's lightsaber, and she had seen very clearly what she could do. It would be so easy to take up his blade, ignite it, and end his life. How many lives would the work of a few moments save? How much darkness would be prevented?

She had stood in the throne room and seen herself doing it—and yet she had immediately known that she wouldn't.

Luke's error had been to assume that Ben Solo's future was predetermined—that his choice had been made. *Her* error had been to assume that Kylo Ren's choice was simple—that turning on Snoke was the same as rejecting the pull of the darkness.

The future, she saw now, was a range of possibilities, which were constantly reshaped by the outcome of events that seemed minor and decisions that seemed small. It was very hard not to see the future that dominated your hopes or fears as fixed and immutable, when in fact it was just one of many. And more often than not, awareness of the Force wouldn't help you find the path through those branching, twisting possibilities.

The Force could show you the future, certainly—but *which* future? The one that was to be? Or the one that you yourself would bring about, drawn to it helplessly? Even if that was the future you most hoped to avoid?

Rey had learned that the Force was not her instrument—that, in fact, it was the other way around.

Just as Kylo was its instrument, despite his determination to bend it to his will. He would learn that one day, she sensed—the Force wasn't finished with him. And that meant Kylo's life was not hers to take, whatever future she thought she saw ahead of him.

Rey would wait, however difficult that would be to do as the First Order warships descended on Crait. She would wait, and the future would unfold as the Force willed.

That had always been true. The difference was that now she understood it.

PART VI

CHAPTER 30

Planetfall always left Leia Organa a little disoriented. She supposed it was the transition between space travel and atmospheric flight that bothered her: Within a few minutes a planet changed from an object below you in space to the entirety of your surroundings, and it was strange to think that the two were in fact one and the same.

But this time, it was a relief to be enfolded by the outer envelope of Crait's atmosphere. Her transport and the five others that had survived were finally safe from the First Order's turbolasers.

But not for long, she knew.

Leaving Poe at the portside windows, she walked across the deck to the cockpit, acknowledging the nods and salutes of the weary soldiers, pilots, and technicians.

Goode and Nell were both exhausted, drained by a journey in which they'd been helpless, surviving only through luck that had eluded too many others. Leia knew there was a price to pay for being spared in such a fashion. All too soon, Goode and Nell would recall their escape from the *Raddus* not with relief at having lived but with guilt that others had not. And Leia knew that guilt would never leave them.

Leia acknowledged the problem and put it aside, out of mind. It was real, and she would do her best to help them, but it would only matter if they survived the coming hours.

So she verified that Goode and Nell had the coordinates Holdo had sent to all the transports, offered them encouraging words and a hand on the shoulder, and then left them alone—flying a brick like a U-55 loadlifter was chore enough without having the leader of the Resistance standing behind you.

She found Poe squinting out the viewport at the brightness around them. They were below the ionosphere now and able to discern surface features: vast white plains streaked with red and shot through with thin ribbons of blue, bordered by high, thin mountain ranges.

"We're not equipped for cold weather," Poe said anxiously.

"We don't need to be," Leia replied. "That isn't snow. It's salt."

Poe frowned, studying the planet below. He wasn't the first to be fooled by the broad expanses of Crait's salt pans.

"You've been here before," Poe said.

Leia nodded. "When I was young. Back before the hyperdrive was invented."

That at least got her a smirk and a dismissive wave.

She let her mind go back decades, to the first time she'd seen this lonely world. She'd been a teenager then, an apprentice legislator in the Imperial Senate and a princess preparing to claim the crown of Alderaan, as per her homeworld's ancient traditions.

Clues in obscure records had convinced Leia that something was happening on Crait, and she'd recklessly taken it on herself to investigate—only to stumble across an insurgent camp. One that had been established by her father, using Alderaanian credits funneled into secret accounts by her mother.

"It was a mining colony once," Leia told Poe. "Abandoned because a labor dispute ate into the profit margins. The mining company built a shelter with blast doors to guard against crystal storms. That was what caught my father's eye, back when he was putting the Rebellion together. His techs added a shield against orbital bombardment, but the real work had already been done."

She had Poe's attention now—he had grown up on his parents' Alliance war stories, and as a young New Republic pilot his disappointment at missing out on the action had been palpable. She doubted he felt that way now.

"So there was a rebel base here?" he asked.

"No," Leia said. "The Alliance didn't exist yet. By the time it did, the Empire had changed its patrols, and my father worried that ship traffic in the area would be detected. We considered Crait as a new principal base after Yavin—did a survey and even brought some equipment. But there were complications."

Poe raised his eyebrows inquiringly, but this wasn't the time for telling tales.

"The coordinates went in my files after the peace with the Empire," Leia said. "The files I kept just in case."

That made Poe nod. Most of the Alliance's military secrets had been turned over to the New Republic immediately after its formation, and had proven critical in the short, savage war against the remnants of the Empire. But Leia, Ackbar, and other rebel leaders had made sure to keep a few things back, as a safeguard against disaster. Their secret files contained navicomputer data for secret hyperspace routes, the location of rebel safeworlds, and any number of bolt-holes and equipment caches. Without them, the Resistance would have ceased to exist soon after its formation.

"Well, I suppose this qualifies as 'just in case,'" Poe said.

"I suppose it does," Leia said gravely, extracting her comlink. "Now let's hope the codes for the blast door still work. Or we're going to look pretty silly camped out on the doorstep when the First Order arrives."

Fortunately, both Leia's codes and the blast door's huge drive mechanisms did still work. The transports flew low over a ridge and Poe spotted the grooves of trenches cutting across the salt plains, leading to a massive slab of a tower with a yawning portal set into it.

The transports came in low across the plain and set down in the tower's gloomy interior. The last soldiers were coming down the ramp of the sixth and final transport when the first alarm was raised.

Leia hurried to the entrance and saw what she'd feared she'd see: the dots of new ships descending through the atmosphere. Holdo's sacrifice had knocked the First Order back on its heels and given them time to reach the planet, but the respite had been temporary.

"They're coming," she said grimly. "Shut the door."

Poc relayed Leia's orders, shouting into the dim interior of the mine. The Resistance evacuees were busy doing any of a hundred things: unloading crates of equipment from the transports, trying to get consoles powered up, and passing out rifles and blast helmets.

"Get that shield door down and take cover!" Poe yelled.

An eerie tinkling noise reached his ears and he spied pinpricks of light at the back of the cavernous interior, in the deep shadows beyond the transports. He looked more closely, wondering if he was seeing things.

But no, it wasn't his imagination. There really were animals back there—dozens of them. They were small—not much higher than a person's knee, with long, pointy ears and drooping whiskers framing their faces. Their bodies glittered in the transports' lights, and Poe realized what he'd thought was fur was actually a dense covering of crystal bristles. When the creatures moved, their fur made a sound that reminded him of the wind chimes of distant Pamarthe.

Whatever they were, they posed no threat—they weren't hostile, just baffled that the quiet of their den had been disrupted by strange, two-legged invaders. Nor did they fear the new arrivals—after a few moments of indecision they snuffled at the Resistance soldiers curiously.

Poe shrugged. The galaxy was full of surprises. One day, maybe, he'd get to sample a few of them in peace.

One day, but not today.

The massive door was creeping downward. Poe silently urged it not to jam on its tracks or run out of power before it shut.

"Poe!"

That was Leia. He hurried across the base's interior, dodging Resistance crewers, and stood next to her, just outside the heavy door. His boots crunched through loose bits of salt, and the air had a tang that was sharp in his nose.

A bat-winged ship was racing across the plains, barreling directly for the base. Six TIE fighters were trailing it. Poe couldn't tell if they were escorts or pursuers, but the Resistance soldiers outside must have seen something he hadn't, because they opened fire.

Poe expected the shuttle to veer off but saw at the last moment that the pilot was too desperate to do so. Poe backpedaled frantically and dived for cover as the shuttle's top wing struck the blast door with an earsplitting screech. The wing sheared away and the craft tumbled across the deck, scattering Resistance fighters, and skidded to a halt in a shower of sparks. Behind it, the door shut with a deep boom.

Leia picked up a rifle and started raking the front of the shuttle with blasterfire. Poe and several soldiers joined her, and the shuttle's viewports exploded.

Someone yelled frantically and a familiar pair of hands emerged from the shattered window, raised in surrender.

"Don't shoot!" Finn cried out. "It's us!"

Once the firing stopped he popped his head out, next to a wide-eyed Rose.

"Finn!" Poe said. "You're not dead! Where's my droid?"

The ramp descended and BB-8 rolled out, whistling energetically.

"Buddy!" Poe said, patting the astromech's head and trying to make sense of the answering stream of droidspeak. "Really? That sounds intense. Look, we're a little busy but you'll have to tell me all about it later."

Finn, still shaken, tried to get his breath. Rose looked around the base's interior, shock and dismay on her face. Six transports, a hundred or so people.

"Is this all that's left?" she asked Finn.

But Finn had no comfort to offer her. No one did.

"You know which end of a hydrospanner is which," Poe told Rose. "That makes you our engineering department. Follow me—we need you."

Leia had remembered the way to the base's control room, but she wasn't prepared for what poor condition it would be in. Years of salt corrosion had left the controls rusty and pitted, and the musk in the air suggested the foxlike creatures had made it part of their home.

Fortunately, the guts of the base's systems had been sheltered and shielded. A few splices and workarounds and a hasty search for batteries got the key equipment powered up and more or less functional.

Poe exhaled and nodded at Finn and Leia.

"All right," he told the Resistance members who had been pressed into service as technicians. "Shields are up so they can't hit us from orbit. Use all our power to broadcast a distress signal to the Outer Rim."

"Use my signature code," Leia said. "This base has sat derelict for thirty years—we meant this to be a hideout, not a fortress. Any allies of the Resistance, it's now or never."

Rose entered the control room, and Finn could see the exhaustion on her face and in the way she held herself. She was barely keeping herself together. But then that was true of all of them.

"What have we got?" Poe asked, though Rose's expression had already told him that he wouldn't like the answer.

"Rotted munitions, rusted-out artillery, some half-gutted ski speeders," Rose said helplessly.

Poe nodded. There was nothing he could say—if the base had a secret stash of gunships or hidden turbolasers, Leia would have known about it.

Finn scowled and Poe knew what his friend was thinking—that they'd traded being dead in space for being dead in a hole. After all, it was what they were all thinking.

"Let's pray that big-ass door holds long enough for help to come," Poe said.

As if in answer, a boom rattled the room—deep, low, and resonant. A trickle of red dust fell from the ceiling.

After a moment, another boom rolled through the caverns. And Finn knew no barrier would keep the First Order out for long. Its leaders would crack the very planet in two to get at them.

CHAPTER 31

A number of exterior cams provided a view of the sodium plains surrounding the base, and a few of those cams had survived the long years of inactivity. Finn peered through a viewing apparatus in the control room, reporting on what he saw.

Leia had been called away to record the request for help that would be beamed to the Outer Rim, and in her absence the tension in the room grew as soldiers and crewers pushed beyond their limits allowed their despair to show.

Poe and Rose, at least, were filling the anxious minutes trying to find something—anything—that might change their situation. The general's message might be heard, but it would do no good if allies arrived to find the base a charred wreck and no one left to save. Poe had sent the droids to find schematics of the base and ordered techs to get the decrepit artillery emplacements working as a last line of defense, while Rose was inventorying anything they might be able to repair and use in a fight, from speeder bikes to ski speeders.

Finn, for his part, was using the exterior cams to study what the First Order intended to throw at them in a ground battle. He was certain those were heavy walkers that the drop ships had landed—AT-ATs, and maybe also the heavy AT-M6s. Depending on the First

Order's assessment of their defenses, there might also be AT-STs and speeder bikes, supporting troops as pickets.

And there would be TIE fighters providing air cover.

One thing puzzled Finn, however: A dozen huge First Order transports were descending in perfect formation. That didn't match any procedure he was familiar with—and after a moment he saw that they were lowering a massive cylinder. It touched down and a moment later Finn could feel the ground shake.

He cranked up the magnification on the scope and shook his head when he saw what they had delivered.

"A battering-ram cannon," he reported grimly. "Miniaturized Death Star tech. It'll crack this door open like an egg."

That was it, then—the instrument of their doom.

"There has to be a back way out of here, right?" Rose asked.

BB-8 rolled up to them, beeping. C-3PO tottered along in the eager astromech's wake. All eyes turned to the droids with whatever hope could be mustered.

Behind the two droids, Finn saw the glowing eyes of more crystal foxes. The creatures had gotten over their fear of the Resistance members and seemed curious about them, though they remained easily spooked.

"Beebee-Ate has analyzed the mine schematics," C-3PO said. "This is the only way in or out."

Another impact rattled the control room as the First Order continued testing the strength of the massive door. The faces around him were bleak with despair—even Poe's.

Finn shook his head. He hadn't come this far just to let the First Order win. And he knew none of the rest of them had, either. They just needed to remember that.

"We have allies," he said. "People believe in Leia. They'll get our message. They'll come. But we have to buy time."

"Time for what?" a pilot asked in despair.

"For help to come," Finn said. "For Rey to return with Skywalker, for Leia to figure out a plan, for the First Order to mess up, for a miracle. What are we going to do, *not* fight? We have to take out that cannon."

Poe nodded, smiling at Finn. And Rose grinned.

"You said the magic word," she said.

"What? *Fight*?" Finn asked.

She shook her head and gave him another smile—one with real affection. Her eyes, he saw, were wet. "*We*."

"Load up," Poe said. "Let's do it."

The ski speeder hangar became an assembly line, with Rose and several other newly minted technicians directing astromechs to check each craft's systems and make a determination: ready to fly, needs repairs, cannibalize for parts.

No ski speeder fell into the first category, but with a little creative thinking and hasty tinkering Rose and the techs were able to get thirteen ships primed and powered, even amid the rhythmic booms of impacts on the shield door and reports that the First Order had landed tug walkers and started dragging their siege cannon across the salt plains.

The ski speeders had begun their existence as civilian craft, built to capitalize on a long-ago fad for asteroid slalom-racing. An oversized engine was set amidships, with outriggers on either side—one for the gyroscopic cockpit, the other for an equipment boom. Below the engine was a halofoil mono-ski designed to keep the speeder anchored. It was locked into a guide in the floor, one that led to a launch chute at the end of the hangar.

The demise of the asteroid slalom craze had consigned most ski speeders to the galaxy's junkyards. But a few had survived and found new life as explorer craft in asteroid settlements, and Crait's anti-Imperial insurgents had put them to use as patrol vehicles. The Crait techs had grafted twin laser cannons onto the equipment boom, locked out the cockpit's rotation, and up-armored the ski speeders with surplus hull plating.

Rose had to salute those techs—they'd done ingenious work. But the ski speeders had been intended to tackle smugglers or pirates. The vanguard of a First Order army was way more than any sane person would expect them to be able to handle.

Poe was helping General Ematt prepare a last line of defense in Crait's warren of trenches. As she waited for him to arrive in the hangar, Rose tried to figure out how to tell him of her reservations.

She'd only stammered through the beginning of her litany when he held up his hand.

"I know, I know," he said. "It's like someone knocked over a museum nobody wanted to visit in the first place. But it's what we've got so we'll make the best of it. Anyway, thirteen birds is a lot more than I thought we could get flying. Great work."

"Um, at least tell your pilots they've got to pick their targets," Rose said, scrubbing engine grease off her hands. "Those fire linkages are brittle, and you'll overload them if you shoot at everything that moves."

"Good idea," Poe said. "But why don't you tell them yourself? Since you're going up with us."

"Me?" Rose looked at him in disbelief. "I'm a maintenance tech, not a pilot. Remember?"

"When's the last time you tightened a pipe?" Poe asked.

"About a minute ago."

"Okay, fine, but that's not the point. You landed that shuttle with six TIEs on your tail and a big damn door closing on top of you, didn't you?"

"Crashed it, you mean."

"A wise man once told me any landing you can walk away from is a good one," Poe said. "Besides, who's going to look after Finn?"

Rose saw that Finn was fumbling with a pilot's headset. He looked up, saw Rose's surprise, and crossed his arms over his chest.

"What? I'm the guy who's most familiar with what they're going to throw at us. And the only one who's ever seen that big cannon of theirs."

"This isn't like flying a shuttle, which you were kind of bad at."

"I'll just do what you do. How hard can it be?"

Poe stepped in before Rose could reply.

"You see? This is why we need you."

Rose started to object, but Poe shushed them. Leia had entered the hangar, C-3PO following behind.

"Red Squadron used these same speeders to fight off Imperial scouts," Leia said. "And I flew one on that mission. According to Poe, that makes me an expert."

A few of the pilots and crewers smiled, though some of the younger pilots looked astonished. Leia saw their reaction and managed not to roll her eyes.

"The ski's there for stability—it's to make sure your engine provides thrust and not lift," she said. "Help it do its job. You go airborne, you're an easy target."

She eyed them to make sure they'd registered that, then continued. "The First Order's landed heavy walkers. They're using TIEs as air support. The walkers are muscle, designed to take out artillery and ground defenses. You can't outslug them, so don't try. But you can outfly them. The TIEs will be a bigger threat. That's another reason to stay close to the deck."

The pilots nodded, though Rose noticed a few studying the ski speeders doubtfully.

"Our objective is that cannon," Leia said. "It's the only thing that can crack our front door, so let's try not to let it get in range. It's being towed by tug walkers—squat, ugly, lots of legs. If we take the tugs out, the cannon stops. If we break the cables they're using to pull it, the cannon stops."

The pilots were listening intently now.

"We've transmitted our message," Leia said. "I don't know who will respond, or when. But I do know we're not alone in this fight—and every minute of time we can steal from the First Order increases our chances. Any questions?"

There were none. Poe stood next to Leia, eyeing his pilots. When she nodded at him, he stepped forward.

"Well, I asked for a dozen T-85 X-wings with cloaking devices," he told them. "Guess they got held up in transit."

Nien Nunb laughed, but he was the only one. The others just stared stonily at Poe.

"Still, you just heard that Red Squadron flew our birds," he said. "I grew up hearing about those men and women and dreaming that maybe I could fly like them one day. Nobody thought those pilots had a chance either. And you know what they did? They took down a Death Star."

Rose smiled. So did a couple of the other pilots.

"Good luck," Leia said. "And may the Force be with you."

The pilots got to their feet and began donning helmets, checking headsets, and pulling on gloves. Meanwhile, techs and astromechs started firing up the ski speeders. The sound of their engines rose from a low thrum to a steady whine.

Poe climbed into the open-air cockpit of the first speeder in line. Finn was next, then Rose. She tightened the chin strap on her helmet, verified she was receiving the squadron channel, and checked her console. All systems were green—for the moment at least.

"Everything good, Finn?" she asked.

Finn turned and gave her a thumbs-up.

"Your comlink works, you know," she replied.

Another thumbs-up. Fair enough.

"Launching," Poe said. "Follow my lead."

His ski speeder slid forward along the guide into the low chute at the end of the hangar, and was lost from sight. But a moment later everyone heard him yelling delightedly over the squadron channel. Rose, familiar with pilots, couldn't resist smiling—if nothing else, Poe would have one last ride behind a control yoke, where he was happiest.

Paige would have been crowing, too, Rose knew. She touched her Otomok medallion and smiled sadly.

If you're out there somewhere, Pae-Pae, I could use your help.

Finn's speeder slid into the chute. Then Rose's jerked forward, hesitated, and began to advance more smoothly. Darkness enclosed her, and then the ski speeder began to move, the thrum of the engine rising to a roar as the walls of the chute blurred past her.

Well, here goes nothing.

CHAPTER 32

General Ematt emerged from a narrow door leading out of the mine into the old rebel trench, blinking at the brilliant light reflected off the white plains. Behind him came Sergeant Sharp, fussing with his blast helmet.

The trench walls were a deep red, dusted with white. Metal planking lined the bottom of the trench, encrusted with accumulated drifts. A pair of artillery cannons loomed over the trenches. Poe had assured Ematt that they'd fire. Ematt decided he'd believe that when he saw it—they looked like the recoil from the first shot would turn them into a pile of rust flakes.

Inside, they were passing out blaster rifles to anyone who seemed like they were more of a danger to the enemy than to the person next to them. Passing out rifles and small arms, and checking a store of old rebel ammunition cartridges to see which had any charge left.

They'd be the last line of defense, after the speeders and the artillery. Ematt hoped it wouldn't come to it, while knowing it probably would.

Well, if so they'd make the First Order pay a price for every millimeter of ground.

Ematt clambered out of the trench and onto the plains, the massive shield door looming behind him. As he scanned the horizon with his quadnocs, Sharp leaned down to pinch a few snowy white flakes. He tasted them and spat.

Sharp looked back and saw that their footprints had lifted away the powdery salt, which now caked the bottoms of their boots. Where they'd stepped, crimson crystal soil had been revealed.

Ematt lowered the quadnocs and spoke into the comlink on his wrist.

"Ground forces incoming," he warned.

"Copy that," Poe replied. "On our way."

Slots opened high in the shield door and the ski speeders hurtled out, their outriggers flexing in the wind. The descent was half glide, half powered flight, and Rose fought to keep her craft stable. Her stomach lurched as she tried to take in her surroundings, from the salt pan rushing up at her to the distant dots of the First Order ground forces.

Then she looked over and saw Finn grinning, apparently hypnotized by the experience of finding himself in the air—and not thinking about what it would be like to hit the ground.

"Hey, dummy!" she yelled into her headset. "Engage your mono-ski!"

Finn looked around, startled, and hunted for the switch. Just when Rose was certain he'd crash, he found the control that deployed the mono-ski. It emerged from the bottom of his speeder's engine mount a moment before their ski speeders hit the salty crust.

The impact of her own speeder's touchdown forced the air out of Rose's lungs, and for a moment she was sure the craft would shed its cannons, her cockpit, or both. But then the speeder had bounced back up onto its ski and she was racing across the white expanse next to Finn, part of a line of speeders advancing across the plains.

Their skis sliced through the layer of sodium atop the ground, kicking up a wake of crystalline dirt beneath the crust and giving each speeder a brilliant red tail that extended behind it like a flag.

Poe had to pull his foot back after a panel gave way beneath it, sending a chunk of hull plating spinning off across the plain.

"What the hell? I don't like these rustbuckets and I don't like our odds. Keep it tight and don't get pulled too close until they roll that cannon out front."

Rose could see the First Order walkers in the distance ahead of them, but not the siege cannon. She reached into her jumpsuit and pulled out her Otomok medallion, hanging it from a lever on her speeder's console.

"Ground forces, lay down some fire," Poe requested.

The Resistance forces in the trenches heard his order and the artillery cannons opened up, blaster bolts streaking across the salt plains toward the First Order lines. A few bolts struck the walkers, but did no damage that Poe could see.

As the wind whipped past his cockpit, Poe considered their situation—and didn't like his conclusions. The bulk of the First Order ground forces were heavy combat walkers. Each leviathan had a massive turbolaser cannon built into the top of its back, and reinforced forelimbs designed to brace against the recoil. Their armor was far too heavy for the Resistance ski speeders' blasters to penetrate.

Above the walkers, TIE fighters circled like predatory birds. And above them, Poe's sensors painted a lone command shuttle—undoubtedly the ship from which the assault would be directed. The speeders' guns were powerful enough to destroy a TIE or the shuttle, but Poe knew the Resistance craft would be shredded if they tried to gain altitude and engage them.

The siege cannon would be more vulnerable—or at least Poe devoutly hoped so. But the First Order was wisely keeping it behind the lines, safeguarded by the walkers. Any attack against it would have to brave both the walkers and the TIEs—which was tantamount to suicide.

It might come to that, Poe knew. But he wasn't going to throw away his pilots' lives unless he could see no other choice. So for now, he'd probe the First Order's line but try to keep his squadron intact and hope the enemy made a mistake—or something changed the odds.

Poe was right about the command shuttle—it housed Kylo, Hux, and several other high-ranking First Order officers, all staring down at the battlefield and monitoring sensor feeds.

Kylo would have preferred to supervise the assault alone—Hux, he knew, would see the relatively straightforward operation as an opportunity for self-aggrandizement. But it was critical to keep the ambitious general close at hand. Hux had eliminated a number of rivals during his rise to power—including his own father—and Kylo had no intention of joining their ranks. With Hux beside him, there was no chance of an accident befalling the command shuttle—and every opportunity to remind the general and the other officers who was in charge.

"Thirteen incoming light craft," Hux said. "Shall we hold until we clear them?"

"No," Kylo replied. "Push through. The Resistance is in that mine. This is the end."

The First Order made its move with the ski speeders still some distance from their lines, ordering the TIE fighters to abandon their holding position over the walkers and engage. Blaster bolts churned through the sodium crust, sending up plumes of red that reminded Poe unsettlingly of blood, and one of the ski speeders blossomed into flame.

"Fighters!" Poe yelled. "Break off!"

The speeders scattered, with TIEs swooping down in pursuit. A dozen chases weaved across the plain, leaving it scarred with crimson pockmarks and slashes carved by the ski speeders' halofoils.

Poe brought his speeder around in a tight turn, the frame of his outrigger emitting a groan of distressed metal, and took aim at a TIE fighter that was looking for an opportunity to strafe one of the speeders. Finding himself too low to line up the shot, Poe yanked back on the control yoke, letting the ski speeder bounce up above the plain.

Still too low. C'mon, baby, gimme a little air.

The ski speeder bounced a little higher and Poe mashed down the trigger, his laser cannon spitting fire. The TIE sheared in two, its solar panels spinning off in different directions.

Poe's crow of triumph was cut short as he had to dodge another TIE swooping down from above, where his guns couldn't reach.

"We can't match this firepower!" C'ai Threnalli warned in his native tongue.

"We've got to hold them till they pull out the cannon," Poe replied.

A pilot screamed as his speeder was ripped apart by cannon fire, the TIE that had destroyed it banking high above the plains. The Resistance artillery tracked it and blasted it to pieces, but the TIEs responded to that threat by wheeling around and raking the vulnerable troops in the trenches.

Finn flinched as the speeder next to his was hit. He peered forward through the windscreen, blinking at the glare, and tried to find the First Order cannon amid the towering shapes of the combat walkers.

Blasts carved through the ground nearby and he juked his speeder back and forth, hoping to spoil the fighters' aim. They were losing speeders—why wasn't Poe ordering them to go after that cannon?

Another speeder vanished in flames, its pilot's cry dissolving into static.

We're losing.

Then his eyes widened.

"Rose! Behind you!"

Three TIE fighters chased Rose's ski speeder across the plains, laser cannons firing deadly bursts. Before Finn could turn to help her, the first TIE was incinerated. Then the second one vanished in a ball of fire. Then the third was gone.

Rose dodged debris raining down from the skies, then looked up to locate her savior. Her eyes widened at the sight of a battered freighter hurtling overhead. The ship looked like it wasn't in much better shape than the ski speeders—but somehow it maneuvered like an X-wing.

She didn't recognize the ship, but apparently Finn did, because he let out a crow of triumph.

Aboard the *Millennium Falcon*, Chewbacca saw the TIEs explode and let loose with a Wookiee battle cry—one echoed by the porg sitting on the console next to him.

Meanwhile, in the lower turret, Rey wheeled and fired at more of the TIEs. Another one exploded and she bared her teeth in a predator's grin. The First Order pilots had been so busy terrorizing their groundbound prey that they'd forgotten the sky might hold other hunters.

"Oh, I like this," she said, blasting yet another TIE.

Aboard her stolen escape shuttle, Rey had waited in increasing frustration as the First Order's Star Destroyers formed a cordon above the planet and drop ships began descending, bearing walkers and a mysterious cylinder she didn't recognize.

She'd hoped that Finn and General Organa were down there and hadn't been caught aboard one of the many transports she'd seen destroyed. It was terrible to think that they might already be dead—or might die while she waited helplessly for the *Falcon* to return. By the time the freighter had emerged from hyperspace she'd been frantic—and annoyed Chewbacca enough that he silenced her with an aggrieved howl as she hurried through the air lock.

The Wookiee sent the *Falcon* spinning away from a pair of TIEs, leaving Rey perfectly positioned to bracket one fighter in her gunsights. She took a moment to admire Chewbacca's grace as a pilot, letting herself sink into the Force and allowing it to guide her actions. As two more TIEs flowered into flame, she spotted more TIEs inbound, having left their position above the First Order walkers. The fighters formed a loose line behind the *Falcon,* jockeying for a shot at its stern.

"Chewie!" Rey yelled into her headset. "Peel off from the battle! Draw them away from the speeders!"

Chewbacca accelerated away from the battlefield, the TIEs strung out behind him like the tail of a child's kite. Below, Rey watched creatures with crystalline fur running along the sodium plains, their eyes intent on the strange avians above them.

Ahead, a crevasse split the salt pan like a great red wound. The freighter dipped down into it and Rey stared at the walls of the canyon in amazement—they were studded with outcroppings of crystal that flashed in the sun.

Behind them, two TIEs collided, the pilots misreading each other's intentions as they sought a safe heading through the rapidly narrowing crevasse. The explosion sent chunks of crystal spinning away from the walls. One block punctured the main viewport of a fighter, sending it spinning into the walls. And Rey peppered the other TIEs with murderous fire.

From the cockpit of his ski speeder, Poe watched in amazement as all the TIEs chased the *Falcon,* vanishing into the skies to the north.

"She drew them all off—all of them!" he said wonderingly.

"Oh, they *hate* that ship!" exulted Finn.

"There it is!" Rose yelled over the comm.

Poe saw what had caught her eye: Two tug walkers were dragging the siege cannon out in front of the main force. The tugs reminded Poe of massive beetles, stumping along on multiple hexagonal limbs. Thick cables connected the tugs to the cannon, hauling it along with minimal help from its repulsorlifts.

Shorn of their fighter cordon, the First Order commanders had apparently decided to press the attack. The walkers sent blast after blast in the direction of the Resistance redoubt, scattering soldiers in the trenches.

"Our only shot is right down the throat," Finn said as the six remaining ski speeders raced for the cannon.

Inside the command shuttle, Kylo was fuming.

The sight of his father's battered ship had filled him with fury, and he'd screamed for the gunners to blow it out of the sky. Hux had promptly dispatched all fighters to do so, stripping the walkers of air cover and leaving their gunners struggling to target the nimble speeders—which were racing for the siege cannon.

Kylo didn't think the speeders could damage the massive cannon, which was almost ready to start the firing sequence. But he'd also thought Starkiller Base was impregnable—and his mother's vermin had turned the superweapon into a debris ring in the Unknown Regions.

"All firepower on those speeders!" he ordered.

"Concentrate all fire on the speeders!" yelled Hux.

Kylo looked at him with distaste.

"Hold tight!" Poe yelled as the walkers turned their attention away from the distant trenches and opened fire on the speeders, sending gouts of red shooting up from new craters blasted into the salt. It felt like his speeder was going to come apart even if none of the laser blasts found its target.

"That is a *big* gun," Rose said in astonishment.

He could only agree. The siege cannon reminded him of a massive gun barrel, two hundred meters in length, with a glowing orange core. Poe banked his speeder and raked the cable connecting the cannon with one of the tug walkers, hoping to see it part under fire. Guns atop the tug walker opened up, forcing him to swerve away.

Undeterred, Poe came around for another pass, heavy fire all around him, and stared at the cable in dismay. He'd merely scorched the surface.

The core of the siege cannon began to glow brightly, and Poe saw smoke rising from it. As he watched in disbelief, the sodium began to melt in front of the cannon, the crust running like liquid. Even at this distance, he could feel the heat of it.

Another speeder exploded, hit by fire from one of the walkers. Poe saw Nien Nunb slide his own speeder over to fill the hole in the formation and admired the cool efficiency of the old rebel veteran's maneuver.

But it wasn't enough to change the outcome, Poe realized. Nothing could do that now. They'd failed.

The cannon was just a couple hundred meters away, but Poe refused to let himself be tempted. His speeder would be cooked before he got close enough for it to matter.

"Pull off!" he ordered.

"*What?*" He could hear the disbelief in Finn's voice.

"The gun's charged. It's a suicide run! All craft, pull away."

"No! I'm almost there!"

"Retreat! That's an order!"

The other three ski speeders pulled away, following his lead, but Finn's continued to race toward the cannon.

"Finn, it's too late!" Rose yelled. "Don't do this!"

"I won't let them win!" Finn said, his voice wild.

"No!" Rose yelled. "Finn, listen to—"

She saw him paw the headset off and fling it aside. He was just fifty meters from the cannon, seeking to fly straight down the barrel—but his speeder was already scorched and blistered. And ahead of him the air itself was burning, ignited by the terrifying heat of the cannon's tracer beam.

No, Rose thought, teeth gritted. They'd come too far together for her to watch while he threw his life away. She banked her speeder hard, following Finn's heading. Her medallion swung wildly on the console. She grabbed it, jamming it around her neck a moment before her speeder smashed into Finn's, just short of the massive cannon's muzzle.

The impact sent Finn's speeder tumbling out of the cannon's path while Rose's slewed wildly, its outrigger coming apart. Then the ground rushed up at her, a crimson-and-white whirl.

Sound.

Rose couldn't tell where it was coming from in the darkness around her, but she knew it was important, somehow. Important and connected with her.

She tried to focus on it, but her head hurt too badly. Everything hurt, in fact. She just wanted to sleep, in the hope that the pain and the noise would recede, would let her be.

She heard the sound again, and realized it was her name.

It was Finn's voice calling her name. Urgently, his voice full of fear.

Rose forced her eyes open. She was slumped in the twisted cockpit of her ski speeder, or what was left of it. The plain around her was a chaotic jumble of salt chunks and red dirt. Finn was running toward her. And behind him, a maelstrom of smoke was rising into the air.

She tried to call to him, to tell him where she was, and that she was okay. But she had trouble making her voice work. And she was pretty sure that she was not, in fact, anything close to okay.

She opened her eyes and saw his face next to hers, eyes wild.

"Why did you stop me?" he asked.

Rose willed her voice to work. This next part was important. She had to make him understand.

"*Saved* you, dummy," she said. "That's how we're going to win. Not fighting what we hate—saving what we love."

The First Order cannon fired, a brilliant scientific sun. A massive bolt of energy crossed the plain between it and the shield door, igniting the air with a roar and sending a hot wind whipping across the salt flats.

As the shield door was torn apart, Rose inclined her head and kissed Finn—just in case he hadn't heard her, or had missed her meaning.

The big goof had a good heart. But he also had a way of missing the obvious.

CHAPTER 33

High above the battlefield, safe in the shelter of the command shuttle, Kylo watched impassively as the siege cannon went dark, its fires spent. The massive door protecting the remnants of the Resistance was riven by a fissure down its center, and huge chunks of stone fell from the edges of the wound.

Beside Kylo, Hux surveyed the damage with a mixture of awe and pleasure.

This was the future, he knew—Resistance dead-enders and New Republic revanchists fleeing the First Order's might until there was nowhere left to run, then cowering in holes on forgotten worlds. It would do them no good—they would be dug out by Hux's machines and dragged out by his troops.

It would be slow work—but never tedious. Because he would enjoy every engagement, surrender, and execution. The galaxy had been hobbled by disease for far too long, but Hux had sterilized the infection. Now he would cut out the dead tissue.

Ren, he sensed, shared his satisfaction at seeing the goal they had pursued for so long finally at hand.

"General Hux, advance," he said. "No quarter. No prisoners."

The Resistance officers inside the mine turned away from the enormous light and heat of the blast, keeping their faces averted until the shaking and the rumble of falling stone had subsided.

Leia lowered her hands from her face and found sunlight streaming in through the breached door. It lent a strange beauty to the gloomy chamber within, as if the site had been transformed into a cathedral.

Connix looked up from her console, where she'd been monitoring their transmissions. "There's no response."

D'Acy looked grave. "Our distress signal has been received at multiple points," she said. "But no response. They've heard us, but nobody's coming."

Leia's face fell. She gathered herself, reflexively reaching back into her memory for a hundred speeches she'd made during a hundred desperate battles, for words that would give these brave fighters the strength and courage they needed to keep on.

But there was nothing. And she wasn't going to peddle false hope to these men and women. They deserved better.

"We fought to the end, but the galaxy has lost its hope," she said. "The spark is out."

An awful silence hung over the mine. Then it was broken by slow, deliberate footsteps from a darkened tunnel in the back of the chamber.

Luke Skywalker walked into the room, clad in black Jedi robes. His hands—one flesh and blood, one mechanical—reached up for his hood and pushed it back. His dark beard was just beginning to gray and his eyes were a bright blue, studying each of the Resistance fighters in turn.

Leia watched her brother approach in disbelief. She was dreaming, and for a moment that made her angry. Here, at the end, her mind had broken and left her seeing things.

But no, everyone else in the room was looking where she was looking, their expressions amazed.

"Luke!" she said.

"Master Luke!" C-3PO said with evident delight, winning a nod and a smile from his former master.

That, finally, convinced Leia—droids didn't hallucinate.

Apparently C-3PO's data banks lacked guidance about the proper etiquette for greeting long-vanished masters who'd somehow conjured themselves halfway across a galaxy: For once the protocol droid chose to remain silent. His photoreceptors followed Luke as he crossed the room to stand before his sister.

"I know what you're going to say," Leia said. "I changed my hair."

"It's nice that way," Luke replied and then his smile faded. "Leia . . . I'm sorry."

"I know. I know you are. I'm just glad you're here, at the end."

Her brother's expression was grave.

"I came to face him, Leia. But I can't save him."

Not long ago, she knew, this would have pierced her to her core. But now there was nothing but a dull ache.

"I know," she said. "I held out hope for so long, but now I know. My son is gone."

Luke's eyes were warm—with understanding and love, but something else, too. It was knowledge, she sensed—a knowledge vast, deep, and strange, but also comforting. It had changed him—remade him utterly—yet the Luke of her youth remained, at the heart of whatever he had become.

"No one's ever really gone," he said quietly, leaning forward to kiss her on the forehead as he took her hands in his.

When they touched, she immediately understood. A slight smile played at the corners of her mouth, and her eyes shone with the secret the two of them now shared.

Brother and sister stood like that for a moment. Then Luke let go of Leia's hands. Offering C-3PO a wink, he walked with those same unhurried steps into the light pouring into the Resistance's refuge, out through the shattered door, and onto the surrounding plain.

Leia opened her hand and smiled at the sight of Han Solo's dice, resting in her palm.

Working quickly, Finn rigged a makeshift travois out of broken hull plating and wiring and strapped Rose to it. He didn't have time to process what she'd said to him, before she kissed him, or to worry about how badly she might be hurt. He had to focus on getting her to a safe place. Fortunately, he remembered his survival training—or, more accurately, he'd drilled enough that it had become muscle memory, with his hands knowing what to do even while his brain stumbled and fumbled.

It occurred to him that, ironically, he had Phasma to thank for that.

There was a long crack in the door to the old rebel base now. Finn double checked that Rose wouldn't fall off the contraption he'd rigged, tilted the travois, and began to pull it behind him, hurrying across the salt plains toward the distant lines of the trenches.

He kept glancing at the towering walkers, fearing that at any moment one of the huge, animal-like heads would tilt their way and open fire. But the walkers simply trudged along without taking any apparent notice of them.

After a moment he realized why.

They don't think we matter. Because they know they've won.

The biggest problem was more mundane—crossing the plain. The battle had opened craters in the salt crust—bowls of red, some of them still crowned with faint coils of smoke. Around them, the sodium layer had been shattered into chunks that grabbed at Finn's feet and left the travois bogged down. Elsewhere, the crust was intact but dangerously slippery. The wind had picked up, and tiny flying nodules of salt stung Finn's face.

He settled into a determined jog—a pace he hoped wouldn't exhaust him or cause Rose too much pain—and tried not to think about what would happen if he got her back to the shattered base. In all likelihood, any medical droid that wound up treating Rose would belong to the First Order, and he'd have accomplished nothing but ensuring she'd be in good health on the day of their execution.

But what was he going to do instead? Leave her to die?

And besides, Rey was still out there somewhere. As long as that was true, they had hope. He wouldn't stop believing in that, or in her.

The trenches were close now, lines of deeper red snugged up against the mountainside.

". . . dragging me," Rose mumbled behind him.

"What's that?" he asked. Finn was breathing hard now and stopped for a moment, to make sure he wasn't hurting her any more than he had to.

Rose peered at him, eyes hazy.

"When we met I was dragging you," she said quietly, and gave him a smile. "Now you're dragging me."

He nodded and smiled back at her, then hurried for the trench.

"We've come a long way, haven't we?" he said.

He reached the trench and half fell into it, then slid the travois over the lip as gently as he could. Rose was peering out at the shield door, puzzled.

"Who is that?" she asked.

Finn looked and saw a man in robes walking across the salt plain. He was making his way toward the line of walkers, looking for all the world like he'd decided this battlefield was the best place in the galaxy for a stroll.

Hux saw the lone figure on the plain and peered down in disbelief as the man walked, seemingly unconcerned, into the teeth of enough firepower to level a good-sized city. Was the man blind, and about to be revealed as spectacularly unlucky? Had some member of the Resistance opted to commit suicide in dramatic fashion?

Amused, he glanced over at Ren—and whatever he had been going to say died on his lips. Because the new Supreme Leader looked like he was staring down at a ghost.

"Stop," Kylo said.

His order was swiftly relayed, and the mighty line of First Order walkers came to an obedient halt. They were barely four hundred meters from the shattered door and the Resistance soldiers huddled within.

The man stopped. He looked up, into the sky, and suddenly the hair on the back of Hux's neck rose. Somehow he knew that the man down there on the scarred landscape was looking straight at them, his gaze fixed unerringly not just on the shuttle but on one person inside.

Hux looked at Ren's face and saw terror—naked and undisguised. That fear meant weakness—and *opportunity*.

"Supreme Leader?" Hux asked, careful to ensure his tone was that of a solicitous underling. "Shall we advance?"

"I want every gun we have to fire on that man," Ren said. "Do it!"

The first walker to receive the order opened fire, its chin guns hammering away in succession. As flames engulfed the lone man on the battlefield, the other walkers began to fire.

As Ren stared wide-eyed at the tumult of fire below, Hux watched him, his mind calculating.

His father, Brendol, had told him how the Jedi had maintained their power by seizing Force-sensitive infants and training them as warriors. The Jedi had agreed to lead the Republic's clone armies, but turned on Chancellor Palpatine and tried to seize control of the Senate. The clones—ironically, another order of soldiers trained from infancy—had prevented this betrayal, turning their guns on their former generals.

The Jedi had deserved their fate, Brendol said—but there was much to learn from their methods. As there was from the training regimens of the Republic's clones. The elder Hux had forged elements of both orders to create an army of soldiers trained as soon as they left the cradle—an army that had originated under the Empire but achieved its full glory under the First Order and the younger Hux.

So, in a sense, the First Order's stormtroopers were the Jedi's legacy.

Hux smiled at that. It would be the sorcerers' final legacy, then.

The First Order had thrived despite Snoke's weakness for mystical nonsense, but that was because Snoke had kept himself largely shrouded from view, letting his directives speak for him.

Ren had never been so wise. He was incapable of it—a slave to his emotions. That wouldn't do in a Supreme Leader. It would endanger all Hux and his technologists had created.

Well, Hux wouldn't allow that. And the more delusions Ren suffered, the easier it would be to arrange for him to be sidelined and eliminated.

As the *Falcon* raced back toward the battlefield, Rey hurried up the ladder from the gun turret and joined Chewbacca in the cockpit. Dread knotted her stomach as she saw the massive crack in the shield door and the lines of First Order war machines so close to it. Then all the walkers' guns began firing at once, focused on one precise point.

Rey and Chewbacca exchanged a bewildered glance.

"Better go around the back," Rey suggested.

The Wookiee barked his agreement.

There was no sign of the man who'd begun his walk across the ruined plain—just a massive pillar of roiling fire and smoke, a conflagration renewed by the energy poured into it amid the continuous thunder of the First Order guns.

In the command shuttle, Kylo Ren had gotten to his feet and was staring down at the strange spectacle below. His fists were clenched and there were tears in his eyes.

"More!" he yelled.

Hux looked at him uneasily.

"We've surely—" he began, but Kylo cut him off.

"More!" he howled.

The firing continued, the fusillade of energy tinting the white salt around the blast point orange and red.

"Enough," Hux said. *"Enough!"*

The First Order commanders looked at one another uncertainly. Kylo said nothing, collapsing into his chair. After a moment, Hux's order was obeyed and the firing stopped.

"You think you got him?" Hux asked acidly, not bothering to hide his scorn.

Far below the shuttle, the column of smoke and flame continued to whirl and churn. Kylo stared down at the salt plains, but his gaze couldn't penetrate the aftermath of the destruction.

Hux eyed Ren with disdain. "Now, if we're ready to get moving, we can finish this."

"Sir . . ." the shuttle's commander said tentatively.

Beside him, Kylo raised his eyes almost unwillingly. As if what was happening below them wouldn't become real if he didn't look.

But that only worked in ancient myths, the kind of stories told to entertain children.

Out of the fiery column below stepped Luke Skywalker, his robes not so much as singed, his gaze still locked on the shuttle. He brushed invisible dust from his shoulders, his face radiating contempt.

Kylo got to his feet, eyes riveted on his uncle.

"Bring me down to him," he ordered the pilot. "And don't advance our forces until I say."

"Supreme Leader, don't be distracted!" Hux urged. "Our goal is to kill the Resistance! They're helpless in the mine, but every moment we waste—"

Kylo harnessed the Force, used it to seize Hux, and hurled him into the wall of the command shuttle's cabin. Hard enough to shut him up, certainly, and maybe to kill him. He didn't particularly care which.

"Right away, sir," the shuttle commander said hastily.

CHAPTER 34

Finn entered the mine with Rose in his arms, yelling for a medpac. Resistance fighters hurried over and took her gently from him, moving her to a hovering gurney that had been brought up for the battle. Finn watched the soldiers bear her away, head hanging from exhaustion. Around them, the crystal fur of the foxes tinkled in the gloom.

Finn looked out through the great crack in the door, where one man with a laser sword had gone to face down the entire First Order. Between the arrival of the *Millennium Falcon* and what he'd learned of Rey's mission, he'd realized who that man must be—a legend come to life, when the Resistance needed one most.

"Was that . . . ?" he asked Poe.

"I think . . . yeah," Poe replied.

Poe knew Luke Skywalker wasn't a figure out of myth, but a real man—his own mother, Shara Bey, had escorted his shuttle away from the second Death Star and accompanied him on a mission after its destruction.

But then Poe had grown up on Yavin 4, playing in the shade of an uneti tree his mother had been given by Skywalker himself, and which he'd told her was a seedling of one that had grown at Coruscant's Jedi Temple. And Poe had honed his flight skills in Yavin's debris ring, dodging chunks of scorched and twisted Death Star plating passed over by scavengers.

Still, Skywalker had all but vanished by the time Poe was an adolescent, pursuing ancient Jedi secrets amid strange stars. What was happening on the plains of Crait, Poe sensed, belonged to a vanished era of the galaxy. It might never be witnessed again.

The command shuttle descended, engines grumbling as its huge wings folded upward. It sat silently in front of Luke for a moment, like a massive black raptor studying him. Then, with a hiss of hydraulics, the ramp lowered and Kylo Ren stepped out into the cracked chaos of the salt flats.

Luke had registered nothing beyond his nephew's presence when he'd found him with Rey, back on Ahch-To. Now he blazed in Luke's sense of the Force, almost radiant with power. It was the kind of power Luke had foreseen for him—first as near-infinite promise, then later as an equivalent peril.

That power was fed by emotions so strong, they seemed almost to pollute the Force around Kylo. Rage poured out of him, and a near-malignant cruelty—a lust to deform and destroy everything around him, to blot it out and erase it.

But those emotions weren't the most powerful ones Luke sensed in his nephew. Even stronger than the anger were Kylo's pain and fear. They filled him, threatening to devour him.

Ben Solo had sought to abandon everything he had been, even casting aside his name. But Luke sensed that Kylo Ren was just a shell around the same broken boy he had tried so hard to reach.

Once, Luke had thought he would be the one who might mend what was broken in Kylo. Later, he had blamed himself for the damage.

Both thoughts had been vanity, he realized now. Whatever had broken in Kylo, it was far beyond Luke's ability to fix.

Kylo had been studying Luke as well. Now he spoke, his voice thick with venom.

"Old man," he said. "Did you come back to say you forgive me? To save my soul, like my father?"

"No."

When he realized that was Luke's only answer, Kylo snatched up his lightsaber. The crimson blade crackled and growled, flakes of salt hitting it and flowering into sparks.

Luke's hand went slowly and deliberately to his own lightsaber, a shaft of blue emerging from the hilt. He and Kylo took up their dueling stances, eyes fixed on each other.

Poe watched the confrontation through his quadnocs. The sun was sinking toward the horizon, stretching Kylo's and Luke's shadows across the plain.

"Kylo Ren," Poe told Finn. "Luke's facing him alone."

"We should help him!" Finn replied. "Let's go!"

Poe wanted to smile—was this the same Finn who'd insisted he wasn't here to join another army? And not so long ago, he would have reacted the same way—looking for anything he could fly and blasting off across the plains. But he'd learned there were other ways to fight— and that those who chose them were no less brave.

Poe studied the two figures standing in front of the command shuttle for a long moment.

"This isn't just a family reunion," he told the remaining Resistance fighters. "Skywalker's doing this for a reason. He's stalling him so we can escape."

"Escape?" Finn asked, incredulous. "He's one man against an army. We have to go help him! We have to fight!"

Leia joined them, trailed as always by C-3PO. She and Poe exchanged glances.

"No," Poe said. "We are the spark that will light the fire that will burn down the First Order. Luke's doing this so we can survive. There has to be another way out of the mine. Hell, how'd *he* get in?"

"Sir, it is possible that a natural, unmapped opening exists," C-3PO said. "But this facility is such a maze of endless tunnels that the odds of finding an exit are fifteen thousand four hundred twenty-eight—"

As he delivered this grim news, C-3PO's analysis of Poe's posture and facial expression indicated the pilot was listening intently. That was a relief—in C-3PO's experience, most organics were notoriously poor listeners.

But Poe was also holding up one finger.

"Shh. Shh. *Shut up!*"

"—to one," C-3PO concluded, feeling it would be irresponsible to leave so important a calculation incomplete. Strictly speaking, he didn't need to listen, not even while his vocabulator was active. He simply reorganized his sensory inputs according to perceived importance. Which was easily done.

"Oh," C-3PO said. "My audio sensors no longer detect—"

"Exactly," Poe said.

He stepped a few paces away from the group, staring into the dark tunnels leading away from the main chamber. It was quiet—eerily silent.

Finn's eyes widened in realization. "Where'd the crystal critters go?"

C-3PO thought of reminding Captain Dameron that the creatures were properly referred to as vulptices, but decided this information would be dismissed as of nominal value given current events. Similarly, the Resistance members probably would be deplorably uninterested if told that the proper term of venery was *a skulk of vulptices*.

Which was most unfortunate. Terms of venery were one of those quirks of organic language that C-3PO found fascinating. He knew of 512 such collective nouns in Basic alone, including the delightful *crash of rancors* and *scold of mynocks*.

Captain Dameron was still listening for something. But C-3PO's auditory sensors recorded no sound similar to the continuous tinkle made by the crystalline fur of the vulptices.

Actually, that wasn't quite true—he *did* detect a faint sound, one for which the most likely correlation was the proximity of a lone vulptex. And indeed, there the creature was, its eyes shining in the darkness.

As C-3PO watched, the vulptex turned tail and hurried off down the tunnel, its fur chiming. This information struck C-3PO as highly relevant given Poe's sudden interest in the creatures, though that interest was decidedly odd.

Still, C-3PO had long ago given up on understanding human behavior.

He started to inform the pilot of the creature's departure, but he'd noticed it on his own.

"Follow me," Poe said, and hurried after the fox.

All eyes turned to Leia, who turned from the distant scene on the plain and nodded at them.

"What are you looking at me for? Follow him."

The ridgeline above the mine had been reshaped over the millennia by salt glaciers, grinding away at the mountains to leave behind a cracked landscape of crags and knobs separated by deep fissures.

The *Falcon* flew slowly over the ridge; inside, R2-D2 had plugged into a dataport in the cockpit so he could access the freighter's sensors.

The astromech whined unhappily.

"The beacon's right beneath us," Rey said. "They've got to be somewhere. Keep scanning for life-forms."

The droid beeped an acknowledgment and urged the freighter to switch its sensors over to focus mode, probing the rock beneath them for matches with human energy signatures.

The *Falcon* responded sulkily, then launched into a diatribe about its inadequate sensor rectennae, power feeds to the dish that remained misaligned more than three decades after the incident that had knocked them out of place, and Chewbacca's obviously deliberate refusal to prioritize repairs the way the freighter thought made sense.

When the *Falcon* mentioned something about barely being able to detect the back end of a bantha at high noon, R2-D2 suppressed an electronic sigh. The *Falcon* had always been cantankerous, its three droid brains quarreling endlessly unless forced to work together. Still, R2-D2 usually got along with the ship well enough. For one thing, none of the brains could stand C-3PO; for another, one of them had a fondness for both romantic gossip and dirty jokes, both of which R2-D2 had learned to provide in large quantities.

R2-D2 gently suggested that—merely as an experiment—the *Falcon* perform a burst scan spatially centered on the mate of the beacon on Rey's wrist. After a show of reluctance, the ship complied.

The astromech beeped to get Rey's attention—the scan had turned up massive life readings.

Rey peered down at the mountainside, trying to match up what R2-D2 had found with what she was seeing.

"Chewie!" she said, pointing. "There!"

Below them, dozens of crystal foxes were streaming out of a fissure in the mountainside.

The Resistance fighters followed the fox through the warren of tunnels. Poe was worried they'd frighten the creature into hiding, but it seemed to understand that they needed to follow it, going so far as to linger when they struggled to keep pace. Rose was toward the back of the group, unconscious thanks to a cocktail of sedatives and pain medication, with Finn trotting along anxiously next to her gurney. At the very back were BB-8 and C-3PO, the latter warning everyone within range of his voice about the hazards of the cave complex.

Threepio had covered cave-ins, ebb nests, debilitating falls, fatal falls, crystal sickness, and starvation when the group emerged from a narrow tunnel into a natural cave glittering with crystal outcroppings. The crystal fox stood atop a large boulder, eyes bright in the gloom. It studied them for a moment, then hopped down from its perch, loping over to a rockfall that filled the back of the cavern. There, it somehow squeezed itself into a crack less than a third of a meter wide, its fur jangling and tinkling against the stone.

"Oh no," Poe said, peering into the narrow exit. He could see light, but there was no way any of them could squeeze into the space.

—————

Rey hurried down the *Falcon*'s ramp and scrambled down a scree of crystal shards and salt chunks into a crevasse. A fox ran past her, its fur chiming and singing, and leapt from outcropping to outcropping to reach the top of the ridge.

Searching for where the animal had come from, she found a small crack in a massive wall of tightly packed boulders.

Rey stepped back to study the tumbled landscape, then smiled.

"Lifting rocks," she said.

CHAPTER 35

Kylo and Luke regarded each other, their lightsabers humming between them. Each methodically adjusted his stance, eyes locked on the other. Around them drifted flakes of salt, light as ash.

"I failed you, Ben," Luke said. "I'm sorry."

"I'm sure you are," Kylo replied. "The Resistance is dead. The war is over. And when I kill you, I'll have killed the last Jedi."

He waited to see what his former Master would say, bracing to defend against a lightning-fast strike. But Luke simply raised an eyebrow.

"Amazing," he said. "Every word of what you just said was wrong. The Rebellion is reborn today. The war is just beginning. And I will not be the last Jedi."

It began with a quaver, and the slightest trickle of dust and bits of rock.

Poe, hardly daring to believe it, gestured for the Resistance soldiers to step back from the rockfall sealing them inside the mine. But it was true—the stones were moving, first one by one and then several at a time. Finn watched, holding Rose's hand, as daylight appeared at the top of the tumbled heap of rock. Leia smiled as boulder after boulder rose into the air, revealing a tunnel. C-3PO shuffled back and forth in distress as the Resistance soldiers hurried past him, rushing out into the crevasse revealed beyond.

Finn emerged from the tunnel to discover Rey standing at its mouth, boulders floating in the air around her. Her eyes were closed and she was smiling slightly, her face serene.

She opened her eyes and the boulders crashed down to the ground.

As the other Resistance soldiers regarded Rey in astonishment, Finn rushed forward, calling her name. For a moment he was afraid that Rose had been right—that this Rey who could lift mountainsides would be utterly changed in other ways, too, with no trace left of the young woman he'd followed across the galaxy from Jakku.

And she *was* different. But the old Rey wasn't gone. And it was that Rey who fell into Finn's arms, sobbing and laughing at the same time, and held him tight.

"Rey," Kylo said, speaking her name like it was poison. "Your chosen one. Chosen over me. She aligned herself with the old way that has to die. No more Masters. I will destroy her, you, and all of it. Know that."

Luke searched Kylo's eyes, found them full of fury and hurt.

Then he turned off his lightsaber. His face was calm, accepting.

"No," he said. "Strike me down in anger and I'll always be with you. Just like your father."

Screaming, Kylo raised his lightsaber over his head and rushed at his defenseless uncle. He brought the blade down on Luke's head and it passed through the Jedi Master, meeting no resistance.

As if it had passed through a ghost.

On Ahch-To, the suns were setting, bathing the peak of the mountain housing the Jedi temple in luminous orange.

On the ledge overlooking the sea, Luke Skywalker floated a few centimeters above the stone. Pebbles hovered around him. His eyes were closed and his legs crossed. His face was strained, and beneath his gray beard the tendons of his neck stood out. Tears streamed down his face as he poured his strength, his very essence, into the Force.

Behind him the peak shuddered, shedding dust and chunks of debris.

Kylo staggered, but recovered his footing and aimed another vicious cut at Luke. Once again, his lightsaber blade met nothing but emptiness.

Luke smiled at his nephew sadly.

"See you around, kid," he said.

And then he disappeared, leaving Kylo alone on the shattered plain, flakes of salt falling around him like snow.

Kylo's blazing eyes leapt to the mine, and the stone door the First Order's cannon had blasted open.

"No!" he howled. "No!"

Luke opened his eyes and fell onto the ledge, the pebbles plunking down around him. He lay on his back, his breathing ragged with exhaustion. The twin suns had touched the horizon and were sinking into the ocean.

Around him the island was wild and alive, a riot of currents and ripples in the Force. Its energies were fed by the birds and insects of the air, the fish and scuttling creatures beneath the waves, and the grass and moss that clung to the ground. All were generators of the Force, yet none were its containers. Its energy escaped the fragile, temporary boundaries of their bodies and spread until it surrounded and permeated everything.

Luke heard the wail of the wind and the cries of the birds. He heard his own faltering breaths as he struggled to get up, and the rhythmic thumping of his heart in his chest.

And he heard a familiar voice. Maybe it was real, or perhaps it was just in his memory.

Let go, Luke.

He did and his body faded away, leaving the ledge empty. In the spot where he had been, the Force rippled and shivered. But a moment later this disturbance was lost amid countless other currents of an autumn evening on the island, and the Force continued as it always had, luminous and vast and eternal.

Rey's hands shook and she sank to her knees, her eyes staring into nothing. The weary Resistance soldiers hurrying up the *Millennium Falcon*'s ramp stopped, staring at the woman who had saved them.

But General Organa was at her side immediately, reaching for her hand. Rey took it as if she were blind, her mouth hanging open. Then the general pulled her back to her feet.

"We need to go," Leia told her, her eyes sad but warm.

Kylo stormed through the rent in the massive stone door, stormtroopers hurrying behind him with their rifles ready, hunting for enemies.

But there was no one to meet them—just empty transports and a jumble of discarded equipment.

Kylo, his face a mask of fury, swept into the control center. It was empty, too—deserted. He stalked around it, teeth bared, and the stormtroopers quickly found a reason they needed to be elsewhere.

Something on the floor caught Kylo's eye. He knelt, his gloved fingers closing on a pair of golden dice linked by a short chain.

As Kylo stared at them he sensed something else—a tremor in the Force, the prelude to a familiar connection.

He stared at Rey. She stared back at him, her gaze level and unafraid. There was no hatred in her eyes, as there once had been. But there was no compassion, either.

A moment later Rey severed the connection, leaving Kylo alone in the gloom with his father's dice resting in the palm of his upraised hand. A moment later, they faded and vanished.

The *Falcon* rose on its repulsors, engine whining, then spun grace-
fully and vanished into the skies of Crait, the shock wave of its passing rippling the fur of several foxes watching from a rocky outcrop.

A few minutes later the battered freighter emerged from the planet's envelope of atmosphere. Before anyone aboard the First Order's
Star Destroyers could issue an order, it had disappeared into hyperspace.

Inside, Leia was puzzled to discover the decrepit freighter was in-
fested with chubby, big-eyed avians. They seemed to be everywhere:
nesting in tangles of wiring, peering out of access hatches, and even
squawking in territorial pique at the Resistance soldiers who dared to
sit around the gaming table.

"Shoo," she said, sidestepping yet another one as she entered the
cockpit. "When did this old rattletrap become a birdcage?"

Chewbacca sat in the co-pilot's seat, his hairy hands drifting over
the controls with a grace that belied his size. The Wookiee chuffed in
amusement, then indicated she should take the pilot's seat.

Han's seat.

Leia's steps carried her to just behind the chair, but no farther. She
stopped with her hand on the seat's back.

"Chewie . . . ," she said, then stopped, needing a moment to control her emotions. "Luke . . . gave his life for us. To buy us time. To
save us."

Chewbacca's hands slowed on the controls, then stopped. The
Wookiee whined, a small sound almost lost deep in his throat. His
hands fell into his lap and he slumped in his seat.

Leia's hand settled on his shoulder as she gazed out through the
viewports, remembering.

Chewie had been in that same seat the first time she'd entered the
Falcon's cockpit. She remembered the chaos, being pressed into service as an extra pair of eyes and ears during their frantic flight from
the Death Star. With the last of the Imperial sentry ships destroyed

she'd flung herself into the startled Wookiee's arms, elated by their unlikely escape.

They'd sat side by side during many long watches on the agonizingly slow journey from Hoth to Bespin, unsure if the Rebel Alliance had survived. And once again when they'd doubled back to Cloud City to rescue Luke.

And here they were again, so many years later. So many years, and so many losses.

"It's just us now," Leia said. "But we'll find a way."

She realized tears were pooling at the corners of her eyes and tried to stop them, irritated with herself. But it was no use. She stood, silent and still, as twin lines of tears ran down her cheeks.

Chewbacca looked up at her, his blue eyes bright. He saw her face and rose from his seat, towering over her.

She tried to tell him she was all right, but the words wouldn't come. He reached for her and folded her against his chest.

Leia buried her face in the Wookiee's warm fur, clinging to him, and finally allowed herself to weep, to surrender to the grief that had filled her to overflowing. She wept for Luke, and for Han, and for Ben. For all those they had lost.

Chewbacca made no sound but simply held her, his embrace surprisingly gentle. They stood like that, Leia's chest heaving, until she was able to master herself and step away. She stared out into the infinity of hyperspace until her breathing was slow and regular again, and she knew she was ready to be what the people waiting in the *Falcon*'s hold needed her to be.

They found the hold crowded with Resistance fighters and pilots. C-3PO was telling R2-D2 about the many indignities he'd endured since they'd separated on D'Qar, while BB-8 listened and clucked sympathetically. As Leia and Chewbacca arrived, Poe looked up from talking with Rey, smiling as the Wookiee reached out a long arm to pull the pilot close.

On the other side of the hold Rose lay in the *Falcon*'s relief bunk, a diagnostic scanner monitoring her vital signs, while Finn rummaged in the compartments beneath the bunks. They were filled

with junk, of course—as Leia and Rey watched, he shoved aside batteries, old tools, and a scattering of ancient books until he finally
found what he was looking for, extracting a blanket and gently drap-
ing it over Rose's sleeping form. Rey turned from watching Finn to
show Leia what she'd been holding in her hands—the halves of Luke's
sundered lightsaber.

"Luke Skywalker is gone," Rey said. "I felt it. But it wasn't sadness
or pain. It was peace. And purpose."

Leia nodded. "I felt it, too."

Her brother had passed into the Force. As she would one day. As
they all would. But the Force remained. It was everywhere around
them, connecting them and lifting them up. And wherever the Force
was, some part of Luke was, too.

No one's ever really gone.

Rey looked from the broken halves of Luke's lightsaber to the
handful of injured, exhausted Resistance fighters.

"Kylo is stronger than ever," she said. "He has an army and an iron
grip on the galaxy. How do we build a rebellion from this?"

But Leia just put her hand on Rey's and smiled.

"We have everything we need."

Every day on Ahch-To, the Lanais cut back the moss and uneti shrubs
that threatened to reclaim the sacred island's stone stairs, swept the
common area outside the huts, and performed repairs as needed.
And if any Outsiders were in residence, the Lanais cooked their
meals and cleaned their clothing, so they could devote their hours to
contemplation.

Alcida-Auka had supervised these tasks for many seasons, since
the day her mother had passed the title of matron and its responsi-
bilities down to her. As one day she would, in turn, pass the title to
her own eldest daughter.

If there was a pattern to the coming of the Outsiders, the Lanais
had never discerned it. There had been long periods in which there
were no Outsiders at all, and brief stretches in which a group of Out-

siders dwelled on the island together. A few of the Outsiders had been kind, as devoted to the Lanais as they were to them. And a few had been mad—the Lanais's secret songs recalled years of fire and ruin that had forced them from their homes until things resumed their proper course. But most had left no particular impression, keeping to themselves and their studies.

The latest Outsider had been a curious one. He had arrived bearing artifacts, some of which the Lanais's songs recalled as having been taken from the island long before. Rather than hold himself apart, he had learned the Lanais's language and ways, appearing each month at the Festival of Return. And he had insisted on doing his own chores, gathering his own food, and performing repairs alongside them.

Eventually Alcida-Auka had accepted that such activities were part of his devotions, and accommodated him. He had been little trouble after that—though the same couldn't be said about his rude, destructive apprentice, the one he'd said was his niece.

Both were gone now. The apprentice had left aboard her skyboat with her two companions, while the Master had simply vanished, his robes discovered on the ledge above the sea. Maybe he had leapt from the peak and given his body to the waves. Or perhaps he had surrendered himself and become shadow, dispersing into the light and darkness from which all had been created. The Lanais's songs recalled that both of these paths had been chosen before.

Whatever the truth, he was gone and no longer Alcida-Auka's charge. But much work remained to be done. There was a hut to rebuild, a fallen lightning rod to restore to its roof—a strike had just destroyed the library in the ancient uneti stump, after all—and the other damage done by the careless niece. There were steps to mend and creeping moss to clear. And there were the routine tasks of the island. It would be winter soon, when the Lanais and any new visitors would be dependent on salted fish, dried kelp, and thala-siren milk gathered during the kindly days that were green and growing.

Alcida-Auka verified that one of the daughters had cleaned the Outsider's robes and put them away in the storage hut, along with his woolens, pack, and boots. She directed another daughter to take his weapon, his star compass, and his strange other gear to the repository, where it would join other items gathered over the generations.

Alcida-Auka checked over the daughters' work and found it had been done as it should be. She cinched her habit against the wind, which had turned cold, singing to her of snow. When the snow came, the Lanais would sweep it away from the huts and the stairs. Alcida-Auka didn't know if the next Outsider would come during her time, or her daughter's, or not until the tenure of a matron yet unborn.

But another would come, and find all in order. Because the Lanais would do their duty.

On a hot desert world, three children sat in a filthy supply room.

Temiri wasn't fond of Oniho—the older boy slacked off whenever Bargwill Tomder wasn't around, forcing Temiri and the other children to work harder to keep up with the chores that had to be done. If they didn't, Bargwill would yell and kick, and maybe go after someone with his whip.

The surly groom had been in a rancid mood ever since the fathier escape—and Temiri suspected Bargwill didn't believe his story that it had been the intruders who set the beasts free and caused all the trouble.

But Arashell Sar liked Oniho's stories, and had asked Temiri to come with her and hear Oniho's newest one. And Temiri would do almost anything if it meant a chance to sit next to Arashell.

Fortunately, Oniho's story was a good one, enacted with the dolls the children made from sweepings and discarded bits of wood and wire. He'd gone all-out, too—there were not just soldiers but also toy walkers and starships in this story.

Temiri couldn't quite follow all of the tale—it had a lot of twists and turns—but the climax was pretty good. It came down to one man with something Oniho called a lightsaber, and that one man was facing an entire army.

Before Temiri could learn what had happened to Oniho's hero—this Luke Skywalker, Jedi Master—the door exploded inward and

Bargwill was screaming abuse in rapid-fire Cloddogran, showering them with spit from his cavelike mouth and mucus from his ingrown nasal tendrils.

Oniho had already fled. Temiri tried to keep his body between Bargwill and Arashell, hoping she'd notice what he was doing for her, and almost got a fierce kick in the backside for his troubles. Arashell didn't need his help anyway—she slipped nimbly past the stable keeper to safety.

As Bargwill ranted and raved at no one in particular, Temiri grabbed up his broom and returned to sweeping out the fathier stables. The beasts were racing, but soon they'd be led back in and need to be washed and groomed. There'd be a lot to do before they could bed down for the night—and maybe Oniho would be too tired to finish the story and tell them what had happened to the Jedi Master who'd fought an entire army all by himself.

The stable doors were open and the stars blazed in Cantonica's night sky, above the racetrack. Temiri kept sweeping, but it felt like the stars were calling to him. The strokes of his broom slowed, then stopped. He looked down at the ring on his finger that the woman he'd helped had given him, the souvenir he'd managed to hide from Bargwill so far.

Studying the rebel insignia, he wondered what had happened to her. Maybe she was having her own adventures out there, among the stars. Like the ones Temiri kept telling Arashell that they'd have one day.

As he stared up at the stars, the boy absentmindedly turned the broom in his hands until he held it at his side, like a lightsaber.

ACKNOWLEDGMENTS

This book exists because Rian Johnson wrote a wonderful story and was so generous about letting me goof around with it. Properly expressing my thanks would demand at least a short story's worth of words. Thank you Ram Bergman for helping so many trains run on time. And, of course, none of this would have happened without George Lucas and Kathleen Kennedy.

Carrie Fisher taught me and every *Star Wars* fan so much about life, love, and loss. May this book honor her memory.

At Del Rey, I'm enormously grateful for my kind, patient, funny editor, Elizabeth Schaefer, who I promise to take to the Tonga Room when it's actually open. Erich Schoeneweiss has been a dear friend and an unflagging champion, while Tom Hoeler deserves all *Star Wars* fans' thanks for his smarts, friendliness, and saint-level patience. And heartfelt thanks to Alex Davis, Nancy Delia, Scott Biel, Scott Shannon, Keith Clayton, Julie Leung, David Moench, and Shelly Shapiro.

At Lucasfilm, I owe so much to so many, starting with Michael Siglain for believing in me and handling a billion things with inexhaustible good humor. Thanks to Jennifer Heddle for keeping me on course and saving me from all too many on-page embarrassments, and to Pablo Hidalgo and Leland Chee for years of lessons about storytelling, lore and genial poise. Thanks also to Matt Martin, James Waugh, James Erskine, Sammy Holland, Phil Szostak, Brett Rector, Caitlin Kennedy, Rayne Roberts, Kiri Hart, Dan Brooks, Andi Gutierrez, Justin Bolger, Dennis VonGalle, Dana Jennings, Chris Argyropoulos, and Anina Walas.

This book is richer and deeper because of contributions from many fellow *Star Wars* authors, a goofball caravan I'm always happy to hop aboard. Thank you Elizabeth Wein, Michael Kogge, Alan Dean Foster, Claudia Gray, Delilah S. Dawson, Cavan Scott, Greg Rucka, Chuck Wendig, Cecil Castellucci, John Jackson Miller, Rae Carson, Saladin Ahmed, Mira Grant, E. K. Johnston, Gary D. Schmidt, and Alexander Freed. I've also been so lucky to get to build on the work of Dave Filoni and Brian Daley.

No author makes it far without tons of kindness, help, and encouragement. I'm grateful to Dan Wallace, Craig R. Carey, Ryder Windham, Frank Parisi, James Luceno, Karen-Ann Lichtenstein, Rob Valois, J. W. Rinzler, Joanne Chan Taylor, Carole Roeder, Sue Rostoni, Kristen Hidalgo, Delia Greve, Scott Chernoff, Jonathan Wilkins, Rachel Barry, Steve Sansweet, Nanci Schwartz, Brian Larsen, Tricia Barr, B.J. Priester, Jay Shah, Chris Reiff, Chris Trevas, Jeff Carlisle, Simon Beecroft, Sadie Smith, Karen Miller, James Floyd, Bryan Young, Cole Horton, Sterling Hershey, Kemp Remillard, Mary Ann Zissimos, Meg Roth, Amy Nathanson, Tom Hutchens, Pete Schay, Allan Carscaddon, Jim and Sarah Jones, and Martha and Robert Bernstein.

Finally, I give thanks every minute for Emily, Joshua, and Mom and Dad.

Acknowledgments come with the terror that you've forgotten someone; I'll be lucky if I've only forgotten a dozen people. If you're one of them, let me know when you want a beer and a groveling apology.

ABOUT THE AUTHOR

JASON FRY has written or co-written more than forty novels, short stories, and other works set in the galaxy far, far away. His other books include the Servants of the Empire quartet and the young-adult space-fantasy series The Jupiter Pirates. He lives in Brooklyn with his wife, son, and about a metric ton of *Star Wars* stuff.

ABOUT THE TYPE

This book was set in Minion, a 1990 Adobe Originals typeface by Robert Slimbach (b. 1956). Minion is inspired by classical, old-style typefaces of the late Renaissance, a period of elegant, beautiful, and highly readable type designs. Created primarily for text setting, Minion combines the aesthetic and functional qualities that make text type highly readable with the versatility of digital technology.